WHAT
HAPPENED
WAS
THIS

ALSO BY JOSH GREENFELD

Fiction

O for a Master of Magic
Harry and Tonto
The Return of Mr. Hollywood

Non-Fiction

A Child Called Noah
A Place for Noah
A Client Called Noah

Plays

Clandestine on the Morning Line
I Have a Dream

WHAT
HAPPENED
WAS
THIS

Josh Greenfeld

Carroll & Graf Publishers, Inc.
New York

First Carroll & Graf edition 1990

Carroll & Graf Publishers, Inc.
260 Fifth Avenue
New York, NY 10001

Library of Congress Cataloging-in-Publication Data

Greenfeld, Josh.
    What happened was this / Josh Greenfeld.
    — 1st Carroll & Graf ed.
        p.   cm.
    ISBN 0-88184-639-2 : $18.95
    I. Title.
    PS3513.R4815W4   1990
    813'.52—dc20   90-40771
                                                        CIP

Manufactured in the United States of America

For Karl

"Show business teaches you to expect the unexpected and to accept the unacceptable. And I've managed to deal with that parlay quite successfully throughout my career. In fact, I wouldn't have had a career if I couldn't."
　　　　　　　　　　—From an interview with
　　　　　　　　　　Lester Rose, *Los Angeles Times*

"Real life is sloppy and messy. That's why we need movies. To tidy up after."
　　　　　　　　　　—Ibid

"Books, plays, art, music, there is nothing more like life—or lifelike—than a movie. Especially one in post-production trouble that constantly requires recutting."
　　　　　　　　　　—Lester Rose,
　　　　　　　　　　Champlin on Film,
　　　　　　　　　　Interview on Bravo Cable

BOOK I

A would-be actor and his two friends
who came of age in the 1950's confront
their destinies and faustian betrayals
in the 1990's.

1

What goes around, comes around, baseball players like to say. But who are baseball players to say anything of consequence? Singles and doubles and stolen bases one might expect from them. And platitudes and cliches and dugout dictums like "Take two and hit to right" or "A walk's as good as a hit." But not enduring universal truths, eternal verities, grand-slam philosophical home runs. Anyway, what happened was this:

On a dry October morning in Santa Monica, Lester Rose was having no major problems with his life, present or past, that he could think of as he stepped up to a teller's window of the Glendale Federal Savings Branch on Montana Avenue—a Spanish-style structure, creamy stucco walls and terra cotta tile roofed, which looked like it housed not a full-service bank, but a fast food taco joint—to pick up some cash. While the girl stamped the back of his personal expense check and typed his account number into the computer beside her before reaching into the till and forking over his cash, Lester's fingers idly fell upon a heap of calendars piled on the onyx shelf before him. They were Jewish calendars with all sorts of vaguely familiar squiggly Hebrew letters in black and dictionary-like illustrations of little candles burning on each Friday in red. Emblazoned near the spiral wire binding atop each calendar in stark black Hebraized numerals was 5750.

Lester should have seized upon those Jewish calendars as a meta-

3

physical warning from afar, a harbinger to be on his guard and be wary of any otherworldly-like visitations from the past. But instead, Lester could only think of a gag he might pull on somebody like Arnie, his business manager: "Don't forget to write 5750 on your checks from now on, Arnie, instead of 5749." Or had he pulled that gag, or a variation of it, on Arnie already? Or had Arnie first pulled the gag on him? Anyway, his memory was leaving him. First with names. And now with dates. Or gags about dates. Perhaps he was coming down with fortyzeimers? Or to be truthful about it and not mince any years, fiftyzeimers? Otherwise, no matter. Because it was only a gag, a one liner, not a concept or a vision. A personal vision. Then he would have been in trouble, deep trouble. Because he had always strived to be a personal film maker and that was why he liked to see all of his pictures start with a personal vision. With something he, Lester Rose, could personally relate to, born—or borne—out of the core of his own life's experience. Something, in other words, deriving from his own sense of deep reality vis-à-vis superficial third-person cinema culture. Which was what would ultimately separate him from the pack and earn him the right to call himself an artist and craftsman, no matter how well his pictures did or did not do at any teen-controlled box office. After all, he'd already had retrospectives in New York and Toronto and his pictures seemed to be developing a growing following abroad. Particularly, for some reason, in Manila. They were always inviting him to Manila. But he had once gone to Teheran on an invitation from the Shah himself. And that was enough. No way was he going to Manila, no matter who sent the nod: Marcos. Aquino. Or some new insurgent President-for-a-day or recidivist right-wing dictator for a lifetime.

After Lester pocketed his cash and picked up the calendar, he ambled from the bank and hopped into his precision-tooled inflation-proof silver Porsche 911, which he figured had to be worth at least twice as much that day as on the day he first bought it fifteen years back in ancient pop history. And that included all the rebuilding money he had since put into it. He gunned the engine lovingly and then roared down rapidly yuppifying Montana Avenue, everywhere a new rice restaurant or specialty food shop or leisure suit boutique, until he hit the broad, expansive ocean, his head leaving behind Teheran and the Philippines and all those gentry trendifying Montana Avenue MBA tastes and instead settling on Cannes. Because that's what the Palisades Park running along Ocean Avenue in Santa Monica always reminded him of: Cannes. Not that it had a flower market. Or that the shore at Cannes was lined with creches at Christmastime. But the fact that the tall palm trees looked out over a sandy gray beach and blue-green semi-tropical churning waters. Just like Cannes. Except that day many fronds lay scattered on the sidewalk, blown down by the Santa Ana winds that each night lately came howling through the canyons, carrying hot, dry desert air out toward the sea where it collected above the waters in a brown smudge, as if the door to a blast oven had suddenly opened, releasing a rush of rusted smoke. Still, to Lester, the Santa Monica Palisades was always pretty as a picture postcard of Cannes. Or an impressionistic painting of the Riviera. Except for the people.

Two bearded men, seated almost at opposite ends of the same bench, were exchanging sections of *USA Today* as a young blond jogger trotted by, her elbows swinging from side to side, her loose breasts bouncing toward each other as if they were cross-eyed beneath her yellow tank top. Lester thought he wouldn't mind getting into her *nookie*. But a white dog was scampering along behind her and he couldn't see himself also chasing after her like some barking hound, so he decided to think of something else. Anything else. The numbers of the new Jewish year, for example. Fifty seven fifty. Which sounded not only like the current price of a Broadway theater ticket, but also like an important year, alot more propitious and portentous than say, 1989. And Lester sincerely hoped it would be a good year because he could certainly use one. Not that 5749 had been a bad year. In fact, it had been a great year. In almost every way. His last picture had done well, if not commercially, then at least critically. No one in his family had suffered a major illness.

And there were no electrical problems in any of his cars. Not that he knew of anyway.

But then he always could use another good year. To be perfectly honest about it, if it were at all negotiable, he would cut a deal for one good day for himself and his family in exchange for the good year due some perfect stranger. He would even be willing to accept one good day for his wife, Jean, and his kids, Monica and Peter, in exchange for a terrible Job-like year for some wonderful stranger, such as Mother Teresa or a Nobel Prize-winning M.I.T. professor to be named at a later date. Altruism was one thing and had its place, but he was also not a saint or a fool. After all, Jean and the kids were part and parcel of any good day he could ever have. And vice versa. But who was Mother Teresa or some Nobel Prize Laureate to him? To humanity, maybe something? Yes. But to Lester Rose, personally? Less than Hecuba. *Bupkes.* And if it made him sound ruthless to say that, very well, then he was ruthless and would accept the rap. Because he was also being ruthlessly honest. He was expressing his own sense of deep reality.

Sure, Jean wasn't everything he had ever dreamed of in a wife. For example, communication was never the hallmark of their relationship. In fact, it was not misunderstandings but understandings that would get them into trouble when it finally dawned on one what the other had been meaning all along. And he could never bring Jean his problems. Not that he had any at the moment. But those were their roles from the word go. She was the problem bringer and he was the problem solver. Because he was the older, the wiser, the more married, the more successful professionally. He was also Jewish and maybe that had something to do with it, too. Not that Jean was a dummy or anything like that; she had alot of straight-arrow *goyishe* sense. But he hadn't married her for her smarts, anyway. Anymore, he assumed, than she had married him just because of his good looks. And call it lack of communication or mis-communication but their marriage worked. As long as he didn't bring his problems, past and present, to her. And just listened to all her problems involving her clubs, her causes, her charities—what his mother used to call her *"shiksa* society lady activities"—and, of course, there were the kids. Jean was terrific with the kids. Better than he was. He couldn't have cast a better mother. And he wanted so much for his kids. He wanted the world for them. Just as his own parents had wanted the world for him. Only he hoped Monica and Peter would be spared the stiff prices they had had to pay. Because Monica and Peter were already living in the kind of dream world his parents had only seen on movie screens: They rode horses, skied, scuba dived, vacationed all over the map, had gone to private schools and went to expensive colleges back East. They had been spoiled rotten and he had been the spoiler. But it was all right. They would have the luxury of pure choice as adults and look at life's menus from left to right instead of starting with the numbers on the right as he had always had to do. The difference between his generation and theirs would be even greater than the gulf that had separated him from his parents. And that was all to the good, too, as far as he was concerned. He remembered the joke about the difference between the International Ladies Garment Workers Union and the American Psychoanalytical Association: one generation. Not a very good joke. Just something that made noise like a joke. But had a lot of truth to it. Except then, why was his most fervent wish—for his kids to have a better life than he had, for them both to enjoy terrific lives—exactly the same as that of his parents?

Lester's own schedule that morning did not happen to promise such a terrific day. It was the first day of his return to the Pritikin diet and he was on his way to their beachfront headquarters in Venice for breakfast. To get off on the right foot. Or rather the right fork. Because there was no doubt about how much he had backslid since his three-week stay there two years ago—way back in 5748.

The weight of evidence was literally before him. No matter how hard he sucked in his stomach, he was still beginning to look like a living Jewish homage to Hitchcock. A far cry from the fleet-footed kid called "Lucky," who as a stickball shortstop was another Pee

Wee Reese, racing into the deep hole behind third to make a back-hand stab. Or, as a touchtackle end, the Buddy Young of his block, outrunning any defender and streaking out past the sewer to snare the football for a touchdown.

Passing the art deco General Telephone building on the corner of Wilshire, which was being remodeled, Lester flashed on the cornerstone of the Jewish community center in the old neighborhood against whose salmon brick wall, while waiting for the bell to ring announcing the start of his after public school Hebrew *cheder* class, he often played Chinese handball. Upon the center cornerstone, if he remembered correctly, a Jewish year had also been engraved in both Hebrew letters and Roman numerals, Ds and Ms and Cs and Ls. Like some Polish name suffering from an acute vowel shortage. It had to have been a fifty-six-hundred year, he was sure, because the old center, which was now a Pentecostal Tabernacle church according to his last driveby when he was in Brooklyn for his mother's funeral, was built before he was born.

Everything changed. Nothing remained the same. The Greeks and everybody else were right. Even the ash brick building along the ocean front at Pico, which was once Synanon, was now Pritikin's. Lester turned right and parked in the lot catty-corner to it. Pinned on his Pritikin alumni badge. Locked his car. Walked briskly across the street. And entered the lobby with its huge picture windows looking out over the beach. Immediately, Lester felt once more as if he was on board a cruise ship that would never leave shore. As usual, the people were friendly, bustling with weight-losing and calorie-shedding camaraderie, as they went down the cafeteria-style lines in their leisure suits and leotards, filling their plates with ample portions of soups and salads, cereals, and high-fiber breads and rice cakes and bran crackers. No question the food was healthy and filling. It was also essentially tasteless, no matter how many tomatoes and lemons had been squeezed in order to try to obscure that fact. But what the hell? You couldn't have everything. And Lester did find himself feeling virtuous, if not sated, by the time he sipped a second cup of herb tea. And as he stared across the table at his fellow diners, he recalled the memorial service held in that very parlor-dining room after the death of Nathan Pritikin himself.

What had happened was this: Pritikin, having discovered himself terminally ill with cancer, registered under an assumed name in an Albany, New York hospital, and proceeded to cut open his veins with a concealed razor, and bleed to death like a Jacobin. No cup of hemlock for Pritikin. Who knew what artery-clogging polyunsaturates hemlock contained? At the memorial service, then as now, people were dressed in designer sweatsuits and exercise togs. A rabbi and a doctor and Pritikin's son and Senator George McGovern all eulogized the deceased nutrition and exercise pioneer, pointing out that the autopsy revealed that, though a victim of cancer, Pritikin still died with clear, plaque-free arteries, devoid of the ravages of cholesterol, "clean as a whistle," not a trace of a light-density lipid in his last drops of blood.

Indeed, after breakfast Lester found himself imbued with a refreshed Pritikin spirit. No more frankfurters, sausages, paellas. Farewell again to ice cream and chocolate and custards. Also cream cheese and Brie and Camembert. He did not enjoy looking down at his protruding stomach and not being able to see his own feet. He knew a little exercise and a great deal of self-control would do him worlds of good. And above all, he did not want to die of heart disease, the exit route of his mother.

It was then he had his vision. Well, not exactly then. But just shortly afterwards. Later he would leave out the Pritikin part completely. Not that he was trying to cloak anything, but it was not germane and could only set people off on the wrong tangent. And, in truth, the vision itself did not really take shape until after he'd eaten at Pritikin's. But rather while he was walking along the water's edge of the beach in the Marina. Well, not the Marina exactly, but Venice. And not the beach if you wanted to be literal. But the promenade, Ocean Front Walk, actually. And he was not walking to be precise. In fact, he was picking his ass off the cement sidewalk after a black skater, who looked as if he was dressed for a

Hells Angels' roller derby, unceremoniously knocked him down and stood over him, his white-gloved hands still clasped behind his big buck ass, while Lester, rubbing his bruised, burning thighs, glared up at him. "Don't give me no fucking attitude," the skater spit out and pushed off, pumping his way down the center of the promenade again.

But Lester would also always leave out that part of the story, too. Because, as far as he was concerned, it was not germane. And why bring in the race issue, anyway? But the fact of the matter was that as he was rising and brushing himself off, indeed, feeling a fucking attitude, he swore that he would never again contribute to the United Negro College Fund. Not that he was that sure he ever had. But it was just the kind of charity that Arnie always urged on him for tax reasons. Anyway, he was lucky that he wasn't hurt, except for a possible raspberry on his thigh. His pants were not torn and that was certainly a good sign what with the cost of imported Italian threads these days. But there was a funny sound buzzing in his ears. And for a moment it was as if he was hearing the faint strains of cantorial chanting very much like he used to hear at the Jewish community center on the High Holidays.

Lester was rarely inside the Jewish community center synagogue itself during the High Holidays, the price of a ticket being too steep for his frugal father to afford. Instead, his father would pray at the spartan Young Israel, which held its services in a cavernous local pool hall above a trolley-lined street. All the tables were pushed together in the back and a temporary ark was set up and chairs were lined up in neat rows. The ticker in the corner was disconnected and masked by a screen, but nothing could obscure the lines of billiard scoring beads stretched overhead. Just enough was charged for worship to meet expenses and have a little something left over for Israel. Lester never liked attending High Holiday services in the pool room. Especially since they did not even hire a professional cantor, but instead had Mendel Mandelbaum, the full-time proprietor of a local drygoods store, performing the cantorial duties. And the moonlighting Mandelbaum had a hoarse rasping voice that always seemed to have phlegm lodged in it.

The Jewish community center synagogue, however, was a stark contrast to the ecclesiastical pool hall. At the entrance to the center synagogue on High Holidays stood private policemen, uniformed Burns or Pinkerton men, whose normal lay duties included guarding the infield after a Dodger game. At Ebbets Field these private dicks deterred possible second-base bag stealers or umpire tacklers; in front of the center's stately oak doors they kept away sneaky supplicants, Jews who might try to pray without having previously purchased High Holiday tickets. Still, Lester preferred standing outside the center synagogue on a hot Yom Kippur day, not far from the cornerstone, kibbitzing with his friends, and eavesdropping—or rather cantordropping. Because, despite the closed portals and unopened windows, the magnificent nasal-tenor voice of some famous cantor, a Moishe Oysher, a Laible Waldman, or a new celebrity refugee survivor from the Holocaust, would seep out—crying, laughing, choking, cajoling, for the sweltering, paying penitents within. And even back in those days, Lester knew a good theatrical performance when he encountered one.

But now, just after being knocked down by that big black buck roller skater on Ocean Front Walk in Venice, Lester was undeniably hearing similar cantorial strains. Which made it twice in a matter of hours that he was thinking of the Jewish New Year which was, of course, half—or maybe even two thirds—of what the High Holidays were all about.

It took more than a moment before Lester realized that the cantorial voice was coming from some place other than a sense memory in his head. In fact, it was clearly coming from a low-slung gray stucco building set among the grocery stores and hot dog stands and art galleries facing the ocean. As Lester approached the building, he could discern a Star of David in the window and Hebrew writing above a doorway with a brass *mezzuzah* implanted on the jamb. But no Pinkerton or Burns men were standing guard.

Lester pushed open the paint-peeling doors and found himself in the rear of a dimly lit synagogue, row after row of pews with reading racks in banked attachment. Jutting out from the center of the front wall was a wine-red satin-covered altar with gold Hebrew letters and the figure of a lion embroidered on it. For a moment, Lester felt as if he was caught in some back-to-shul time warp. Or as if he was suddenly looking at the wrong piece of film in the editing room. It seemed surreal. The dim gray interior just did not match visually with the bright sunlit Venice Beach exterior of the previous shot, so to speak.

And neither did the sound track. Rocking on the raised platform —the *bimah*—before the altar, his back to Lester, holding onto a rostrum with both hands, kneeling and bending as his voice trilled, was the source of the cantorial voice. Not a Moishe Oysher or a Laible Waldman, but still a powerful *shtima* with a cantorial *niggun,* nevertheless.

Standing motionless near the entrance, Lester did not dare to interrupt. Instead, he suddenly meditated—or rather found himself reflecting—about what it was to be a Jew. Even though he himself was married to a *shiksa* and doubted if his kids had ever even been in a synagogue except to attend a peer's *bar* or *bat mitzvah,* he had never allowed himself to forget for a single second the lesson of the Holocaust. Which was that Jewish identity was a deterministic result, not some free-will decision. That, when push came to shove, it was the *goyim* who ultimately decided who was and who was not a Jew according to their own needs. The *goyim*—the gentiles—were always the definers and that was something that every Jew had to be ready to accept personally. In other words, the *goyim* could always fuck the Jews. At the same time, no one knew better than Lester that his old neighborhood had been a ghetto consisting of no one but Jews who were out to fuck each other. Thus him, by definition. In fact, it was his fellow Jews who had taught Lester early on that the world itself would never be more than a long shot in any galactic congeniality contest.

The cantorial voice suddenly broke off in the midst of a Hebrew prayer and began to sing the scales: do-re-mi-fa-sol-la-ti-do, and the cantor himself turned around, wiping his brow with a large, floppy blue-polka-dotted handkerchief. Lester was about to leave, feeling as if he had somehow inadvertently intruded upon some actor's private moment exercise. But the cantor smiled and blinked toward the back of the synagogue where Lester was standing. "Les?" he called out. "Les Rose?"

Lester stopped. "Yes?" So they knew him here, too. Anywhere in Los Angeles they always recognized an important film maker. No matter where he went. As opposed to say, New York, where he could walk the streets for weeks without being spotted as a person of stature, a world-class figure, a major director worthy of recognition.

After all, he had made some important pictures. *Compassion* and *Kid Alabama*, for example. Flukes, some critics called them. But his champions described them as his ouvre. And they were good films by any standards. Because he was never a *shlock meister,* he always tried to do good work, he never sold out. Was it his fault that the really good material rarely came his way? And in order to keep working, to build a career in a business where at bats counted even more than hits, he had to accept film assignments that were not always up to his own aesthetic standards? But that was the nature of the beast. And he had never been powerful enough—or given his roots, secure enough—to enjoy the luxury of walking away from pay-day turkeys. And if some of the turkeys he made never flew, at least they waddled. They were better films, not worse, because he had made them. He had done the best he could.

And contrary to popular opinion, most people in Hollywood always did their best. Actors, writers, directors, everybody worked at the top of their talent. No one ever set out to make a bad picture. Because the wear and tear involved in making even the lousiest of films, required the same intensity and thick-skinned concentration as a quality film with a fine script. Perhaps even more. Because it was more exhausting, energy sapping, brain draining, soul depleting.

Which was one reason he sometimes turned to producing. It

could be more lucrative without being as demanding. And he could at least try to come up with his own projects. Projects he could relate to personally. That he didn't have to direct in order to make his statement. Lately the teenage mentality that ran the studios seemed to prefer it that way, regarding him as some sort of dinosaur, a television relic from a pre-existing era. Meanwhile, he could still always direct television movies. But even though that was where he had come from, he was not very happy doing it anymore. Not enough set-ups, never enough time, and it would always wind up a fart in the wind anyway. Features had spoiled him, features could become art; he yearned for a feature project that would stir his own directorial juices and, at the same time, find him acceptable to the studio and the principals.

The possessor of the cantorial voice stepped forward into a gray shaft of slanting light. He was a full-faced, handsome man with a thick head of curly silver hair. "Myron," he said and smiling, tapped his chest with his index finger. "Myron Feldstein."

"Myron Feldstein?" Lester repeated out loud. Then he shook his head. He just could not automatically remember names anymore. And that name drew a blank even though the face was familiar. For a split second he had the feeling he might be an actor who had once auditioned for him. But how could that be? The man was a cantor. He had never been involved with a script calling for a cantor. "Myron Feldstein?" Lester searched his memory. "Give me a hint?"

"Michel DuChamps," the cantor said, still smiling.

"Of course," Lester stepped forward. "Michel. How are you, Michel? It's been a long time."

2

How could he have possibly forgotten Myron Feldstein? Or Mickey
Feldstein? Or Mickey Feldstein or Myron Feldstein as Michel
DuChamps? It was only for a moment and soon the sluice gates of
his memory unlocked and in torrents of montages and freeze
frames and quick dissolves it all came pouring back to him. Their
whole bloody youth together—and apart.

In a way it was strange, Les thought, that he had recalled the
name Michel DuChamps, and his offstage nightclub persona, more
readily than the real Myron Feldstein. Because he had known Myron as Mickey since high school, long before his Gallic incarnation
as Michel DuChamps. But it was almost as if after Mickey chose to
become Michel, Les, too, had accepted that self-casting and never
looked back. After all, every artist had the right to create—or
recreate—himself. That was part of the lure, it went with the
territory. Hadn't he himself wanted to escape his own Brooklyn
Jewish background just as quickly as possible? Hadn't he chosen to
portray other people on stage in order to become another person in
real life? No wonder Michel's early success had driven him crazy
with envy.

But that did not mean Les was necessarily stricken with amnesia
either. Not with all those strips of film hanging in the cutting room
of his mind. He remembered, for example, appearing with Mickey
Feldstein in assembly hall productions of the "Thespians," the

15

Rutherford B. Hayes High School Drama Society. And he and Mickey had also once been cast together in a drama class exercise from "Of Mice and Men," with Mickey playing Lennie to Les's George in one scene and their roles reversed in another. They had worked very well together, too. Mickey was an instinctive actor. In fact, at that stage of their development, when they were both untrained and inconsistent and had to rely mainly on sheer intuition, Mickey was, if truth need be told, a better actor than Les. And also better looking. Mickey had curly black hair which would rise in a pompadour before cresting on his swarthy brow. His eyes were gray green but otherwise, his face, always sun bronzed, had a Latino cast, like Tony Curtis. Like Alain Delon.

They were both infatuated with Vivian Davis, too. Vivian Davis of the flowing black hair, full rosy cheeks, thick ruby lips, dark hazel doe eyes that glinted invitingly in any light, and ample breasts that always promised to break the bounds of their peasant blouse enclosure or explode through tight cashmere sweatered restrictions. Vivian looked like a Jewish Carmen and both Les and Mickey would have gladly faced the horns of bulls on the off chance that she might blow gently into their left ears. Not only was Vivian *zaftig* beautiful, she was unquestionably the best actress at Rutherford B. Hayes High. She also happened to be the most active Communist.

On wintry Friday nights Les and Mickey would join some of the other young "Thespians" in the finished basement of Vivian's two-story red brick house, one in a row of attached houses that looked across the street at mirror images of themselves in what was considered the classiest development in the neighborhood, one of the very last tracts of houses to be built before World War II. There they listened to records of Paul Robeson singing "Ballad for Americans," as well as paeans to the courage of the Red Army and the indomitability of the Long Marchers of the Chinese People's Republic. Also, a live guitar or banjo player who would pick at Woody Guthrie and Leadbelly songs while letting his cigarette burn down to his lips Humphrey Bogart ash-length. Everyone would join in the singing and applaud lustily afterwards. Then someone would make an announcement of a picket line to be joined and someone else would take up a collection for some indicted anti-fascist freedom fighters or disenfranchised Negroes who usually came in numerical bunches. These evenings were called *hootenannies* and Les considered them an important part of his introduction to the world of sophistication. Sprawled on a throw rug or leaning back against a sofa or a settee, puffing away on a cigarette as a gallon jug of cheap red wine was being passed around, the real sophisticates slipping the jug over the back of their hands and drinking from it Spanish gypsy-style, Les could not help but feel that he had at last begun his own long march out of his tangled childhood roots into his own individual artistic adulthood. It was still a Brooklyn neighborhood basement, though, and sometimes the voices of Vivian's parents, particularly that of her father, a prominent local *kosher* butcher, who it was rumored had become wealthy because of black market activities during World War II meat rationing, could be heard through the pinhole board accoustical ceiling, proudly proclaiming, "Gin!" or hotly demanding of his wife how in hell she could knock with such a hand.

Meanwhile, petitions were signed and picket lines assembled and collections made for the exploited and the downtrodden and the victims of injustice everywhere. Especially when Vivian's older sister, Laura, was present. Les always looked forward to her appearances. Because Laura was every bit as provocative in her own way as her younger sister. She was slimmer than Vivian and cut her hair short like Ingrid Bergman in "For Whom The Bells Tolls" and was always dressed in black. Black slacks and black skirts and black sweaters and black blouses. Even wore a black beret sometimes, which really drove Les wild. But Laura never looked as if, like a Chekov character, she was in mourning for her life. Rather, it seemed that since she simply didn't have the time to worry about her wardrobe, she had decided to follow Henry Ford's dictum and wear anything as long as it was black. Besides, clothing styles were ephemeral, a passing bourgeois conceit; it was the impoverished and the subjugated, the exploited and the enslaved, the disen-franchised and the downtrodden, who demanded the complete fo-cus of her energies. A senior at college with an A average, Laura had decided to become a doctor, to lead a life in white so to speak, in order to further the revolution. Which struck Les as ironic con-sidering her fix on black. Down to her boyfriends. She always came with a handsome Negro in tow.

Les sometimes wondered as he looked up at the pinhole board acoustical ceiling if Laura's parents, laying down their gin rummy hands, knew exactly what was going on below in their finished basement with its separate entrance: What seeds of future revolu-tions were being sown, not only economically but socially. Laura always seemed to favor him with a provocative Jewish Giaconda smile as she observed Les sign the petition she was circulating or the membership enrollment cards to organizations she was forever handing out. Les would barely read the cards and petitions before quickly signing them. He never even considered not signing the material before him in the light of Laura's entreating, join-hither glances. Even his native street smarts, his built in danger detectors did not warn him to do otherwise. Besides, he was never that interested in politics anyway. It was not his particular form of theater.

Still, he might have been even more actively sympathetic to the many causes the Davis sisters espoused if Vivian had shown more interest in him. But somehow, she always seemed to have an older boyfriend, a college man, whose knees she would lean back against as she smiled over to Les while the four insurgent generals were betraying the Loyalist cause or Guantanamera was under attack or the peat bog soldiers were having a hard time of it. Sometimes Les thought he was just invited to those evenings for the sole purpose of being teased. Along with Mickey Feldstein.

Indeed, one night after a Davis soeurs soiree they walked out together into a cold February evening, suffering both the bluster of the Brooklyn winter wind and the pangs of the unrequited love—or, at least, intense infatuation—they shared for the Davis sisters.

And as they headed toward an all-night cafeteria to soothe their rejections, Mickey unfurled the long striped muffler which had been coiled about his neck and snapped it like a locker room towel at the corner lamp post. "How long must I wait?" he shouted suddenly, a dog baying at the moon, a Job beseeching his trying God. "How long must I wait?"

"Wait for what?"

Before answering Les, Mickey rolled the muffler into a loose coil and unsuccessfully tried to skip rope with it. "Two things," he said, unfurling the muffler and wrapping it around his neck again. "To fuck Vivian Davis. And to get the hell out of Brooklyn."

"What about Laura Davis?"

"That's for after I get out of Brooklyn."

Les nodded solemnly. "But if you could have your choice of fucking one, and only one of the Davis sisters ever, which one would you take?"

Mickey buffed the back of his collar with his muffler as if he were shining a shoe. Looking up, he stopped, and said, "Vivian."

"Why?"

"Because I think she would make me laugh."

"And Laura?"

"I'm not sure she would make me laugh—or cry."

"Tell me the truth, Mickey," Les followed through quickly. "Have you ever gotten laid?"

"Of course," Mickey laughed. "Haven't you?"

"Of course," Les lied.

Later, at the all-night cafeteria as Les watched Mickey drink Postum while he sipped his own heavily sugared coffee, Mickey spelled out his plans for the future. He had no intention of going to college. He was not the least interested in getting a job with a future after high school graduation in June. Instead, he was going straight to Paris.

"Why Paris?"

"Why not Paris? I've had to breathe enough of the bourgeois *shmutz* around here to last me a lifetime."

"What will you do there?"

"Work. Study. Live. Act. They got show business over there, too, you know."

"Do you have enough money to go?"

"I have my *bar mitzvah* gift money. I've never touched a penny of it. That'll get me there."

"What about getting back?"

"Who knows if I'll ever come back? Hey," Mickey leaned forward, "why don't you come with me?"

"I wish I could." Les poured another spoonful of sugar into his cold coffee and stirred it. "I wish I had the money."

"It would be great," Mickey continued in a rush. "We'd get a pad, a big studio with a slanted glass roof like in the movies, and we could send for the Davis sisters to come live with us."

"And who would I have? Vivian or Laura?"

"Either. Or both." Mickey laughed. "We all could have each other."

That spring, a week after their high school graduation, Mickey actually did leave for Paris. And Les went down to the boat to see him off.

3

It was the first time Les had ever been on a boat larger than the Staten Island ferry. And he was impressed. If this was just the tourist lounge, he imagined, as he looked up at the huge chrystal chandeliers descending from the tall arched ceiling on heavy, gold-plated chains, what must it be like up in first class? And the floor he was standing on was covered with a thickly woven red carpeting of an intricate geometric design that he assumed came from Persia or India or someplace expensive. And along the walls were swirls of murals depicting ships at sea and tropical islands and coral reefs and bare white sandy beaches with palm trees hovering over them. It was as if, Les thought, all the WPA artists whose familiar renderings of the Boston Massacre and the construction of the Erie barge canal and the surrender at Appomatax and the raid on Harper's Ferry were hanging in public school auditoriums and post office lobbies throughout Brooklyn, had suddenly been shanghaied into service on South Seas pleasure cruises and ordered to paint what they saw there instead.

Beneath the muraled walls stood sturdy leather couches, the kind Les had previously only seen in bank managers' and school principals' offices and dentists' and optometrists' waiting rooms. And all around the large room were clusters of glass-topped tables surrounded by rattan-weaved cane chairs. Les spotted Mickey sitting unhappily in one such chair, beside two smaller figures, a man pouring whiskey into a white paper cup and a woman with a fist pressed up against her eye. When Mickey saw Les, he sprang to his feet and ran over and embraced him joyously. "Am I glad to see you, Les," he said, patting his back in welcome.

"Why me?"

"Anyone then," Mickey said. "Just to get away from her." He turned to point at one of the smaller figures, the pink-faced woman dabbing at her eyes with the tip of a lace handkerchief. "But c'mon," Mickey steered Les toward the table. "Meet my parents, anyway."

Mickey's father held out a paper cup to him and Les accepted it with a silent nod as they were introduced. The woman offered him a sandwich wrapped in waxed paper from a wicker picnic basket covered with a linen napkin. When he refused it, she sighed and removed the handkerchief from her eyes and blew into it. "Tell me Lester," she asked, wiping her nose from side to side. "Are you entering college?"

Les looked over to Mickey for a signal of sorts, but none was forthcoming. "I start in September," he finally replied.

"See," Mickey's mother addressed her son. And then she returned her attention to Les. "So tell me, Lester, do you think it's right?"

"Do I think what's right?"

"A boy," the tip of her handkerchief was at her eyes again, "should go to Paris instead of entering college?"

Mickey's father was pressing his paper cup against Les's. *"L'chaim,"* Mr. Feldstein said and downed his shot in one gulp. Les took a small sip. It was rye, which he really did not like.

"I don't understand," Mrs. Feldstein wept.

"Enough, Ida," her husband said.

"Bar Mitzvah money is for Paris? *Bar Mitzvah gelt* is maybe for Israel, but never for Paris. Who ever heard of such a thing? Who ever heard of learning a profession in Paris, France?"

"C'mon," Mickey took Les's arm. "Let me show you my cabin."

An elegant, carpeted wood-framed elevator slowly carried them below deck. And then they seemed to be walking forever, as if they were changing lines at an unusually clean subway stop but one as complicated as Canal Street, until at last Mickey pushed open the mahogany louvred door of his cabin. Les was shocked by its size, or rather lack of size. There was barely enough room to move between two double-decked bunk beds and four small dressers. Still, as Les looked out the porthole window across the gray slivering waters of the Hudson at the bleak New Jersey shoreline, he was intensely jealous and wished he was the passenger about to sail off on a romantic journey, instead of a visitor who would have to return to his own mundane world in just a few hours. Les turned away from the porthole. "Who are your roommates?"

"A South African, an Australian, and a Frenchman. *Veddy* international," Mickey said, and sprawled out on the bunk bed nearest the door. And then Les heard her, recognized her laugh before he saw her. "This must be it," Vivian was saying as the door pushed open and the Davis sisters appeared.

Vivian was wearing jeans and a man's white shirt; and Laura, of course, was dressed in black. But it was also one of the few times Les saw Laura without a Negro. In fact, he was still half-expecting a Negro to follow the girls into the cabin when, indeed, a Negro steward did appear in the still opened doorway with a telegram for Mickey from Victoria Levine. Vicki Levine was the faculty advisor of the "Thespians" and she was wishing Mickey a bon voyage.

"Isn't this exciting?" Vivian said, examining the cabin as if she intended to rent it. "Do you know where you'll live in Paris?"

"I have the addresses of some cheap hotels," Mickey said.

"I mean what section?"

"The Left Bank."

"I have some names and addresses of people you should look up," Laura said. "People who are politically aware." She opened her purse and handed Mickey a list.

"Thanks," he said, and consulted the piece of paper before placing it in his wallet. "Any of them good for a meal?"

"They all are, I'm sure," Laura said. "But more important, they'll offer you food for thought. There is a lot of work to be done in Europe yet."

Mickey laughed uncomfortably. "I'm not going there just to work."

"Mickey's going there to learn, too," Vivian volunteered.

"Learning is work," pronounced Laura.

A bell clanged as if to signal the end of a class—or a round. And an announcement followed requesting that all visitors go ashore. "Maybe we should join your parents," Les said.

"I guess so," Mickey grimaced, and left the cabin with Laura. Then Vivian slid her arm inside Les's and they followed after them. Les wondered if he was rubbing against Vivian's breast or her underarm, but he did not want to chance disturbing the pleasurably erotic sensation he was feeling by looking down to check it out.

Les had expected to find the lounge half-emptied. Instead, it was twice as crowded with visitors like themselves, converging there from all parts of the ship. Children raced back and forth between the muraled walls with an antic desperation—as if they had only a very few moments left in the world to have any real fun. Champagne and wines were flowing everywhere and at a table near the entrance a group of girls was singing loudly in French. It was not even noon, yet it seemed like a New Year's Eve. Over the P.A. system in English, and then French, came announcements again requesting all visitors to go ashore immediately since the ship was about to sail. Tugboat fog horns blared as if to echo the warning. But the only visitors who seemed about to respond were Mickey's parents. They had repacked the picnic basket they had brought and were standing beside their table looking about forlornly. When they spied Mickey emerging from the elevator, they rushed toward him as if he were someone who had just arrived in time to bid them a last farewell before *they* sailed away, instead of vice versa. "Where were you so long?" Mrs. Feldstein greeted him. "I thought I'd never see you again."

Mickey laughed. "You're seeing me again."

"Maybe it's for the last time." Her handkerchief was once more at her eyes. "I remember once I lost you at Brighton Beach when you were a boy," she suddenly recalled. "Do you remember?"

Mickey smiled. "I remember. The policeman bought me an ice cream cone. Strawberry."

"Strawberry ice cream cone," Mrs. Feldstein repeated. And then just as abruptly as she had dipped into the past, she dived into the future. "Who knows if we'll ever see each other again?"

Mickey put his arm around his mother's waist. "We'll see each other again, Ma," he assured her. "I'm not going to the beach. I'm going to France."

"They have beaches there, too," said Mrs. Feldstein.

"Beautiful beaches," Mr. Feldstein suddenly agreed. "Better than Brighton. Better than Rockaway. Better than Jones, even. You ever hear," he whispered as if he were revealing some privileged information, "of the Riviera?"

"We've all heard of the Riviera, Pa," said Mickey. "C'mon," he began to propel his parents toward the exit to the deck, "you people have to get off the ship."

"Isn't it a nice room he has?" Mr. Feldstein said, falling into step beside Les. "You should have seen what I had coming over."

"Where did you come from Mr. Feldstein?" asked Laura.

"We sailed from Antwerp."

"But where did you live originally?"

"Russia."

"The Soviet Union?"

Mr. Feldstein shook his head. "No," he repeated, "Russia."

At the gangplank, they all embraced Mickey. First, Mrs. Feldstein and Mr. Feldstein kissed him on the lips. Les shook his hand and bear hugged him. Vivian buried her head more in Mickey's neck than in his face. But Laura, surprisingly, seemed to give him a real kiss. From where Les was standing, he couldn't tell if it was a French kiss, as if Laura may have decided it would befit the occasion. But if she had been wearing lipstick she would most certainly have left a mark, some telltale smudge. Once more, Mrs. Feldstein kissed Mickey and whispered something to him. He nodded and patted her on the shoulders. And then Mickey stepped back and seemed to wave and shrug at the same time as they all walked down the sisal-covered gangplank.

A few moments later the gangplank was raised like the entrance to a castle and soon the distance between the ship and the dock opened up like that of a moat as the vessel set sail, serenaded by the toots of escorting, pennant-flying tugboats. Les had the sensation that the dock was moving and the ship was stationary. But it was Mickey leaning against the rail on the upper deck, who was alternately blowing kisses at them and shaking his fist in the air, while they were all waving up to him as if he was some departing leader, a great warrior of renown off on some heroic quest. Until gradually, as the ship slid down the Hudson, he became just an indistinct speck, a vague dot, and finally just a blur. Then Mr. Feldstein turned to Les and the Davis sisters. "Anyone want a ride back to Brooklyn?" Les looked at the girls, shaking their heads, and shook his head, too. "No, thanks."

"Well, then take this." Mrs. Feldstein pushed the wicker picnic basket into Les's hands. "Delicatessen sandwiches. But nobody ate nothing. And what am I going to do with all this food? I thought maybe Myron would take something with him. But," she sighed as if reporting the rejection of a deathbed request, "he told me he didn't want it."

Les tried pushing the basket back to her in a reverse tug of war, but Mrs. Feldstein dropped her hands, insisting, "Take it."

Mr. Feldstein had already begun to move away. "Good-bye and thanks for coming," he said. "It's good to see Myron has such nice friends."

And Mr. and Mrs. Feldstein hurried away in surprisingly quick steps and were gone, with Les left still holding the basket. "What am I going to do with all this food?" he asked the Davises.

Vivian looked at her sister. "We could have a picnic?"

"Why not?" agreed Laura.

And soon Les was in heaven—or his idea of heaven at the time: a Davis sister on each arm, with the prospect before him of spending an afternoon—or at least a picnic lunch—with both of them.

4

First they sat on a blue-gray rock overlooking the lake in Central Park, eating the sandwiches, drinking beer, and munching on oranges and grapes. Then they walked over to the Museum of Modern Art where they saw "The Last Will of Dr. Mabuse." While on the screen the automobile traffic stalled and a silent gunman took aim at a fellow driver, in the dark, underground auditorium of the Museum Les felt a marvelous sensation. Vivian Davis, leaning forward, was reaching over and taking his hand. And it remained in hers throughout the rest of the film. Afterwards, on the long ride back to Brooklyn, as their fellow passengers fanned themselves with their *Telegrams* and *Journals* and *Posts,* Les and Vivian were swelteringly pressed together in subway intimacy.

At their stop, they climbed the iron-lipped stairs of the subway and emerged from the kiosk onto a tree-lined parkway. In those days, their Brooklyn neighborhood truly felt like a suburb, a development planned to combine the air of the country with the proximity of the city. Less than thirty-five minutes earlier they had been bound by the hot canyon walls of Manhattan's massive stone buildings, then they were trapped in the dungeonous subway, but now they were on an expansive Parisian-like parkway that could have been designed by Baron Hausmann himself, walking beneath silhouetted trees that offered the comfort of a gentle evening breeze.

Les hated to see the day end. For him, it had been a teeming day with the romance of a shipboard farewell to a friend and the reality of a picnic lunch in Central Park with the two most beautiful girls he knew. Not to mention the foreign film, a silent one, different in tone and texture from any movie he had ever seen before. And, of course, there was the hand-holding during the picture, too. He did not want to forget that. No, he did not want such a rare day to end just yet. He certainly was not ready to go home to his family and eat a silent supper laid out on a porcelain-topped table. So, when he saw an unoccupied bench he suddenly sat down upon it, placing the empty wicker basket in his lap. "I don't know why. But I'm tired," he said, leaning back and letting his legs sprawl forward. "Mind if I rest?"

Laura quickly sat down beside him but Vivian remained standing, hovering over him as if they were still in the subway and she was a straphanger who had yet to find a seat. "What do you think will happen to Mickey?" she asked, her wide, round eyes moving back and forth between him and Laura. "I mean will he change?"

"If change is growth," said Laura. "Then he'll certainly change."

"It'll be interesting to see him a year from now," said Vivian.

"It'll be interesting to see all of us a year from now," said Laura.

"Mickey could change a lot in a year," Vivian told her sister. "But you won't change much."

There was a chill in her voice and Les sensed a tension between the sisters he had never noticed before. "You'd be amazed how much I could change in a week," he intervened banteringly, "in France."

"I'm serious," said Vivian.

"I'm serious, too," Les said.

"Why should I change anyway?" Laura addressed her sister. Then she rose and turned to Les. "You don't have to walk us home."

But Les insisted on walking the Davis sisters home. It was not that much out of his way, he said, and would be his pleasure. But the walk to their door, despite his constant chatter, was not a pleasurable one. Laura was in a sulk and Vivian seemed more interested in stealing glances at her sister's pouting face than in picking up on any of Les's jokes. So, as he climbed the four brick steps to the front porch of the Davis house, he was relieved, prepared to say a quick good night and go his way. But Laura suddenly invited him in, and he quickly followed the girls into the entrance hallway, saying he could only stay for just a moment or two.

Having invited Les into the house, Laura then immediately excused herself and went upstairs, leaving Vivian to watch over him and both of them to watch the gin rummy game fiercely being waged in the dining room opening off the center corridor. Across the corner of a long walnut table, confronting each other, sat Mr. and Mrs. Davis. Oscar Davis had an oval, sunburned face and was bald on top with a greying fringe on the sides, striking Les as a Jewish Dwight D. Eisenhower. For his part, Oscar Davis was inspecting Les with his watery gray eyes as if Les was a card which he had not anticipated drawing and for which he could not foresee any possible use. On the other hand, his wife, Bea Davis, whose rimless glasses gave her angular face an intelligent cast, seemed more interested in Les. At least, she smiled over to him congenially before looking down at Oscar's discard, rolling a piece of gum about her mouth, and picking up the card. Then, matter-of-factly, she announced in the same breath that she was knocking with three and that there was plenty of food in the kitchen if anybody was hungry. Vivian said they weren't hungry and took Les's hand and led him to the doorway opening onto the stairway down to the finished basement.

Les had never really examined the Davis sisters' record library before. On Friday nights the program had always seemed to have been literally stacked in advance. But now, as he examined the pile beside the record player, he discovered not only folk songs and red anthems but pop records, many without jackets.

"Find anything you like?" asked Vivian.

Les held up a record.

Vivian squinted as if she could possibly read the label from across the room. "Put it on," she said.

Les carefully placed the record on the turntable. He didn't want to scratch any of the records in the Davis sisters' collection. That could certainly foul up things. Because who knew what they considered collector's items or were sentimentally attached to? And when the smooth, smoky tones of Nat King Cole began to issue from the speaker, Vivian joined him in front of the turntable as if it were an actual bandstand and they were at some college hop, like in the movies. Then, once more, she took his hand, committing him to the action before he even had a chance to make the decision. "Want to dance?"

Les knew he was not a terrific dancer. But he also knew how to act as if he was one. Dancing for him, like every other aspect in his life, was a performance—or, at least, an opportunity to perform. Even as a would-be actor he knew a strong characterization, even the wrong one, was better than none at all. So on the dance floor he acted as if he found boundless joy in movement. And in the execution of even the simplest two step, he managed to impart a sense of style and panache by simply overdoing it. Exaggeration, he had already learned, always did wonders. And he was like an artist who sketched in bold, heavy strokes in order to mask a native inability to draw the lines of an anatomy precisely. Most of Les's partners could never tell the difference between a good dancer and a poor one, anyway. Nor did they care to. After all, to most of them, it was only a dance.

But not to Les. For him it was a rhythmic excuse to neck standing up. A driving opportunity to dry hump. A first step toward actually scoring.

Les had never danced with Vivian before. Not one-on-one. On a Friday night some East European refugee had presided over a folk dance in which they all had joined hands in a semi-circle and hopped about. Something like the *hora* done at Jewish weddings, only with very loud foot-stamping and deep-knee bending. But this was different. Dancing with Vivian alone. And she was a good dancer, too. He had but to touch her lightly and she would follow. And when he dipped, she trusted him completely. Impulsively, he put his lips against her cheek. When the record ended, she pulled her head back and smiled at him. Then she moved her lips forward and they kissed.

For a moment they stood there without music until, as if embarrassed by the silence, Vivian went over to the record player, and turned it off and the radio on, twisting the dial until she found some band music. Then Les flicked off the light switch at the foot of the stairs and led Vivian along the paneled wall to the couch. It was almost completely dark except for a spill of light, seeping in from the half-windows facing up to the driveway. "Wait," Vivian said. She pulled the cord dangling from the lamp beside the couch. A weak red bulb came on.

When they sat down, Vivian snuggled into his arms and leaned back against his shoulders. Her high apple-round cheeks, caught in the eerie glow of the bulb, looked rouged. Les placed his fingers gently there and they became red, too. He pointed to the bulb. "It's like a gel."

Vivian laughed. "You can never forget about the stage for a single second."

"It's my dream," said Les. "It's what I want to do." And he made the mock face of a gallant lover and theatrically kissed her on the mouth. But after a moment, his tongue left his mouth and pushed gently between her lips. Surprised to find give there, it quickly entered and darted after her tongue, like one tadpole giving chase to another. Then their two tongues met, each warm and moist and very much alive, until Vivian pulled back her head with a sigh and Les buried his head in her neck and blew into her ear. He had once heard that drove girls crazy.

Vivian did not seem to be driven crazy at all, so he kissed her once more, their tongues meeting again, but this time like old friends, warm and welcoming to each other; and at the same time Les pressed down lightly on Vivian's left breast, rotating his hand slowly over the cotton shirt that covered her bra, and becoming more conscious of a hard-on forming between his legs, his own flesh rubbing against his jockey shorts, than of any other sensation. Wondering how Vivian was reacting, her lips still almost suction locked on his, his tongue still swirling within her mouth, he tilted his head ever so slightly upward and opened his eyes. But all he could see was the shadow of the lamp string on Vivian's nose. He could not tell whether her eyes were open or closed. Not that it mattered. But it was something he was always interested in knowing. He himself sometimes enjoyed kissing with his eyes closed because then he could imagine he was kissing someone else. Usually, Vivian. Was that what Vivian was now doing? Imagining she was kissing someone else? Like Mickey Feldstein, for example. He had been surprised that afternoon to see the Davis sisters come down to the boat to see Mickey off. He had not suspected Mickey was that close to them. But then again, maybe the girls had just enjoyed the idea of participating in a shipboard farewell? Anyway, what was past was past and maybe tonight would be more than just prologue.

Les placed his hand on Vivian's neck, just above her shirt whose top button was already open and undid the two buttons beneath it and slid his hand down between her pink brassiere and her bare white skin, fumbling for her nipple. Vivian moaned softly when he touched it and Les feared that he soon might come in his own jockey shorts. He was trying to twirl the nipple between his fingers in that cramped, constricted space when Vivian sat up and removed her shirt and reached back behind her neck with both hands and undid the clasp. Then she wiggled her shoulders and the straps slid down and the brassiere cups fell, magically revealing the most beautiful sight Les had so far seen in all his young life.

He stared idolatrously, like a shaman at a pagan shrine. Vivian's tits were terrific. Perfectly formed. Round and white and supple and firm, they reminded him of some proud, happy, fun-loving baby sea animals. He kissed one, then the other, teething the nipples as they hardened in his mouth. Vivian gasped in short audible breaths, her head rolling from side to side, and his own throbbing giant animal threatening increasingly, if pleasurably, to explode.

So he slid his hand down under Vivian's jeans. Just two fingers. And suddenly those terrific tits disappeared, the lovely milk-colored breasts were gone.

"That's enough," Vivian said, as she seemed to sit up, reclasp her brassiere and rebutton her blouse, all in a single flowing, constant motion.

"What's the matter?"

"I'm only seventeen."

"I don't understand."

"I'm still a virgin," Vivian slipped her blouse back into her jeans. "I don't go all the way."

"Who said anything about going all the way?"

Vivian rose. "If you want somebody who goes all the way then try my sister. She fucks."

Les was not so much surprised by that intelligence as he was astonished by the manner in which it was delivered. He just did not expect the word *fuck* to be used so precisely. He had heard girls say *fuck* before, but as an expletive or a judgement. Never as an action, or rather, *the* action. And he wondered if he should ask Vivian to put in a good word about him in connection with that action verb with Laura. But before he could say anything, the basement was bathed in light and Vivian was standing near the staircase beside the switch.

"When I'm eighteen I'll fuck, too," Vivian announced pleasantly. "But not until then. I've promised myself that."

Les tried joking: "I never keep promises I make to myself."

"I always do," Vivian said seriously.

"When are you going to be eighteen?"

"Soon. In December."

"December!" Les jumped to his feet. Why, that was practically next year! He would be almost finished with the first semester of his freshman year at college by then. He could barely imagine a future that distant. It was aeons of light years away and he knew it would be impossible to endure his virginity that long without a destructive disruption—or eruption or explosion—of some sort. His impulse was to scream and rant and rave and implore. But instead, he made an actor's choice and attempted reasoning as calmly and matter-of-factly as he could. "That's just a few months from now," he said. "A sheer technicality. Not even enough to be a technicality."

"To me, it's more than just a technicality."

"Why eighteen?" Les asked, his shoulders hunching together, his palms extended upwards. He was like a lowly beggar, an innocent supplicant, a small alms mendicant.

"Why not?" Vivian answered. "It's my virginity."

"It's also mine," Les shouted to himself the words he dared not say aloud. And instead, touched the switch on the turntable and held out an invitation to Vivian to dance again. "Can't you make an exception?" he asked as she walked into his arms. "For a friend?"

Her head moved wistfully from side to side and her lips twisted into a pout. "Not even if I wanted to."

"Why?" They were barely moving in place.

"Because I don't have a diaphragm."

"Couldn't you borrow your sister's?"

Vivian pushed him away and regarded him incredulously for a moment. Then she emitted a full-throated laugh. "That would be funny, wouldn't it."

"It would be more than funny," Les said, pulling her back into his arms and dancing over to the lamp where he pulled the string. "It would be great."

"Not till I'm eighteen," Vivian said decisively, and pulled the string, turning the light back on again. Still, she put her cheek against his as Nat King Cole resumed his crooning about the sweetness of Lorraine, Lorraine . . .

5

Like most adolescents, Les viewed his prolonged state of virginity as some cruel and unjust punishment meted out to him for some minor crime he could not even vaguely recall committing. It was not as if he had ever been caught red-handed masturbating, or detected eating ham on Yom Kippur, or discovered talking on line in the hallway of his grade school, or apprehended cheating on some high school examination. But rather, he was the victim of some completely false and trumped-up accusation. And, oh, how despite his innocence, he was made to suffer for that alleged transgression! But still, Les did not mark Vivian's eighteenth birthday on a calendar and check off each day toward that promised date—or date of promise—like a GI waiting for the termination of a tour of duty, or a prisoner awaiting the end of his sentence. He had too many other things to do at the moment. After all, he had not sailed off to Europe like a Lucky Pierre Mickey Feldstein. Instead, he would be starting college in the fall. And although Brooklyn College was tuition free, there would be a great many other expenses: Les wanted to take private acting lessons, he yearned for a car, he thirsted for a new wardrobe. And he dreamt of an apartment in Manhattan, a place of his own, where he could develop into a theater artist and get laid alot—or, at least, for the first time.

Which all required money, the long green, gold, shekels independently earned, jingling into his pocket from an outside source rather than grudgingly extracted by his mother or father after ringing up the "No Sale" key of the store register and then, in almost the same abrupt motion that slammed the National Cash Register drawer shut—as if that prevented the escape of further monies—slapped into his waiting hand.

In accepting such money, Les always felt guilty. Because he knew his parents were justifying those cash drawer withdrawals as contributions to the career of a one-day lawyer or some-day accountant-to-be, an upstanding professional whose future they were underwriting so that he would never have to put in long, hard days working behind the counter in a retail store, his feet and back aching as he dealt with rude and vulgar customers and beat off aggressive salesmen from six A.M. to ten P.M. daily, seven days a week.

Les had never even tried to share his dreams with them. After all, what could they possibly know about his visions of art? How could they ever understand the exaltation he felt appearing on a stage? Who could expect them to accept the fact that he wanted more out of life than just money when they had spent their lives dedicated to making just enough money to get by? They often accused him of being a dreamer without even knowing half the truth. Just imagine if they knew all of it!

But no, he did not simply spend that summer dreaming of one day fucking Vivian Davis in the backseat of a car he did not yet own. Or in front of the fireplace of a studio apartment in Manhattan he had yet to rent. Or of some year becoming another Marlon Brando, a star on Broadway going on to garner even greater acclaim in films. Les still had those dreams, but they were on a siding of his mind, as he faced the immediate reality tracking him. He needed a job.

That summer, the summer of his graduation from high school, the first summer of his real life in a sense, did not begin well. Mickey was gone, Vivian would be gone soon, too, off to work as a counselor at camp in Vermont, and he had no summer job in sight. The first few days after graduation he had halfheartedly answered the ads in *The New York Times*—not even knowing whether to look under "Boys Wanted" or "Young Men Wanted"—because no job seemed to pay enough to enable him to stash away any savings. If he was going to have to earn so little, Les considered spending the summer helping out in the store. In that way his conscience, at least, would be partially free of his mother's literal long-standing complaint: her aching feet. How many times had he returned home to find her seated in the back of the store, her chubby, bowling-pin legs crossed, and a chiropodist's paring instrument in her surprisingly long fingers as she scraped away at the planter's corns on her blue-bottomed feet. Les believed Ida's podiatric problems derived not from the time she spent on her tired feet behind the store counter, but rather from the high-heeled, tight pumps into which she always insisted upon squeezing those tired feet from the moment she first awakened in the morning. In fact, Les could scarcely ever remember seeing his mother in flat, no-nonsense shoes, not even slippers. Sensitive not only about her excess poundage but also her diminutive stature, she somehow had picked up the mistaken notion that by enhancing her height she need not take off weight. As a result, her excessive bulk still showed, but reeled on unsure spikes, her squozen flesh seeping over the sides of her calf pumps like slow-moving lava issuing from a grumbling volcano.

Late one afternoon after a feckless day of job hunting, Les returned to the store as Ida was preparing a sandwich for Chicago Mandelbaum. Chicago was a deeply suntanned man in his late twenties, a decade older than Les, whose curly red hair always seemed freshly permed. That day he was wearing a short-sleeved white-on-white shirt, wide flowing pleated tan gabardine slacks, and brown-and-white pimpled oxford shoes, shined and polished to a high gloss. By neighborhood standards, Chicago was considered well-dressed, a "sharpie." And, indeed, Chicago could afford to indulge himself sartorially because he never had to worry about sullying any of his costumes in connection with his line of work. He was the neighborhood bookmaker.

Chicago's natty dress also served to enhance his reputation as the

great neighborhood lover. He was involved in all manner of romantic intrigues and peccadillos with married women, young wid-
ows, skittish virgins, and still sexually active grandmothers. One
rumor had it that Chicago had dodged the draft by feigning epi-
lepsy; another asserted that he had been legitimately rejected for
military service because he was the possessor of a solitary testicle.
But the rumor concerning the deprivation of a testicle was only a
matter of conjecture. No one had ever come forth with corroborat-
ing eyewitness testimony.

The origin of Chicago's nickname was also open to conflicting
explanations. Some held it derived from his hustler's skill at Rota-
tion, the popular pool game also known as Chicago; others attributed it to his having once vociferously espoused the cause of an
underdog Cub team in a long forgotten three-team parlay. In any
event, that's what everyone called him; Les could never remember
hearing Chicago referred to by his real name.

Despite—or perhaps because of—his well-known, self-publi-
cized philandering, Chicago was a popular local figure. He had
many friends among horseplayers, sports fans, legitimate business-
men, and storekeepers such as Ida. The fact that he was reputed to
have substantial underworld ties in connection with his line of
work, rather than diminish his popularity, only served to abet it.
Also, everyone appreciated the fact that he was personally instrumental in arranging for the rental of the pool hall to the Young
Israel for High Holiday services every year. For it was a widely
accepted piece of neighborhood lore that Chicago, like a regular
Jewish Robin Hood, picked up most of that rental tab himself, both
as a form of neighborhood reputation-enhancing philanthropy and
as a deferential tribute to his Orthodox father, Mendel Mandelbaum, who always served as the lay cantor, presiding over the
services in his rasping voice.

"Your mother makes some sandwich." Chicago lifted his poppy
seed roll, which was thickly laden with lox and cream cheese, as if
it were a pony of port and he was proposing a toast with it. "Anyone figure out a way to bottle it, would be rich as Coca Cola."

Ida accepted the compliment by spitting out the words, "Coca Cola" as if they constituted some sort of curse better reserved for Cossacks and Ukrainians, and dipped her head toward Les. "Any luck?"

"No," Les replied as he went to the large red steel box, with *Coca Cola* in swirling white semi-script embossed on its side. He dropped his hand into it and fished in the melting ice until he came up with a Mission Orange soda.

"What are you up to, Les?" asked Chicago.

"He's looking for a job," Ida answered for him. "Know of any?"

"I thought you were going to college."

"That's not till fall. He needs a summer job." Ida answered for Les again, as if she were speaking for a child or someone who was not even present. "Know of any?"

Chicago wiped a spittle of lox from his lips with a paper napkin. "The best summer jobs are in the mountains," he announced, as if he were a judge asked to render a verdict.

Ida waddled around the counter. "Know anybody in the mountains?"

As Chicago looked about for a place to put his soiled napkin, Ida leaned forward and abruptly snatched it out of his hand. Chicago studied his suddenly bare hand. "Maybe I do." He finally looked up and repeated to Les, "Maybe I do," adding as an afterthought, "Check in with me tonight, Les."

That night Les checked in with Chicago in the pool room, where he found him perched on a high stool beside the bell-shaped, glass-domed ticker, scanning the tape spewing out the night baseball scores. While waiting for the Dodger half of an inning in Cincinnati to come in, Chicago informed Les that he did happen to know somebody in the mountains, someone with whom he had often chased *nookie*—Heshie, the headwaiter at the Levine Family Diplomat. Chicago said he would call old Hesh to see if he might have something up there for Les. "But I've got to warn you," he looked up from the spewing ticker, "you've got to be ready to bust balls if you want to make out in the mountains."

Les quickly assured Chicago that he was quite prepared to strain his gonads to the point of implosion in the mountains, or any place else for that matter, in order to make out.

"Smart," adjudged Chicago, fingering the yellow ticker tape like a priest counting the beads of a rosary. "No wonder your mother is sending you to college." And then he tore off the tape and watched it fall in a curling heap to the floor like the inevitable ending of an Indian rope trick. "The Dodgers might as well go to college, too," he said. "Because they ain't doing shit in Cincinnati."

6

If Les had a preconception of "the mountains"—or "the country" as that area of the Catskills was also called—it was of a mini-Switzerland with winding streets and rolling hills and verdant knolls, where cows and bullocks and goats and sheep, shepherded by derby-wearing, black-clad *Chassidim,* nibbled on spotless stream-fed pastures under cloudless azure skies. In the background loomed Alpine lodges from whose shuttered windows issued the fresh-voiced trills of milk-fed sopranos in song. Some times these chesty maidens, their golden pigtails hanging over their apron-covered frocks, would actually fling open the shutters wide and wave down to their *Yeshiva bucher* shepherd lovers, who, caught between the demands of their otherworldly pursuits and animal husbandry, playfully twirled their own earlocks with one hand while intoning from the leatherette-bound prayer books they held in the other. In short, it was a Walt Disney "A Sound of Talmud."

So much for Les's prescient images fostered—or foisted—by pop culture. In reality, the Levine Family Diplomat was one in a row of hotels—the others were Schwartz's Mountainside, the Claridge, the Plaza, the Feinstein Flamingo, and the Sir Arthur Balfour—all set back along a strip of traffic laden blacktop that led into the main street of the town of South Hillsburgh, less than a half mile below. Some of the hotels seemed to have been originally designed for Miami Beach and Las Vegas and even Israel itself, having a turf-

and-surf desert oasis motif in their sand-stone-stucco construction. Others, at first glance, like the Claridge and the Sir Arthur Balfour, seemed more appropriately suited to their north temperate zone environs. But after the sun went down and the garish neon signs proclaiming their identities hissed on, the touches of Tudor in their facades, derivative more of the Forest Hills Inn than any structures to be found in the English countryside, vanished completely in the night mountain sky.

What perhaps distinguished the Levine Family Diplomat most was the fact that it alone seemed to have no single architectural antecedents. The main building, which housed the dining room, looked like the giant wing of an old monoplane, which somehow had managed to have landed safely on an island of cleared woods on the side of the road. The annex, large and red, resembled an antiquated barn converted into a summer theater. The low-slung casino, which actually served as the theater, nightclub, and dance hall, could have been mistaken for a Southern Californian supermarket or a Santa Fe restaurant. Yet somehow taken all together, this eclectic amalgam did manage to suggest summer sun and mountain fun. In addition, the Levine Family Diplomat included an almost Olympic length swimming pool, a regulation size basketball court, and a nest of clay tennis courts. Also out of sight, beyond glinting stainless steel chain-link fences that bound the pool and the mesh wires enclosing the tennis courts, were a cluster of small shacklike buildings carved into the side of the hill behind the annex. These shanties, as Les was to soon discover, housed the hotel laundry and served as the sleeping quarters for the hotel's staff.

To reach the Levine Family Diplomat, Les had boarded a Short Line Bus at the Hotel Dixie Terminal in Times Square. An hour and forty-five minutes later, the bus stopped for twenty-five minutes at the Red Apple Rest, a large diner on Route 17 just outside of Middletown. Les rested there by drinking a Pepsi Cola and then pissing into a pine-scented urinal. Standing at the adjacent urinal was the bus driver who informed him, in the course of an otherwise idle exchange, that Les and his fellow passengers would be dropped by the bus at their exact destinations, the bus functioning much like a cab once it reached "the mountains," except for its station stops in the towns of Monticello, Liberty, and South Hillsburgh. And indeed, an hour and ten minutes later, Les found himself deposited at the bottom of the driveway that curled up to the entrance of the Levine Family Diplomat, with the large Gladstone his mother had insisted on packing down to six changes of underwear, unloaded at his feet. He followed the white curbstones, still smelling of their limestone markings, up the driveway where, instead of being greeted by *Chassidic* shepherds singing, *"L'chaim* to Life!" he was met by a solitary tall, lean semi-uniformed bellhop with an emaciated, but vaguely familiar, pin-head face who was wearing a Napoleonic maroon and gold tunic over gray gym shorts and high-topped black basketball sneakers. "Let me take that," the bellhop said, grabbing the suitcase out of Les's hand. Then he looked back over his shoulder at Les as he began to trudge up the driveway. "How is it in the city?"

"Hot," said Les, wiping his brow, as if he still personally bore within his pores some of the heat of the City of New York.

Silently, they reached the top of the driveway until the bellhop turned around and asked, "Do you know if you're booked in the main building? Or the annex?"

"I don't know where I'm booked. I'm just going to work here."

"Shit!" The bellhop dropped the suitcase immediately, as if suddenly discovering he had been carrying one hundred pounds of stones. "Why didn't you say so?"

"You didn't ask."

The bellhop touched Les's suitcase lightly with his toe. "What do you have in there anyway?"

"Underwear," said Les, picking up the suitcase. "A lot of underwear. My mother believes in underwear."

"All mothers do." The bellhop nodded knowledgeably and hurried under the protective shade of the canopy that extended out from the doorway. "I hope you're not another bellhop," he said, when Les caught up with him. "Don't tell me they've hired another bellhop?"

"No," said Les, "I'm a busboy."

"Good." The bellhop pushed open the front door of the hotel and Les followed him into a long, narrow lobby crammed with white wicker furniture adorned with pillows covered in a design of large orange and green flowers. "You can leave your bag there." The bellhop pointed to an empty spot near a wicker rocker.

Les dropped his bag. "Now what do I do?" he asked, and idly pushed the empty rocker as if it were a swing with a young child perched upon it.

"Well, if I was a new busboy the first thing I would do was go to the dining room and report to the headwaiter. Is Heshie expecting you?"

Les laughed nervously. "He better be."

The bellhop held up a finger. He had a thought. "Say, where do you go to school anyway?"

Almost automatically, Les was about to respond with the name of the high school he had just graduated from, Rutherford B. Hayes High. But he caught himself in time and announced instead his new educational affiliation, the college he would soon attend, "Brooklyn College."

"Brooklyn College?" the bellhop considered. "You're not on the team there."

"What team?"

The bellhop smoothly pantomimed a dribble and then after passing an imaginary basketball over to Les, flounced down onto the swinging rocker, all but crushing the imaginary child Les had just pictured perched upon it. Les, stuck with the imaginary basketball he had just mimed catching, turned it over as if to examine it. "Hey," Les suddenly looked up at the bellhop, as if he had just read something other than a brand name, such as Wilson or Voit, inscribed on the imaginary basketball. "Aren't you Artie Rabinowitz? NYU?"

The bellhop looked up from the rocker pleased. "Yeah," he said and smiled.

Les had seen Artie Rabinowitz play against both Notre Dame and St. Johns in Madison Square Garden doubleheaders. "I'm Les Rose," he introduced himself. "You have a hell of a hook shot."

"Don't I though?" Artie admitted proudly. Then he pointed over his shoulder and to the left. "You better check in the dining room if you want to work dinner."

Les nodded. "Think fast," he said, and push-passed the imaginary basketball back to the bellhop, who caught it airily with one hand.

In order to reach the dining room, Les had to walk through a long alcove whose walls were lined with various candy, soda, and pinball machines. Standing alongside one of the pinball machines was a small old man wearing a *yarmulke;* on the other side of the same machine was a fat child in a bathing suit, waving a Coke bottle in one hand and an Oh Henry candy bar in the other. Both were peering intently over the glass top at the pinball machine player, who was the tallest person Les had ever seen, taller even than Artie Rabinowitz by a good six inches. The giant was leaning over the machine, his long arms and enormous hands firmly gripping its wooden encased sides, as if they were the thighs of an easily excitable woman, his fingers working the flippers dexterously, his lean, rail-thin body swaying back and forth in suggestive English. He had blond hair fashioned in a crew cut over his gaunt, hollow-cheeked face and seemed to breathe by sucking in air between the thin lips that framed his small mouth. Although he could not place him exactly, Les knew immediately the giant, like the bellhop Artie Rabinowitz, had to be a basketball player, too. Evidently the Levine Family Diplomat was loaded with basketball players.

When the giant straightened up before shooting his next pinball, he sharply instructed both the old man and the fat boy to "Get off the machine." Then he smiled at Les, revealing a missing front tooth. Les thought of passing him the imaginary basketball in return, before remembering that he had left it with the bellhop rocking away in the lobby.

One of the muslin-curtained French doors at the entrance to the dining room was half-opened and Les slid through it. At once, he was amazed by the size of the room. Table after round table, eight settings to each, goblets and glasses at each setting, spread out before him on every side endlessly, like a wallpaper pattern. It was bigger than Dubrow's Cafeteria, than Hoffman's Cafeteria, even bigger than some Times Square cafeterias. And without mirrors. But it was also utterly silent. Les saw no signs of human existence until he spotted a small teak desk with a large figure sitting before it along the near wall running down from the entrance doors. At first, from a distance, the figure seemed to be sorting cards, as if dealing out a hand of solitaire. But as he approached the desk, Les could see that he—the figure was definitely a man—was actually placing business-sized cards in the slit pockets of an oversized binder, like a high school teacher arranging classroom seating.

Les coughed to announce his presence. The large figure froze his card dealing, and turned around. He had a pink face and wore a large emerald ring and a shining gold wristwatch. "Who the fuck are you?" he barked. "And who the fuck sent you?"

Les answered the second question first.

"How the fuck is Chicago? Is he getting a lot of *nookie?"*

Les hesitated for a moment. He had no idea of the quantity of *nookie* Chicago was getting. But he nodded affirmatively anyway.

"Good, because if he's getting his *nookie* it means he won't be coming up here, which will save me some pinochle money." The large figure appraised Les as if he were some stray dog. "I hope you're not some fucking basketball player."

"No."

"Good." The man rose and extended his hand. "I need dining room help and they keep sending me hoop stars. But what good are fucking dribblers in the dining room? Tell me, *boychick,* do you have any experience as a busboy?"

Les hesitated again, just a second before answering. "Yes."

"Where? What houses did you work?"

Chicago had instructed him to say that he had worked as a busboy at the catered affairs held at the local Jewish community center and he replied to that effect.

The headwaiter laughed in his face. "Whose bullshit is that? Yours or Chicago's?"

"Chicago's," Les admitted.

"Never shit a shitter," the headwaiter said, "and I can bullshit with the best of them. Meanwhile, I can use you on the floor tonight." He reached into a drawer, extracted some tax forms and handed them to Les. "Fill these out for Uncle Sam and be here in uniform at five o'clock and I'll show you your station. Also, ask the fucking hoop star in the lobby to show you where the help bunks and to fix you up with bedding."

With that, the headwaiter sat down and resumed his peculiar game of solitaire, a game which Les later learned demanded both the art of the matchmaker and the crafts of the pimp. It also turned out Chicago knew not only the headwaiter, Heshie, but also the Levine Family itself and was a frequent guest there in quest of summer *nookie*. In fact, the parting piece of advice that Chicago had favored Les with before he took the subway to the Hotel Dixie Bus Terminal for the Short Line Bus that bore him to the mountains was, "Save your money. And get good *nookie.*"

7

Les worked hard, busted his balls, and in a few weeks had accumulated more money in savings than he had previously dreamt possible. He also managed to come in contact with sufficient *nookie* to unburden himself—at least technically and semantically—of his long-smoldering virginity. But still, it was Vivian Davis and her precise form of *nookie*—by this time it was a firm promise in Les's imaginative, rapturous mind, a definite commitment for delivery upon her eighteenth birthday—that was the consummation he was most devoutly wishing—and waiting—for.

Indeed, it was that dream that sustained him during the long days in the dining room of toting them dishes and lifting them trays, and carried him through those tiresome, boring nights in the casino where he would dance with guests and bullshit with his fellow busboys before shuffling off to sleep. He knew that the present was only transitory, as fleeting as summer itself. That he, Lester Rose, was made for better things, a future that was as golden as the Catskill sun shining down upon the bathers in the Levine Family Diplomat almost Olympic length pool at noon. After all, he was an artist interested in more than just the passing pleasures of the mundane and the banal. He bore within him the call—or the curse—of art. And he would succeed as an artist, too. The time would come when his name would be a household word, like Kirk Douglas and Marlon Brando and Burt Lancaster. Meanwhile, he could mix and mingle and fake a South American dance alot easier than most of his fellow busboys. Because he brought his actor's skills to the tasks. He could confide with a straight face to a septuagenarian guest that he planned to be a doctor, an internist; in fact, a gerontologist, specializing in the illnesses that afflict the old. Or with equal sincerity intone to a bearded religious zealot that he was determined to become a rabbi and go to Israel. Or on the dance floor he would praise a buxom guest on how lightly she moved her feet. He would flatter one, he would flatter all. Lies came to him effortlessly. Because they were not really lies. It was all a shell game in which he was his own shill trying to promote a larger tip. And he became quite adept at it.

The guests loved him, his fellow busboys accepted him. Only some of the sleazeball *anti-semitten* derelicts, hired by the Levine Family to work in the kitchen, would give him a hard time. Once, a drunken salad man named Higgins threw a knife at Les, narrowly missing his head as it whirred past his earlobe and bounced off the hardwood freezer doors. And all Les had done was just reach for a whitefish that somebody else had ordered. No big deal. But there was something about food, preparing it and having to be about it all day, that brought out both the worst in people and the worst of people.

Working around food also induced horniness. As if the attempt to service one vital need immediately stimulated another. As if the headquarters for all the sensory needs were located in the same neighborhood and any alarm sounded for one was responded to by all. And as he toiled to accrue enough money to satisfy one set of dreams, Les also finally managed to unburden himself of another set of singular obsessions, those dealing with his long-festering virginity. But only technically, not even completely, and certainly not emotionally.

All summer Les was chiefly focused on money. The making of money. He wanted to keep making money. And more money. Filthy lucre. The long green. *Gelt.* As in *Gelt ist der velt.* Why else was he enduring the dining room servitude practiced at the Levine

Family Diplomat? Putting up with all the shit the guests were throwing at him? Plus suffering countless indignities because of the legendary cheapness—the legend being that of the exploitive Jew —of the Levine Family?

The routine was constant and unchanging. Up at six-thirty. The dining room opened at seven, the guests ambling in for breakfast until nine thirty. Then, always a last minute flurry—God forbid a guest should miss a meal he would be charged for on the Jewish-American plan.

So, Les could never leave the dining room before ten. But he had to be back by eleven-fifteen to have his own lunch at the work-benchlike staff tables, oilcloth-covered doors laid down over carpenter horses, in the kitchen pantry. Guest lunch was served from twelve to two. And in the afternoon, thankfully, there usually was a decent break before dinner. During which Les could pose as a vacationing guest himself and play basketball or tennis or swim. Or take care of his personal chores, such as laundry or letter writing.

But Les could never really keep up with his letter writing. Because he was bombarded almost daily with communiques from Mickey Feldstein over in Paris, France, chronicling his adventures, near adventures, mis-adventures. Sometimes they were real letters with hotel stationary letterheads; but just as often they were napkins, menus, picture postcards, all urging Les to come join him at once. Or failing that, at least visit him. Les's other chief correspondent was Vivian who was working as an assistant dramatics counselor at an interracial camp in Vermont, where she seemed to be having a great deal of fun but kept insisting she was bored.

Les was not so much bored as tired. Tired because he had to return to the dining room by five. Work dinner from six to eight. And it would be eight-thirty before his working day was over. A long day. Even for someone brought up living above a retail store. And a long week, too. Because there was never a day off. In fact, Vivian in her very first letter had suggested that they might plan their days off together, that it would be great fun for him to hitch over to her camp. Or that they could at least meet halfway—she had looked at the map—in some place like Albany or Pittsfield. But Les had to write back that he could never make it. Not even if Vivian were suddenly, by some miracle, ready to declare herself officially eighteen. Because he simply never had a day off. Not even Sunday. Sunday ironically was the one work day Les actually looked forward to. Sunday was the day when the guests usually tipped for the week—or the weekend—of service.

Les worked six tables, two stations, for two waitresses, Millie and Glenda, busing for as many as forty-eight guests at a time. Ideally, just as the waitress was supposed to be tipped at least five dollars, the busboy could expect a tip of three or four dollars. Sometimes more; but more often less. Yet each Monday morning Les was able to bring at least one hundred dollars in cash to the South Hillsburgh Post Office, purchase a money order and send it home. When Vivian learned of his schedule, she described his lack of a day off as *exploitive.* Certainly it was *exploitive.* But by Labor Day, Les hoped to have been exploited sufficiently to salt away over a thousand dollars.

For a new wardrobe. For tuition for private acting classes. For a payment on a car. And, of course, for that one particular vision which was sustaining him all summer long: The rapturous post-eighteen date, or rather night—with Vivian.

Meanwhile, he lived the life of a busboy, serving stewed prunes in monkey dishes with underliners and glasses of hot water and lemon to soothe the under-functioning stomachs of the overstuffed guests; pouring third and fourth cups of coffee and tea, cocoa and postum, fresh unpasteurized milk and cultured sour buttermilk; stooping under the loads of the heavy trays stacked with dirty dishes in a shell or floral shape, like the carapace of an overturned turtle, which he toted on his shoulder on the long journey through the cavernous dining room to the swinging door entrance of the noisy kitchen, where the waitresses were all standing in lines clamoring for their orders, and back to the steel sinks where the "pearl divers," as they called the itinerants who washed the dishes, looked up unsympathetically, soap grease frothing on their tattooed arms, smoke curving upwards from the cigarette butts lodged between their lips. And finally, Les would lower his tray and empty it in a cacophonous clutter and crash onto the wooden drainage racks and emit a long sigh of relief.

As a busboy, it was also Les's duty to fetch anything that was not on the menu, a "special" requested by a guest that would interrupt the waitress's normal routine, no matter how many dirty dishes were piling up on the tables. And so the first law of vocational survival that he learned from the more experienced busboys was to never go into the kitchen empty-handed. The second law he learned was never to believe anything his fellow busboys told him.

Especially, about money or *nookie,* two of the three subjects most constantly discussed by both the guests and the help. When a fellow busboy told him how much money he had earned that week, for example, Les quickly learned to either multiply or divide that figure by two in order to arrive at the neighborhood of the truth, depending upon the personality of the teller. When it came to *nookie,* the multiple—or divisor—factor employed had to be even larger.

A third subject ever present on the tips of all tongues, not surprisingly, was food. The guests chattered on about it in terms of the skill of the chef and the artistry of the pastry baker. They discussed its quality, abundance, variety, preparation and, of course, taste. The staff simply complained about its lack. Because they were rarely served pastry or bread that was less than stale.

Indeed, Les found it cruelly ironic that he was supposed to work around food all day, yet never get anything good to eat. Except that which, like a smuggler, he managed to bootleg out of the kitchen: a special order of smoked white fish. A side of belly lox. A fresh piece of fruit. A helping of pie. An untouched cut of steak or a chop. He would carefully secrete his napkin-draped bootie behind a bread basket on the bottom shelf of a serving station; and after the dining room had emptied, facing the dining room wall as if he were indulging in some illicit sex practice, surreptitiously gulp and chomp it down. Les had seen several of his fellow busboys even snatch up the remnants on guests' plates. But he never resorted to that.

After each meal Les quickly cleared the tables of livestock, those staples salvageable for reuse such as butter, marmalade, milk, cream, horseradish, mustard. Then he helped his waitresses, Millie and Glenda, set up for the next meal. First, he brought the dirty silverware, which throughout the meal he had deposited into stainless steel buckets at the foot of each of his waitresses' serving stations, into the kitchen. Next, he added soap powder and hot water and strenuously swirled the silver in the mix. Then he rinsed it twice and called it a wash. Millie and Glenda wiped the silver as they set the tables with it, while he polished the goblets with linen napkins and restocked the salt and pepper and sugar dispensers. When he finished those tasks, he poured black coffee onto any new stains showing on his black twill trousers, pealed off his hotel-issued white linen Eisenhower-like jacket, unclasped his black bow tie, and dashed off for an evening of freedom—and possible adventure.

8

One August night, after rushing from the dining room to the unpainted wooden shack in the hillock behind the casino that served as the busboys' bungalow, and fighting his way to a place before the single jagged, broken mirror still standing above one of the two sinks in the john, Les spotted a familiar but unexpected image peering over his shoulder behind him. As he continued combing his hair, pushing it up in front above his forehead to form a slight pompadour and then slicking it down flat in back, the image produced a smile by lifting the toothpick that issued out of one corner of its mouth like a cat's whisker and rolling it over to the other side. Les followed the moving toothpick the way he would observe the cut of a deck of cards, his own head reflexively swirling in a similar circular motion. "When did you get in?" Les addressed the mirror. "I had no idea you were coming up."

"Neither did I," said Chicago, still shuffling the toothpick about his lips. "But it just got too fucking hot in the city. "Here," he poked Les in the back. "Your mother asked me to give you this." Les turned around and Chicago handed him a large box wrapped in thick brown paper and bound with a white stringy twine of coarse pealing strands. Les jiggled the box tentatively. It was light, too light to contain food: a salami, a loaf of rye bread, a jar of pickles. Oh, how he would love to have a salami to *nosh* on before going to sleep on a cold mountain night. He was always particularly hungry then. "What is it?" he asked Chicago hopefully.

"I just brung it," Chicago said. "I didn't open it." And followed Les out of the latrine into the small cubby containing two beds, one splintery dresser, and studs with nails from which clothing was descending everywhere, which Les shared with Lionel "Happy" Feigenbaum. There was no question as to how the dour "Happy" might have acquired his nickname. He never smiled. Not even on a Sunday with terrific tips rolling in. Not even after passing off for a winning basket in a Friday night game against Tamarack Lodge. And, for all Les knew, not even when he was scoring with his girlfriend in the city, Betty, whose peculiar sexual preferences he always used to like to describe to Les in vivid detail before falling off to an adenoidal sleep.

Les quickly unwrapped the bulky package and emptied the contents onto his unmade bed. Nothing but underwear. And more underwear. T-shirts and jockey style shorts, underwear up the ass. Of all his needs, the only one his mother diligently sought to fulfill was the supplying of sufficient underwear to last him a lifetime. No other woman would ever have to buy him underwear again. Perhaps in college he would someday take a psychology course and find out the reasons. Meanwhile, he tossed his new underwear into the air as if it were freshly falling snow. Chicago caught a flake and inspected it. "Fruit of the Loom," he read approvingly. "But boxers give more ball room than jockeys. And I always get mine monogrammed."

"Your balls?" Les asked in feigned amazement.

"My boxers." Chicago corrected him seriously. "With my initials. It adds class. And the chicks like it."

Les wondered what possible class initialed underwear could add and why "chicks" could possibly like them. But all he said was, "Maybe you should tell my mother about boxers."

"Be glad to," Chicago offered sincerely. "But your mother is a very smart woman already. I'm sure she knows that. Meanwhile, c'mon. Get dressed. Aren't you going to the game?"

Les had not planned on going to the hotel basketball game that night. Not that he did not like basketball. But he was always a bit embarrassed to appear before the Levine Family Diplomat Hotel guest public as one of the few males in the dining room who was not a college varsity basketball player. During his first week as a busboy, Les did, in fact, suit-up for a game and even played in the waning minutes. But who needed that? Just as Les had no intention of becoming a bit actor, always cast in small roles, he did not find it very pleasant to be a substitute hunched forward on a cold, bare bench on a chilly summer evening. Nor did he relish the possibility of making a fool of himself in a sport that was never his strong suit. Baseball was his game. "Anyway, I'm not on the team," Les said.

"Neither am I. But when I come to the mountains, first I always like to watch a basketball game. Next, I like a nice piece of *nookie*. And then a good game of pinochle. That's what I call a vacation."

Les did not see how the bill of pleasures Chicago sought on vacation was any different, given his reputation and avocation, from those he normally pursued during his usual workday non-vacation schedule, except perhaps for a variance in the order. But Les did not say anything, and agreed to go to the game with Chicago. After all, Friday night, basketball night, was *the* night at the Levine Family Diplomat. There was also show night (Saturday), movie night (Wednesday), bingo night (Monday), band night (Thursday), and Latin American night (Tuesday). But basketball, Les had learned, served as one of the great lures of the Levine Family Diplomat. Year in and year out, with players drawn chiefly from New York City colleges, the hotel boasted one of the best teams in the mountains.

The games were played on an outdoor cement court laid out beside the pool. Along the sidelines the bellhops set up folding chairs, some of which backed onto the pool area. A few of the card-playing guests preferred sitting in that area at pool-side tables so they could watch the basketball game and, at the same time, carry on their card games in the shadowy spill of illumination provided by the egg-box clusters of lights hung atop the aluminum poles at both ends of the court.

Since the game that night was against the neighboring Sir Arthur Balfour, a large contingent of their guests were also on hand, having accompanied their team on the after-dinner walk of a distance less than the length of a football field that separated the two hotels. There was, as one would have expected, a good-natured rivalry, not only between the two basketball teams, but also between the guests, so not surprisingly many "friendly wagers" were negotiated as the players warmed up. Also, a few "unfriendly wagers" in terms of the sums involved. A chubby Sir Arthur Balfour guest named Jackie Gordon, who wore sunglasses even though it was twilight and who described himself as "The King of the Cut-Rate Optometrists" was eagerly seeking "action," loudly offering to take Sir Arthur Balfour and eight points for *any* amount. And, at that price, by game time he had covered over five thousand dollars of Levine Family Diplomat money. But not any of Chicago's money.

"Give me a break," Chicago had said, declining the Optometrist King's invitation to bet. "I'm on vacation. Besides," he leaned over and whispered to Les, "I smell something and it ain't *kosher.*"

"What do you mean?"

"You'll see," Chicago nodded knowingly. "You'll see soon enough."

Most of the talk taking place around the court, as the players milling under their respective baskets shot their warm-ups, did not involve the comparative merits of the teams or wagers on the likely outcome of the game, give or take eight points. Rather, it was about the virtues of the respective dining rooms. And these discussions evoked far more competitive spirit than talk of the impending game itself.

The Sir Arthur Balfour had originally been a *Glatt kosher* hotel, frequented only by the most pious bearded types, East Side and Williamsburgh *Chassidim*. But in recent years, a new ownership had converted it into a hotel that, like the Levine Family Diplomat, was strictly kosher but not *Glatt kosher, kosher* beyond the slightest scintilla of the shadow of a doubt. Still, the Balfour seemed to cater to a generally older, more "family type" crowd, than the Levine

Family Diplomat. And no one expected it to compete with the Diplomat on the social front. Because the Levine Family Diplomat was as famous for the ample social opportunities it provided its theoretically younger crowd to mix and mingle and "make out," as it was for its basketball team. In fact, it was often described even by the help itself as a "make-out," "muffkie-fuffkie" house. But many of the Diplomat guests were not quite willing to acknowledge that fact to others, especially to neighbors paying lower rates.

So, as they shmoozed with the visiting Balfourites, they boasted about the excellence of the Levine Family Diplomat's pastry chef ("I know I shouldn't eat them, but who can resist such strawberry shortcake tarts and lemon meringue pies."); the imagination of its salad man ("What that man can do with artichokes and avocados. Any vegetable beginning with 'a.' Such as 'a carrot' or 'a stalk of celery.' "); the sheer magnitude of the portions ("If I only ate half of the steak, it would still be double the normal portion I get at home."); the endless varieties offered ("We have more different soups to choose from at each lunch than Campbell makes in a year."); and, of course, the service ("Those busboys out there are better than any of the professional waiters in the finest restaurants on Broadway. They guess what you need even before you know you want it. And as for the waitresses, each one of those girls is a genuine beauty.").

Beauty was not the first word that came to Les's mind with which to describe the waitresses in the Diplomat dining room. Rather, he would have used adjectives such as *hardworking* and *industrious* and *tough.* And if he were limited to the use of just one word, it would have been the noun *shiksas.* The older "girls" were actually women, professional waitresses who worked in either Miami Beach or Manhattan during the winter; the younger girls were from Pennsylvania and Kentucky, from places such as Allentown and Scranton and Louisville. Millie and Glenda, the two waitresses Les worked with, for example, were of each type.

Millie was a chesty divorcée in her late twenties with red hair and a mean mouth. She had been married to a sailor in San Diego and now had two young children who were staying with her mother in Astoria. Les had liked Millie from the start because she was fair, never blaming him for any of her own goofs, the way so many other waitresses would get on their busboys for their own mistakes.

Also, she was ballsy. Never afraid to put an out-of-order guest in his place. One day, for example, Harry Sasonkin, a sleazeball radio tube manufacturer who was nobody's favorite, began giving Millie a hard time over a burnt steak. This was after he had twice sent it back for not being sufficiently well done. At that point, Millie refused to take Sasonkin's guff and told him what he could do. Only the intervention of two members of the Levine Family plus that of Heshie, the headwaiter, succeeded in placating the aroused and offended Sasonkin. He was finally moved to another table where Heshie personally served him another burnt steak offering. Still, Les was proud of the way Millie had stood her ground and afterwards told her so.

"You could have said something, too," she said.

But he had seen no need to risk getting fired in the middle of the summer when there was no way he could count on getting another job where he could be making as much money. Why jeopardize his dreams? "You were doing so well yourself," he said. "I didn't think it was my place."

"Who's place was it, then?" Millie asked. "The fucking *shik-sa's?*" And she had turned her back and walked away.

And Les decided to let the matter rest. True, he had served one of the well-done orders, but Sasonkin's quarrel had been with Millie, not with him. So, he had seen no point in intervening and adding his two cents. Especially, when she seemed to be handling the matter just fine.

Les could never have imagined his other waitress, Glenda, a tall blond girl from a Pennsylvania mill town, ever talking back to a guest. Glenda was extremely quiet anyway, speech always seemed a genuine effort for her, and she would sooner nod or point or shrug than say anything. Les had never held a single conversation with her beyond "Good morning" and "So long" or "See you later." It was only from Millie that he learned that the slim silver band on Glenda's ring finger signified her engagement to her high school boyfriend, an all-state second team tackle, who was presently in the Air Force over in Wiesbaden, West Germany. According to Millie, Glenda was hoping to save enough money to go to Germany and marry him. And though Glenda rarely spoke to anyone, not even Millie, she was forever reading letters from or writing letters to the grid star. It was the only activity in which Glenda seemed to show any interest; otherwise, her face was a constant study in vacuous, gum-chewing boredom. It sometimes occurred to Lester that if a glimmer of the light of interest were ever to dance into Glenda's eyes, if a hint of an expression of animation could ever crinkle in the corners of her mouth, Glenda could possibly be considered beautiful.

Not that blank-faced she was unattractive, or a dog, or anything like that. Nor was Millie, for that matter. Les often wondered if he should put a move on Millie. He sensed she might be attracted to him, detecting a possible interest in him on her part beyond professional camaraderie. Or was that just his imagination? Because everyone else on the staff who had tried to get to first base with her, including the giant Solly Ryan, had been snubbed. In a world of libidinous rumors, rife with exaggerated tales of sexual conquests, Millie's reputation summer-wise was unsullied. And Les did not want to chance the discomfiting prospect of having to work alongside her after a rebuff. Millie had a quick enough tongue as it was, without possibly furnishing her any additional ammo.

None of the other waitresses at the Levine Family Diplomat appealed to Les personally, but there certainly was not a *dog* among them. Heshie would never have employed a girl, he once confided to Les, "Unless she helped dress up the dining room in one way or another." The very reason he employed waitresses rather than waiters was "to give the floor a hornier air in keeping with the hotel's make-out reputation."

"A single guy checks in for the weekend," Heshie explained to

Les as if he was conducting a seminar on dining room management. "On the one hand, he's looking for a nice Jewish girl he might marry. On the other hand, he wouldn't mind getting laid. So, I sit him at a table next to an eligible-type chick, who might not be the best looking broad in the world. And I let him get served by a *shiksa* with nice tits in a tight-fitting short skirt uniform that shows off her cute *goyishe* ass. Because there's always something about a uniform which turns guys on. So, even if he gets no action—can't come up with even a fingerful of *nookie*—it'll still take him two days before he realizes what isn't happening and go back to the city to jerk off. And then he can tell his mother he met a nice Jewish girl at the Levine Family Diplomat and, at the same time, bullshit his buddies how he practically got a blow job while eating his *blintzes.* And everybody's happy." Heshie laughed with self-satisfaction. "Even old man Levine."

9

Old man Levine, the patriarch of the Diplomat-owning family, was a running—or rather slowly prowling—joke among the help. On a day-to-day basis, the hotel was in the hands of his two sons, Moses and Aaron, and his daughter, Miriam, and their families. And the modern, "make-out," "muffkie-fuffkie" Levine Family Diplomat was very much their operational creation. Except the land on which it stood still belonged to their father, having originally been the site of his *kuche alain,* a cluster of cabins in which families cooked their meals in a communal kitchen.

Old man Levine still spent most of his time in the kitchen, either a shot glass of rye or a glass of steaming tea before him, a *yarmulke* on his bald head, glowering at his sons, his daughter, his grandchildren, and the kitchen help, bestirring himself only to clutch at a passing waitress's ass. Most of the girls quickly learned to give him a wide berth, but he still could move surprisingly fast for a man in his late eighties and sometimes his whoops of success, combined with the startled screams of the waitresses, could even be heard in the dining room, which was off limits to him. The staff had strict orders not to allow him to enter it during a meal. But these orders, of course, were also strictly unenforceable. Often meals were interrupted by sudden shrieks—another waitress falling prey to old man Levine's sudden goose attack. It was strange though; despite his lack of restraint and the fact that he was supposed to be out of control, old man Levine never pinched or snatched at the rear cheeks of Jewish-female, paying clientele. Only the waitresses and their *goyishe tushes,* both on and off duty, were his targets. Les wondered whether it was because he had enough of the Jewish ass in his lifetime? Or because, like an old pet, he knew the bounds of behavioral excess his family would tolerate.

The star of the Levine Family Diplomat basketball team was Solly Ryan, the gaunt, long-armed, pinball machine playing giant Les so often observed in the hotel arcade, intently hunched over the flippers. Solly Ryan spent so much time at the pinball machines, and had become so adept at operating them, that he was always referred to by other employees as the "pinball pro." Actually, Solly was a pro, a professional basketball player of some renown with the Hawks. Unlike the other members of the staff, it was his sole duty at the Diplomat to play on its basketball team. And no matter how much he was getting paid, it was a very good investment for the hotel. Because Solly Ryan's presence not only attracted basketball-loving guests from all over the country, who could not get enough of the sport during its long fall, winter, spring regular season, but he also provided the linchpin for the assemblage of the Levine Family Diplomat Hotel team itself. College ball players, such as Artie Rabinowitz and "Happy" Feigenbaum, were only too eager to be recruited to work as busboys and bellhops for a hotel whose team featured Solly Ryan. It would give them a chance to hone their talents with the very best, get a leg up on potential professional careers. And, of course, the gamey image that went with a winning basketball team contributed synergistically to the reputation of the Levine Family Diplomat as a youth-oriented hotel.

Les had planned on spending a quiet night of near solitude writing letters to Vivian and Mickey. He could not match Mickey's letters in terms of breathless descriptions or sheer excitement. Mickey still made everything seem an adventure, even getting across Paris to the American Express office to pick up the money order from home that always seemed to arrive just in the nick of time. And since he was constantly changing hotels, the c/o American Express address was the place where he could best be reached. In addition to being on the constant verge of running out of money, Mickey was also always full of plans. In his last letter, he had written of perhaps taking a train to Barcelona and then sailing to Turkey where he had heard things were really cheap. The people he would travel with were Americans and there was very little mention of any particular Frenchman, or woman, but a great many comments about the French in general. Also, about the Germans and the British and he used the words *European* and *international* a great deal.

Vivian's last letter had dealt with crazy campers and intelligent counselors, who had prevailed over the camp director by talking him out of dividing the campers into two factions, the blue and the white, and having a "war." She also confided that though she was looking forward to college, she was not sure that was the right path for her to take if she was serious about becoming an actress. Somehow, what Mickey was doing seemed a much more splendid preparation for an artistic career. Meanwhile, she was helping the dramatics counselor stage a production of *Oklahoma.* Only they weren't calling it *Oklahoma,* but *Camp Nee-wa-nee* and rewriting the lyrics and the plot to fit camp life. It was fun, but it was not art. A far cry from Steinbeck or Ibsen or Chekov or Odets.

But, as it turned out, Les did not spend the evening in a deserted lobby or abandoned casino writing letters to Vivian and Mickey. Instead, he was watching the Balfour basketball game with Chicago. After all, he owed his job to Chicago, and if for some reason Chicago had expected him to accompany him there, then that was where he had to be.

It was far better than the game itself and it was over in a matter of seconds, yet that mini-happening would forever stand out boldly in Les's memory. Which proved that one could not dictate priorities to memory of what was and what was not supposed to be important; of what to hold on to and what to discard; and that memory did its own independent edit. Because, even though it was literally just a walk-on, that minor moment would loom far more vividly in Les's memory in years to come than anything else that transpired that evening. Including the event of seemingly far greater significance that occurred a few hours later, his finally getting laid, at least technically, for the first time.

What happened was this: With just a minute left to go in the game, Old Man Levine suddenly scampered out onto the basketball court and, like a toddler out of control, bit Solly Ryan, who was busy establishing himself in a post position beneath the Balfour basket, in the ass. Since the wizened Old Man Levine barely had to bend over in order to achieve the feat, it was not easy for Solly, whelping in pain like a wounded terrier, to wrench himself free from the patriarch's Polydent grip. But he finally succeeded in shaking himself free and the referee called "Time!"

With Solly doubled over, his teammates huddled around him in protective cover, commiserating as they inspected the damage. Fortunately, it did not seem to involve the breakage of any skin. Meanwhile, the Levine family en masse rushed out onto the court to retrieve their patriarch who was ranting away in Yiddish, directing a broadside of curses at the doubled over Solly Ryan, which linked him with both Hitler and the Tsar Nicholas. And as the old man was being ushered back to the sidelines, his *yarmulke* askew atop his bald head, he was chastised by his heirs. "That's it, Poppa," his youngest son Aaron reprimanded the old man in the manner of a coach removing a veteran athlete from a game. "No more basketball for you."

What had propelled old man Levine to go after Solly Ryan's ass? And then proceed to assault him verbally? At the time, Les could only attribute the behavior to either senility or some misunderstanding that may have occurred around the pinball machine. Perhaps the old man had caused a tilt during a winning game and been chewed out because of it by Solly? Or the fact that Solly Ryan was neither Jewish nor a paying guest could have contributed to that particular choice of target? Whatever the cause, Les could only laugh at both the incident itself and the many sideline comments it evoked. "That calls for three shots," shouted one wag. "Two foul and one rabies." But Solly Ryan did not seem to find anything to laugh about as he finally trotted up court, grimly rubbing his ass.

Until that incident, the game had been uneventful. The Levine Family Diplomat should have been easily outclassing the Sir Arthur Balfour quintet, with Solly Ryan controlling the boards on both ends and Les's roommate, "Happy" Feigenbaum, leading the Levine Family Diplomat fast break up court and Artie Rabinowitz pulling up and popping them in. But Solly Ryan had consistently been out-hustled under the boards, and when he did get a rebound, his outlet passes were wild and erratic. And Artie Rabinowitz seemed to be having an off night shooting. As a result, in the closing minutes, the Diplomat was still struggling to hold on to a slim three-point lead. Les was glad he had not suited up because it was turning out to be the kind of close game he would never have gotten into. Mel Trachtenberg, a fellow busboy who played for Pace and possessed far greater basketball skills than Les, never even got off the bench. But in the waning seconds, Solly Ryan, as if energized and spurred by the old man's assault, scored two quick baskets, enabling the Levine Family Diplomat to win by seven points. But still a point shy of the eight points spotted to the Balfour backer, Jackie Gordon, "the King of the Cut-Rate Optometrists."

"I could smell that one a mile off," said Chicago, as the buzzer sounded. "C'mon, let's get some *nookie*. Who are those two chicks?" To Les's surprise Chicago was pointing past Fat Jackie Gordon, triumphantly lighting a long Cuban cigar, to Millie and Glenda.

"My waitresses."

"They serve you?"

"I serve them. In the dining room. I bus for them. They're both my stations."

"No shit," said Chicago, turning to Les as if he had suddenly discovered some new and marvelous, previously undisclosed facet of his personality. "I really got you a good job, didn't I?"

"And I appreciate it."

"And I'll really appreciate it," Chicago smiled salaciously. "If you can fix me up with the tall blonde. She's beautiful."

"Glenda?" Les asked incredulously.

"Beautiful name for a beautiful blond." Chicago continued. "Introduce me." And before Les even had a chance to give his acquiescence, Chicago, with a firm grip on his elbow, was already propelling them toward Millie and Glenda, who had turned their backs and were walking in the direction of the casino. Chicago would soon see for himself, Les thought, that there was a lot less to Glenda than first met the eye.

10

It was not the first time Les had been in a guest's room. Not that he made a habit of frequenting them. But like the Himalayas of India, the Catskills of New York had a caste system. Guests usually did not invite the hired help into their rooms. Nor did they really mix with them. Except, of course, for the muffkie-fuffkie purposes the hotel was famous for.

But even then it was strictly a relationship based upon class position. The married woman out to enjoy a little summer romance during the long work week, while her husband was toiling away in the sweltering city, bestowed her sexual favors upon the hired help of her choice. Never vice versa. It was always her whim. No busboy or bellhop could ever dare initiate the pursuit of a guest. Even a busboy's hint had to be a reaction to a guest's wink. He was never the conquistador, no matter how great his subsequent macho boasts of amatory conquest. The power was all in the hands of the registered guest, he or she was as dominant as any ruling-class Brahmin across the world, and the hired help, expendable as any pariah, could be fired for any alleged transgression. It was strictly a one-way relationship; the guest could always check out because of an imagined slight.

Still, a few weeks earlier Les had tried to come on with a guest. But, unfortunately, he had picked the wrong guest. Lillian was a fifteen-year-old about to enter her second year at Midwood High

School. A tall, slim girl who wore her braided hair in long pony tails that ran down past her deep-set eyes and high cheek bones and smooth, tawny neck, Lillian struck Les as being on the precise verge of becoming spectacularly beautiful. Just like her mother must have been. Not that Anita Heller was still not beautiful. Especially, in her white latex bathing suit, which showed off her dark womanly figure to its best full effect. But Anita Heller had to be almost forty, if she was a day, and with her daughter about it seemed there was absolutely no chance that she would be playing around. So, while Anita looked on smiling benignly, Les danced with Lillian in the casino; and afterwards strolled with her behind the tennis courts, talking of his future in the theater, while she held forth about her plans to avoid taking a required science course in the upcoming semester. And later, Les would deliver Lillian back to her guest room in the annex, never getting more than a close-lipped good-night kiss, before Anita Heller, usually already pre-pared for sleep in a nightgown which clearly revealed the contours of her sun-burnished body, would invite him in for a slice of cake or a piece of fruit. And then, after the nightcap *nosh,* Les would return to the busboy's bungalow. Another evening passed. Another night spent.

And not until the day the Hellers checked out, while Ben Heller, husband, father, and pharmacist, was placing the baggage of his wife and daughter in the trunk of his Buick, did Les realize what a terrible mistake he had made and what a terrific opportunity he had blown.

What happened was this: He and Lillian had just finished ex-changing simultaneous farewell handshakes and light kisses on each other's cheeks. And Ben Heller's head seemed to have disap-peared permanently in the mouth of the opened trunk as he strug-gled to fit in one more suitcase. When Anita Heller, saying good-bye to Les, suddenly leaned forward and began to embrace him with her full womanly strength, her breasts pressing hard against his T-shirt, her tongue twirling in his ear as she hurriedly breathed into it, "What a fool I was! What a summer it could have been!"

And then she kissed him, her lips moving vigorously, before stepping back, turning slowly, her rounded *tush* gyrating, as she walked toward her daughter in the waiting car.

Ben Heller finally extracted his head and slammed the trunk shut and came over and shook hands with Les, and then got into the car beside his wife. The Roadmaster started, and with Les waving sadly at both mother and daughter, rolled down the Levine Family Diplomat driveway. When Les stopped waving, he examined his right hand. If he had temporarily forgotten about the two-week tip coming to him, Ben Heller had not. There was a twenty dollar bill between his fingers.

Chicago's room was different from that of the Hellers. Not only was it a single rather than a double room, but it also lacked the lived-in quality even a hotel room can assume when the guests have decided to make it as comfortable and homelike as possible. In the Heller's room, for example, in addition to the bowls of fruit and boxes of chocolate on top of the dressers, there had been toiletries of all sorts on the night stands and stuffed, pastel-colored animals on the twin beds. In Chicago's crowded room, two bottles of hard liquor, Wild Turkey and Canadian Club, were precariously resting atop a suitcase on a chair. A platter of cold chicken and a sliced loaf of rye bread were on the dresser next to an open jar of Gulden's mustard, a dining room knife dipped into it at a forty-five degree angle. If he got no more than a chicken sandwich out of the evening, Les decided, as he picked up the knife and swabbed a slice of bread with it, he had already come out a winner.

The gathering in Chicago's room was born out of Chicago's very first words upon meeting Glenda and Millie. "I asked Les to introduce me to you girls for a very important reason," Chicago said very solemnly as they were exchanging nods. The basketball game had just ended and they were all standing at the entrance to the casino.

"What reason?" asked Millie.

"I wanted to give you both an invitation."

Millie's eyes narrowed. "An invitation to what?"

"An invitation to a party."

Millie regarded Chicago warily. But he was too busy to notice, his own eyes glued to Glenda's as if he had become completely hypnotized by some wondrous jewel, such as the Star of India. And to Les's surprise Glenda seemed to be returning the same fixed stare of enthralldom.

"What kind of party?" Millie asked.

Chicago turned away from Glenda for a micro-second. "Why, a terrific party," he said, almost simultaneously putting his arm about Glenda and leading her onto the dance floor of the casino. Les asked Millie if she wanted to dance because it seemed the thing to do. But she said she was too tired and he did not push it. Anyway, they both knew the Levine Family frowned upon the help socializing with each other, especially on the dance floor during weekends when there always was a surplus of wallflower singles registered.

Les and Millie picked up Cokes at the bar and found an empty table out on the corner of the terrace where they could still hear the blare of the horns and the persistent samba beat laid down by Buddy Cohen, the dance band drummer.

"You don't usually go to the basketball games?" Les said.

Millie nodded. "But sometimes you got to do something otherwise you'll go crazy."

Les agreed. "Yeah, the dining room day in, day out, is too much."

Millie gave a deep you-can-say-that-again sigh and lit a cigarette. Then she motioned toward the opened doors at the dance floor. "Who's your friend?"

"Chicago? He's the neighborhood bookmaker. I mean, he's the bookie in my neighborhood."

"No kidding." Millie continued looking off in that direction, as if she could actually still see him. "He's a good-looking guy. If you like the type."

"What type?"

"The good-looking type," Millie exhaled. "And he has some line."

"Seems to."

"But does he really expect anyone to go for it?" Millie smiled, "I mean in this day and age."

After the dance ended, Chicago came over to their table, his arm still about Glenda, as if they were ready to dance off together at any moment.

"I've got some terrific news," he announced. "That party I was telling you about is going to be tonight."

"Not with me there," Millie said.

Chicago reacted in shock, as if some important treaty was being violated, an ironclad commitment suddenly severed. "But you were invited," he insisted.

"Yeah," somebody suddenly said. "You were invited."

Millie and Les together looked up at Glenda who was smiling down at them in her dumb, silent way. They could hardly believe that she had spoken. But there was no one else around. So it had to have been her, unless Chicago had suddenly become a ventriloquist.

"And I'll get Heshie," Chicago was saying. "He'll be our caterer." And with his arm still about Glenda, he turned to go. "In a half hour. In my room." He stopped and pulled out his key and read it. "Three twelve. Main building." And then he whirled Glenda back into the casino, rhumba-ing onto the dance floor.

"You going to the big party?" Les asked.

Millie yawned. "I'm too sleepy."

"Glenda's going."

"She's a big girl."

Les caught himself yawning, too. He was as sleepy as Millie and her yawn was infectious. But unlike Millie, he could not just turn down Chicago's "invitation." And for some reason, he could not quite fathom at the moment he wanted Millie to go with him. "C'mon," he entreated, "there'll probably be food. And nobody has to stay long."

"Well, if I'm still awake," Millie had said, "and hungry."

Les bit into his sandwich. The bread, as always, was too hard, almost stale, even though he could tell by the water stains on its crust that it had been wrapped in a moist cloth napkin to preserve the illusion of freshness. But the chicken was fine, and as always at this hour of the night, he was hungry. He turned to Millie, "Shall I make you a sandwich?"

Millie laughed. "You mean you want to serve me?"

"Certainly." Les mock bowed. "The pleasure is mine."

"Also the bother," said Millie. "Just give me a bite. That's all I should have. I'm getting fat."

"You don't look fat. Not by Jewish standards."

"I'm not Jewish."

"That's what I mean." Les held out his sandwich to her. She took a bite and nibbled on it. Les took another bite himself and held the sandwich out to her again.

Millie held up her hand like a traffic cop. "That's enough. You'd be surprised how fat I am. It's all in here," she patted her thighs. "And here." her hand slowly described her own ass.

Another hand with a large emerald ring and a shining gold watch on it fell upon Millie's hand and froze it in place. "Hey, what are you doing with your *tush,* Millie?" Heshie asked. And before his question could be answered or his hand removed, he was declaring, "This is the nicest *tush* in the dining room."

"What about my *tush?*" asked Marilyn, the bespectacled assistant bookkeeper, who was Heshie's girlfriend.

"I said the dining room," Heshie's hand left Millie's ass in a tentative, testing way that seemed to suggest he had placed it there only to provide emergency support and that now, if suddenly deprived of that scaffolding, Millie's *tush* might actually fall, crashing to the floor. Then he turned and embraced Marilyn, cupping her ass firmly. "Dining room," he repeated. "Not bedroom."

Heshie had once pointed out to Les, in one of those instructional seminars he liked to hold as they stood waiting for the dining room to open on an evening, "Notice how I don't let my girl work in the dining room. She could make more money as a waitress than book-keeping, but I don't let her wait tables in the dining room. You know why? *Cack nisht ver mir est.* 'Don't shit where you eat.' In other words, don't mix business with pleasure. Now stand back," he then mock warned as always, "here they come." And he opened the dining room doors and stood back as if he actually expected a thundering herd—or hoard—to come charging in. And instead, as always, only a few of the older guests, straggled in, one by one. No one ever wanted to be first, to give the appearance of a chowhound. Especially among the younger set. The younger the guest, the later he or she would arrive at a meal; in that way, they indicated they had much better things to do than just eat. For breakfast, of course, the young always showed up at the last possible moment. Because an early appearance would be a dead giveaway that they had not had anything better to do the previous night but go directly to sleep.

Dining room entrances were not isolated behaviors. So much was ceremony and show, appearance and performance, Les had thought, as he watched Heshie rubbing his horny hand up and down Marilyn's ass. In fact, what had drawn Les to acting in the first place was that he noticed that people were always acting, performing in roles, following preconceived scripts. Here he was, for example, standing around eating a cold sliced chicken sandwich on stale rye in the middle of the night when he was tired and sleepy, just because Chicago was trying to make one of his wait-resses. He and Millie and Heshie and Marilyn were all supporting actors brought on to fill out the background, to complete the set-ting of Chicago's stage, so to speak. But they were also cast there to provide the social context of an audience, to bear witness to the enactment of his intentions. Indeed, smiling silently on Chicago's lap in the easy chair in the corner as he sipped his Canadian Club was Glenda.

"I'm really sleepy," Millie yawned again. "Time for me to go to bed."

"Me, too," said Les. "I'll walk you back." He swallowed the remainder of his sandwich and walked over to Chicago. "Terrific party," he lied.

Chicago bounce-eased Glenda off his lap and sprang to his feet. "Don't tell me you two are pooping out already?" he asked, smiling at Millie, who Les had not realized was trailing behind him. "Just when I was thinking we might all drive down to Philly for a cup of coffee."

Glenda seemed to find that notion hilarious and her silent smile actually grew larger as she continued to gaze on Chicago with utter admiration.

"Not tonight," said Les.

"Not any night," said Millie.

Chicago laughed, "Okay." Then he smiled and said to both Millie and Glenda, "Excuse me," and led Les out to the hall.

Where he pressed a key into his hand.

"What's this for?"

"It's for an empty room you and Millie can use."

"I don't need it."

"You got some place else?"

"There's nothing between Millie and me."

"Take it from me," said Chicago, wrapping Les's fingers around the cold metal of the key. "There should be."

11

Owning a jeep never figured in any of Les's automotive—or extra-automotive—fantasies. No place in Manhattan or Brooklyn required a four-wheel drive. Except perhaps the beach at Coney. But he had never secretly harbored any intentions of racing along the surf in a mechanical horse. In fact, he could easily picture the carnage that would result by any vehicle running amok at crowded Coney on a sunny summer Sunday afternoon. Nor had Les ever dreamt of straying far from the city either. Rugged hills and craggy dales and sand swept deserts and flooded marshlands were not for him. He was no nature boy and his summer in the mountains had provided him with enough country to last a lifetime. And if, for some reason, he had to take a trip to the hinterland, he never imagined using anything less than well-paved roads all the way. Certainly nothing less than a blacktop. No thin lines on the road map for him.

But nevertheless, there it was, parked in front of the store like a sentry on guard duty, his newly acquired, freshly painted, khaki jeep, which was a constant source of wonder and embarrassment to his parents. They wondered what on earth he was doing with a "machine" they had never seen before except in the movies or on television. They were embarrassed because its distinct military hue and different shape and design were not like any "normal, ordinary car" of their acquaintanceship, such as a Ford or Chevy or Plymouth or Buick or Oldsmobile. "We don't need no invaders on this block," his mother said upon first inspecting the new jeep. "Bring it back to wherever you got it."

"I can't. The sale was final."

"Your brain is final," she snorted. "Take it back."

And since she kept shaking her head in disgust, Les did not even begin to try to explain why he could not return the jeep and just how final the sale had been. Because then she really would have had visions of a neighborhood invasion by platoons of United States Army troops, hugging the delicatessen and the appetizer store as they battled their way up the sidewalk shop by shop, first assaulting the bakery and the candy store and then Glick, the *kosher* butcher, hurling grenades and firing mortars and bazookas in vicious street fighting. All to reclaim possession of a single stolen jeep, and return it to its rightful place in the Fort Hamilton motor pool.

"I bet you didn't even have a mechanic examine it."

"Of course, I had it checked out. Besides, it's practically brand new," Les insisted, the second half of his statement, at least, being true.

"No doors," his mother snickered again. "And where is the roof?"

"It has doors. And a roof. Just like a convertible, if I want to put the cover on."

"And how much did you pay for this convertible jeep?"

"It was a bargain, Ma. Believe me."

"So tell me: how much of a bargain?"

"What's the difference? If I told you, you wouldn't believe me."

"Tell me and I'll believe you."

"Fifty dollars," he smiled.

"I don't believe you," she said. "More like five hundred dollars?" she guessed.

"I'm not going to tell you."

"Oh, my God." She slapped her hand to her cheek and addressed that invisible third personage she was always summoning to serve as her witness. "For that thing the boy paid more than five hundred dollars!"

"Less. And it's not a thing. And that's all I'm going to tell you."

"If it was less than five hundred dollars," she suddenly switched gears like a clever attorney during a cross-examination, "how come so cheap?"

"The guy who had it wanted to get rid of it quickly," Les replied.

"Because it looked like rain?"

"I told you, I have a cover for it. Want to see?"

"No." She turned and headed back into the store. "I still don't think that convertible thing is the proper car for a college boy."

"You're right, Ma," Les called after her. "I should have got a Stutz Bearcat.

Actually, almost any other model or make car would have appealed to him more than an army jeep. But Les had not been presented with the opportunity to pick up a "normal" Chevy or "ordinary" Ford half so cheaply. No one had approached him with a comparable deal. If the jeep was "hot," so to speak, it was not Les who had stolen it. And if he had not picked up on it then, someone else would have. Besides, how could he have known it had been stolen? The paperwork on it certainly appeared authentic enough. And what was he supposed to know about the buying and selling of cars anyway? It was the first car he had ever bought. And even if —according to the worst case scenario—something did go wrong, since he was under twenty-one nothing could possibly happen to him except some sort of mild slap on the wrist.

What had actually happened was this: Chicago had learned of the existence of the "hot" jeep through a fellow bookmaker. It seemed an army sergeant had put it up to square an over nine-hundred-dollar gambling tab. The sergeant was able to produce the necessary false papers certifying the vehicle as army surplus so that it was properly registered. Still, the Bay Ridge bookmaker, not being a used jeep dealer, was anxious to quickly turn it over for cash. Chicago passed that military intelligence along to Les, with the recommendation that he act on it immediately.

At first, Les was reticent, telling Chicago that he had some moral qualms and reservations. But Chicago had just laughed: "Qualms? Isn't that some dessert in Chink restaurants? And reservations? You think you're still working for a hotel or something? And what's morals got to do with buying and selling, especially when it comes to the golden opportunity of picking up a bargain? Otherwise, the churches and *shuls* would be empty, completely shutdown, out of business. A bargain is a bargain and has nothing to do with morals or qualms or reservations or anything else. Especially in this case. Besides," Chicago nudged him in the ribs, "have I ever steered you wrong?"

That was true. Les certainly could not argue with that. Hadn't Chicago gotten him the job at the Levine Family Diplomat? Hadn't Chicago handed him the key that historic night, which enabled him to break, at least technically, his cherry? And now, by helping him get wheels of his own, it would be three in a row he owed Chicago.

But even as a steal, the jeep turned out to be a problem. Because it was an ongoing money drain. Not only did Les have to meet hefty monthly insurance payments, he also had to house the jeep in a garage and keep it properly fed with gasoline and oil. What he had on his hands, Les soon discovered, was nothing less than a mechanical pet demanding constant care, a very dumb animal with a leaking fuel pump and a carburetor always in need of a fine-tuned adjustment. But just as with any dependent animal, a dog or a cat or even a hamster, he gradually fell in love with his Toledo-bred pet and even gave it a nick name: *Monty*. He didn't exactly know why he called it *Monty*. Except *Monty* sounded right to him. Perhaps because it reminded him of the beret-wearing British general of desert battle fame who had always seemed to be standing in the back of a jeep, his calvary riding crop under his arm. Or perhaps because of the actor Montgomery Clift, whom he idolized, especially since a girl once told him that he resembled the new star?

One thing was certain: The name *Monty* evoked for him the gallant image of a man climbing on a horse and then riding off to perform the heroic feats of a star actor. So, the name stuck and Les rarely referred to his jeep in any other way and his friends and parents did the same, too. And soon, just as Tom Mix and Tony, Roy Rogers and Trigger, the Lone Ranger and Silver, they became Les and *Monty*. But in this case, instead of a Hollywood he-man and his horse, it was a Brooklyn boy and his jeep.

"Where are you and *Monty* going tonight?" his mother asked him one evening. She had just finished lighting the *Chanukah* candles in a brass Menorah on the kitchen windowsill, the handkerchief she used as a head covering still resting lightly atop her perm. His mother never said *Yizkor,* the memorial prayer for the dead. Nor did she fast on *Yom Kippur,* or ever worry about whether food was *kosher.* Lighting *Chanukah* candles was the only Jewish ritual she steadfastly observed and performed. Les once asked her the reason. "Because," she had replied, "it beats Christmas."

"Oh, I'm just going over to see a girl I know," Les said matter-of-factly that *Chanukah* evening. He did not say that the girl was Vivian Davis and that no ordinary night loomed ahead. But rather a night as special as any of those fabled nights of ancient Judeah for which she had just lit the commemorative candles in the window. Because even if he was not quite a Maccabee taking on the Romans, it would still be an achievement of legendary proportions in his book. He would be realizing at last the dream of his high school lifetime. Tonight was Vivian Davis's eighteenth birthday.

He had set up the date a week earlier in the Brooklyn College cafeteria just before the Christmas vacation break, figuring that would give Vivian sufficient time to pick up the eighteenth birthday present she had told him she had long promised herself. And then with that newly-fit diaphragm in place, she could receive a second birthday gift. Namely him. In preparation, Les even bought a book of poetry which he had heard from a CCNY senior was pretty hot and worked every time. The book was called *This Is My*

Beloved and Les inscribed in it, "This guy may say it better. But I mean it more. Love, Les."

Now, driving through the familiar streets of his boyhood, past the salmon brick colored Jewish community center and the movie theater with its multi-bulbed marquee and the bowling alley next door, the neon arrows on its sign pointing downward to its basement location in a constant flow of alternating flickers, it seemed his whole life had been but an extended prologue for the curtain that would be raised that night. He regretted not having a Buick or an Oldsmobile, a Chevy or a Ford, a "normal" or "ordinary" car with ample enclosed backseat space instead of *Monty,* whose top was always difficult to batten down, despite what he had told his mother, making it forever prey to whatever Arctic-like storms bellowed through Brooklyn. Fortunately though, the Davises had that finished basement, and since it was a weekday night, certainly the parents would be going to sleep early. Besides, fate was on his side. Had not almost every movie he had ever seen, and practically every song he had ever heard—not to mention, every poet he ever had to study—instructed that Destiny always favored young lovers?

But there was also the possibility of a slight snag, of some sort of hitch or snafu. Because perhaps he had violated the sanctity of young love Destiny so favored by fucking Millie. But then again, that was only during the summer in the mountains and certainly Destiny did not count that. Like spring football practice or the grapefruit league of baseball, it couldn't possibly figure in one's ultimate moral standings. Besides, losing one's virginity was above and beyond the usual strictures of morality because it was a sociological imperative and a biological necessity—Les could argue it either way. And it was not as if it had been a long-planned seduction into which he lured Millie or anything like that. It had just happened that night after Chicago handed him that key to a vacant guest room over in the annex.

Les was genuinely surprised when Millie noticed the key in his hand and asked him what it was for. They were walking back to *Pennsyl-tucky,* the waitresses and chambermaids' bungalow, where he planned to drop Millie off and then continue on down the path to the busboy's shack. What with the party in Chicago's room, it had already become a later-than-usual night. But then Millie asked him what he was clutching so tightly in his hand.

"This," he held it up in the moonlight, "is the key to a guest room."

"Whose?"

"Nobody's."

"Where did you get it?"

When he told her, Millie asked, to his surprise, if they could go look at it because she was curious, never having seen the inside of a guest's room in the annex before. So, Les took her arm and guided her back toward the annex, sneaking another peek at the key in his hand and the imprinted leather attached to it:

RETURN POSTAGE GUARANTEED
THE LEVINE FAMILY DIPLOMAT
SOUTH HILLSBURGH, NEW YORK
IF FOUND DROP INTO ANY MAIL BOX

And then what happened was this: He had to jiggle the key for what seemed an unbearably long time before he succeeded in unlocking the door. It also seemed to take him a lifetime before he could find the switch that turned on the single forty-five-watt overhead light source. Then together, he and Millie poked their way around the dim room making disparaging remarks about how chintzy the curtains looked and how sparse the furnishings were—not even a bed lamp—and how dumb the guests had to be for paying the exorbitant rates the hotel charged for the annex. They sat down on the bed and tested the sinking mattress, bouncing up and down on it, as if they were considering buying it. And just as they were about to rise to their feet again, they suddenly embraced clumsily and kissed, their lips barely meeting, Les's landing mostly just beneath Millie's nose and hers glancing against the top of his chin. And then they both lay back against the pillow and kissed again, this time getting it right.

But that was just about the last thing they did get right. Or Les got right anyway. Because he foofed and fumbled, wondering whose clothes to get off first—his or Millie's, and where he should start: go straight to home plate or try to get there a base at a time—when he felt Millie's lips moving moistly against his cheek. She was saying something, but he could not quite make out her muffled words. He pulled his head back and asked: "What?"

"The light." Millie pointed her finger up past his eyes at the dim bulb. "Put it out."

Les push-lifted himself up from the bed and went to the light switch beside the door. On the way back to bed, he began to remove his snug-fitting sweater, pulling the long sleeves up over his head in the darkness. Suddenly, at the same time, his head snagged at the narrow crew-neck opening and his knee bumped against the room's only chair, turning it over with a bouncing thud and sending a pain shooting up his right leg. "Son of a bitch!"

"What's the matter?"

"Nothing." Les finally extracted himself from the sweater and leaned over and rubbed his leg. "I just bumped into something."

"The chair?"

"Yes."

Millie giggled.

"It's not funny," Les said and got back in bed beside her.

"It is, too," Millie insisted.

"My right knee really hurts."

Millie's hand slid down his thigh and gently massaged it. "How does that feel?"

"Better," Les said. And Millie began to laugh again. "What's so funny?"

"Everything," she said. "You. Me. Your knee. And I don't even know what we're doing here in the first place. Do you?"

Les did not quite know how to answer that question. It was not as if he had any special pent up yearning for Millie. Certainly, she was attractive enough in her pert *shiksa* way; and at that moment, for some reason, she was obviously accessible. But there was also something missing. And it was not because she was not Jewish, or her skin was a trifle coarse, or her red hair was too stringy, or anything like that. It was simply that she had never been cast in any of his dreams, featured in any of his fantasies. Also, Millie lacked the soul of an artist. How could that taut, hardworking body with the muscular calves built to stride across the floors of life even begin to understand his aetherial fancies and spiritual longings? He could never imagine soaring away with Millie on some idyllically romantic flight. Going off to Paris together, for example. Not that that was important at the moment. What was important was to keep going and take advantage of the opportunity that was presenting itself. And he was not thinking about a deep-knee massage either. It was breaking his cherry at long last. Getting laid, fucked, *shtupped,* scoring for the first time. Les rolled over and kissed Millie as gently as he knew how, as if somehow the less pressure his lips exerted, the more sensual would be the effect.

"I mean," Millie was saying, "we've been working together all summer and getting along fine, so why should we start fooling around now? I mean, it doesn't make any sense."

"Sasonkin," Les whispered back. Referring to the guest who had caused all that trouble by insisting upon having his steak so well-done that it was finally burnt to the point of charring.

"Wasn't he something though?" Millie laughed and stopped rubbing Les's wounded knee and began tickling his thigh instead.

"Cut it out," he giggled.

"Sasonkin," Millie said. "He was a prick. I don't know."

"You don't know what?"

Millie's hand flitted over his penis lightly. "I don't know if I should let your little Sasonkin get too fresh," she laughed. "Oh my," she said, her hand resting on his stiffening penis again, "it's too late. Your Sasonkin is getting awfully fresh already."

When Les had returned to bed in the dark, his knee aching, he half expected to find Millie welcoming him back with open arms to

her receptive nude body, having somehow in his brief absence un-
dressed herself completely. But she had not removed a single stitch
of clothing. But now, after he kissed her again and played with her
breasts, massaging and squishing them between his palms and his
fingers, and then boldly reaching down and feeling his way along
the inside of the surprisingly soft underflesh of her thighs to the
slippery smoothness between her panties, still kissing her all the
while, and then fingering her cunt until she became moist and
leaned back and squiggled her panties away from her waist and
rolled them down past her knees to her ankles where in the moonlight seeping in through the window they seemed to form a puddle,
he wanted to return to her breasts, to those proud and previously
inaccessible tits he had so often admired in her dining room waitress's tight-fitting uniform, lifting a tray or stretching across a table
to serve a grapefruit or a scoop of sherbert. But she was wearing a
tight, fleecy sweater and his own sweater had just given him so
much trouble. Besides, she was really becoming gooey wet now,
and moaning and groping for his excited penis, which he was
afraid he could not keep from coming very much longer. Les rolled
onto his knees and quickly unzipped his fly and half pushing off
his underwear and slacks mounted her.

"Wait," Millie breathed out. "Do you have anything?"

"Huh?"

"A rubber. Like a Trojan, I mean."

Les had carried a prophylactic, an unused condom, in his wallet
throughout his last two years of high school, not so much to use, as
it turned out, but rather to have available as a credential to pull out
and show like a G.O. card or a driver's license, whenever the guys
got around to boasting under the corner street light or on the stoop
of a brownstone in the middle of a side street block about their
fictional sexual exploits. But now, at the brink of this crucial moment in his real sexual history, as he was actually about to plunge
his penis at long last into the aperture of his dreams, he was caught
with his condom gone, his silver-cased Ramseses II so long stashed
away within the leathery folds of his Moroccan green wallet that it

left stretch marks, having just expired a few short weeks before by drying up and cracking into dust, like an ancient artifact exposed too long in the hot desert sun. And given his previous lifetime batting average of .000, Les had not bothered to rush out immediately and purchase a successor wallet stasher. So now he, who had so often mocked the Boy Scout motto of "Be Prepared," was not. But he also could not see blowing this golden opportunity to claim his manhood. What the hell to do? Should he take his chances and lie? Would Millie be able to tell the difference? Or should he take his chances and tell the truth? Les decided to go with the truth and panted, "No."

Millie stirred uneasily beneath him. "You don't you have any protection?"

"No," he repeated. "Do you?"

"I'm Catholic," she replied. As if a diaphragm was something as peculiarly Jewish as a *Chanukah dreidel* or a potato *latke*. "And it's my worst time of month." She began to try and sit up. "Maybe some other time."

"No," Les cried out and pinned her shoulders back. He did not know what else to do, so he kissed her again, if only to buy time. But as if heightened immeasurably by the suddenly imposed limitations and restrictions, every sensation intensified and his nerve endings rose to an exquisite explosive state.

And something very similar it seemed—her head rolling from side to side, her body thrashing spiritedly beneath his—was happening to Millie. "Okay," she breathed out. "Do you think you can pull it out before you come?"

"Sure," Les said.

And slid into her.

And came immediately.

"Hey," Millie was punching him hard in the back, screaming, "What the fuck have you done?"

"I couldn't hold back, I guess."

Abruptly, she pushed herself out from under him. "Put on the light," she commanded, rising to her feet.

Les jumped out of bed and rushed toward the wall switch. Again hurting himself, this time bumping his other knee against the protruding side of the dresser. "Shit!" he shouted, as he pushed the switch on.

"Shit is right," echoed Millie. She was wiggling back into her panties. "I should the fuck have known better."

Les stood before the light switch beside the door, watching her dress. Les never imagined a woman could dress that quickly, it was like watching a film at silent picture speed. "I'm sorry," he said contritely, but not moving an inch toward her.

"You don't know how sorry," said Millie, slipping into her loafers. Then she brushed by him, pulled open the door, and started down the hall.

Les poked his head out the door and followed after her, unable to take his eyes off the muscular calves of her short but sturdy legs. "Where are you going?" he called out.

"To *douche.*" Millie flung back over her shoulder. "And I hope it's not too late." Then she broke into a trot, like a school girl late for class, before disappearing through a side door with the red and white letter sign marked: EMERGENCY EXIT.

When Les limped into the dining room the next morning, favoring his now swollen right knee, Millie acted not only as if the previous evening had never happened, but as if he simply no longer existed. Silent as Glenda, she walked right past him into the kitchen, refusing to acknowledge his presence in the slightest. During the meal itself, her communications to him were barely civil, limited only to the barest situational essentials such as: "Get Epstein coffee." "Schweidel wants pickled lox." "Mrs. Turanski is asking for her hot water and lemon."

Glenda, on the other hand, had actually wished him a "Good morning! Good morning!" an usual enough greeting by ordinary standards but one, coming from her, which was like the spouting of volumes of verse. It was two words more than her sphinxship had ever previously uttered to him on any one occasion all summer long. And when Glenda leaned forward and touched his jacket lightly with her left hand, while still balancing the tray bearing three orders of baked apples and a half of grapefruit above her shoulder with her right, the gesture reverberated through him with the dramatic impact of a burglar alarm going off. It was as if she was proclaiming the fact that together now they shared some special intimacy.

The intimacy, of course, was Chicago. And at any other time and with any other person, Les might have enjoyed trying to work into the ensuing conversation references to the lure of mono-grammed boxer shorts and to the exact number of testicles that might have been encountered the previous evening. But with Glenda, he knew no more possible conversation could ensue. There would be no further breakout from her subterranean silences. She had exhausted her communicative powers in the double salutation and soft tap.

Besides, he soon had another problem to deal with: Heshie was on his case. As Les limped by Heshie, bearing Mrs. Turanski's hot water and lemon, the headwaiter shook his head and wagged a finger at him. "You got to walk better than that. I can't have a gimp in my dining room."

"I just bumped into something," Les insisted. "I'm okay."

"Okay or not," Heshie frowned. "It don't look right. How can people enjoy eating food a cripple brings them? Get yourself an Ace bandage or something."

But what really hurt Les that morning was not the acute pain in his right leg. Or the cold shoulder Millie was giving him. Or even the veiled threats Heshie was making. No, what was killing him was the fact that he felt so utterly depressed on what should have been the greatest morning in his young life. After all, he had finally busted his cherry, gone all the way, crossed pay dirt; he had unbur-dened himself, at least technically speaking anyway, of the unbear-able weight of the megaton cargo of his own virginity. Which had for so long governed his every behavioral action in terms of both fraudulent poses and actual quests. But instead of feeling proud and free, emancipated and liberated, carefree and ebullient, exhilarated and exuberant, elated and ecstatic, rapturous and radiant, manly and virile, and potent and princely, Les felt like shit.

Was that all there was to the loss of virginity? No, Les decided as he dragged one leg after the other around the dining room that morning. There had to be more. If there was such a thing as true love—and he did not doubt that for a single second—then there also had to be true sex. Or, at least, the deep reality of true sex. As the end all and be all of true love. And somehow it all had to do with Vivian Davis. Perhaps he had not completely spent—rather than completely misspent—his virginity with Millie Meagher because of Vivian Davis? Perhaps he had let go prematurely because he was really holding back, so to speak, since he was saving the full ripeness of his sexual bloom for Vivian Davis? Just as she had all but promised hers to him. Together one day soon back in the city, perhaps on the very date of her eighteenth birthday, they would unfold each other's blossoms, petal by petal like in the e.e. cummings's poem he had once read. Because he did not doubt in the slightest that he and Vivian together shared a date with Destiny, true Destiny, sexual Destiny.

12

It was a chilly evening, but not so windy as to require *Monty*'s blanket, the canvas top with the plastic windows that theoretically could be fastened into the jeep's steel frame. Anyway, Les was actually enjoying the breeze that washed against his face. And, shifting in and out of gear at each stoplight, every control at his fingertips, he was glad that he had bought the jeep after all. The symbolic instrument of American power and conquest, highly maneuverable yet daringly vulnerable, it really was the proper vehicle for him to be driving that night.

The Davises lived on one of the few mixed blocks in the neighborhood, one that housed both Jews and gentiles. Some of the windows showed *Chanukah* candles, others displayed Christmas trees and had strings of bulbs wired about their frames. From the street he could see no lights of any kind glowing within the Davis house; it almost looked as if no one was home. But as he parked *Monty,* Les still tingled with excitement.

He ran up the front stoop, taking the steps two at a time, and rang the bell. Pounding his gloved hands together, he peeked in through the damask curtains that furled against the living room front windows. A sliver of light slanted in from the dining room across the hall. And at last he heard foot steps. Mrs. Davis, wearing a housecoat in a floral pattern, was coming to the door. He quickly resumed his position in front of it as she opened it.

"Oh, hello, Lester."

"Good evening, Mrs. Davis."

"I'd ask you to come in but the girls aren't here."

"Oh."

Mrs. Davis smiled. "They flew off to Paris Monday."

"Paris?"

"Isn't your friend Mickey there?"

"Yes," Les nodded, wondering what Mickey had to do with Vivian and Laura's flying there. He still associated Paris more with Charles De Gaulle and Edith Piaf and Marcel Cerdan and even Oscar Wilde, than Mickey Feldstein.

"Well, her father and I asked Vivian what she wanted most for her eighteenth birthday and she said—" Mrs. Davis stopped and interrupted herself. "—Come in, have a cup of tea, you'll catch a cold standing out there—"

"It's okay, Mrs. Davis, I just happened to be in the neighborhood and—"

"No, no. I was supposed to call you and in all the *tsimos* I forgot. Come in, even if you think you won't catch a cold out there." she folded the housecoat more tightly around her thin, angular body. "I'll catch a cold standing here."

Les followed Mrs. Davis down the hall to the dining room where Mr. Davis sat, the ever-present scowl on his face, brooding over the disrupted gin game. "Oscar," Mrs. Davis said, "I was telling Lester about Vivian's birthday present."

"Hello," Mr. Davis grunted.

"Are you sure you don't want any tea?" Mrs. Davis turned to Les.

"No, thank you."

"Anyway," Mrs. Davis, picked up her hand and resumed her seat at the dining room table. "It was all a spur-of-the-moment thing. Vivian said she wanted to go to Paris. Laura said she was willing to go with her. As her chaperone. There was no school this week and next week because of the Christmas vacation. It was her eighteenth birthday. And it was also *Chanukah* . . ." She turned to her husband, "I forgot if you're saving nines or not," she said and laid down the nine of spades.

"I'm not saving nines of anything," said Mr. Davis and drew from the pile.

"And they're having a wonderful time there," Mrs. Davis continued. "I don't know what time it was over there, but they called me this morning. They told me they saw your friend Mickey already and he was like a regular Frenchman. I knock with three." And she laid down her cards like an Oriental dancer opening a fan.

Mr. Davis slapped his hand down in disgust. "Nineteen. Do you want to play or do you want to talk?"

"I'm going," Les said, rising.

"So long," Mr. Davis waved and collected the cards.

"Wait," Mr. Davis was on her feet again, holding the folds of her housecoat tightly. "Let me see you to the door, Lester. I'm sure Vivian will be calling you the first thing she gets back."

Les fled from the Davis house as if some furies were pursuing him. He had never felt so utterly disappointed in his life. Far worse than the night after he had made it with Millie. This was a new, record low. Because on her eighteenth birthday there was Vivian in Paris with her new diaphragm along with Laura and her old diaphragm. And Mickey was there amidst all the diaphragms. And he was still in Brooklyn and all he had was a hot jeep named *Monty*. Suddenly, Les wished that things had worked out better with Millie. After all, as it turned out, she was reality, everything else just passing fantasy. Wishes and dreams that weren't worth shit.

But Millie had been so angry that she completely ignored him for the rest of the summer. Except the one day she sidled over to him some three weeks after Chicago's party, while he was sneak-eating some chopped liver near her server. "You may not be good," she said, staring straight ahead as if she was standing lookout in a spy movie, "but you're lucky. I had my period yesterday, so we're all off the hook. I wasn't going to tell you yet either, but what the hell?"

"That's great," Les said. "I was really worried," which was only partially true. How could he really have been worried about the possibility of Millie's being pregnant when she was scarcely acknowledging that he even existed?

"Anyway, it was all one big mistake from beginning to end," Millie said, and walked away, her muscular legs leading up to her round ass as appetizing as ever.

And Les's clearest memory of that first unhappy morning after he had finally scored would remain that of limping through the alcove toward the lobby after working breakfast, his knee still killing him, and feeling a hard nudge on his elbow. It was Chicago wearing white shorts and a V-necked tennis shirt. "What did I tell you last night?" Chicago said, shaking his fist in the air.

"About Millie?"

"No." Chicago blocked his passage. "About the game with Sir Arthur Balfour. It was a set-up."

"What do you mean?"

"It was a dump. Fat Jackie Gordon fixed it with Solly Ryan. Paid him a few bills for shaving the points enough so he could win by the spread." Chicago laughed. "That's why the old man bit him."

"Old Man Levine bets basketball?"

"Sure. Solly Ryan was costing him money and he didn't like it. Old Man Levine had the Diplomat and was giving eight points and he could see what was happening. His money was going down the tubes because Solly was dumping. So, he was furious. He's still furious." Chicago moved his head about. "Notice anything missing?"

Les looked about the alcove. All the candy and Coke machines were still there. But there were gaping holes where the three pinball machines had stood. There were only the markings of their former presence, indented black squares in the arabesque carpeting where they were formerly implanted.

"The old man had them taken out first thing this morning," Chicago laughed. "He figured that ought to teach Solly a lesson."

Les was not really interested in the moral lessons that might be imparted to Solly Ryan. Instead, he told Chicago his concern about the fact that his limping in the dining room had upset Heshie.

"Don't worry. I'll take care of Heshie," Chicago assured him. "I'll tell him you have a case of blue balls from last night. By the way," he winked, "how did you do last night?"

Les winked back and answered Chicago's question by repeating it. "How did you do?" He assumed he already knew the answer, but wanted to head off any further inquiry into the details of his own "success."

"I got a problem there," Chicago said. "That girl's in love."

Les was genuinely surprised. After Glenda's behavior that morning, he expected to hear a tale of great conquest. Instead, he apologized for not having warned Chicago about the high school boyfriend over in Wiesbaden.

"Not with him," Chicago threw up his hands. "But with me. The girl's in love with me. It always happens. Give them a one-night stand and they want you for life."

"It must be your underwear," Les said. "Get new underwear."

"It ain't the underwear," Chicago replied seriously. "It's what's in them."

Les wondered if it might have been the rare beauty of a seldom encountered, solitary testicle that caused Glenda—in fact, all of Chicago's previous, countless conquests—to become so hopelessly smitten? After all, it was a well-known fact that women were strange creatures, most vulnerable to cripples, most susceptible to kinks. Or did Chicago's alleged lonesome testicle simply exert a remarkable potency and prowess? But that morning Les asked no further questions. Instead, as Chicago drifted off toward the pool in search of a pinochle game, Les limped on down the path toward the busboy's shack, his head down, his knee aching, but the perpetually gnawing reminder of his virginity, at least, temporarily, if only technically, was gone . . .

Les pulled away from the curb in front of the Davis house—on the vacant seat beside him the undelivered birthday gift, the book of love poetry—U-turned sharply, and headed back in the direction of his own block and the poolroom. He hoped he'd find Chicago there. He had to see him right away. There was something he had to ask him. Or rather ask for him to arrange. Even though it would mean owing Chicago another big one.

BOOK II

1

As Lester and Mickey stepped out of the synagogue onto Ocean Front Walk into a bright morning sun, Lester flashed on blinking into the glare of similar suns after leaving the Saturday temples of his youth, the neighborhood movie house in Brooklyn which they had called the "Itch," now a twin theater featuring hard-core pornos, according to his last driveby.

"Have you had any breakfast yet?" Mickey was asking.

In the full flush of exterior lighting, Lester could perceive how dramatically Mickey had aged. Not that he was not still good-looking in a French Latino way. But now Mickey looked more like a craggy and mature Jean Gabin, than a smooth, young American Alain Delon.

"As a matter-of-fact," Lester lied, "I haven't."

Mickey pointed. "There's a terrific deli down the block."

"Is there?" Les squinted into the sun. As if he didn't know exactly which deli Mickey was referring to. As if when he had stayed at Pritikin's two years before, he had not more than once guiltily sneaked over to that very deli with a fellow Pritikinite, a best-selling writer, who suffered from high blood pressure in addition to several other ailments that afflict the obese. The writer, Dom Fazio, wrote serious books about politics, but never seemed to take Pritikin seriously. The first day they met, Lester had asked Dom how he found the food at Pritikin's. "Who eats it?" the writer shrugged. "What about the exercise program?" "Who does them?" the writer replied. But Lester, with the exception of the few transgressions he committed with Dom at the deli, had pretty much stuck with the Pritikin program. And it had done wonders for him. Blood pressure down. Cholesterol down. Weight down. Sex up. As for Dom, the last Lester heard, he had written another best-seller, this one about Irangate, and was in North Carolina on the Duke rice program.

"How many years is it?" Mickey asked. "We haven't seen each other?"

Lester looked out at the ocean. Surfers in their black wetsuits, looking like sea creatures from another planet, were bobbing up and down on the waves. "A long time," he said. "The last time we saw each other, I had never even seen a surfer."

Mickey laughed. "Not even at Coney?"

"Especially, at Coney."

"Remember the Davis sisters?" Mickey said.

"Of course. How could I ever forget them?"

Mickey stopped and kicked at a candy wrapper which had attached itself to the bottom of his shoe. "Laura's dead."

"I didn't know that." Lester lied. "Or maybe I did and forgot. Sometimes all that," he gestured toward the beach as if their past had once sprawled there on the sand only to be washed away by an incoming tide, "seems like another world: Brooklyn. Our youth. the Thespians. All that. I'm very far removed from it."

"What about *Monty?*"

Lester smiled. *"Monty* was my Rosebud."

"What about your parents?"

"They're both long gone."

"Oh, I'm sorry to hear that."

Lester accepted the tribute with a sigh, as if he were still in mourning. "What about your folks?" he asked politely.

"Indestructible," pronounced Mickey. "Right down to their gall bladders and prostates." They had reached the deli and Mickey pushed open the door and said, "Now, enjoy."

Lester did enjoy his white fish. He would have preferred chopped liver, but he had manfully restrained himself from ordering such a delicious mountain of cholesterol. And he had his bagel toasted dry and ate only half of it. Which made him feel rather virtuous. It was not every day he exerted such fine self-control, even if he had just eaten a Pritikin breakfast an hour earlier. Mickey, poking at his own lox omelette, smiled. "You've put on a pound or two, Les, haven't you?"

"Not really," Lester said. "Not lately." He pointed down at the lox omelette bathed in a moon of butter. "If I remember correctly, weren't you once into health food?"

"Still am." Mickey picked up a heaping forkful of eggs and inspected them. "Except for lox and eggs." He deposited the forkful into his mouth and proceeded to chew on it with winks of delight, shaking his head from side to side in exaggerated motions of sheer pleasure. "Mind," Mickey's fork suddenly reached across the table like a three-tonged spear, "if I finish your bagel?"

Lester snatched up the remaining half of his bagel. "As a matter-of-fact, I do." He had abstemiously endured its cardboard, shirtback dry taste and he was damned if he would let Mickey enjoy it in any other way. Especially with his gusto way of eating. Lester picked up a knife and slid it under a pat of butter. Anyway, except for the white fish, he had not really had breakfast yet, not if you were seriously counting calories.

"Well," Mickey sipped his tea, "I seem to remember you much thinner."

Lester added a dab of orange marmalade jam to his bagel. "Fatter, thinner," he lifted the bagel to lips. "After all these years is that all we have to talk about?"

Mickey nodded solemnly. "You're right."

"So, tell me about yourself," Lester stirred his black decaf as if it actually contained a mixture of cream and sugar. "Like how come I find you singing in a synagogue?"

"Because that's where cantors sing." Mickey laughed.

"Michel DuChamps is a cantor?" Lester asked incredulously.

"No, but Ben Sirota is."

"Ben Sirota?"

"My cantorial name."

"Cantors have stage names?"

"We also have agents."

"Of course," Lester nodded, and bit into his bagel again. Not bad, but it could still use a little more marmalade. As he reached for the plastic cup and scooped out the rest of it, he watched Mickey slowly push away the remnants of his unfinished lox omelette. "The portions here are colossal. I can't finish this."

Lester retrieved the platter. "I can't stand waste," he explained. They'll only throw it out. You don't have AIDs, by any chance, do you?"

"Just herpes."

Lester's fork, about to plunge into the lox omelette, froze in mid-descent. "Really?"

"Not really."

What to believe? Lester considered for a moment. Michel certainly looked healthy enough. But still, what did he know about his health record? It was reason enough to lay off the leftover lox and eggs. Also there was the matter of C and C, calories and cholesterol. But what the hell? It was only a few bites, couldn't be more than an ounce or two. And it would all even out anyway. After all, hadn't he taken his decaf black? Not even with NutraSweet. He picked up a forkful and began to place it in his mouth. Even his lips could tell the eggs were cold, the lox too briny, and that the taste would certainly not be worth all the C and C. But his tongue, his teeth, his jaws, all seemed to operate with minds of their own. They proceeded to chomp down and devour it ravenously, every last scrap on the plate.

Lester had not seriously thought of Mickey in years, and now in the banquette of a Venice deli it was as if he was seated across from a Lazarus. "And you've been a cantor all these years?"

"Oh no," Mickey shook his head. "After I was blacklisted . . ."

"Oh, yes, the blacklist," Lester said. It had been a long time since he had heard that phrase. Not that he had forgotten about the blacklist for a single minute. "Then you seemed to drop out of sight."

"I went back to France for awhile," Mickey said, "and tried to pick up there. But it didn't work. I went to England, but nothing happened for me there, either. Then I went to India—"

"India? Were you looking for the truth?"

"No. A show business gig."

"And what did you find?"

Mickey smiled: "The truth. Which is that show business is the truth for me. It's my karma."

"I can understand that," Lester agreed. "But how did this cantor thing come about? Did you go to Israel, too?"

"No. I went to a synagogue in the old neighborhood."

"Which synagogue? The community center?"

"No," said Mickey.

"The Young Israel in the poolroom?"

"No," said Mickey. "Do you remember the *B'ais Chaim?*"

"That mosque-like building with the balcony for the women?"

"That's right. I went there with my folks one year for the High Holidays. I was at loose ends at the time. I was down to even giving voice lessons to school kids. Not ordinary school kids. Elizabeth Irwin kids. Little Red kids. Dalton kids. I had a pad in the Village at the time.

"Anyway, they always had a cantor in that synagogue, not a big timer like at the center or an amateur like Mendel Mandelbaum up in the poolroom, but a trained cantor. However, they never had a choir. And every year since I was a kid, several members of the congregation were recruited to serve as a choir. I was a former choir boy himself, so to speak. And they pushed me up to the *bimah* and I became a part of the choir again, grouped around the cantor. And almost immediately it all came back to me, as if I had been rehearsing for three weeks straight. And as we sang, I couldn't help but notice how all eyes—and ears—were on the cantor, center stage. He was bathed in attention. My mother and the other women up in the balcony were all staring down at him in his white satin robe, hanging on to his every phrase and trill, and it was as if the energy of their interest was forming some sort of metaphysical spotlight around him. And the ham in me—you should pardon the expression—enjoyed being a part of it, having some of it wash off on to me, too. Afterwards, the cantor himself nodded to me appreciatively and he complimented me. Said I had a good voice, sang with a traditional cantorial *niggun,* and it was a shame I was using my gift just that once a year to serve God and the Jewish people. He told me there was an acute shortage of cantors and even suggested I might train to become one. That I wasn't too old. And he suggested a conservatory I should study at."

"So you had," Lester extracted a green tomato from the pickle jar set on the table, "a religious experience?"

"No," Mickey laughed. "A show business experience. All my religious experiences came later. I had liked singing in the choir that day. It was the first audience I had performed before in months and months. So, that winter I enrolled in a cantorial conservatory. And it hasn't been a bad life. But now I'm going to give myself another shot."

"Another shot at what?"

Mickey extended his hands palms upwards. "At show business, of course. Real show business."

"As a singer?"

"I would sing some, if necessary. But I've always regarded myself primarily as an actor."

A half laugh escaped from Lester, despite the fact he tried to cover over it with a cough. "Don't you think you're a little old?"

"How old is Dustin Hoffman?"

"Younger than you."

"Maybe a year or two, but not by much. And I'm a better actor than Dustin. Just give me the chance."

"I don't have anything going at the moment," Lester said.

"I'm not talking about you, fatso. I didn't even think of you when I came out here. I'm talking about the movies in general."

"As an old friend, I've got to warn you, Mickey. It's still a tough business. Very tough."

"I know," Mickey nodded. "But God is tougher."

He had to be kidding. Lester stared deeply into Mickey's eyes. But his soft gray-blue eyes gave away nothing.

"He's prepared a scenario for me," Mickey continued. "A scenario that can't miss."

Lester began to plot his getaway. This was California and kooks popped up everywhere. Even high school friends in the synagogues of Venice. He looked at his watch and inquired politely, "God's written a script for you?"

"Of course not," Mickey said, regarding Lester as if he was the kook. "But He has prepared a scenario that would give me access to reentry into the business."

"You mean by meeting me?"

"No," Mickey continued to regard him as if he was being the absurd one. "By giving a concert here."

"Where?" Lester decided to play along with him. "At the Hollywood Bowl? At the Greek Theater? At the Universal Amphitheater? At the Santa Monica Civic?"

"No," smiled Mickey. "Those places would be nice. But they aren't necessary. Besides, who would come to hear a cantor in any of those theaters? Don't you think God knows the business well enough to know I couldn't draw gnats in any of those places?"

"So, where will your concert be?"

Mickey pointed back over his shoulder. "In the synagogue. Where we just met."

"If you pardon me, I'm sorry, but I don't understand how a concert held in a synagogue could launch you into the movie business."

"You obviously are not religious."

"Not very," Lester agreed.

"You'd be surprised, Les, at how many important industry people are members of that congregation. They will come to my concert. They will hear me sing. They will be moved by my performance. And there will be a rush to employ me in a major motion picture."

"Or," Lester could not restrain himself, "in a new hit TV series?"

"No," Mickey said solemnly, "I don't want to do TV just yet."

This time Lester did not even bother coughing to mask his snicker-laugh. He rose and said, "I have to run."

Mickey studied his costume. "Jog?" he asked.

"No, run," Lester said. "I really mean *run*. I have to go. I'm late."

Mickey nodded understandingly and picked up the check. "This is on me." He waved away Lester's offer of money and dropped several bills on to the table. "Is this enough?"

"More than enough," Lester assured him. "And thanks."

As they walked out of the deli back onto the promenade on Ocean Front Walk, the strong sun all but blinding them, a bearded vagrant held out his hand. Mickey reached into his pocket and handed the man a dollar. "Promise me you'll buy a drink with this."

The vagrant smiled with blackened teeth. "You got a deal." And then he tipped his hat and moved on to another prospect.

Mickey looked after the seedy vagrant. "Thank God that isn't either of us."

"So far. At least, not yet anyway." Lester held out his hand. "Good to see you again, Mickey."

"Good to see you, too, Les. Although I don't think it's healthy that there's so much of you to see. And I'm sorry you don't think my concert plan will work."

"I thought it was God's plan, His scenario."

"Same thing." Mickey nodded. "Anyway, if I recall correctly, you didn't think I could make it as a French singer, either."

Lester smiled. "That's true." And that was as far as he wanted to let it go. "See you." He pumped Mickey's hand vigorously and turned and jogged back toward Pico in the direction of Pritikin, where he had parked his precision instrument, hoping that no druggie or derelict had vandalized it in his absence.

2

On the first day of classes at Brooklyn College after the Christmas–New Year's break, Les ran into Vivian Davis on the fourth floor of Boylan Hall. She was wearing a cream-colored pleated skirt and a blue sweater, and looked as if she had just stepped out of the pages of *Jardin du Mode* magazine. "Hi!" she greeted him cheerfully. "Bonne Année! I have so much to tell you. Can we meet after the two o'clock?"

Les nodded.

"In the lounge. Okay?"

Les nodded again. And she was gone, heading down the hallway toward the staircase.

All during his two o'clock which was, ironically, French, Les made doodles in his spiral and seriously considered standing Vivian up. But what was the point? Inevitably, he would soon see her again. After all, having registered for it together, they were in the same speech course on Mondays, Wednesdays, and Fridays. There was simply no way to avoid seeing Vivian again, even if he really wanted to. And he was not so sure about that. He had dreamt of Vivian too intensely and for too long, and if his dream was dying, it still contained the breath of lingering life. He had yet to learn just how badly Vivian had let him down. In fact, he somehow felt he was still in the ball game. Also, he was curious. Not about her reactions to Paris. But about Mickey. What he was doing? How was he making out? His condition seemed to change from letter to letter. At one moment, he would be totally depressed and describe only how desolate his life was under the gray sunless Paris skies. In the next letter, he couldn't be happier, full of artistic aspirations and show business hopes and cultural pretenses of all sorts, as he urged Les to drop whatever he was doing and come on over and join him.

A few minutes before three, Les spotted Vivian in the corner of the student lounge, leaning over a desk intently. "Hey," she smiled, "I'm writing Mickey a letter. Telling him how I'm about to meet you here." She capped her ballpoint pen and closed her spiral notebook.

"How is Mickey?"

"Oh, he's fine. He's wonderful." She rose and picked up her books and wrapped her black raincoat tightly about herself. "C'mon," she said, taking Les's arm. "I have so much to tell you."

Les slowly surveyed the lounge. Several couples were dancing; most students were just sitting on the couches, smoking, but one couple was seriously necking. Les wondered how much further they would go in public. "What's wrong with here?" Les asked.

"Oh," Vivian prodded him toward the door. "The dreary records, the lousy ambience." She pronounced ambience in French, as if the word had never crossed over into the English language. "Besides, I need some fresh air."

"It's raining."

"Oh, don't be so chicken, Rose," she said. "Don't tell me you're afraid of a little rain, Rose." During that first semester of college, it had become their custom to address each other by their surnames, the adult names the teachers called them in class.

"I'm not afraid of the rain, Davis. *Monty* has his top up."

"Then let's go for a ride."

"Where to?"

"Anywhere. I don't mind."

"I have a class next hour."

"So do I. But let's cut. Our vacation was too short, anyway. It's too soon to be back in school.

As they stepped through the side doors of Boylan Hall onto the granite steps that led down to the quadrangle, a cold snap of wet drizzle hit their faces. *Monty* was parked over on the other side of campus and they walked past the library in the rain. When they came to the lily pond, Vivian stopped. "Wait," she said.

The lily pond behind the library was where lovers would stroll on pleasant autumn or warm spring days. On a cold, dismal Tuesday in January it was deserted. Also overflowing. But Vivian insisted Paris had taught her to open her eyes, to see everything as if for the first time. And after they had walked around the artificial pond once, she paused and peered down into it. "I never appreciated how really beautiful this place was before."

Les pulled his collar up higher about his neck and hunched his shoulders. "I don't appreciate how beautiful it is now." On the contrary, to him it seemed quite the opposite, miserable and dreary to the point of ugliness. Not a single lily in sight. Only some floating twigs and fallen leaves, and an ice cream pop stick drowning in its own cellophane wrapper. "C'mon." He firmly took Vivian's arm and tried to steer her away form the lily pond toward the direction of Campus Road, where he had been lucky enough to find a parking space.

"Wait," she again said, "I want to tell you something while we're here."

"What?"

"First," she stepped at a right angle to him, "tell me if I look different."

They were on the gravel path that ran along the edge of the lily pond. The rain was coming down hard now, in pellet-like drops that exploded into small overlapping whirlpools upon hitting the surface of the gray shallow waters. Les stared at Vivian. Now, as always, she wore little makeup. No eye shadow or mascara around her large hazel eyes. Not even the slightest hint of rouge on her high cheeks. Only cleanly drawn lines of a thick, but pale lipstick, marred her otherwise natural look. The rain, streaming down her long hair, rendered it stringy. Otherwise, she looked her beautiful, natural self. "Different from what?" Les asked.

"Different from what I was?"

"When?"

"Before I went to Paris?"

Les studied her again. Aside from her hair, she still seemed marvelously impervious to the cold, falling rain. He shook his head, "No."

"Well, I feel different."

"Soaked?"

"No," she shifted her weight from one foot to the other. "I'm serious."

"I'm serious, too. Let's get out of here."

"But first I want to tell you something and swear you to secrecy."

"I'm sworn."

"I'm serious, Rose."

"So am I, Davis."

"Well," Vivian said quickly, "I'm no longer a virgin."

Her announcement was greeted with no sudden peal of rolling thunder and no great flash of lightning. The rain just continued to beat down hard. "Since Paris?" Les asked.

"In Paris," she said. "And I want to tell you all about it."

"Not here," Les said. "Not now." And taking her arm again, he began to lead her toward Campus Road and his parked jeep. There they could get out of the rain—if *Monty*'s top was not leaking—and he could hear her story. Not that he really wanted to.

Down Flatbush Avenue Les drove, *Monty*'s top leaking every cobblestone of the way. When he spotted a parking place just past the entrance archway to Erasmus Hall High School near Church Avenue, he pulled over and parked in it. Then he and Vivian ran across the trolley-track lined street together, holding their hands over their heads to shunt off the slanting rain, and pushed their way through the revolving doors of Garfield's cafeteria.

Even though it was long past the lunch hour, it was not easy finding an empty table. Les remembered the old Milton Berle joke: "It was raining, so I went into a cafeteria for a cup of coffee and an umbrella." But in the back of the mirror-walled side room, far from the steaming counter opposite the tiled mosaic mural in the main room, Les took off his London Fog and placed it over a vacant chair, before an unoccupied table, to stake their claim. Vivian, still wearing her black raincoat, accompanied him back to the high-topped beverage section of the counter. They both ordered coffee and agreed to share a piece of poppy seed strudel, but when they returned to their table, Les showing off by not using a tray but instead professionally carrying the coffees in one hand and the strudel in the other, they found two middle-aged women seated there, one eating apple pie and coffee, the other having rice pudding, heaped in cream, and tea.

"Excuse me," Les pointed with the coffees, "but this table is taken."

The chubby lady in a brown dress, whose beefy pink jowls immediately reminded him of a sixth-grade teacher he had hated, held a suspended forkful of pie before her mouth. "Oh, yeah?"

"Couldn't you see my coat here?"

"Oh, is that your coat?" she said, and her mouth closed down over her forkful of pie.

"Of course. Why do you think I left it here?"

"I thought maybe somebody forgot it or something."

"Nobody forgot it," Les said. "Are you going to get up?"

"Go away, sonny," the woman rasped, her eyes narrowing. "This is a cafeteria, not a restaurant. You think you're in a Schrafft's or a Child's or something? You can't make reservations here. And your wet raincoat can't do it for you, either." Now she addressed her rice-pudding-spooning companion across the table. "You ever hear of such a thing?"

Les stared down at her, the coffees still balanced professionally in his hand, not quite knowing what to do. And then, he simply seemed to go out of control. But not before calmly handing Vivian behind him the dish containing the poppy seed strudel, and placed one of the cups of coffee down on the table as if he were serving the woman a second cup of coffee. Then, he reached down and scooped up his London Fog with his left hand. And emptied the second cup of steaming coffee onto the lap of the woman, who emitted the scream of a wounded cat, her wails resounding from mirror to mirror.

"C'mon, let's get out of here," Les grabbed Vivian's hand, as a crowd quickly began to form around the woman, now screeching hysterically like a wounded crow, and they ran into the main room, past the cashier's protective perch, and right out the entrance door. They could not re-cross Church Avenue to *Monty* because there was too much traffic running and the light was against them. So instead, they rounded the corner and ran under the protective marquee of the Flatbush Theater next door, ducking into the outer lobby. In the far wall was a legitimate theater-style box office. Les quickly slapped down money for two tickets and pushing Vivian ahead of him, hurried into the theater.

"What's playing?" Vivian whispered to the elderly usher, who was tearing up their tickets.

But Les did not give the ticket taker a chance to answer. Taking Vivian's hand, he raced up the stairs and did not stop running and tugging until they were seated in the pitch-black balcony. On the screen was the face of Dan Duryea. And soon, Yvonne de Carlo came into the picture.

"I think I've seen this," whispered Vivian, shifting to get comfortable in her seat.

"Then see it again."

"I think," said Vivian, studying the screen intently, "they're on the lam."

"So are we."

"What should I do with this?" she produced the dish with the poppy strudel she still had in her hand.

"Eat it," Les said. "It's evidence."

"Say, you have some temper, don't you, Rose?" she whispered, unevenly breaking off a crumbling piece and handing it to him.

"I don't know."

"You really exploded at that lady."

"She reminded me too much of all the shit I had to take in the mountains."

"Was that all?"

"That was enough."

Vivian touched his arm lightly, almost scratching it like a kitten. "I hope I never remind you, Rose, of too much shit." How could she ever possibly think that? Les wondered, as he put the strudel in his mouth, rubbed his hands against each other and sank back into his seat.

After the movie, while Les was driving Vivian home in *Monty* in the rain, she finally told him what she had been bursting to tell him all day—about her trip to Paris and what an adventurous one it had been. The high point being the fact she and Mickey had made love in the Montmartre atelier of a painter he knew, while Laura had gone off to a Communist Party meeting in Ivry. "And you know something," she said. "It was the most marvelous experience in the world. It was everything I ever hoped and dreamed making love for the first time would be. I will have that moment to treasure for all the rest of my life. A true souvenir of Paris and—"

"And what?"

"Youth," she said and smiled brightly.

"Did you have a diaphragm?" Les asked. He didn't know what else to say.

"I came to Paris prepared," she said.

"And you're in love with Mickey?"

"I was in Paris."

"And in New York?"

"I've just been back two days," she shrugged.

"Were you in love with Mickey before you left New York?"

"I don't know."

"Whose idea was it to go to Paris, anyway?"

"Laura's. She told me to ask my parents for the trip as a birthday present. I think she did it so she could come along as my chaperone."

"Some chaperone."

"I'll say," Vivian said.

They drove on in silence in the rain until they reached her house when suddenly Les asked, "How does Mickey feel?"

"About what?"

"About you."

"I don't know. He said he was in love with me. But you know Mickey."

"What do you mean?"

"He's always such an actor. Besides, I think he's half in love with Paris. And completely in love with the idea of being in love in Paris." She gathered her books and prepared to leave the jeep. "Anyway, do you want to come in?"

"What for?"

"Have dinner with me. I'm sure there's plenty of food left over."

"No, I better get home, too."

Vivian leaned over and kissed him. "Thanks."

"For what?"

"For listening to me. I had to tell someone. I've been dying to tell someone ever since I got back. I've been dying to tell you."

"Why me?"

"Because you're my best friend."

"Am I?" Les was genuinely surprised. "What about your sister?"

"Are you kidding?" Vivian said, "I would never tell Laura anything in a million years. Especially about something like this." Les watched as she stepped down from the jeep, turned to wave goodbye, and headed up the walk to her house, clutching her books with both arms like a schoolgirl, though she was definitely, as he now knew all too painfully, a woman.

3

One day, shortly after Mickey had returned to America, Les met him for coffee at Cromwell's drugstore off the lobby in 30 Rock, the NBC building. As Mickey's eyes scanned the booths, he told Les he was thinking of changing his name and coming on like a Frenchman. Because in Paris he had been able to get a few singing gigs as an American. So, why not try to get work in this country as a Frenchman?

Les pooh-poohed the idea. "Just because someone's been cast in a Pirandello play, doesn't mean they should come on like an Italian from then on. Or because they might be in a Chekhov, they automatically turn into a Russian."

But Mickey had insisted. "You've never been abroad, Les. You don't understand the appeal of a foreigner to civilians. To most people, a foreigner is exotic."

"A *mockie* is exotic? A greenhorn is exotic?"

"Maybe a greenhorn isn't," Mickey admitted. "But an American in Paris is exotic. And a Frenchman in New York might be, too. Anyway, I figure it's worth a shot. If I strike out again, at least it'll be on different pitches."

Les kept putting down the idea as ridiculous, but Mickey remained dead serious. He really wanted to get started in show business in the worst way and he figured that was the way for him to go. "Meanwhile," he smiled, "do you think you can get me a job upstairs?"

"Things are tight." Les stirred his coffee. "I'm lucky to have my job." And he slid the check over to his side of the table.

What a difference, Les thought, a year made. A year before he had been like any young artist, as innocent and idealistic as a poet. Until Vivian Davis broke his heart twice in two different places. By not fucking for him, as he thought she had all but promised. And by fucking for Mickey instead. Thereby, not only smashing his lyrical dreams, but also seriously bruising a ball or two. And then, to really ram matters home, Vivian had even insisted on telling him about it, gushing it all out to him as if he were her closest friend and she had no other possible confidant in all the world. How was that for a complex castration?

But, yes, what a difference a year made! Les had spent the previous summer as a busboy in the mountains, making good money but hating every minute of it, having to rise daily to the same sordid routine of clearing dirty oatmeal bowls and sweeping up cracked egg shells, while Mickey was in Paris, waking up each day to a new adventure. But this past summer, Les had been luckier. While Mickey was dreading the necessity of returning home to America, Les had been acting in summer stock on the Cape. And while he had not made a single penny, he had loved every second of it. And now, as a floor manager at NBC Television, Les was standing on the fringes of the best of all possible worlds, and loving both every dollar and every minute of it.

Between his summer jobs of busing and acting, Les had spent a year in college learning two important lessons. The second was that a year of college was enough for Les Rose. The first: The world spinned on contacts. And show business was no different from the mountains; it wasn't what you could do, but who you knew. For example, it was a college contact that got Les into summer stock. And it was a summer stock contact that led to his job at NBC. And who knew where the contacts he was developing at NBC would lead him to? True, he wasn't in quite the slot he wanted at the moment—Les still yearned to act—but he was definitely in show business. And he was in on the ground floor of the medium that everybody was predicting would soon replace movies, just as surely as it was already supplanting radio. So meanwhile, he did not dwell too much on the past; he was just too happy enjoying the prospects of the future.

All of which he owed to Lisa Ormont. Lisa was the contact who opened the way for him to get out of Brooklyn and put his own personal show, so to speak, on the yellow brick road. And it had all happened so casually; Les had barely known Lisa Ormont, who was a senior member of "Varsity," the Brooklyn College drama society that he aspired to someday join. But Les had always admired her from afar, a respectful freshman distance. After all, Lisa played leads in "Varsity" productions; it was obvious she was unusually talented; and the only question about her potential career-wise was her height—or lack of it. Because aesthetically she was a trifle too short. Not that she was quite grotesque. Just short. Dwarf-esque and midget-esque in an era when statuesque was to be queen. Whatever the fashion, as far as Les was concerned, Lisa was beautiful. Her boobs were large and generous in proportion to her foreshortened body, her dark skin gave a distinctive Latin cast to her oval face, and she wore her straight black hair long, flowing down her back like gleaming cascades of wet coal on a shining chute. So what if she was missing a vital inch or two? She always wore such spike-heeled shoes that her acute shortness was rarely too noticeable.

But the most striking image Les would always carry of Lisa had nothing at all to do with her brevity altitude-wise. It was the way she held a cigarette. Between drags her wrist upturned, the cigarette dangling behind her fingers as if banished from sight until cued. Les imagined Tallulah Bankhead smoked that way and he attributed to Lisa's characteristic gesture a sophistication, which came from worlds of experience far beyond his ken. And why not? Lisa lived in Manhattan. In an apartment with an actor, an older man who had once been married and who worked regularly on Broadway. While the only people Les lived with were his parents in Brooklyn, who worked eternally in their store.

One afternoon Les was standing outside the entrance to the Little Theater, studying the sliding glass curtained cork bulletin board, looking for casting calls he might answer. So far, his stage career at Brooklyn College had consisted solely of serving on backstage crews and assistant stage managing. He had been the assistant stage manager on the production of *The Three Sisters* that starred, if one could use that word to describe a role in a college production, Lisa as Natasha. As for his own acting hopes at the moment, he would have even killed for a decent role as an anything in a student original one-act performed during the college club activity hour on Wednesdays. Just to break the ice. Just to start acting again. Most of the money he saved during the past summer in the mountains, which he had planned to spend on acting classes in the Village, had been blown instead on his untrusty jeep *Monty* in a long series of repairs.

"Hi," Lisa greeted Les. "I haven't seen you since *Three Sisters.*"

True, she may not have seen him since *Three Sisters,* but Les had seen her just the week before at a bill of student one-acts, standing in the back, her arms clasped about her books which she held before her chest, peering judgmentally up at the stage as if she was a critic or even the playwright herself. Les turned from the bulletin board and nodded down to her.

"How are you doing, Larry?" she asked.

"Les," he corrected.

"Of course, Les." She smiled. "I can always remember lines, but never cues." She touched him lightly on the chest. "Do you have a second, Les?"

"Sure."

"I'd like to talk to you, Les. Let's go in there and sit down." She pointed at the double doored leatherette entrance to the Little Theater.

For a wild moment, as they entered the aptly named Little Theater—the stage was small, the seating capacity was no more than double digits, and backstage was mostly just a stairwell—Les wondered for a moment if perhaps Lisa had been delegated to ask him to join "Varsity." But how could that be? One had to acquire a certain number of points earned through stage appearances and crew work to be eligible for invitation, and he knew he still lacked sufficient units by a large margin.

Les followed Lisa into the last row and took the aisle seat. On the shallow stage, two actors were rehearsing a scene with a student director who was walking about them with his thumbs joined together horizontally and the rest of his fingers spanned outward vertically, as if he was framing the scene for a movie through a viewfinder. When the student director saw Lisa the imaginary viewfinder turned into hands waving at her. Lisa waved back as she sat down, opened her purse and extracted a pack of cigarettes. She offered Les one but he refused it. "I should stop, too," she said but lit up anyway and inhaled deeply. Then Les watched the cigarette disappear behind her hand, which she placed on the cheek removed from him. "Are you majoring in speech, Les?"

"Probably."

"Do you want to act?"

"Definitely."

Lisa smiled back. "So do I." She waved the cigarette back into view and drew in on it. "Do you have any plans for the summer?"

"Not really. I might go back to the mountains," Les said, boosting an imaginary tray to his shoulders, "and work as a busboy again."

"Do you like doing that?"

"Not really," Les said. "But the money is good."

"So I've heard," said Lisa. "But how would you like to join a group of us in summer stock on the Cape, instead?" She then mentioned a few of her fellow heavyweights in "Varsity." "Plus, there'll be some kids from NYU and Hunter and a few from out-of-town schools like Cornell and Boston University and from acting classes like Paul Mann's and Stella Adler's. We're calling ourselves the Inter-Collegiate Players and it'll be a one-in-a-million once-in-a-lifetime opportunity. This rich woman has an estate on the Cape with a theater already built on it, and she'll give us all free room and board." She paused. "But that's all. There won't be any money, no salaries at all for the actors, but it will give us a chance to do good stuff. Shaw and Shakespeare, as well as contemporaries like Miller and Williams and O'Casey. Are you interested?"

"Are you kidding?" Les said. "Except I have one question."

Lisa smiled, unveiled her cigarette again, and inhaled deeply. Then exhaling slowly, she returned the cigarette to its dangling place of banishment and asked, "What's your question?"

"Why me? Why are you asking me to join this group? You've never really seen me act."

Lisa looked him in the eyes. "I can always spot talent. And more important, drive. Besides," she smiled, "we can't all be stars, even in summer repertory. We need players for the minor roles, we need reliable stage managers."

"And assistant stage managers?"

"And assistant stage managers," she said and smiled again. "We also need transportation and I understand you have a jeep."

"Monty," Les said.

"Excuse me?"

"Monty," said Les, "is the name of my jeep."

"How charming," Lisa said, and went through the gyrations that brought her cigarette to her mouth and inhaled.

One thing about being an assistant stage manager in summer stock, Les quickly learned, you might not get to play star roles with pages of sides to learn, but you did get to act. And in good, quirky, compact roles, too, that enabled you to showcase your own talents. For example, Les was Howard, the boss's son, who fires Willy when he comes for a raise in *Death of a Salesman;* and he was Fuselli, the gangster in *Golden Boy,* who owns Bonaparte. Not that he did not have to assistant stage manage also. At rehearsals, he would chalk draw the floor plan of a set, trot off to find missing actors, run lines with the actors present until the absent ones appeared. During performances, Les was a boy scout backstage, flattering here and cheerleading there, while setting up props, arranging for storms to thunder and phones to ring, and making sure everyone entered on cue. In addition, at the end of each week's run he would stay up all night with hammer and nail and brush and paint helping to build new sets and strike existing ones. And with seldom trusty but always available *Monty*, he was frequently scooting off on emergency production errands during the day or providing vital cargo services along the beach at night, bearing the necessary provisions for midnight bonfire parties and cookouts. Les worked hard, he was humble, everybody loved him.

Lisa was especially proud of him. How well he fit in and how popular he had become. Les was her protege and she was his *kvelling* surrogate mother. And Doug, her actor boyfriend, who was also one of the company's three directors, became Les's summer surrogate father. Doug was a big, hairy man who always seemed to be bending over and not only in deference to Lisa; it was as if he were a chubby puppet who was forever dangling on loose strings. He was hunched over as he checked into his pockets for cigarettes or turned the pages of a Samuel French playbook, looking for a speech or just searching the barren stage floor for answers to an actor's questions. Doug and Lisa always saved a place for Les at their table in the dining room and he would sidle in next to them like a son returning home late from school. Sometimes, as if they were actually a real family, Doug would lean over and help himself to some of Les's dessert.

By the end of summer, Les was stage managing Doug's shows exclusively. No matter what Doug's faults, and he was no great brain for one thing, Les enjoyed watching the way he handled actors. Doug never treated them as if he were some sort of supervisor or boss. Nor was he subservient or obsequious to them in any way. At the same time, he was not their co-equal buddy. Doug was more like a co-conspirator, a fellow member of a circle of thieves or a gang of bank robbers, but the only one who for some reason seemed to have been entrusted with the secret road map or getaway plan.

Doug had many friends in the city and shortly after they all came back to town at the end of the season, he was set up for a job as a stage manager in the new medium of television over at NBC. But a few days later, in one of the ironies that is fact in an actor's life, Doug landed a major role in a Broadway show about to go on tour. So, he sent Les to keep his appointment instead, to see the network honcho his friend had arranged for him to meet. And somehow that executive, a distracted and harried man, confused Les with Doug, thought Les had both Doug's extensive experience and his friend's enthusiastic recommendation. Les wisely did not disabuse him of either notion. And a week later, instead of registering as a sophomore for the fall semester at Brooklyn College, Les Rose was a floor manager—the television equivalent of an assistant stage manager—at NBC.

The base pay was not great, the hours were long, but everyone was young—almost if not quite as young as Les himself—and it was never boring. The production procedures derived out of theatrical tradition; and the first two days of rehearsals, when the actors would walk through their roles on any of the weekly half-hour shows Les worked on, for example, weren't that different from summer theater—or even Broadway theater. Rehearsals were in midtown hotel ballrooms or in other halls rented out all over town. But then the day before air, when working with the facility's equipment at 30 Rock, it became different. 8H was the most fabled of the studios, the one Toscanini had used, custom-built especially for the maestro on a delicately balanced system of springs to absorb any off-key shocks or rumbles caused by the Sixth Avenue subway running beneath the building. But there was also 3A and 3B and 6G, formerly radio studios but now filled with thick coils of wires that snaked to and from the stolid cameras and flimsily constructed sets that overflowed into the cluttered institutional hallways. Les laid down the marks for the actors to hit and relayed the wishes and instructions from the godlike director in the booth. And after the run through and the dress, it was all live, on air, and Les would feel the tingle of excitement and the adrenalin of panic when an actor suddenly went up on his lines and skipped two pages right to the end of a scene with the next set not ready yet, not one of the three cameras in position, and he would have to implore the actors through desperate hand signals to wing it until an adjustment could be made. Or suddenly a camera itself blew, the little red light becoming black as an equatorial night and he would have to commandeer another camera and whip it across the floor and reposition it like an artillery replacement in the midst of battle. And, indeed, it was a constant battle, disaster never lurking far away, the cast trying to keep pace with the clock, while suffering opening-night jitters at the same time. But there was also joy. The joy of collaboration, the joy of tension and creation, and Les loved it.

Les was still too new on the floor when Mickey asked him to try and get a job for him; so there really was not much he could do. He was lucky enough to have his own job and he still dreaded losing it because someone would discover the case of original mistaken identity—or referral—in hiring him. But, as each succeeding week passed and Les was as helpful and useful in the studio as he had been in summer stock, he became more secure about his position. Meanwhile, Mickey was becoming more and francophiled, wearing a beret and passing himself off as a complete Frenchman by speaking a broken English. But he had yet to pick up any work.

Mickey would drop by NBC on his way to and from auditions at supper clubs, where he was trying to sell himself as the second coming of Chevalier. And if Les was not on the floor working on a show at the moment, or busy in his floor manager's hutch, one of endless cubicles in which each floor manager had a desk and a phone to work with while planning and prepping his assignments, they would go downstairs together to Cromwell's Drugstore for coffee and talk of career dreams.

Les would never bring up Vivian and what had happened in Paris. He thought mentioning it would be betraying a confidence —Vivian's. Not that there was any great continuing romance between Vivian and Mickey—that had ended even before Mickey's return to America. Or any great continuing romance between Les and Vivian, for that matter—that had never got off the ground.

Since Les had been away all summer on the Cape, and then dropped out of college completely because of his TV job, he was seeing less and less of Vivian. Their friendship may have very well have peaked the day of her Paris–Mickey revelation. Also, Vivian had changed. She was still majoring in speech at Brooklyn College and speaking fervently of her dreams of acting, but she had also recently begun considering law as a career possibility. In law, she told Les, not only could she make a good living, but also work to improve the living conditions of others. A lawyer, realistically speaking, she had decided, could be far more effective in the class struggle than, for example, a doctor, the profession her sister Laura had chosen. Les saw a connection, even then, between Vivian's first tentative steps toward a practical career approach and her retreat from the idealism of art; and he attributed it to Mickey. Mickey had let Vivian down, disappointed her, shattered her innocence and destroyed her idyllic dreams—just as surely as she, and Mickey— had annihilated his. Les remembered the fantasy Mickey once held out to him on a cold winter's night in Brooklyn that somehow Vivian and Laura, and he and Les, would all live together in Paris "and have each other." Instead, they were all living apart in New York and no one seemed to have very much. Except he did have his job, his foot in the show business door, which Mickey still so desperately wanted to enter. At least, he had that.

One day, as Les and Mickey were catching a breath of the damp gray air after a drugstore counter coffee break, watching the ice skaters below in the Rockefeller Center rink, Les mentioned that Vivian had told him about what had happened in Paris. He really didn't know why he brought it up. Except Mickey seemed especially miserable and depressed that day—he had just been turned down for the role of a bellhop in a farce set in a Parisian hotel for which he thought he had auditioned brilliantly—and perhaps he was trying to cheer Mickey up, pump up his ego, even if it was at the expense of his own.

Mickey looked up from the ice skaters below and turned to him. "Did she tell you about Laura, too?"

"You mean that Laura was in Paris with her?"

"No," Mickey smiled. "That I made it with Laura, too. But then, I guess she still hasn't found out about that yet."

While Vivian was out buying theater tickets one afternoon, Mickey said, he had slipped it to the chaperoning Laura. Les stared at him in utter shock, admiration, and envy. "How did you manage to pull that off?"

"It was easy." Mickey leaned forward over the rail again and peered out at the promenade running into Fifth Avenue where the Christmas tree would soon be standing. "She smelled her sister's *nookie* on me."

Les didn't understand. "Huh?"

"Like, likes, like."

Les still couldn't understand what Mickey was saying. "What do mean?"

"Cunt likes cunt," Mickey explained.

Les nodded slowly, as if Mickey had just imparted words of great wisdom and depth. But he still wasn't quite sure what Mickey meant. So, he asked the question whose answer he knew he could surely understand. "How was it?"

"With Laura? Or with Vivian?"

"With either?" Les spread his hands. "With both?"

Mickey pursed his lips together tightly and the effort of consideration showed in his wrinkled brow. "They were both terrific in different ways," he finally decided. "Fucking is always terrific. Even when it's not so great, it's still great. Like the movies when we were kids."

Again Les could not understand him.

"When we were kids," Mickey smiled. "Did we ever see a bad movie?"

"No," agreed Les. "Some were just better than others."

"Exactly. It's the same with fucking. Even when it's bad, it's good and when it's good, it's great. Right?"

Les did not want to betray the paucity of his sexual experience during Mickey's stay abroad. Especially, most recently. There had been only two actresses he was really interested in that past summer. One didn't care the slightest about him; she had been involved with the company's leading-man type, Eugene Stephens from Cornell; and the only intimacy the other actress had shared with Les was that she was a lesbian, had a girlfriend in the city, and would appreciate it if both that fact and he went no further and that they would just be friends, no matter what the others in the company might think.

Les was still considering the response to his previous question when Mickey raised one of his own. "But you know what really would have been something?"

"What?"

"If I could have had a sandwich."

Again Mickey was beyond him. Les didn't have the vaguest idea of what he was talking about now. "A sandwich?"

"A sex sandwich. If I could have gotten both sisters, Laura and Vivian, into bed with me at the same time. Now, wouldn't that have been something?"

Les nodded slowly. After all, Mickey was articulating, in a way Les had not dared to imagine, the dream of his adolescent lifetime.

"That really would have been something beautiful."

"For you," Les said.

"Not for me," Mickey dismissed his words with a brusque wave of his hand and moved away from the rail. "For them. It would have been beautiful for them. It would have finally brought them together as sisters. I wish I had suggested it. But I guess I was still too petite bourgeois. Even in Paris. Especially in Paris."

Mickey seemed so genuinely upset with himself that once more Les actually tried to console him. "At least you made it with both of them separately," Les said.

"Yes," Mickey agreed. "And it was terrific."

"So you say."

"Fucking someone," Mickey pontificated as if he was just uncovering a great truth, "fucking anyone, can certainly tell you a lot about that person's character."

"I don't doubt it," Les said. They straightened up and turned away from the skaters, Les headed back to 30 Rock and work; and Mickey, looking far from a conquering Frenchman in New York, leaned into the wind and slowly walked toward the subway. But just a few weeks later, the world turned over for Mickey. His career as Michel DuChamps was launched in a nightclub. What happened was this:

Wearing a tux that reminded Les in a way of the busboy's uniform he had worn at the Levine Family Diplomat, with a michrophone in his hand, Michel would dance and prance between the girls of the chorus, who were somehow both overdressed and scantily clad at the same time, singing a song proclaiming that this was Paris and that these were the girls of the Follies Bergère. He also had another number in which he was dressed as a sailor in a waterfront Marsielles bar singing "La Vie en Rose" before two Apache dancers went at it.

The nightclub was on Forty-eighth Street and Les came over one night and, standing beside the stage manager who also doubled as a clown in one of the production numbers, watched two shows from backstage. The purpose of each production number, as far as Les could discern, was to give the dancers an excuse to change from one more revealing costume into another. After the last show, Les waited for Michel to change into his civvies in a telephone booth size dressing room on the floor above the nightclub. Then he wandered with him through the dancers' dressing room, where he perceived a lot more nudity than the people downstairs had been paying for. Mickey hugged and kissed each girl as he introduced Les to them as both his friend and an important television director. And then he leaned over and asked Les if he saw any girl he wanted.

"What do you mean?" whispered Les.

"You see one you want?" repeated Michel. "Just tell me."

Les surveyed the scene once more. In the crowded room above Times Square, lights flicking on and off outside the windows covered with oil cloth shades, and brightly colored costumes hanging everywhere, from nails, from racks, and from screens, there was something indescribably cheap about the setup. But also present, up close, were the most beautiful girls Les had ever seen. One statuesque girl reminded him of Virginia Mayo. Mickey seemed to be following his eyes. "Except Sonya," he said. "She's the governor's."

"Which governor?"

"What's the difference?" Mickey laughed.

"You're kidding?"

"Why should I kid about a thing like that?" said Michel. "But you want anybody else. The redhead?" he pointed suggestively at a girl who smiled and wagged her finger back at him. "That's Doreen." In both shows, Les had watched Doreen with awe and wonder do an up-tempo featured strip as a silent film siren, the lights flickering away, to the tune of "The Flight of the Bumble Bee," until she finally revolved each bared breast in opposite directions. "Doreen," Michel was already introducing him into her makeup mirror, "this is my friend, Les. He's an important TV director. He went to college just like you."

And Mickey embraced Doreen from behind as if to reward her for an exemplary academic record. "What college did you attend?" asked Doreen, as she resumed rubbing off her makeup.

"Brooklyn College," Les said. "But only for one year."

"That beats me," said Doreen. "I only attended for one semester. Bowling Green."

"I know the subway stop," said Mickey. "But I didn't know it was also a college. I attended South Ferry myself."

Mickey was truly happy and expansive that evening. A few hours earlier he had learned that he would be going with the same show to Miami and then Las Vegas. And who knew what turn his career might take next? After all, how far was it from Las Vegas to Los Angeles? Doreen and Andrea, a sullen, black-haired girl from the chorus line, joined Mickey and Les for celebratory coffees and desserts at Hector's Cafeteria across the street. And Les was beginning to wonder about what further stages the evening—or rather night —might progress to. But as they left the cafeteria, to Les's great surprise, the three of them, Mickey, Doreen and Andrea, hailed a taxi and quickly boarded it together, closing the door behind them and leaving Les still standing on the sidewalk, as the taxi sped away. Later, Mickey explained to Les that Andrea was suddenly not feeling well, suffering from an attack of food poisoning, but Les did not know whether to believe him or not. Because he knew by this time that when it came to women, no matter how seemingly altruistic his original intentions, Mickey could not be trusted.

After Vegas, Mickey was booked into Ciro's in Hollywood, an engagement which led to his being cast as a French POW in the sitcom that became one of the top-rated shows in those early days of television. And the next time Les saw him in a New York nightclub, it was downtown in the Village—and downstairs—as a featured singer, with his own accompanist seated at the piano, while he crooned "C'est si Bon" and "La Vi en Rose" to the squealing delight of otherwise seemingly adult and intelligent women.

4

Les's career, too, was moving along. In addition to his floor manager job at NBC television, he continued his involvement in theater by taking over another gig that had been meant for Doug.

All summer long Doug had been promising some of the actors in the company that he would run a class in scene study back in the city. Now they wanted that class. But Doug, off touring on the road, could not conduct it. The actors decided to meet by themselves and hold their own class. And then, late in October, Lisa came to Les and asked him, not so much to preside over the class but to manage and administer the group, schedule the dates, make the phone calls, send the postcards, and finally to assign roles in the scenes. After all, Les had been Doug's assistant and the group needed a leader, even if the leader in this case would be somewhat less than his equals. Les's function was to be that of a secretary. Or, perhaps more precisely, that of a stage manager who after opening night always took over and actually managed the life of a show.

The class met Monday nights in the Greenwich Village apartment that Lisa shared with Doug. On Ninth Street up four flights in what once had been a painter's garret, complete with a skylight against which every drop of autumn rain would reverberate like a falling stone. An Indian screen of sandalwood isolated the small bedroom section of the studio apartment from its living room and dining areas. The kitchen was a hot plate on a rack and a refrigerator near the sink. There were radiators hissing steam, but it always seemed cold, even in October.

At the very first meeting, an actor brought the copy of an unproduced play written by his girlfriend. It was a play highly derivative of Tennessee Williams about a Jewish middle-class girl whose parents were driving her toward a bourgeois marriage with a crude and vulgar and boorish washing-machine parts manufacturer, while she has all sorts of artistic and aetherial dreams personified most vividly by her attachment to a homosexual poet who eventually commits suicide. Les would sometimes think of the play disparagingly as *The Class Meshuggeneh,* while he heard others invoke the heroine's patronymic and refer to it as *A Streetcar Named Epstein.* In any case, the group began reading the first scene from the manuscript play and somehow it seemed to have just the right breakdown of parts for the group; soon, they invited the playwright to the class and were working on the second scene and then another, before taking on the whole play. The playwright, a wispy blond with Coke-thick glasses, would always hunch up inobtrusively near the hot plate, a pencil in her hand and an opened copy of the play on her lap, observing most intently her boyfriend, Stuart, who Les assumed was the prototype for the poet, and was indeed playing him. Either Beth, the lesbian Les did not have an affair with that summer, or Lisa, was usually cast in the main role.

Beth would always give Les a hard time whenever he made the slightest directorial suggestion, glaring at him as if he was purposely trying to veer her off some private course to the truth. Or she would ask impossible questions. In one scene, for example, the script had the stage direction: *She opens the window.* A simple enough action and since the actors were not on their feet, Les had scarcely noticed it.

But Beth looked up from the script one night and insisted upon knowing which window she was supposed to open before proceeding any further.

"Any window you want to," Les told her.

"How many windows are there in the room?"

"Two, I guess," said Les.

"Then does she open the one on the left? Or the one on the right?"

"The one nearest to her."

"That's the right window then," said Beth, intently marking her script. "And does she open it from the top or the bottom?"

"From the top," Les answered quickly.

But Beth was still not finished. She had one more question. "But why does she open the right top window?"

"To let in air, I guess." Les whistled out.

"Oh," replied Beth. "But are you sure?"

"Let's ask the playwright," Les said, turning to her.

"I never thought about it," said the playwright. "I just wanted to be sure she could hear the sirens and react to them."

Lisa, on the other hand, was a dream to work with. She was just as concerned as Beth with both the extrinsic details and the inner life of her character. But she did not make such a big deal about it. One night, when Les thought her reading was a bit portentous, he did not have to present her with an elaborate Method "as if" scenario—"It's as if you are a bird and you've had a broken wing, but suddenly it's healed and you discover you can fly again." Or ask her to explore—and exploit—her own private sources, resources, and neuroses. No, he just had to suggest that her character had a sense of humor and Lisa promptly made the adjustment and lightened her performance.

By Christmas the play had become the class project and someone made mention of the availability on Monday nights of a certain off-Broadway theater housing a long-running hit for staged readings. Immediately, the informal scene study class turned into the rehearsal process and somehow, automatically, it was understood that Les was in charge. Everyone worked hard, as if they were preparing for something much more than a bare stage one-night stand. Les humored the actors; he motivated them, too, so they would not, at worst, fall upon their collective faces. And when they were finally as ready as they could be considering the time and logistical limits,

it also seemed to fall upon him to see to it that there were mimeo-
graphed programs with small cast bios on hand to give to the
invited guests on performance night. Les considered for a long time
exactly what credit to give himself. He knew he did not want a
stage manager credit. But taking a director credit might offend
some of the actors. Finally, he decided to give himself a "Staged
by" credit.

The Monday evening staged reading went well. After all, the
audience consisted solely of friends and colleagues. And there was
not a peep either way about his program credit. Les had invited
both Davis sisters and Laura came with a Negro who was obviously
homosexual; after the performance he rushed over to Les at the
back of the theater, gushing about how much he loved the play and
would have gone on talking endlessly about it if Les had not interrupted to ask Laura why Vivian had not come. Laura just replied
with a shrug, "Am I my sister's keeper?" And the Negro found that
remark so hilarious he was still giggling when a cluster of people
who Les worked with at NBC gathered around him, compli-
menting Les on his directing work. Les was particularly pleased to
see George Hecht in the group. George was an independent pack-
ager and producer on whose crime show, *Homicide,* Les worked.
Les had sent him an invitation more pro forma than anything else,
hardly expecting him to show. But there he was, a beautiful Puerto
Rican actress beside him, firmly gripping Les's right hand and
telling him what a fine directing job he had done and that it would
not be too long now before Les might be directing a show for him.
And the actors, still milling about on stage when Les joined them,
congratulated and praised him as much as he congratulated and
praised them. It was a terrific night for all the members of the
scene study class—especially Les.

Lisa, too, was in a state of post-performance high. Les had cast
Lisa in the leading role for the reading, despite the strenuous objec-
tions of both Beth and Stuart, and she had performed it very well.
And a staged reading, Les realized, was her dramatic forte; with the
vocal elements assuming precedence, her height disadvantage

seemed to show least. Especially after Les had decided to let Lisa sit on a tall stool. The rest of the cast, seated on plain cane chairs, rose while delivering their lines and speeches, while Lisa remained perched on her stool as if it was a throne and she was a queen—or a queen bee—with all the action revolving around her. Anyway, she really had been brilliant and she knew it. And, as far as she was concerned, Les had definitely contributed to that brilliance.

After scene study classes, the group usually adjourned to the Waldorf, an all-night cafeteria on Sixth Avenue near Eighth Street for *coffee and.* But this evening, along with friends and well-wishers, they reassembled at Julius's for beer and hamburgers. Most of them had the usual type of actors' temporary jobs to get to the next morning, so the cast party, so to speak, did not last very long. There was a self-congratulatory celebratory drink or two, a belated snack, and then good-bye waves to one another. In front of Julius's, Les offered to walk Lisa, who lived just a few short blocks from there, home.

At the foot of the steps to her building on Ninth Street, Lisa looked up at Les and said: "I'm still too excited to even think of going to sleep. Why don't you come up and share a nightcap?" When Les hesitated, she pulled his hand gently and he followed her up the steps, hovering behind her as she unlocked the front door, and then up the four steep flights of stairs to the studio she shared with Doug, who was still on the road, touring with the bus and truck company.

Les had never been in the apartment before with just Lisa alone, without Doug or someone else from their scene study class present. And suddenly the apartment seemed much larger to him, abundant spaces everywhere, especially if you included the area he had rarely seen before behind the sandalwood Indian screen that divided the room. While Lisa rinsed glasses and emptied an ice cube tray, he glanced down through the tilted casement windows at the corner of Sixth Avenue. In the doorway of the Chinese laundry below, a couple was smooching.

Lisa came to the window with two drinks in hand. She had

unknotted the braided bun in which she had compacted her long black hair and was still shaking it loose. It flowed down her back all the way to her waist. "I put a little water in your Scotch," she said. "That's how Doug always takes his. And we don't have any soda, anyway. Imagine," she shuddered, "having to lug bubbled water up four flights of stairs."

"This is fine."

"Well," she clinked her glass up against his. "Here's to tonight. May it have been the first of many."

Les saluted her with his glass and took a long sip. He really did not like the taste of Scotch. To him, its smokey, charred-wood taste seemed more appropriate for some prescription medicine. But he did not mind its effect. He still had an opening-night high himself and could use a little coming down to earth, before he literally went underground to take the long subway ride back to Brooklyn. Because, naturally, over the weekend the temperamental *Monty* had failed him again and was back in Ralphie Miller's garage. Ralphie, who had sat next to Les in the first grade and was the last one in their class to learn to write his own name successfully, had finally dropped out of school completely during the eighth grade and was now forever endorsing the repair checks Les had to make out to him. Ralphie owned two gas stations and a body-and-fender shop and was also, he had confided to Les recently, looking around for a new car dealership.

Les remained standing as Lisa sat down on the green couch. "Sit down," she patted the gray-green serape covering the back of the couch. "Relax."

Les sat down opposite her on an antique maple rocker she and Doug had picked up that summer at one of those New England lawn sales. "This is comfortable," he said.

"Isn't it?"

"You were really good tonight," he said.

Lisa smiled. "I could have been better."

"I don't see how."

"I could have been taller."

Les couldn't tell whether she was joking or not so he said, "Nonsense."

Lisa laughed and sprang to her feet, holding out her hand to take his glass. "Some more?"

"I'm fine."

Les rocked back and forth as he watched Lisa pour a refill for herself from the bottle standing on the small drop-leaf kitchen table. Behind it was a poster for a Klee exhibition in Zurich. "Are you sure?" Lisa held up the bottle before putting it down.

"Okay," Les said. "Just a little more."

Lisa came over and replenished his drink. "Do you want more ice, too?"

"No, thanks." Les had no intention of doing anything more than nursing his drink. He had accepted the offer of a refill because their efforts at conversation seemed to be dying and he always felt a bit uncomfortable with Lisa. After all, she forever seemed to be doing favors for him. He was afraid that perhaps one day she would present him with a due bill and he had no idea in what area or in what manner it would be coming. Lisa was always physically free with her hands and arms and body about him, *touchy touchy* and *huggy kissy* whenever they met. But no matter how often she rubbed her boobs against him, he never felt the least bit horny about her. Les didn't know whether it was because she was almost a midget, or like an artistic mother figure to him, or simply because she was Doug's girlfriend. But he just never did feel that way about her. Or even think about her that way. As Les sat on that old New England rocker, sipping the Scotch distastefully, he foresaw no potential developments in the sexual sphere, immediately or prospectively. He would soon lay down his drink, give Lisa a fraternal —or filial—kiss upon the top of her head, and return to Brooklyn.

But suddenly he felt nauseous. "Excuse me," Les said rising.

"What's the matter?"

"I don't know." He rushed toward the bathroom. "But my stomach's upset."

Les opened the bathroom door and leaned over the toilet. Soon the bowl was a spatter of half-digested Scotch and beer and hamburger.

"Are you all right?" Lisa called in.

"I'm fine." He finished bringing up the dregs within him, flushed the toilet, and wiped around the edges of the bowl with toilet paper. Flushed the toilet again. And washed his face and rinsed his mouth at the sink. When he turned to the towel rack to wipe his hands, Les saw panties and stockings hanging there instead. And in the bathtub, from the shower nozzle, a white slip floated down over the water tap handle. He unrolled some more toilet paper and dried himself with that and dropped it into the toilet and flushed once more.

When Les returned to the studio room, Lisa was folding the serape and laying it down on the rocker. Then she spread a sheet across the couch and lay a pillow down on top of it.

"Hey, what are you doing?"

"I can't let you go home in that condition. You sleep over here." Lisa fluffed up the pillow like a maid in a play. "How are you feeling?"

"Better."

"Well, take some Pepto Bismol, I have some someplace. Brush your teeth, we've got plenty of extra toothbrushes. And go to bed."

Les yawned and said that perhaps he was allergic to Scotch. Or it could have been something he had eaten, like the Julius hamburger. Or it was just the beginning of a stomach cold. But in any event, he didn't feel that sick and could certainly manage the ride back to Brooklyn.

"Nonsense," said Lisa. She lay down a blanket atop the couch and hurried past him, soon reappearing with an absurdist bouquet of a toothbrush in a cellophane box, a half-filled bottle of Pepto Bismal, a teaspoon in a glass, and a towel. "You're staying over. No problem," she smiled. "Besides . . ."

"Besides what?"

Lisa shrugged. "Who likes to be in an apartment all by herself? I'll sleep better knowing you're here."

5

If, as Mickey had proclaimed, there was no such thing as a bad fuck, Les decided, then there certainly was great fucking. But he had never known that until Lisa. Because his sexual experiences before her had ranged from almost nil to just meager. In addition to the technical but official episode with Millie, there had just been Ethel. Who Chicago had "fixed" him up with on the night he learned Vivian was celebrating her eighteenth birthday in Paris with Mickey—and his dickie—as it later turned out.

After Les left Vivian's house that night, the unwrapped gift of love poetry on the empty seat beside him, he had driven *Monty* over to the poolroom. There, he found Chicago atop a stool near the ticker, gristle and spittle and mustard-streaked doughy bread together dangling from his mouth. Les told him, more or less, exactly what happened, and explained his urgent and pressing need in most immediate terms. "I got to get laid," he said. "Tonight."

Chicago lifted his head from the waxed paper wrapped corned beef club sandwich he was about to bite into again, picked up a bottle of Pepsi Cola, took a long swallow from it and finally belched out, "No problem."

So instead of Vivian, Les had Ethel, one of Chicago's neighborhood girlfriends, a doughty, dumpy, dirty blonde in her twenties who sullenly performed a favor for Chicago by going to bed with Les.

She was wearing a cotton quilted housecoat, had her hair in curlers, and was chewing gum when she greeted them at her door that night. "Lucky for you my parents are in Miami."

"Lucky for you," Chicago had replied, "Les is with me."

Ethel looked him over. "Who is Les?" she asked Chicago, without taking her eyes off him.

"Les is one terrific guy," Chicago said.

They had entered Ethel's house by a side door that faced a similar side door across a narrow alley and were standing near the entrance to the kitchen. Ethel's bland, bovine face in the fluorescent kitchen light reminded Les of the British Queen Elizabeth. But her accents and diction were distinctly Brooklyn "Whyn't cha call first?" Ethel asked Chicago.

Chicago smiled. "Because I wanted to see you right away."

"Then how come you stood me up Saturday night?"

"I didn't stand you up." Chicago protested, his face showing an expression of great pain. "Didn't you get the message?"

"What message?"

Chicago turned to Les. "That Albie. You heard me tell Albie to call Ethel when I had to go to Pennsylvania all of a sudden on business last Saturday night."

Les nodded dutifully.

"See," Chicago spread his arms open expansively.

"Bullshit," said Ethel. "I don't see nothing."

Chicago took her in his opened arms. "Honest. Don't you believe me?"

"Why should I believe you?"

"Because why should I lie?" He kissed her hungrily on the lips and then dipped into her neck like a famished bird.

"Cut it out," she said.

"C'mon," he said.

"I don't feel like it," she said.

"C'mon," Chicago said again. But this time it was addressed to Les. Chicago had removed his hands from Ethel abruptly, looked away from her distastefully, and stepped back and motioned Les toward the door with a quick movement of his head.

"Wait," said Ethel.

Chicago winked at Les before turning back toward her. "Okay," he said. "But be a little friendly with Les here first."

"What do you mean?"

"He's my friend. You're my friend. We're all friends. So be friendly." He put his hand in the small of Les's back and pushed him toward Ethel.

Again, she was looking past Les at Chicago. "I'm not a who-ah, Leon."

"Don't say such a word. Who said you was anything? Nobody said such a thing. You're my friend. Les is my friend. I just asked you two to be friendly, that's all. Is that asking too much?"

She turned the gum over in her mouth. "Okay, Leon," she said. "But just this once."

"Of course," said Chicago.

"That's what you said the last time," she said, and began to lead Les down the hallway. Les turned around and Chicago was winking at him and flashing the Mel Allen Ballantine three-ring sign at the same time.

Ethel's bedroom, at the end of the corridor past the bathroom, was crammed with furniture: a maple dresser, a white dressing table and chair, and a huge cherry-wood armoire that completely dominated the room. Ethel pushed aside the teddy bears and stuffed animals and Raggedy Ann dolls that lay on top of her bed and pushed on the radio that stood on the nightstand beside it. "I like music," she explained. "I like the Make Believe Ballroom."

"So do I," Les said.

She listened to the music coming over the radio for a second. "But it isn't on now," she said regretfully, and then lay back and touched the curlers in her hair. "You don't mind these?"

"No."

"I don't suck," she said. "Not even Leon."

"Of course not."

"You can ask him."

"I believe you."

"I'm not a who-ah."

"Of course not."

Les took off his jacket and kicked off his shoes and wondered if he should kiss her. He certainly had no desire to. But perhaps she expected some sort of preliminary. Up close, her smell somehow reminded him of the wax fruit his mother kept on their dining room table. When he did try to kiss her, she averted his lips, protesting. "What are you doing?"

"Nothing," Les said.

"Just take it easy," she said, and unloosened the rope-like belt about her quilted housecoat and it flapped open. Beneath it she was wearing a long flannel nightgown. "I was getting ready for bed," she said.

"Of course," Les said.

And then the room went dark as she clicked off the bedside lamp. Les groped under the flannel for her breasts, but she was already pushing the gown up past her hips and was shimmying out of her underpants. "Hold on," she said.

Les held on.

"You can take it out now," she said.

Les took it out and was both surprised and relieved to find it hard.

"You can put it in now, if you're ready," she said.

Immediately, Les push-slid it in. She wasn't very moist, but he seemed to be supplying sufficient lubrication of his own as he grunted away. When he was about to come she said, "Don't get it all over the bed."

"Where should I come then?"

"Come in me."

"Is that safe?"

"Sure. I always douche after."

Les's shoulders twitched as if in instinctive disbelief, but he came right away. In her. And then Ethel moved quickly, pushing him back off the bed and wiping around the spread with Kleenex before rushing off to the bathroom. Les dressed and went back into the kitchen where Chicago was seated studying a Yiddish newspaper. Chicago looked up, "Everything okay?"

"You bet," Les said smiling. "Your turn." But Chicago just dipped his head back into the Yiddish newspaper.

For some reason Les was suddenly very thirsty, his throat as dry and parched as if he had just crossed the Sahara. He went to the sink for a glass of water, asking over his shoulder. "Where'd you get that paper?"

"It was here. It just keeps coming, I guess, even while Ethel's parents are gone."

Les picked up an old commemorative *Yahrzeit* glass that had been laying face down on the white-grooved, enamel surface covering the laundry side of the sink. "Can you actually read it?" Les asked, as he rinsed the glass.

"Sure," replied Chicago, turning a page. "But I don't understand all of it." He put the newspaper down and rose and came to the sink beside Les. "I think I'm going to hang around here for awhile."

"Sure." Les had finished his drink, but was still holding the empty glass. "Say goodnight to Ethel for me."

"She was okay?"

"She was terrific, thanks."

"I told you she would be a lot better than some who-ah over in Jersey City someplace."

"She was terrific," Les repeated. "She must really love you."

Chicago laughed. "They all love me. Be careful where you put the glass. This is a *kosher* house."

"I'm glad it isn't *shabbos,* then."

"Are you kidding?" said Chicago. "Getting laid on *shabbos* is a *mitzvah.*"

"Leon!" Ethel called out.

Chicago shrugged and winked at Les, then ambled down the hall. Les picked up the Yiddish newspaper Chicago had been reading. He knew all the Hebrew letters from *cheder* yet he could not read a word of Yiddish, not even any of those in the thick headline on the front page. But, moments later, when leaving the house he noticed a brass plated *mezuzzah* on the threshold of the door, he made an actor's point of kissing it.

Les was never tempted to ask Chicago to arrange for a repeat with Ethel. Or ask Ethel herself, for that matter. One day months later he did run into her on the street not far from her house and nodded, "Hello." She stared at him as if he were a complete stranger—which, of course, in all truth he was—and quickly hurried past him.

Lisa was extraordinary sexually, making up in intensity and inventiveness what she lacked in size. Inch for inch, ounce for ounce she was the best lay Les would ever have, including a Yoga instructor from Studio City who once had him fucking her while she stood on her head. Not that he knew very much about fancy fucking when he was making it with Lisa. There had been Millie, Ethel —never Vivian—and then Lisa. So, he was more or less a sexual naif. But even that first night, headache and nausea and Pepto Bismol and all, Les could tell that fucking with Lisa would be more than just racking up another historic milestone, technically or otherwise.

He later once asked Lisa during an intermission, when they were waiting for his dormant penis to rise again, her hand gently caressing him around his thighs and ass, why it had taken her so long to go to bed with him. After all, she could have had him months before just for the asking. In retrospect, hadn't she picked him out for that very reason? Wasn't that why she had invited him in the first place to join the Inter-Collegiate Players? Hadn't she had her eye on him even then?

Lisa replied she had been waiting for Les to ripen and develop before plucking him. Her word. Develop in what way? Les wondered. Because in all honesty he told her that he had not garnered any additional sexual experience to speak of since the day they had first met at Brooklyn College. Indeed, he had squandered a good part of his freshman year hung up on his high school crush, Vivian. And in stock that summer, for some perverse reasons, only the lesbian had seemed to attract him and he had struck out with her. And since working at NBC and running the scene study class that fall, all he had really been doing sexually was sublimating.

Lisa stroked his pubic hair and said something he found most interesting: "By developing I meant becoming used to your hunger, so you could know how to be hungry again." Which, of course, was her way of telling him that their days together, almost by definition, were numbered. Until Doug returned, to be precise.

But since Les was not yet twenty, no fuzzy future could be as vivid as an active sexual present. Especially—to use the word of that period—an existential one. Each day after work he would return to the apartment, *Monty* more or less on rest leave in a Brooklyn garage. Or he and Lisa would meet in a Village restaurant. Have dinner at Chumley's or The Blue Mill in the West Village, the San Remo or Monty's or Minetta's down on MacDougal Street, the Grand Ticino or Filene's over on Thompson Street. And then they would climb the four flights to the apartment together and make love.

For some reason Les had always assumed that Lisa came from The Bronx. Perhaps because he could not conceive of anyone just living in Manhattan without having come from someplace else first. And, indeed, Lisa's family had come from someplace else first, before settling in Manhattan's West Side up in Washington Heights; Argentina where Goldberg had become Ormont. Midway in her junior year, Lisa cut down the long subway ride out to Brooklyn College by moving in with Doug in his Village apartment. And it was still Doug's apartment when it came to every gas and electric bill in the mailbox and every ring on the apartment telephone. On the few occasions Les was there without Lisa, he did not answer the phone. Suppose it was Doug calling from the road?

Les felt queasy about Doug. Doug had been his mentor and his friend and his savior almost every bit as much as Lisa. And there he was fucking Doug by fucking Lisa. Whenever he would start to broach the matter while they lay next to each other or in each other's arms, Lisa's finger would come to his lips admonishingly: "Let's not talk about such things in bed." But if he mentioned his concern about the problem at dinner or while they were walking through the Village, she would say, "I know more about these things than you do. Don't worry. These things always take care of themselves."

But Les was never that sure. And that discomfit only seemed to enhance his sexual life with Lisa, give it that sharper edge of pleasure that comes with a sense of eventual menace and danger. He knew their days together were not endless, that their dalliance would one day suddenly end. Unless, of course, they were in love. But Lisa would never allow love to be part of the vocabulary of their lovemaking. If Les just whispered the word, her finger was on his lips immediately.

Height is a vertical property and lovemaking is basically a horizontal activity—except perhaps for Yoga teachers in Studio City. So Lisa's diminutiveness—she once told Les she was four ten, but he mentally subtracted an inch or two from that—never bothered him in bed. But sometimes, when they were walking down the street, he would suddenly feel a frisson of embarrassment as he looked down at her beside him. To some of the passersby, he had to be in the company of a freak or some kind of midget or a grotesquely dressed child. In bed, such feelings never crossed his mind—or heart. Especially when Lisa was riding atop him, her muscular thighs churning and grinding, her long hair brushing from side to side, her eyes blinking down at him with love and gratitude and intense purpose all at once. Then she—and they—were nothing less than magnificent. Yet somehow Les knew, even if Doug had not been looming in the picture, their future together was limited. He could not dream ahead of a life outside of bed and theater with Lisa. When it came down to deep reality, in the long run Lisa would always be too short for him.

In February the play Doug was touring in closed and he returned to New York, moved back into his apartment and resumed his life with Lisa. And she resumed her life with him. Doug also took charge of the scene study class. And although Les continued to attend it, more or less as Doug's stage manager once again, inevitably, Lisa and Les became more and more distant. Sometimes she would press his hand with secret warmth when they would meet within a group. And once she vaguely suggested that she might be able to borrow an apartment where they could meet if Les was still interested. But he was no longer interested in her. He was in a way even embarrassed by their former intimacy. Glad that they had succeeded in keeping it a secret. Because now, whenever he saw Lisa in a group of people of normal height, it was obvious that she was hyper-short, to the point of abnormality. And only her extraordinary acting ability to seem otherwise had obscured that fact to him. Just as some actresses, not particularly pleasing in the aesthetic department, can play beauty, Lisa knew how to act tall, to appear normal. But basically Lisa was a grotesque of sorts. Almost a freak physically. And he was still much too young and far too insecure to deal with that.

6

Les had not planned on going to Vivian's wedding. And perhaps shouldn't have. But he was curious, to say the least. And he would be treated, he was sure, as a most honored guest. After all, very few of those invited would know both the bride and the bridegroom independently and he didn't think anyone could possibly know either as well as he knew both.

Naturally, it was a catered affair. At the Jewish community center. The movable walls that enabled the synagogue to expand into the ballroom and become as huge as a gymnasium for the High Holidays had been pushed aside. Now it was the ballroom that was arena size and the synagogue that was of almost locker room proportions, just big enough to accommodate the daily *minyan* and Friday night and Saturday services held there throughout the long retail part of the Jewish year.

As Les passed through the ballroom, his summer as a busboy not that far behind him, he automatically checked out the tables. The goblets all sparkled and there were two forks and two teaspoons, double settings at each place. On the bandstand were the drums of Murray King and His Musical Princes. Les wondered if he would actually stay around long enough to hear their music. Because he really didn't feel comfortable there; he was going to send a telegram pleading sudden illness; and it was only at the last minute that he had decided to attend at all. After Mickey—or Michel—

called him: He was in town just for the wedding. He was dying to see Les, too. How could Les not come?

After his fling—or affair—with Lisa, Les had other extended encounters with both actresses and civilians. But his feverish adolescent obsession with sex per se was more or less in check for the moment. Instead, most of his waking energies were concentrated on advancing his career professionally in the burgeoning but highly competitive new field of television. And he had been progressing rapidly. Within a year he had become an assistant director and now had his sights set on getting a show of his own. Oh, how he craved such an emblem of success! Early success. After all, what good was success if it came too late for you to really enjoy it? Or after most of your friends already had their taste of it? Les looked forward to getting his own show before his twenty-first birthday. Which would be the equivalent of the end of his junior year had he stayed in college. Directing his own TV show would make up for a lot of things.

Still, his career was in slow mo compared with Mickey's. Because as Michel DuChamps, Mickey had really taken off. While most of his peers were still struggling with their tenuous show business toeholds like Les, Mickey had already literally landed on his feet in Variety, where he was reviewed as a featured production singer in cabarets and nightclubs in New York and Chicago, Las Vegas and Miami. He had appeared on television, too. Not only on numerous locals shows, but on the Arthur Godfrey Show and Steve Allen Show. And he even had a press agent who plugged his name in gossip columns. Michel was the only person Les actually knew to either drive a sportscar or to be linked romantically with a movie star. The sportscar was a flaming red Austin Healy with impressive grillwork. And the film star was a flaming redhead, famous for her low bodice work, who although never quite a household word, once played a leading role in some of Les's early adolescent masturbatory dreams.

The item linking Michel and the star was in a Paul Dennis

column in the *New York Post*. And years later Les purposely would go out of his way to set up a meeting with the redhead on the pretense that he was considering casting her in something other than a dream-like fantasy. Her hair was still red, if not afire, and Les found her hadable, easily doable, but not really desirable. She was simply too old. But he did ask her about Michel and if she recalled him. "Michel who?" she responded.

However, at the time of the wedding, Michel was definitely en route to stardom; and he was already a star in the neighborhood. As much as one of the pitchers from the Rutherford B. Hayes High School baseball team, who had signed on with a Cleveland Indians farm club and had recently been accused of rape by an Iowa farm girl on page four of the *Daily News*. And Michel was a star to Les, if for no other reason than his return address: Studio City, California; in his innocence, Les somehow pictured Mickey actually living on some studio lot.

The last time Mickey was in New York Les had received a call from him one morning. He didn't have much time, Mickey gushed, but he was dying to see him. As it happened Les was working that day, getting a show on its feet, in one of the rehearsal halls at Central Plaza down on Second Avenue in the heart of the old Yiddish theatre district, and he told Mickey to come by for lunch. After all, there were all sorts of great dairy restaurants in the area, the kind Les was sure he could not find in Los Angeles, such as Ratner's and Thau's and Rappaport's. No, said Mickey, he was just too busy, what with agents and publicity people and the fitting of a new suit, every stitch hand-tailored. Well then, Les suggested, just drop up any time, they would be rehearsing on the third floor. No, Mickey said, he couldn't do that, the actors might recognize him and his presence would prove just too distracting and be disruptive. Les held the phone away from his ear for a moment and looked at it. He couldn't believe what he was hearing. Who the hell did Mickey think he was—Frank Sinatra? Marlon Brando? Laurence Olivier?—that he would disrupt a rehearsal? But could they have a

drink or coffee together? Mickey was asking. Fine, said Les, there
was a candy store just downstairs from the rehearsal hall and he
would meet him there around three o'clock but only, insisted Les,
if he could get away at the time.

Les did get away at five after three that afternoon, but by a
quarter past three he was still nursing an egg cream at the counter
when he watched Michel park a red Austin Healy before the hy-
drant at the curb, as if he was pulling up in front of the Stork Club
itself.

Mickey removed his sunglasses and looked up through the windshield, as if to test the afternoon sun, before returning the specs to
the bridge of his nose. He bounced out of the car as jauntily as Fred
Astaire on his way to meet Ginger Rogers. And he swept into the
luncheonette—like an ingenue making an entrance—sailing up to
the counter where, health conscious long before it became fashion-
able, he ordered an orange juice with a spritz of seltzer.

Instead of sitting down on the vacant leatherette stool beside Les,
Michel twirled it around with his index finger like a record on a
turntable. And while still standing, hastily drank the concoction
handed him by the counterman as if it were some sort of medicinally necessary task to be dispatched as quickly as possible, down-
ing it in just one big gulp. Next, wiping his lips with the back of
his hand and wetting his fingers at the same time, he made an
acting point of reaching into his pocket and extracting from it a
thick Guys-and-Dolls roll of bills from which he peeled the top
one, a single, and slapped it down on the formica-topped counter
and waved away any possible change—all in the same fluid motion.
And then, only then, did he finally acknowledge Les's presence. By
clasping his arms around his chest and embracing him in a bear
hug from behind, while whispering into his right ear, "Lester,
baby."

Les swiveled around on his stool and pointed out at the flaming
red Austin Healy. "Nice wheels."

"It's only rented," Michel made a sour face. "But you ought to
see the job I tool around in in California."

"A Ferrari?"

"Not yet. Just a Porsche. But one that handles real well. When are you going to come out and visit me?"

Les noisily sucked in the froth of his egg cream. "I'm pretty busy."

"No excuses," he said, draping his arm loosely over Les's shoulder. "Did I tell you, Les, I'm up for a series? In your medium."

"Television?"

"Yes."

"As a Frenchman?"

"Naturally, what else?" he laughed. "They have enough Jews in L.A. to play the usual *goyim.*"

Entering the synagogue Les now spotted Michel, a white satin *yarmulke* pasted on his head like a piece of dot candy, nodding vigorously to Rabbi Solomon Samuels, who was wearing a wide-peaked, fully-inflated black *yarmulke*. Rabbi Samuels was a stocky man with an aggressively rosy coloring and a shuck of red hair that fell down over his forehead, making him look like a sort of Jewish Huckleberry Finn. As a student he had played semi-pro soccer on Sundays with a team of Irishmen up in The Bronx, the New Hiberians, and it was easy to see how he could have passed for one of them. Rabbi Samuels was reputed to have been so adept at the sport which he had learned as a boy in Israel that he had had to make the Golden Boy-like choice between soccer and the rabbinet. The women in the congregation were very pleased at the choice he made, but some of the older members had their doubts, questioning Rabbi Solomon Saumels's scholarly ability. After all, how much *Yiddishkeit* could they expect from a man with a proven record of athletic inclinations? Chicago's father, Mendel Mandelbaum, had led the exodus of that schismatic group to the Young Israel congregation, which convened in the pool hall on the High Holidays where Les's own father would *daven.*

When Michel saw Les he motioned energetically for him to come over and join him and the rabbi.

"What is this 'La Vie en Rose'?" Les overheard the rabbi asking.

"It's a French song."

"I have heard of 'Promise Me' and 'Because' and 'Always' sung at weddings, but this will be my first 'La Vie en Rose.' "

"It's a terrific song," said Michel. "You'll love it."

"Well, if that's what the bride wants . . ." The rabbi waved his hands helplessly. "But we have a lot of wonderful Jewish and Hebrew and Israeli songs. I'm sure you can understand why I would have preferred a wonderful Hebrew song to any French one."

"But it isn't just any French song. It has a great deal of meaning and significance for the bride. It's one of her particular favorites," Michel said. He paused and put his arm around Les's shoulder. "Rabbi, I would like you to meet Les Rose. Les is in television."

"Les Rose. La Vie en Rose. Is that a coincidence?" the rabbi said, gripping Les's hand and pumping it vigorously. "So, you're in show business, too? How exciting. What do you do?"

"I work for NBC TV."

"Channel four?"

"Yes."

"Wonderful. Could you by any chance get tickets for *Howdy Doody?* My children love that show."

"Maybe," Les offered. "I can try."

"Wonderful," the rabbi judged once more. "Please send them to my home address." He pulled out a card and handed it to Les. "Nice to have met you, Mr. Rose. Now, if you'll please excuse me." He pumped Les's hand once more before hurrying off toward the door, as if he had just spotted a soccer ball rolling toward an open net.

The synagogue was filling up and Les recognized several members of the "Thespians" clustering around Vickie Levine, the teacher who had been the faculty advisor of their acting group in high school. Vickie was a tall woman who walked with a masculine stride and Les suddenly realized that there might have been an unconscious correlation between his attraction to Beth, the lesbian actress that summer in stock, and the fact that Vickie had been his first drama teacher, his introduction to the world of theater, which he had come to love fervently. When the group saw Michel and Les, they made a beeline toward them and soon Les was all but lost in a circle of nostalgia, with most of the crowd playing up to Michel, telling him how they had caught his act at some nightclub and how wonderful he was in his television appearances, although a few people did mention that, while waiting to see the news, they had noticed Les's name on the credit crawls that rolled on endlessly from the previous show.

When the rabbi took his place in the center of the *bimah,* the holy ark behind him, a *chupah*—or mini-tent-like construction supported by four ushers, each holding a corner pole—Les withdrew from his old high school group to a back row. Michel remained up front at the side of the *bimah,* like a manager perched at the edge of a baseball dugout, waiting to join his team as the last of the formal pre-game introductions.

"Dearly beloved," the rabbi intoned, "we are very pleased to have with us this evening a long-time personal friend of the bride from this very neighborhood, a star of stage, screen, radio, and television, that internationally famous singer," here he paused and fumbled through his pockets until he came up with a batch of index cards, "Michel DuChamps, alias Myron Feldstein, who will sing that great hit 'La Vie en Rose,' which is French, I'm sure, for *Zol zein mitt glick.*"

Michel rose and ascended the *bimah,* directing his biggest smile toward the former "Thespians." For a moment, as he stood showing off his dental work, Les thought he was actually going to sing *a capella.* But then a piano accompaniment of "La Vie en Rose" oozed out of the two speakers set near the wood-beamed ceiling in opposite corners of the synagogue. Michel first sang in French rather delicately, waiting until he hit the translated English lyrics before really belting it out in a crooner boffo Eddie Fisher-style.

Hold me close and hold me fast
The magic spell is cast
This is La Vie en Rose.

When you kiss me heaven sighs
And though I close my eyes
I see La Vie en Rose

When you press me in your heart
I'm in a world apart
A world where roses bloom

And when you kiss me angels sing from above
Every day words seem to turn into songs of love
Give your heart and soul to me and life will always be
La Vie en Rose.

Michel sold the song with a surety and confidence, a profession-alism Les had rarely associated with Myron Feldstein before. His nightclub act included a patter in which he spoke English with a phoney—"how-do-you-zay-it?"—French accent. And he sang the English with the same phoney pronunciations. Yet, it all seemed to work. And why not? A synagogue assemblage, accustomed to He-brew chanting it rarely understood at all, welcomed any kind of English translation.

As Michel retreated to the side of the rabbi, out of the loud speakers came the familiar organ strains of the Wedding Proces-sional. First Mendel Mandelbaum, wearing a black homburg, half-tottered down the aisle, his eyes narrow slits, his lips moving rap-idly in a mumble of Hebrew prayers. As if he were already petition-ing the Almighty for forgiveness for the many sins committed by his son, the latest of which was probably allowing his sacred mar-riage ceremony to be performed by that muscular *bulvan* Rabbi Samuels whose entire Hebrew learning, as far as Mendel was con-cerned, could fit into a small thimble with room left over for a few drops of *shnapps*. Mendel opened his eyes completely just long enough to safely ascend the two steps to the *bimah* and assume his place besides the rabbi, whom he did not even look at. Instead, he put a finger into his ear as if to ward off the music—to Mendel, piped-in instrumental music was for *goyim* in their churches, not *yiddin* in their synagogues—and continued to rock in prayer even more earnestly.

Next came Judah, Mendel's elder son, heir and partner in the store, Chicago's big brother who bore little resemblance to either his brother or father. Whereas Chicago had a thick mop of curly red hair and Mendel had a fine head of straight silver hair, Judah had no hair at all. The black derby he was wearing showed like a licorice Black Crow against his white nape and forehead. Judah, also obviously uncomfortable in his striped pants and Prince Albert best man's uniform, seemed to be wearing on his pale, worried face a fixed smile of apology for that costume. When Judah reached the *bimah,* Mendel stopped his rocking prayers just long enough to roughly pull the uncertain Judah over into the proper position beside him.

Chicago looked handsome as a prince, a very nervous prince to be sure, one who lived in constant fear of a sudden military coup that would lead to his instant assassination. Since he always wore clothes well, his black-tie outfit suited him perfectly. But his face was as blanched as the dough of a water bagel, and he kept looking from side to side as if seeking an avenue of last minute escape. As he approached his row, Les flashed the Mel Allen-Ballantine three-ring sign to him. But Chicago just stared at him uncomprehendingly and walked on by, as if he were being tugged by some invisible rope. Les felt sorry for him; he had never seen Chicago display so total a lack of confidence. And as he mounted the *bimah,* Mendel opened his narrow eyes wide and glared at his son.

Then came Laura, the sister of the bride, in a lovely mauve dress. She looked neither to the right nor the left as she walked in a proud regal manner, her gait slow and solemn, her eyes fixed directly ahead. The expression on her face was somber and serious.

Too serious. She seemed more like an unhappy bride on a forced march to the altar than the maid of honor.

Next in the procession was the father of the bride, proud as Eisenhower leading an academic procession as president of Columbia University. As he promenaded down the aisle, he looked first to one side than the other, like a nightclub performer switching a mike from hand to hand, nodding but tight lipped, only the barest of smiles escaping from the corner of his lips.

On his elbow, beautiful as any bride Les had ever seen, in a shining white gown of the finest satin, all lacy and frilly at the edges, was Vivian, gently carrying her bouquet of American beauties before her, as if she were cradling an infant. And she was smiling happily, lustrously, radiantly, all her teeth showing and her hazel eyes sparkling. She looked past the other former "Thespians" and when she saw Les she winked at him and smiled broadly as if they shared some intimate joke. Which they did, Les guessed in a way, and winked back.

After welcoming the bride to the *chupah,* the rabbi cleared his throat and began to talk about what a particularly happy occasion this was for him because the assemblage before him was gathered not only to celebrate the union between two wonderful young Jewish people, "this beautiful bride," and he turned to Chicago, "this fine, upstanding young Jewish man," but also to pray for what he hoped would eventually result in the return to the fold of "our wandering friends." For he earnestly hoped the appearance of Mr. Davis and Mr. Mandelbaum together on the *bimah,* representatives of both opposing factions in the synagogue strife, was a symbol of the future and meant an end to the plague of *goyishe* divisiveness which had so stricken the neighborhood Jewish community like a cancer by splitting "Jew from Jew in two." In any event, it was still not every marriage ceremony that he could conduct with such great confidence. Because he knew these two beautiful young Jewish people, no matter where their parents prayed during the High Holidays, "whether in this beautiful *bais midrash* or in some who-knows-where-you-should-pardon-the-expression poolroom?" would maintain a traditional Jewish home in which they would raise their own beautiful Jewish children in the traditionally beautiful Jewish values. Which was no easy task these days, considering how so many of the cutest and smartest Jewish children from even the best Jewish families seemed to prefer watching *Howdy Doody* rather than attending *Talmud Torah.*

The rabbi then, invoking his proud position as "a preacher and teacher in Israel" in Hebrew and "the powers vested in him by the laws of New York State" in English, asked the couple individually if they would love, honor, and obey each other no matter how sick one of them became. And upon receiving affirmative responses, he asked the bridegroom to slip a wedding band on the bride's fingers and he soon pronounced the couple Jewish man and Jewish wife. Together the bride and bridegroom sipped wine from a small shot glass which was then placed on the floor and Chicago stamped on it with the heel of his shoe, missing it once, but then sending shards of glass flying in all directions.

Later, as the wedding guests were seated around the circular tables, pushing aside the rinds of their grapefruits and waiting for the soup course to be served, Murray King called to the bandstand "that internationally famous singing star and personal friend of the happy couple, Michel DuChamps." Michel, seated beside Les, blushed innocently as his fellow guests applauded and then stood up, pushed in his chair and walked around the perimeter of the dance floor to the bandstand. Where he conferred with Murray for a moment before accepting the microphone, adjusting it to his height while smiling over to the bridal couple at the head table. Finally, he began singing in English with the Musical Princes faking behind him:

> *C'est si Bon!*
> *Lovers say this in France.*
> *When they thrill to romance.*
> *It means it's so good.*

Les studied Vivian as Michel sang, her eyes completely rapt on him, her mouth opening slowly, her lips slightly parted. And then Les turned to the end of the head table, where beside best man Judah Mandelbaum, the maid of honor, Laura, was seated, drawing in nervously on a cigarette while still waving away the smoke of her previous exhalation. "C'est si bon," Michel sang out in chorus and French verse before concluding in English:

> *So I say it to you.*
> *Like the French people do.*
> *It means it's so good.*

The bride applauded wildly, ecstatically, blowing kisses up toward Michel. The groom, looking down into his soup, stirred it and smiled, as if suddenly and pleasantly surprised to find a matzoh ball floating there. And the maid of honor churned out her cigarette into her untasted grapefruit.

7

Chicago had first informed Les of his impending marriage in the lobby of the old Madison Square Garden between halves of a Knick basketball game. The news shocked Les not only because of who the prospective bride was, but also because Chicago was still pretty much screwing everything in sight. Hopping off to Pennsylvania to meet Glenda. Continuing to *shtup* Ethel in the neighborhood. And who knew what else he had going for him? Because it had not been that long ago when with Glenda and Ethel, both pregnant at the same time—so much for the efficacy of the douche—Chicago had boasted to Les of getting the same abortionist for both at a special discounted price. Besides, Chicago had also always pooh-poohed marriage, putting it down "as a sucker's game," describing it as "the kind of action it was always wise to lay off and stay away from." So, Les's reaction in the Garden lobby was very much to the point: "What about an abortion?"

Chicago immediately seized Les by his shirt collar with one hand, his fist in the other hand coiled before his face. "Watch your language. We're not talking about some *who-ah*. We're talking about my fiancée." He soon loosened his grip and told Les the brief history of their romance: How he had seen Vivian many times about the neighborhood. How he had always admired her classy looks, but considered her "in another league" because of his lack of education. But then how one day he had boldly stopped her on the street and told her how much he was impressed by her and how anxious he was to get to know her. And to his great surprise she agreed to go out with him.

"Where'd you go?"

"No place. Just a movie."

"Vivian likes movies," Les observed. "And then what happened?"

"The first time?"

"Yes?"

"Nothing. I took her home and said good night."

"That's all?"

"That's all."

"Didn't she invite you in?

"Are you kidding? We're not talking about some *who-ah*. I didn't even kiss her good night. We just shook hands," he laughed, "like we was making a bet."

"Did she tell you she knew me?

"Your name didn't come up until after way later."

When Chicago and Les returned to their seats for the start of the second half, Les had a hard time following the game. Especially as Chicago continued to ramble on about their great romance and how proud he was to find such a terrific girl, a college girl at that, and how happy he was that she had agreed to marry him.

Les sneakily smiled at him and poked him in the ribs. "College girls make the best screws?"

Chicago cast him a sidelong glance, "That's a stupid thing to say," he said, still looking intently down at the court below, as if the action there demanded his full and immediate attention. But after Ernie Vanderweighe sank two foul shots, he leaned back in his seat and smiled. "Anyway, you don't screw your bride-to-be," he said. "You make love to them. Or sleep with them. And I'm not saying I have. Because even if I have, I would keep my big mouth shut. Anyway, I love Vivian. I'm going to marry her. And that's enough. Except you forgot one thing."

"What?" Les asked as Cousy dribbled the ball up court.

"You forgot to congratulate me, *shmuck.*"

"Congratulations, *shmuck,*" Les said, extending his hand across his lap. "I mean it."

Chicago gripped his hand and shook it firmly while they watched Cousy drive toward the basket and dish off to Lostocoff, of all people, who scored over Gallatin.

As shocked as Les was to learn Chicago and Vivian were marrying, he was even further surprised when Vivian called him a few days later saying that she wanted to talk to him about something important. He and Vivian had rarely seen each other recently. Vivian was still going to Brooklyn College and he had his job at NBC, not to mention his affair with Lisa. But now Vivian wanted to see him as soon as possible. He could easily have driven over to her house one night or picked some neighborhood cafeteria or ice cream parlor at which to meet. But he wanted to impress her, to show Vivian that if he was no longer a student of Brooklyn College and not yet a citizen of the world, he was at least a familiar denizen of Manhattan and Greenwich Village. He suggested they meet at the Cafe Reggio on MacDougal Street near Washington Square.

When Les arrived there, Vivian was already seated at a table near the window, like the subject of a French Impressionist painting, in a light green suit with a lemon-colored foulard wrapped about her throat, her hair parted in the middle and combed simply to each side like a nun or schoolgirl, her face devoid of makeup except for her hazel eyes, clearly articulated by underliner and eye shadow. She was dropping a sugar cube into her espresso when Les joined her.

"This is a nice place," she smiled.

"I like it."

"Come here often?"

"Sometimes."

"Spend alot of time in the Village?"

"As much as I can."

The waitress came to take his order and he pointed to Vivian's espresso and asked for the same.

Vivian regarded him for a long time across the table, "I hardly know you anymore, Rose," she finally said.

"We're both busy people, Davis."

"How long ago high school seems."

"College, too, for me."

"I've missed you." She reached over and squeezed his hand. Her fingers seemed smaller than Les remembered.

After their coffees, Les and Vivian left the cafe and strolled through Washington Square Park, the limbs of its leafless trees stark black silhouettes in the gray air. As Vivian poked her arm through his, Les wondered if he still loved her in that special way one always loves one's first love. Or if he had simply not yet gotten over her initial rejection of him in the same way one never quite recovers from any rejection. But soon, listening to her explanations and justifications, it suddenly seemed to him as if he were a prospective lawyer consulted by a client seeking help in finding loopholes.

"Leon is very nice," Vivian had begun.

"He's my friend," Les agreed.

"I never imagined you had such friends."

"What do you mean?"

"Such—" She removed her arm from his and groped toward the sky as if the precisely descriptive words she was searching for might be dangling from some low-overhanging cloud. "—Such real people."

"Chicago's the salt of the earth," Les said in half jest.

"Exactly," Vivian said in dead seriousness. "He has such elemental energy. I can't tell you how attractive I find him."

"More attractive than Michel?"

"There's no comparison. Leon's a man and Mickey was a boy."

"That's not how you once felt about him."

"I was just a girl then. What did I know? But now I'm a woman. And I can tell a real man." She laughed and took his arm again.

"But that's not what I really wanted to talk to you about. Let's sit down."

Vivian had stopped near the end of an empty bench. Les watched the wind lift a scrap of newspaper and sweep it against the side of a wire mesh trash basket. And then, as if actually trying to Help Keep New York Clean, blow the torn paper up and over the rim and into the receptacle itself.

"Anyway, I'm in love now," Vivian said, rubbing her hands together as she sat down. "In the way I always imagined it would be like to be in love. I mean, the love the poets and playwrights speak about and all the songs are written about. Leon makes me deliriously happy. And I can't imagine a happy life ahead for me without including him in it forever. Does that sound strange to you?"

Les did not know what to say. He said, "No."

"I guess it's ironic, but I never thought it would be someone like Leon I would fall in love with. I mean really fall in love with. But I don't care if he's never gone to college or never reads anything more than a newspaper and has no desire to go to the theater. As far as I'm concerned, Leon's still very wise and very smart. But, most important, he's very caring. And instinctive. He's instinctive in an uncanny way. Can you understand?"

"Chicago's my friend. You don't have to sell him to me."

"I just want you to understand how important he is to me. And how important my marriage is to both of us."

"Chicago's told me."

"I know. But still I'm not sure how—" again she seemed to look to the sky for verbal help "—how sophisticated he is about certain things. How he might take them. I mean, he's such a basic creature. That's why," she turned to Les, her hazel eyes slightly moistened, "I want to be sure you never say anything to him about me and Mickey."

"Why should I ever say anything?"

"Exactly," she said. "Thank you."

"But," Les could not help but smile, "does Chicago think you're still a virgin?"

She laughed. "He knows I'm not a virgin anymore."

"Does he think you were a virgin before him?"

"I haven't told him differently. Why should I possibly want to do that? So, Leon doesn't know anything about Mickey. And nobody else knows besides you."

"And Laura.

"Laura? What does she know? I never tell her anything."

"But wasn't she your chaperone in Paris?"

"Not really. We pretty much went our separate ways in Paris. We always do in most respects."

"Not all," Les said.

"What do you mean?"

"Nothing," Les stretched his legs forward and stood up. "Anyway, you have nothing to worry about. I'll never tell anyone your little secret. But could you do me a small favor and tell me something I've always been curious about in return?"

"Depends," Vivian said. "What?"

"Do you really like monogrammed boxer shorts?"

She laughed. "I think they can be cute. Especially on Leon."

"And what about his balls?"

"Leon's balls?" She raised her eyebrows.

"I'm curious. How many does he have?"

She frowned. "I never noticed."

"Oh, come on."

"Then I never counted," she said. "And even if I had, I could never tell you." She once more stared at Les's eyes unremittingly. "I just told you, Rose: I love Leon. I really do. And I don't want him hurt in the least way."

"I was only kidding," Les said.

"Well," she mock shivered, "then let's get some coffee."

Les pointed back in the direction they had just come. "But we just had coffee."

Vivian stood and threaded her arm through his again. "I mean real coffee, Rose. Cafeteria coffee. With tons of sugar and loads of cream and a big piece of strudel."

"You mean Jewish coffee, Davis."

"That's right, Rose," she said. "Jewish coffee. Not the Italian *dreck.*"

8

When Les danced at the wedding with Vivian, who was positively radiant in her flowing white bridal gown, her face flushed with joy, he was genuinely happy for her. They both commented about how well Michel looked and how wonderfully he had sung and agreed that there would be no stopping him career-wise, but neither mentioned the little secret concerning Mickey and Vivian. Instead, as Les passed Vivian on to her next dance partner, she patted his hand and insisted that he was very special to her "and Leon" and that she wanted him to be the first person they had over for dinner after their return from their honeymoon in Las Vegas and they were settled in.

So, Les was not very surprised several weeks later when Vivian phoned him with just such an invitation. Les asked if anyone else was coming.

"Just my sister," Vivian replied. And Les made no smart-ass comment. But he had also danced with Laura at the wedding and found her somewhat less than jubilant. A scowl creased her brow whenever she glanced over toward Chicago as they moved across the floor in silence. Finally, for want of anything better, Les said, "You look terrific."

"I don't feel so terrific," she smiled up at him sadly.

Les nodded sympathetically. "I guess it must be difficult to see one's kid sister marrying."

"It's not that," she said, her gaze flitting back over to Chicago again, who was dancing with a gawky teenage cousin. "It's who she's marrying."

Les felt defensive. "What's wrong with Chicago?"

"I know he's your friend, Les. But he's not like you. Or like Michel, for that matter," she said. As if on cue, Mickey glided by them with his dance partner, an elderly relative of Chicago's, and smiled over to them. Laura smiled back at him before returning her attention to Les and the subject at hand. "Chicago's so crude."

"Crude?"

"He has no intelligence. No class sensitivity. Indeed, he's completely lacking in a sense of history. So, please don't try defending him. Chicago's an animal. Like Marlon Brando in *A Streetcar Named Desire.*"

"Well," Les laughed, "at least you're certainly no Jewish Blanche Dubois."

"I certainly am not. I'm no Jewish anything. I'm just disappointed in my kid sister. I didn't think she could be so—" she searched for the word "—frivolous with her life."

"You two never got along anyway."

"But that doesn't mean we still don't identify with each other," she said, as Murray King and his Princes ended the song "Amapola" with Murray himself reaching for an Artie Shaw note on his clarinet—and missing it.

When Vivian had described the apartment house on the Parkway to Les over the phone, he recognized the building at once. An elegant pre-war structure with gray stone cornices and a little gatehouse at the entrance. Carrying the Ebinger's chocolate cake he had picked up on the way over, Les presented himself to the doorman seated in the gatehouse, who was still bent over the *Daily News* crossword puzzle as he called up to the apartment to clear Les before grudgingly imparting, "You're okay. Mandelbaum is 5C."

The ceilings were higher than Les expected and the rooms larger, but the apartment itself was somehow smaller. There was a master bedroom and a kitchen and a dining room and a living room, each furnished to the modern hilt, all flowing into one another through archways and swinging louvre doors. But still a room seemed to be missing. A place where one could go and be alone. Except for perhaps the bathroom. But even that, shaving cream and hair sprays stocked together on the common shelves of the open cabinet, wreaked of community property. So this is marriage, Les thought. No matter how much space for two, there is no privacy for one.

Vivian led him through the dining room into the kitchen where Laura was busily mixing a salad. "Do you think it's done yet?" Vivian asked. Laura put aside the salad and together they opened the oven door and peeked into it.

"Give it another few minutes," Laura advised.

"Hmmm," Les inhaled theatrically. "Smells good. What is it?"

"Roast beef," said Vivian.

"Did you get it at your father's?"

"No," Vivian smiled. "My father got it here himself. Delivered it personally."

"Taste this," said Laura, holding up a forkful of salad to Les.

It was a trace too vinegary. "Maybe just another drop or two of oil," Les suggested.

Laura tried the salad again herself. "I think it's fine as it is," she decided, smacking her lips like a gourmet. "Who wants a gooey dressing?"

Then why had she asked him to try it? Les wondered.

There were sounds at the door, then footsteps, and Chicago was in the kitchen, clutching a *New York Post* in one hand and holding out a bottle of wine to Vivian with the other. She placed it on the counter and held up the cake Les had brought. "Look what Rose brought."

"Ebinger's," Chicago nodded approvingly. "Terrific. How you doing, kid?"

"Good," Les said. "But not as good as you."

"Who is?" Chicago beamed and pecked Vivian on the mouth.

Then he seemed to remember Laura who, despite her admonition about gooeyness to Les, was adding oil to the salad. "How are you, honey?"

"Fine."

"You better hurry up and finish medical school. I think there's something wrong with my back," Chicago said, rubbing his back against the door jamb by way of evidence.

"We know what's wrong with your back," replied Laura. And everyone laughed.

"Oh, come on," said Vivian. "No newlywed jokes, please."

"I had this back thing long before we married," said Chicago.

"I'm not surprised," said Laura. And everyone laughed again.

The dinner was good—even though the wine was a little too sweet for Les—and they all made much over how delicious everything was. Vivian told how a woman who had played the same slot machine she had been playing in Las Vegas won a jackpot just seconds after she had walked away from it. Laura discussed medical school and how it was a difficult place for any woman with an ambition to become anything other than a pediatrician. Les talked about television and how exciting the medium was and how he hoped to get his own show soon so that he could really do something. And Chicago expressed serious doubts about how much the Dodgers had helped themselves during the off-season, especially in the way of much needed pitching. And everyone congratulated Vivian on what a great job she had done in such a short time in fixing up the apartment, considering that she was still going to school full-time.

So the conversation had not been exactly stimulating up to the point the girls went into the kitchen to do the dishes before serving the dessert and coffee. Chicago and Les adjourned to the living room, the ex-bachelor settling into the maroon easy chair, while Les relaxed on the long buff couch behind a glass-topped coffee table, and thumbed through the *Post*. Les was feeling a trifle impolite in ignoring Chicago, even though he was the host and Les was the guest, but Chicago seemed very content just sitting there silently. Still, Les realized he never really had a discussion with Chicago about anything other than sports—and, of course, *nookie.* And he didn't feel like talking about either just then. But he felt he should talk about something. So he put down the newspaper and observed, "Married life really seems to agree with you."

"Sure," said Chicago. "Why not?"

Les laughed. "But you were a bachelor for so long."

Chicago pursed his lips together and considered before finally deciding, "That's true. You got a point there."

And Les thought for all intents and purposes, even though in a sense he had brought up *nookie,* their mini-discussion was over. But Chicago then leaned forward, looked back toward the kitchen, and with his hand half covering his mouth, whispered: "I want to ask you a favor, Les."

Les spread his hands wide. "Sure. Anything Chicago."

"Remember," he waved his finger in the air. "You owe me."

"Sure," Les repeated. "What do you want me to do?"

"I don't want you to do anything," Chicago lowered his already whispering voice. "I want you to tell me something. You know Vivian for a long time, right? Since high school, right?"

"Right."

"Tell me the truth." Les had to practically lip read as Chicago kept glancing furtively toward the kitchen and lowering his voice even further. "Was she a virgin before me?"

"How should I know?" Les whispered back.

"You know," Chicago fixed his eyes upon him. "I know you know."

"How?"

"Call it a hunch bet. But I can tell you know. Am I wrong?"

Les hesitated. There was no right thing to do. He would either have to betray Vivian or lie to Chicago.

"Remember you owe me," Chicago repeated.

Les also may have had the right to remain silent, sphinx-like silent. But Chicago kept staring at him like a pitcher looking in for the sign. Les shrugged. Chicago shook his head as if to reject that sign. Finally, Les put his left index finger on his chest and raised his right hand, as if he were taking a solemn oath, then slowly and sorrowfully shook his head.

"So, she was no virgin?"

Les nodded.

"I know it wasn't you," Chicago nodded back. "But was it the singer? What about the singer?"

How much did Chicago really know and how much was he fishing? Had he been able to tell physiologically that Vivian was not a virgin? And if he had made the discovery before marriage, what difference did it make now? Unless Vivian, for some reason, had only recently decided to raise some specter of doubt in Chicago's mind? But why would she want to do that?

"Remember," Chicago said once more. "You owe me."

What was his responsibility? And who was it to? Les wondered as he mechanically nodded.

"Was it by any chance," Chicago whispered slowly again, "the singer?"

Les nodded.

"The singer," Chicago whispered. And then, as if only by voicing that intelligence aloud could he complete the process of internal communication, he said, "Michel."

"Michel what?" asked Vivian brightly, entering the room with the tray of coffee and cake.

"Michel nothing," said Chicago innocently. "He's some singer. The dessert looks terrific." Vivian set down the tray and turned with a sisterly smile to Laura behind her. "The men have their secrets," she said, seeming to take Les in accusingly. "And we have ours."

"It just might work after all," Laura said.

Les was driving her home after the dinner with Vivian and Chicago; to her parents' house where she planned to stay the night, instead of returning to her Manhattan apartment near her school, NYU-Bellevue Medical.

"What might work?"

"The marriage. My sister's marriage. What do you think?"

Les stopped for a light and turned to face her. Laura was dressed in her usual color: a black cloth coat topped by a black beret framing her angular but attractive face, which exuded greater intelligence and energy than her sister's. But her eyes were cold, narrow all-seeing slits compared to Vivian's softer hazel does. She was sitting upright, a model of good posture, her hands clasped on her lap.

Les was no great expert on marriages and their prospects and did not know what to think or say. But basically, no matter how unlikely a coupling, Vivian and Chicago's marriage was still a neighborhood marriage and in their neighborhood marriages lasted. Couples did not divorce. They moved out to the Island, they retired to Florida, but they did not divorce and their marriages endured. Les pursed his lips together. "I don't see why Vivian and Chicago's marriage shouldn't work. They have a nice apartment to start out in."

"Less than ten minutes away from my parents," Laura said and shivered. "I wouldn't want to live there a single second."

"Neither would I," Les agreed. "But then, I can't see living in Brooklyn a day longer than necessary."

"Then why don't you move out?"

"I've been looking for a place for months," Les said, shifting into gear as the light changed.

"Manhattan *is* expensive," Laura said understandingly. "You can fit my whole apartment into Vivian's living room."

Familiar storefronts, their display windows reflecting the headlights of the passing traffic; stately brownstones set back behind pointed iron picket fences; red brick tract houses hunched together, separated only by their gray driveways, all passed in a quick blur. And Les pulled up in front of the Davis house, remembering the hope and anticipation with which he had once parked *Monty* there. How long ago that seemed. And now it was Laura, not Vivian, beside him and he was not about to pick up a Davis sister, but rather to drop one off. Down the block the moon showed over the chain link schoolyard fence, and the bare trees silhouetted behind it and the air had a cold, moist tinge. It felt as if it might start snowing at any moment.

Les waited for Laura to step down. He would drive *Monty* home, perhaps watch television with his mother who always stayed up later than his father, and then go to sleep and end another long commuting day. But Laura did not move. Instead, she was smiling hesitantly. "Say, do you want to see it?"

"See what?"

"My apartment?"

"Why sure," Les responded automatically.

"But it'll be way out of your way," she reconsidered, "and it'll take you forever to get back to Brooklyn."

"If it gets too late, I can always stay at a friend's in Manhattan," Les lied.

"Oh, good," she said, and Les put *Monty* into first again. "Because it'll save me a lot of time in the morning."

"Me, too," Les lied again.

So, it was down the parkway and onto the avenue and then over the bridge with very little traffic at that hour. Snow was now falling lightly and Les asked Laura if she wanted him to stop and put the top up but she said no, she liked it as it was, as if they were in a mechanized sleigh, and soon the pristine, fresh fallen flakes, shimmering as they landed on her beret and coat, contrasted sharply with their stark blackness. "This is fun," she said.

Les turned off the bridge and drove uptown over cobblestoned streets, the snow seeming to polish them individually in the yellowish glow of the phosphorescent lamps that arced out over the avenue. "Over there." Laura pointed toward a cleaning store that proclaimed in flashing neon lights, MARTINIZING SAME DAY SERVICE. Les parked in front of it wondering if he should put up *Monty*'s top. The snow was beginning to come down hard.

"I better get the top up," he decided, holding out his hands to catch the falling snow as proof of that need.

"I'll go up and put on coffee," Laura said. "Just ring the bell in the hallway—2A."

Les helped Laura down and watched her disappear into the doorway between the dry cleaners and a liquor store with an expandable barricade fence stretched across its entrance and attended to battening down *Monty*'s top, wishing he had gloves, wondering why he had driven Laura back to Manhattan, as the snow falling in thick clusters now piled up on the sidewalks and against the curbstones.

The apartment was small, as he had expected, just a single room —no larger than Vivian's living room as Laura had said. It was directly over the cleaner's with an area near the front windows set aside for a dining area and a bathroom. It was also messier than Les had anticipated. Somehow, he assumed Laura would be neat and tidy. After all, she was studying to be a doctor and he associated the practice of medicine with antiseptic bandages and white uniforms and steel sterilization tanks and boiling vats of water. Also, Laura's personal appearance always wreaked of order, no single strand of her well-coiffed hair ever seemed to be out of place. But the bed was unmade, kapok was oozing out of the corner of a musty couch, and everywhere there were newspapers at his feet—not to protect some Persian rug or newly-waxed parquet floor—but rather the result of having simply fallen there as randomly as the snow flakes now gathering on the cobblestones of the avenue block below. Laura handed him a teacup and Les sipped from it, inhaling the spices and the alcoholic fumes before even tasting it. "This isn't coffee."

"No," said Laura, holding her own cup with both hands. "It's grog. I thought you might prefer it."

Les took a second sip. "I do."

"I wish I had a fireplace," Laura said. "Otherwise, this place suits me fine."

"It must be very convenient."

"It is. I should take better care of it, though. But why bother? I mean, I'm hardly here except to sleep."

Les made an acting point of looking around. One wall, he now noticed, was bare brick. "Still, you could do a lot with this place."

"That's what I thought when I moved in," she laughed. "But I haven't done a thing. More?" She offered him a refill and he accepted it. "It's a big difference between this apartment and Vivian's, isn't it? But then deep down she's always been more bourgeois than me. You've always known that, haven't you, Les?"

He didn't say anything as Laura returned to her seat, an old leather sling chair, and scrunched her legs under her thighs yoga-style, before twirling her cup around slowly and peering over it. "But then, you've always been in love with my kid sister, haven't you, Les?"

Les could sense his cheeks aglow with a sudden rush of warmth and wondered if she could actually see him blushing in the weak light. The kitchen fluorescent was not on. Only a lamp near the bed on the far side of the room was lit.

"I always used to tease Viv about it," she continued.

"I was young," Les said, imagining his cheeks now positively afire in the dark.

"Don't be ashamed," Laura said. She climbed out of her chair and came over and placed her hand on his shoulder. "One is not always responsible for one's emotions."

"What then is *one* responsible for?" Les asked.

"One's actions. That's why I thought Viv's marrying Leon was such an irresponsible thing to do. He just isn't our sort of person."

This was really ironic, Les thought. Here was this great egalitarian, a champion of leftist politics of the most extreme sort, someone who was always going out with Negroes and minorities of every kind, smugly putting down Chicago as if he were of a class beneath them. When actually, of course, he was of a level far above and beyond them both, someone who could pluck his living abstractly out of the air itself, carving numbers and creating angles in an exercise every bit as scientific as her medical pursuits and as imaginative and artistic as his own theatrical dreams. Les could not help but smile.

The hand on his shoulder lifted and then slapped down again hard. "I know what you're thinking. That I'm talking like some sort of bigot or snob. But what I mean is, Leon isn't our sort of person when it comes to sensitivity. Intellectual sensitivity. Class-conscious awareness. He is a political and cultural illiterate, and you know it." She turned and walked away from Les, as if he had been a witness on the stand and she was a cross-examining attorney who had just scored a point.

"You're casting yourself as Blanche DuBois again," Les said.

"Analogue and metaphor," she said, wheeling around, "are the weakest form of argument."

"Maybe," Les said. "But why do you always have to compete with your sister?"

"Don't get Freudian with me, mister," she laughed and went to the window and jabbed her chest with her index finger. "I'm a Marxist."

Les laughed, too, and placed his cup on the edge of the sink. Then he joined Laura at the window, studying the falling snow. "The kids will have a lot of fun tomorrow," he said. "It'll be good packing snow."

"I don't know about you, but I still am a kid when it comes to snow," Laura laughed. "And why wait for tomorrow?" She ran to the closet at the back of the apartment and reappeared wearing a Navy pea jacket over her jeans. Soon, she was binding her hair under a black kerchief, pulling on gloves and pushing Les out the door and down the stairs.

A siren greeted them as they hit the street, the sounds of an ambulance rushing to the hospital nearby. Also, it had become colder and a strong wind was whirling the snow in drifts up against the storefronts. Les turned up the collar of his London Fog, which was without its liner, and rubbed his gloveless hands. Also, he was wearing just loafers and had no hat. He could see himself paying for this whim with double pneumonia.

Laura had already rushed to the curb, where she was leaning over and scooping up snow to make a snowball. Les followed after her, naively wondering what her target might be, when she wheeled and threw, with a girl's awkward vertical motion, at him. Les ducked. She would not have hit him anyway. And he bent down and hurriedly made two skimpy snowballs and hurled them both at her, the first missing but the second hitting her back and leaving a chalklike mark on her jacket.

Les prepared two more snowballs, his cold hands now stinging, and raced forward to attack while Laura threw another snowball, catching him on the side of his neck. But by then he was upon Laura, grabbing her with his left hand as he dropped one snowball and threatening to wash her face with the other, still cocked in his right hand. Trying to twist away, she sank to the ground pleading, "Fingers." Which in the Brooklyn neighborhood lexicon of their youth meant "Time out!" or "I Surrender!" or both.

And Les immediately released Laura. Whereupon she flung the snow she had evidently garnered in her descent to the pavement up into his face. Then she sprang to her feet and ran down the middle of the avenue. Les pursued after her, chugging hard, his moistened hands throbbing with cold, snow seeping into his loafers. At the end of the block, he finally caught up with her and they both sank to the ground panting hard. "No more fingers," he rasped. "This time I really am going to wash your face."

"No, you won't." Laura laughed brightly.

"Give me one good reason why I shouldn't."

"Because then I wouldn't sleep with you."

Les released her as suddenly as he had caught her. "That's a very good reason." Then he kissed her. Their lips were numb with frost and their noses burnt, but their mouths were very moist and warm. "C'mon," Laura took his hand, "let's go upstairs and get out of these things.

"You always appealed to me in your poochy kind of way," Laura was saying. They had just made love and Les had not found it nearly as pleasurable as he had once dreamed it might be. Laura's body, what he saw of it now in the half-light, did not disappoint him. Her breasts were almost as abundant as her sister's and her skin was every bit as soft and pliant as he had fancied it to be. But perhaps it was because it was all literally coming too late, a few years too late, and some dreams had built-in time limits, expiration dates before which they must be realized for best results, otherwise they should be discarded like old supermarket products. Or perhaps it was because he was acutely aware of the gel in Laura's diaphragm, her cunt feeling too medicinally lubed? Or maybe it was just because after Lisa, Laura's performance seemed mechanical and uninspired? Les did not know. And if Laura, on her part, found him disappointing in any way she showed no signs. Unless her insistent chattering implied some negative judgement factor.

"Why do you think I asked you to drive me home? To see my apartment? What am I, a real-estate agent?" she laughed. "I guess I have always been jealous of my sister's hold on you."

"Were you jealous of her appeal to Mickey, too?"

"Why do you ask?"

"No reason." Les hesitated. "Except, he did tell me about Paris."

"What about Paris?"

Now, under her comforter in the warm apartment, Les had no desire to hurt her in any way, especially after the favor she had just bestowed upon him, but he did feel a need not so much to expose Mickey as to begin to claim some parity with him. "Mickey told me," Les said.

Her hand, which had been lightly touching his chest, stopped moving. "What did Mickey tell you about Paris, Victor Lazlo?"

Les ignored her joking reference to *Casablanca*. "That you and he . . ." he began, ". . . like you and me," he finished.

Her hand began to move again. "And you believed him?"

"Shouldn't I have?"

"That's not the point, this is," she said. And her hand traced down past his stomach and touched his hardening penis. "But I just think anyone who tells someone of fucking someone else is just trying to fuck that person again."

"I won't tell anyone we fucked," Les promised.

"Not even my sister?"

"Especially your sister."

"Then maybe I will tell her," Laura laughed. And began to play with his penis again.

Les lay back and enjoyed her play, but couldn't resist asking her one more question. "You've made love to Negroes?"

"Yes."

"Is it true or is it just a myth that their penises are bigger than those of Caucasians?"

"In your case," she laughed, "it's no myth."

They were even. And the second time they fucked it was better, but still not the sex he had enjoyed with Lisa, and not the sex he had always imagined having with Vivian. And when they fucked again in the morning, somehow knowing it would be for the last time because the scorekeeping was over as far as they were both concerned, Les still could not dispel completely the lifeless lubed feeling of her cunt.

When he left Laura's apartment and looked up and saw her black-clad figure waving down to him on the white snow-covered avenue below, Les thought of what Mickey had once said about how the smell of one's woman's *nookie* on one's penis invariably attracted another woman to that penis, and Les decided that a head smell or an emotional aura could also work in very much the same way, making the ideal every bit as real as any real. Which was as deep as any reality could get.

Les shook the snow off *Monty*'s top, started without any trouble, and while cars careened and taxis skidded all about him, with the four-wheel drive finally coming in handy, he easily breezed his way uptown to work.

9

"What did I tell you? Wasn't my instinct right?"

Even though Les had always been unusually good at recognizing voices, he could not tag this one. It was agonizingly familiar and he almost had it. He knew who he thought it was, but he wasn't that sure it was her. Because he had not spoken to this voice over the phone recently. Just another speech or two and he would certainly nail it down, though. So, he let the caller continue on without answering her questions, waiting instead for the telltale click of recognition. "I told you it wouldn't last, didn't I?" she was saying. And now Les knew precisely who it was. He had been close in his mental bet. But no cigar. It was not Vivian, after all, her voice somehow altered through the state of marriage, as he had wagered to himself, but Laura.

But hell, he was entitled to be off. It had been months since Les had last spoken to either of the Davis sisters. Or seen them. The snowy night with Laura, as he had anticipated, turned out to be just a one-night stand. Not that he didn't make another pro forma move for the record, calling Laura a few times but always finding her "busy." Until he got the message.

Anyway, he was also very "busy." Because at last a show of his own was in the works. A father and son cop show. In fact, it was called *Looey and Son*. With the leads a hardboiled New York City police lieutenant, who had come up the hard way, and his Ivy

League lawyer son. Together they solved crimes. Not a very original concept, but not the worst. And one with good pedigree, its bloodlines being Ellery Queen with a twist. Which meant it met the formula for success—the same but different. The father was going to be played by a veteran Broadway actor and the son by a "B" movie star who had come East seeking the art of theater, but was now ready to settle for the paycheck of television. George Hecht had sold the package to both the network and the ad agency, insisting that he wanted Les on board to direct it. All thirty episodes. It would be a lot of work. But it was also, to put it bluntly, the opportunity of a lifetime. And it was his young lifetime. How far he had come and in so brief a period! And how much further could he expect to go! Les was very proud of himself. But not too proud to work night and day to make sure that he didn't blow it. Because once the show was launched with him at its helm, not only could he afford the apartment of his dreams in Manhattan but also any car he wanted. Even the kind of sports job he had last seen Mickey driving. What was it? An Austin Healy? Or the car Mickey said he owned in California, a Porsche? Anyway, he would get rid of *Monty,* that was for sure.

"I feel sorry for my sister," Laura was saying.

"Whoa, there! Would you mind backing up a little, Dr. Davis," Les said. "I walked in during the middle of the picture."

"I'm talking about the Davis-Mandelbaum marriage and how it's phhhht."

"You mean Vivian's left Chicago?"

"Viv didn't leave Leon," Laura laughed. "Leon walked out on Viv. Rather ran out. And went off to Pennsylvania to some *shiksa.*"

"What do you know?" Les breathed out. "How is Vivian taking it?"

"Her pride is hurt but otherwise I think she'll come out of it fine. Eventually. Meanwhile, you might give her a call. She needs all the friendship she can get now."

"That's me. Mr. Friendship. Shirley Temple will play me when they make a movie of my life."

"Don't be bitter," Laura said.

"I'm not. I have nothing to be bitter about." They talked on for awhile, Laura bringing him up to date on her medical studies, while he boasted of his prospective career advance.

"That's terrific," she said. "You could be another Orson Welles."

"Citizen Rose."

"I mean it. Only I hope you're an Orson Welles who doesn't forget his social conscience. And social responsibilities. Now, you should definitely call Vivian. She'll be very proud of you. It'll give her a good reason not to be depressed."

"Is she depressed?"

"For her, she is. And I don't like seeing her so—" she searched for the phrase—"so down in the dumps."

Les couldn't resist it. "Since when are you so concerned about your sister?"

"I always identify with her in one way or another. Why do you think I went to bed with you? It's all part of the same sibling shit."

Laura was getting even with him, dig for dig. But he wasn't going to let matters end there. "Yet usually you're never so happy as when she's—" Les paused until he could recall her expression "—down in the dumps."

"That's true," Laura quickly agreed. "More sibling shit. It's all so very complicated. You're lucky you never have to deal with it."

In any event, Les promised he would call Vivian right away. But the moment he hung up, his phone rang again. It was George Hecht. George had become Les's rabbi in giving him his first shot out of the box. And Les already had him down for profuse expressions of gratitude—along with Doug and Lisa—in having such great faith in little Les when Lester Rose made his Academy Award acceptance speech. But all kidding aside folks, he really did appreciate the great opportunity George was giving him. A show of his own to direct.

But what George wanted to talk with Les about that day had nothing to do with *Looey and Son* per se, but everything to do with it in the long run. Les soon forgot all about Laura's call and his promise to talk to Vivian. Because what was at stake was nothing less than his entire career in show business. Having barely started, it could already be over.

10

Theatrical producers never had any problems filling the empty spaces on their office walls; they adorned them with framed posters of their hits and—if their offices were big enough—their flops. But what could TV packagers and producers do? They did not even have a poster to show for all their efforts once a production was aired. It was as if they had just been farting in the wind. Or pissing in the ocean. George Hecht's solution to the blank wall problem was a simple one: blow-ups of Variety reviews and Jack Gould columns from the *Times* and John Crosby reviews from the *Trib* extolling the virtues of *Homicide* and other Entertainment Associates productions. Also a small office.

The office on Forty-eighth Street off Sixth Avenue was just one flight up marble stairs in a building that housed mostly jewelers and diamond dealers. In the anteroom sat George's secretary and receptionist, his Bronx cousin Pearl's daughter. And in his crowded office there were two desks, one for himself, of course; and one for his partner and money man, Marvin Sussman, a second cousin from Newark who looked after the company's books when he was there. But he was rarely there because his heart and soul and body were with the ponies. Marvin was forever spending long afternoons out at the track. Les wondered how secure he would feel in George's position, having a compulsive gambler as the partner in charge of the books. But that was George's worry, not his, and their partnership, Entertainment Associates, was successful. In addition to *Homicide,* it turned out one-shots for all the dramatic anthology shows.

George was always puffing away on a Meershaum pipe, pressed between his thin lips as if it were an extension of his own pearly white teeth. He had shaved every hair on his head like Yul Brynner —or the Swedish Angel—to give himself an exotic look. And like Yul Brynner and the Angel, he was in good shape physically too, swimming laps daily over at the Hotel Sutton. Under ordinary circumstances, meeting him cold, Les might have had his doubts about George's basic masculinity. But he did not have to work with him very long before discovering that George dated and bedded the most beautiful actresses in town with the same compulsive fury as his cousin Marvin bet the horses. Compulsion must have been a family trait. Even cousin Pearl's daughter in the anteroom was no ordinary looking receptionist. A small-boned girl, weighing close to 200 pounds, she had an ever-present box of chocolates beside her desk.

"You will know that the Jews have finally arrived in America, not when one become president or breaks Babe Ruth's home run record as Hank Greenberg once almost did," George said in greeting Les. "But when they begin to drink like *goyim.*" He lifted a cardboard container of black coffee from his glass-topped desk and toasted, *"L'chaim."*

George was always peppering his speech with Yiddish and Yiddishisms and forever making allusions to baseball to show that though he was a Canadian he was still as Jewish and American as a New York *knish.* And he also always took his time in getting to his point, as if there was never anything better to do on the tundra. Now, he asked how Les was and how *Looey and Son* was coming along. As if he didn't know. Next, he suggested a possible candidate for one of the minor roles, which had not yet been cast. Something he could have done anytime. But Les made a big point of how great that idea was. And then George blew a cloud of some clove-smelling Danish tobacco across his desk toward Les, and asked if he thought that Y and R, the agency packaging *Looey and Son,* would clear that actor.

Television was in the midst of a blacklist scare. But Les had never heard even a hint of any possible problem in connection with the actor George was suggesting. He reminded George, come to think of it, hadn't they used the same actor not too long ago on a *Homicide?*

"Well, some strange things have been happening lately," George said, removing his pipe and examining it as if he were a surgeon suddenly discovering some strange instrument in his hand in the midst of an operation, "and I wouldn't get too concerned about this just yet." He returned the pipe to his mouth and spoke out of the side of his mouth. "But when we finally got around to submitting your name pro forma for *Looey and Son,* it bounced."

"What do you mean?"

"You weren't cleared."

"How could that happen? There has to be a mistake."

"That's what I thought. So we resubmitted it." George slid open a desk drawer, removed a sheet of paper and leaned over and handed it to Les. "But look, *boychik:* Do any of these organizations look familiar?"

There was Les's name and a dossier after it. Communist front organizations Lester Rose had allegedly joined, pinko petitions Lester Rose was supposed to have signed. Les scanned the list slowly, shaking his head. Then he stopped and slowly nodded. "I know where this comes from," he said.

BOOK III

1

There was not a mark on his car.

And perhaps Lester should have left it that way, with Mickey just a sudden blast from the past on the Venetian sea of Bohemia, another rag-tag curio among the flotsam and jet-setters that constantly washed ashore, beaching themselves on that continental edge—and returned Mickey to his proper place of deposit, some rusting file in a distant corner of his own memory bank. After all, he and Mickey had long since left each other's life, and in a deep sense for Lester it was good riddance. There was little point in renewing their friendship except for nostalgia. And there was a great deal Lester did not care to remember. Besides, since they no longer shared an abiding interest in the Davis sisters, at least fifty percent of whom were now gone, their greatest link no longer existed. Anyway, what was past was history. Over and done with. Caput. Also, Mickey had obviously wound up some sort of weirdo, confusing certain traditional aspects of the Jewish religion with a belief in a George Burns sort of God.

But still, there was also no telling the creative process how to work. Or not work. And who could truly say how a motion picture began? Usually it derived from the success of a previous motion picture and was a conscious attempt at cloning. A homage to larceny that was called genre. The same but different with the difference dignified by being described as *spin*. The whole bloody notion

encapsulatable in a single sentence and labeled *concept*. But sometimes ideas—and these were the best ideas—would spring directly
from life full blown—or grown—and you had to be a fool to walk
away from them. Because it was your unconscious telling you
something. And you had to assume that your unconscious was not
that different from anybody else's unconscious. That it was the line
that hooked you into the great multitude, the homeless and the
rooted, the eggheads and the Republicans, the seedy unwashed and
pimpled teenagers and sophisticated yuppies, all with no other
place to hide but in the communal dark. You had to listen to your
unconscious, especially when it was operating against your so-called
better sense, when it would constantly gnaw at you and not let go.
Yes, Lester wanted to forget all about Mickey and their meeting at
the beach for a great many reasons. But unfortunately, that meeting
had sparked a vision that could become the engine for an entire
movie from Fade In to Fade Out. It even had a base in successful
genre. Mickey's story, as Lester was conceiving it, was nothing less
then *The Jazz Singer*—the same but different—only backwards
and with a contemporary twist. Which was all to the good.

According to his vision, Lester saw it as the tale of a rock singer
in the fifties . . . the very first rock singer, perhaps . . . sort of
an Elvis who predated Elvis . . . who becomes a great star, and
then is blacklisted . . . His world comes down on him . . . No
place to go . . . Nothing to do . . . He is lost completely . . .
But then he finds God and becomes a great cantor . . . and finally
gives a comeback concert at the Felt Forum . . . Or the Garden
itself . . . Or even at Shea Stadium . . . There would be hoards
of groupies in the story, but there is one girl who has stuck by him
. . . And there would be his parents . . . And maybe give him a
sister . . . It would be an old-fashioned movie full of sentiment
and emotion, a crossover film generationally . . . Of course, there
were still a few details to be fleshed—or flushed—out, but what
were writers for? A few words on paper and it would be eminently
marketable. And already in his mind's eye, Lester could see long

lines forming all around the block in Westwood and on Third Avenue. Yes, there was definitely a movie there.

But how to approach it? First, he had to get some more material from Mickey. All those years—how had he actually spent them? Had he been married? Did he have kids? Where had he lived? And how sincere was he about the whole God bit? Deep reality was the mother lode for which there was no substitute. The imagination of even the best writer always came in second to the experience of a man's life itself. Perhaps he might even have to spend a little seed time with Mickey. A little down time. Not too much, though. But he had not even taken Mickey's address. No problem there. He could always contact him through that industry outpost Mickey had mentioned, the Ocean Front synagogue.

As it happened, Lester was unusually busy that week. His daughter, Monica, was getting ready to return to Princeton and his son, Peter, to go off to Sarah Lawrence—even though it sounded to Lester as though it should have been the other way around. But times had changed utterly, gender distinctions completely eliminated—or at least blurred—and Lester, for one, was all for it. He always thought Monica was a lot smarter than Peter, anyway. So, she should be entitled to her shot. For example, even though she had another year to go, she had already mentioned to Lester the words that strike in terror in the heart and pocketbook of any parent—almost as much as the phrase, root canal—graduate school. Monica said she wanted to go for an advanced degree in European history. Peter, on the other hand, didn't have the foggiest notion of what he wanted to do, undergraduate let alone graduate. Which gave Lester the sneaking suspicion that he could wind up in show business as an actor, a producer, a director, perhaps even a writer. But Lester was not pushing either kid in any way. And when and if the boy decided to take the plunge into show business, there was always the William Morris mailroom. But until then, Lester knew his money and position could always buy his kids hang time, the economic luxury of drift and quest, of being able to knock around for awhile and do all the things Lester himself could not afford to do when he was their age. And as long as the kids did not get hung up in the drug culture, or whatever they were calling it these days, Lester would be happy. At the same time, the kids still did piss him off a great deal. For not really appreciating the non-monetary, as well as monetary, richness of such a gift. For taking everything too much for granted. Peter, for example, was already talking about needing a car. In New York?

On the last Saturday night the kids were home, Lester also had a social duty to perform. Marie Carol, the French actress, was in town. When Lester had needed to cast someone who could bring instant off-screen recognition to a character in *Alice In Paris,* he had approached Marie Carol almost as a lark. After all, it was just a cameo role as a mock femme fatale. But to his delight and the film's good fortune, she had agreed to do it. And he and Marie had hit it off. Not sexually—even though Lester would not have minded tasting her *nookie* either—but famously. As artists. As people. As citizens of the world, or at least, the cinema world. The mademoiselle had a quirky sense of humor and Lester adored her for that. Jean had liked her, too. And two winters back, when they went to the south of France, they borrowed Marie's villa in Bandol for two weeks. Afterwards, when Lester suggested some form of payment, Marie simply dismissed the notion as absurd, saying something about the house being unused or underused anyway, so it was she who should be grateful. But Lester, in addition to genuinely enjoying her company, still knew he owed Marie one. And while she was in town, the least he and Jean could do, he figured, was to arrange a little sit-down dinner for her. Not a big affair, nothing too formal, but for starters they did invite several studio heads, a few top agents, three tennis-playing lawyers, two name producers, a fellow director and, of course, a sprinkle of bona fide film stars. Soon, it escalated into a whole *shmeer* with caterers, a tent in the garden, rented tables and chairs, outdoor heaters, and who knew what other expenses? It would probably wind up costing him a lot more than the tab for two weeks in the Marie Antoinette suite of a Riviera hotel would have been. But what the hell, Lester decided, *C'est la vie.*

On Friday afternoon, Lester had his girl, Rhonda, call the synagogue and leave word for Mickey that he would be welcome at the dinner party. Lester was not even sure Mickey was still in town, but thought he would give it a shot anyway. Because somehow the idea of using Mickey's story as the germ of a film had not left him. It had refused to fly out the window, the ultimate destination of transient story ideas. Instead, despite the fact that he had his head into three other projects, Lester constantly found himself returning to the notion at odd moments. No mistake about it, there was something that grabbed him there. Call it nostalgia, call it his Jewish roots, call it his leftist past. Call it the Davis sisters. Call it autobiography. Call it deep reality. Anyway, there it was. A successful film in the making.

Mickey came to the party for Marie Carol, and not only stole the show while he was there, but also stole her at the end of the evening, the two of them leaving together. Marie had eyes for no one else throughout dinner, completely ignoring the horny studio head, Dan Weisberg, Lester had seated next to her. Instead, she was constantly fluttering her famous eyelids in the direction of Mickey's table at the end of the garden, definitely not the power table, the one, presided over by his own daughter, Monica, who also seemed to take a fancy to the *Galatzianah* Gaul. And how was that for a new wrinkle to the plot?

What had happened was this: While the guests were gathering on the patio before dinner, spearing hors d'oeuvres from the passing waiters and sipping Chardonnay or Perrier, Mickey had sat down at the piano in the Rose den and started running through the standards of his old night club/wedding act, opening with "C'est si Bon" and "La Vie en Rose" and segueing through "C'est Magnifique" to "La Seine." Lester could not believe his eyes—or ears. In thirty years Mickey, or rather Michel, had not changed a single sy-la-ble of his old routine. His francophiled English was still imitation Chevalier. But everyone seemed to be falling for it.

One by one his guests came tripping into the den, savvy studio heads, killer agents, hot-shot directors, superstars in tinted glasses. And Mme. Carol, who Lester certainly thought would spot the counterfeit franc. But instead, she joined Mickey at the piano, as if he was Gilbert Becaud or Jacques Brels, himself, alive and well in Santa Monica, singing the familiar words along with him. Then Mickey slid over on the piano bench and made room for Marie to sit down beside him. And by the time dinner was served, they were laughing and hugging each other in joy and everyone was applauding them.

"Class act," Lester overheard the writer, Max Isaacs, standing beside him. "Reminds me of The Blue Angel." Lester had invited Max because he figured the evening needed at least one writer and Max was a writer, who not only looked like one—wild wavy hair, tortoiseshell glasses, tweed jacket with leather patches—but also always had a pretty girl at hand.

"The movie?" Max's date, probably one third his age, asked. She was a little Oriental or Latino or maybe even a little Negroid or African, but however she was tinged racially, it worked. She was terrific looking.

"No, the nightclub," Max was saying. "Back in New York." He became aware of Lester beside him. "Remember The Blue Angel, Lester?"

"Sure." At the moment Lester would have said "Sure" to anything Max said. He was too busy staring at the girl who had green catlike eyes. "Marlene Dietrich and Emil Jannings," Lester said and began singing, "Falling in Love."

"Jeezus. First frog songs and now heinie tunes." Max laughed, "I mean the nightclub back in New York."

"Of course," Lester said, still staring straight into the girl's green eyes, waiting for her to be the first one to blink into a smile. "I had a girlfriend who lived down the block from it."

Finally, she did break into a smile, peewee-sized dimples forming on the bottom of her round cheeks. "Lester," Max was saying, "I want you to meet Susannah Troy. She's a very talented girl."

"Actress?" Lester asked taking her hand and shaking it as if he was sealing some sort of business deal. She had a large hand with long, slender fingers.

"No." Her voice was husky and she spoke barely above a whisper. "Writer."

"I have a great admiration for writers," Lester said. "Why do you think I invited Max here this evening? Without writers, the human race is just one big, dumb tongue-tied animal. I wish I could write myself. What do you write?"

"Poetry mostly," she whispered.

"Nothing like poetry, right?" said Max, as always overplaying the writer-cynic role.

"Exactly," Lester said with all the sincerity he could muster, before surrendering Susannah's hand.

After dinner Mickey and Marie were back at the piano again, a regular duet, and Lester wondered if Mickey would soon run out of French songs, exhaust his repertoire completely, and have to resort to a medley from the High Holiday services. And, who knew, maybe Marie, despite the cross dangling from her neck, was Jewish after all and would join in with him? You could never tell about the French. According to Lester's experience they were always either virulently anti-Semetic or strongly pro-Zionist.

On the fringe of the crowd gathered around the piano stood Max and Susannah. Lester smiled over to her and Max smiled back at him. But just moments later when Lester looked back in that direction, both Max and Susannah were gone. And then, after a flourish of chords, Mickey and Marie, rose from the piano and together threaded their way away from it. Mickey stopped to hug and kiss Lester like a Frenchman on both cheeks as he thanked him for inviting him. And Marie embraced Lester like an American starlet, rubbing her French tits hard against his blazer, as she told him what a formidable home he had and what a magnificent time she had and that he was welcome to her villa anytime he was in the south of France. And then she and Mickey were gone, too, sweeping out the door together.

"Who was that charming Frenchman?" his daughter Monica asked Lester the following morning.

"A cantor."

"You've got be kidding."

"No. We went to high school together."

"I don't believe it."

"We were Thespians together."

"You were Lesbians together?"

It was an old joke, old even back in high school, and Lester put his arm around his daughter and laughed anyway.

"Seriously, Dad. Is he really a cantor?"

"He's really a cantor and we went to high school together."

"I can't believe you're the same age."

"We're the same age. Believe me."

"But he's so sexy."

"What about me?"

"You're my father."

On Monday morning Lester had Rhonda make two calls. The first was to Mickey at the number the synagogue had given him. Because Lester was curious as a teenager, wondering if Mickey had "made out" with Marie. But there was no answer, Rhonda said, not even from a machine. The second call was to Max, asking for Susannah Troy's phone number, explaining that Mr. Rose had a project that could use the touch of a poet.

Good old Max. At first he was evasive. Questioning Lester's motivations, which Lester quickly assured him were strictly professional. "Look, Max, if I just wanted to get laid," he told him, "frankly, I can think of a lot of people I would call for help before dialing you. Also, even though I know diddley dick about splitting infinitives, I definitely know better than to literally fuck a writer. Because I never saw a writer who could keep his or her or their grammatical mouth shut for very long."

Including Max. Like all writers he could never keep a secret. It went with the territory. Not that Max could have kept Susannah Troy's phone number a secret from Lester for very long anyway.

Lester had to find out soon enough. Because that's what girls—or rather assistants, which was what, it seemed to Lester, anybody with access to a Rolodex insisted upon being called these days—like Rhonda were for. They loved the chance to show off how shrewd and resourceful they were. But anyway, as Lester had pointed out to Max, giving him Susannah Troy's number would actually be doing the girl a favor. Because it was to the girl's advantage career-wise that Lester got in touch with her ASAP. And at last Max weakened and agreed to give him a phone number. Not Susannah's home phone number exactly, but someone who could put Lester in touch with her, as Max put it, "career-wise pronto." Lester buzzed Rhonda to pick up on the line and take the number down.

"That sounds vaguely familiar," said Lester, as he overheard Max giving a Beverly Hills number.

"It should," said Max. "It's William Morris."

"I didn't know William Morris was into poets."

"They are if they also write screenplays. Talk to you later," said Max and hung up.

Not only had Susannah Troy written a screenplay, it turned out, but the script was one which the agent, Gary Adelman, was very high on and would be glad to messenger over to him ASAP. Nothing surprised Lester anymore. Not in Hollywood, anyway. If Keats and Shelley and Byron were alive today, Lester was certain, they'd all probably be turning out scripts, too. Unless they were heading rock groups as lead singers. Times changed. And so too did literary conventions. Why shouldn't a pretty young thing, who calls herself a poet, also be writing for the movies? It went with the geography and the generation.

Lester's own generation, as he recalled, had been different; much more idealistic. Especially the poets. They didn't expect to make a living except for perhaps someone like that poet, whose book of love poetry he once bought as a gift, who wrote a free verse marshmallow pre-porn that had to be very tame and mushy by today's standards. But the real poets of Lester's day either howled on street corners or starved in dark ivy towers, their work emerging only in readings delivered in the back of small bookstores, or in anthologies theoretically studied only in college lit courses.

But Lester had read them. He read the poets. For just as down through the years he had made up *nookie-wise* for that extreme case of coitus disappointus foisted upon him by Vivian Davis, he also compensated culture-wise for his failure to complete college. And as an autodidact, he prided himself on reading voraciously, certainly reading more library books than were on any college curriculum. Still, Lester regretted not finishing college. Just as he regretted not having a sensational memory of rapturously fulfilled youthful fantasy to carry around within him. Maybe that would have enabled him to retain his youthful idealism a little longer.

2

Lester sold the studio on the reverse jazz singer concept. No big deal for him. He was a good salesman and knew how to pitch. Because pitch was just the Hollywood word for peddle, and Lester always felt comfortable doing so. By just reminding himself that was all part of his genetic tradition.

Then Lester carefully picked the restaurant, a Mexican bistro run by a Canadian couple in Venice. Because he wanted a funky, out-of-the-way place. Something that showed that he was still a regular guy even though he moved in a movie maker's world of acquired sophisticated tastes. In other words, this time Lester would peddle himself as someone who came from the streets, but had picked up all sorts of polish along the way. Which was an easy sell for him because it was not too far from the truth. But far enough. Because then when the real truth, the deep reality, that he was a lot smarter and much more cultured than he seemed to let on slowly emerged, it would come as a plus in his favor. After you've carefully laid it all out for them, Lester had long learned, people always gave themselves great credit for discovering the very obvious and then liked you all the more for it.

The Canadians always treated Lester very well there, too. The maitre d', who was an out of work actor and loved hockey, knew exactly who Lester was. There was a certain ring of deference and respect in his Peter Jennings voice whenever he greeted him with

207

an "And how are you today, Mr. Rose?" Almost as if Lester was an LA King goalie. And the food there wasn't bad for the money, either.

During dinner Susannah told Lester about herself. Not surprisingly, it turned out she was mostly Jewish, which was what probably had attracted him to her in the first place. And in a way she did remind him of the young Vivian Davis. Not physically, but there was both a poetry and an intense practicality to her. It was always amazing where one's instincts could lead you, especially your baser ones. Susannah's real name was Cohen and the Troy came from U.S.C.—as in the Trojans—where she had been, just a few short years ago, believe it or not she said, a song girl. And Lester told her about himself. Some career facts she may not have known, a credit or two she might not have been aware of, and how he always worked closely with writers. Very closely.

Afterwards, as they walked with the people along Ocean Front Walk in Venice, which Lester pointed out was where the idea first sprang to life, so to speak, he outlined what he wanted the story to be—in short, *A Jazz Singer,* with reverse Jewish—and asked her to consider helping him flesh it out. She would have to spend some research time with Mickey, find out how he actually had spent all his cantorial non-show business missing years, in other words dig into the deep reality—the basic source of all art and a few hit movies.

"But how do you know I'm the person for this assignment? You haven't read anything I've written," she said.

"I don't have to," Lester told her and asked her if she wanted a frozen yogurt. She shook her head as Lester stopped in front of a dairy stand. "It's non-fat," he said. "Just fifteen calories an ounce." But she still shook her head. "I go by instinct," Lester explained to her and then asked the chubby girl behind the counter what flavors they had in non-fat. She pointed with an empty cone at the wall behind her.

Lester didn't know whether to chose Chocolate Passion or Orange Amaretta and asked Susannah again, "You sure you don't want any?"

"No, thank you," she said firmly.

"I'm not so sure you're Jewish," Lester told her.

"Small, medium, or large?" asked the chubby kid behind the counter.

"Large," Lester told her. "A large Chocolate Passion. Make that a huge Chocolate Passion."

"Any topping?" asked the counter girl.

"No," said Lester. "I'm on a diet."

As they strolled away, Lester greedily licking at his Chocolate Passion, Susannah said, "Give me a few days to think it all over."

After Susannah thought it all over, business affairs came to terms with her agent for just a slight bump above minimum with the usual cutoffs. Lester figured he had nothing to lose. The best thing that could happen would be that Susannah came up with a terrific script. The worst thing that could happen would be that he didn't get to fuck her. And as both a businessman and an artist he could deal with such adversities.

3

Lester didn't get to screw Susannah and suspected Mickey did. So much for his brilliant instincts and hunches.

Lester had tracked Mickey down through the Ocean Front synagogue and called him in the East. Mickey was excited by the concept and agreed to help in the development. Lester told him that all he wanted him to do was talk to a writer and Mickey said he had no problem with that. Lester made it clear that Mickey's life wouldn't be the basis of the picture as such per se, but that he could be very helpful as a research resource. Mickey readily agreed, and seemed completely unconcerned about any questions of rights, although he did ask Lester to remember him when it came to casting. Lester told him that it sometimes took longer than an elephant's capacity to remember from Fade In on paper in the script to an actual go picture before the cameras, but that in this case he would certainly do so. And they left it at that; although there was some talk about Mickey's coming on board as a technical advisor when the time came. Lester did not promise Mickey any definite role because there was no character he knew of yet written that Mickey might play. Besides, it was not in his nature to cast roles of an unwritten script.

Susannah went back East to see Mickey in New Jersey. It seemed his wife had died a year or so back, and his kids were grown, one living in Israel and the other in Wyoming or some similar place. Mickey was the cantor emeritus of the congregation and so had a lot of time to screw around. Which he apparently seemed to do despite—or, in addition to—all of his protestations of deep religious conviction. Susannah spent only a week with him. But that was enough. Mickey was obviously taken with her. And she by him. As far as Lester could make out, the only thing not all over the script she eventually turned in was his come. But his influence, in the form of his crazy religious ideas, was on every page. Also her fascination with him. Susannah had swallowed Mickey's heavenly line completely. Her first draft might have been called, *God Was His Co-Cantor.*

The studio was no more enthusiastic about the draft than Lester. There was the usual vague talk about ordering a rewrite when the right writer became available, but for most intents and purposes the project was set for limbo. So much for Lester's brilliant notions of subject matter and writer casting. And that's how matters stood, both the project and Mickey very much on the dark crater side of Lester's mind. And, of course, the mindless studio's.

But then one day Mickey, who Lester had still assumed was back East, showed up at his office. He was in tennis shorts and sneakers and looked more like an out of work actor to Lester than a retired cantor, or rather cantor emeritus. Mickey told him how wonderful he thought Susannah's script was and that she was a wonderful writer. For the sake of non-argument, Lester decided to act as though he agreed with him.

"But that's not why I'm here," Mickey smiled, "just to talk about your movies. It's my career I'm interested in. And I wonder if I can ask you a favor?"

"Depends," Lester replied non-committally.

"I want you to prepare a list for me," Mickey said.

It struck Lester as a strange request. Was Mickey trying to tease him in some way? "What kind of a list?"

"I want a list of the most important Jews in the industry."

"Are you planning a *pogrom* by any chance?"

"No," Mickey laughed, "more like a program. Remember my concert idea?"

"Vaguely."

Mickey then reminded Lester of his scheme, God's scenario as he had called it. For his reentry into show business, Mickey was not banking on any picture conceivably based loosely on his life, even though that certainly might help. Rather, he was banking on a concert he would be giving in that synagogue in Venice or Santa Monica—wherever it was—which would attract all sorts of industry biggies under one temple roof. And there, with God's personal sponsorship so to speak, he would deliver such a dynamite performance that every Jew in town who was anybody would be clamoring to hire him. To star in anything. It would be Mickey name your tune—or flick—time.

To Lester, Mickey's plan made his own notion of a reverse *Jazz Singer* seem like a *Star Wars* by Shakespeare in comparison. "I could help you with a list," Lester said, "but isn't that a pretty racist approach on your part?"

"Put down any *goyim* you want, too." Mickey spread his hands. "As long they wear *yarmulkes* in the *shul,* they're welcome to my concert."

"Will God's scenario apply to them?"

"Of course," Mickey said seriously. "God's very ecumenical."

"When will this industry-shaking concert take place."

"Chanukah."

"Chanukah?"

"Chanukah. You remember when Chanukah is?"

"Sure. Around Christmas."

Mickey shook his head sadly. "On behalf of the Maccabees, I forgive you."

Lester walked Mickey out front to where Rhonda sat and told her to assist Mickey in any way they could. "My Rolidex is your Rolidex," Lester said. And after suggesting that they get together for lunch one day soon, he left him there with Rhonda. Then Lester went back into his office, closed the door, and in spite of himself began thinking of people to put on the list for Mickey.

4

Peering down at the paper, now flattened out on the glass-topped desk in George Hecht's office, Les recognized the name of an organization or two and some of the countless petitions cited. "These names," he told George, "they come from the basement."

George was confused. He crushed the empty coffee container in his hand and threw it in the waste basket. "What basement? What kind of lower depths are you talking about?"

"The Davis sisters' basement," Lester said, and explained the Friday night hootenannies that were held there.

George listened carefully, tamping his pipe. "What you say is very funny, Les," he said. "But as matters stand, I'm afraid it's no joke."

George, of course, was right. The blacklist was no joke, and the situation in which Lester found himself was nothing less than absurd. He was not a well-known performer, a world famous artist, an international name. Lester Rose was not an Elia Kazan, a Clifford Odets, a John Garfield, a Lee J. Cobb, or a Jerome Robbins. Neither was he an Arthur Miller, a Lillian Hellman, a Zero Mostel, a Paul Robeson, or the Weavers. Lester Rose was not a household word, except perhaps in a solitary apartment above a retail store in the backwaters of Brooklyn. Lester Rose was just a backstage nobody who should never even have been considered important enough to be blacklisted. Or so Les would have thought. But there it was. That was the deep reality of the matter and there was no escaping it. Suddenly, he had to come to grips with the very same plague that was afflicting show business greats who were the stuff of legends.

And he approached the problem in much the same way they did. He sought advice and counsel. Naturally, he could not go to any high-priced lawyer. Instead, he tried to rely on the wisdom of old friends.

But first, Les followed George's suggestion and called the ad agency and, surprisingly, found a very sympathetic ear at the other end of the phone. The man Les spoke with at Y and R, who was in charge of clearances, said he was just doing his job and had nothing to do with the mechanism. The agency was too busy, he explained, to investigate each performer and director and producer working in television. So, they hired an outside organization, paying them a monthly retainer fee to do just that, and Les's name had not cleared with them. It was that simple. And if Les felt that some sort of error had been made his best advice to Les was to take it up with them directly. And he gave Les their name and their office address and phone number and told him the person to ask for.

Les hung up and dialed that number. Instead of a female secretary or switchboard operator coming on, a youthful, male voice answered the phone. And when Les asked for the name he had been referred to, it turned out to be that man himself.

Les told him who he was and why he was calling and asked if he could see him as soon as possible.

"We charge for both consultations and further checks," Les was told. And since the figures mentioned didn't sound like very much to him, considering it was not only his present but his entire future that was involved, Les made an appointment to meet the youthful, male voice whose name was Harrigan the next day during his lunch hour.

The address was on Forty-second Street and Les walked the few blocks downtown along Sixth Avenue, past the jewelry district and men's clothing shops and hardware and back number magazine stores. The building entrance was off the lobby of a Forty-second Street movie house that showed triple features. Les found the listing in the downstairs wall directory and took the elevator up to the top floor. When he got off the elevator Les hesitated, not knowing in which direction to turn. "Counterattack?" he asked the operator, who pointed down the hall to a double-frosted glass door with AMERICAN BUSINESS CONSULTANTS stenciled across it in simple black type. Beneath that in red, white and blue streaked italics were the words *Counterattack*.

Les pushed open the door and a gray haired receptionist/typist looked up from the letter she was typing. On her desk was a half-eaten apple.

"I'm here to see Mr. Harrigan," he said. "Lester Rose."

She told Les to sit down and disappeared down the hall. It was a small anteroom and there was just a single bench with an end table cluttered with recent copies of *Counterattack*, the weekly newsletter that listed alleged Communists and Communist-front sympathizers with their dossiers. Les turned the pages of a few issues. He was surprised to read the records of unknowns which seemed as innocent and no more incriminating than his own.

The gray-haired receptionist returned, a smile on her face, as if she had enjoyed her brief excursion away from her desk, and motioned for Les to follow her. She opened another frosted-glass door revealing a large room, clutters of files with publications and periodicals stacked on top of them, and several steel gray metal desks pushed up against the walls. Evidently, the people who sat at the desks were out to lunch. In one corner was an ink-stained mimeo machine and against a far wall was an old rolltop wooden desk, each individual compartment over-brimming with papers of all sorts. Sitting on a swivel before it was a baby-faced man in his thirties with thinning brown hair which he tried to wear in a crew cut and part at the same time. He had a slight build and looked like a priest who had been dipping into the collection plate. Les was disappointed at first sight. Somehow, he had expected a blacklister to have a full head of blond hair, the powerful body of an interior lineman, and ooze with moral rectitude.

Les told him he was sure that some mistake had been made. Harrigan smiled and went to one of the smaller files and extracted an index card. Then he took the index card and went to a larger legal-size file and riffled through it until he found a sheet of paper. "We don't usually make mistakes," he said, inspecting the sheet. "You made the mistake when you joined those subversive groups and signed those unpatriotic petitions." Then he handed the paper to Les. It was the original of the carbon George had shown him.

Les waved the paper back and forth as if in that way he could somehow make it disappear. "I was just a kid," he said.

"That's not my fault," Harrigan replied. "Normally, as I told you over the phone, we charge five dollars for a check. But since I already ran one on you for Y and R and you're just an individual, I'll charge you only two dollars." And he held out his hand.

Les resisted thanking him for the bargain in a wiseass way and just paid him the two dollars, watching as Harrigan pulled a wallet out of his back pocket and slid the bills into it. "I had no political views then," Les insisted. "And I'm certainly not a Communist now."

Harrigan looked up as he was replacing his wallet. "I'm glad to hear it. But look, kid, I'm busy. And there's nothing I can do for you. I'm just a talent consultant. I checked your background. I didn't make your background."

"But how can I get my name cleared with the agency and the network, so I can go ahead and work on the new show?"

"I don't handle that," Harrigan said. But he sat down at his desk, pushed aside some papers, scribbled on a pad like a doctor writing out a prescription, tore off the page and held it in the air. "This is a consultation," he said.

"I don't understand."

"I only charged you two dollars for the talent check. But a consultation is always five dollars. I told you that, didn't I?"

Les could hardly believe what was happening. His entire life and livelihood were being threatened because he was allegedly a dangerous enemy and posing a great threat to the entire American political system. And this self-appointed bulwark of democracy was trying to nickel and dime him out of a few bucks. The mimeo machine suddenly somehow made the office look like the kind of place in which revolutions were plotted. And Les suddenly felt like hatching a revolution or two himself. By smashing the platen of the mimeo machine. Upending the file cases. Throwing the file drawers out of the windows. And hacking the old rolltop into pieces like a Jimmy Durante piano. But instead, he gave Harrigan a fiver. Again, out came the wallet, in slid the money, and back into the pocket went the wallet. Only then did Harrigan hand Les the slip of paper he had been dangling before him.

On it was written just a name and phone number. But no address.

"For five bucks," Les said half joking, "I expected at least an address, too."

Out came Harrigan's wallet again and with the other hand he reached for the slip of paper. "Do you want your five dollars back?"

"No."

"Believe me," Harrigan said, "I'm referring you to the one person who can help you."

Les looked down and read the name on the slip aloud, "Herbie Moscow?" he asked. "Is that a code name or a joke?"

"The position you're in," Harrigan said, sounding like an elementary school teacher, "is no joke, Mr. Rose." Then he turned and sat down at his desk, as if suddenly he didn't have another moment to spare.

"Do you mind if I use your bathroom?" Les asked his back.

Harrigan's hand shot up and pointed to the front of the office. "It's down the hall. But you'll have to ask the receptionist for the key."

Boy, Les thought, it really was like an elementary school. But he borrowed the key and pissed in the john. Which was normal enough. It was the blacklist business in the office that was shitty.

When Les returned to his own office cubicle, he closed the door and dialed the number five dollars had just bought him. Again a male voice answered the phone, again a very youthful one, but this time one breathless and full of energy and high-pitched excitement.

"How'd you get my number?" Herbie Moscow immediately asked. "And how much did the Irisher make you pay for it?" When Les told him, Herbie Moscow said, "Don't worry. You weren't cheated. I'm worth it. Tell me where you are and I'll see if I can fit you in this afternoon." Les thought that he would have to go see him. But "No," Herbie Moscow said, "I make house calls, I love networks, you see I'm basically an actor myself, so I'll come by NBC this afternoon."

Les was beginning to feel like Philip Marlow or Sam Spade, and was expecting some sort of Peter Lorre character to walk in through his cubicle door. Instead, entering his office hutch that afternoon was a chubby, curly-haired young man about his own age in a tan raincoat toting a brief case in one hand and a Charlotte Rouse in the other. Les knew the situation he was in was very serious, but this Joe Cairo seemed a seedy joke.

Les pointed to the Charlotte Russe. "I thought they went out of business years ago."

"No. You just got to know where to find them," Herbie Moscow said, biting into the whipped cream-topped sponge cake, which rested on a paper cardboard cone base. "Like Communists," he added, and sat down on the corner of Les's desk, the whipped cream spotting his lips.

Les leaned forward intently, "I am not a Communist."

"I was a Communist," Herbie Moscow said, his tongue licking the whipped cream on his upper lip like a windshield wiper. "Now tell me your problem."

A typist-actress from Texas, passing down the corridor, waved to Les through the glass divider. And his Joe Cairo immediately waved back, saluting her with his Charlotte Russe. "Pretty," Herbie Moscow nodded, somehow dividing the word into three glottal syllables. "That's one of the reasons I joined the Communist Party.

The gash. I thought I'd find great gash. Get laid alot. But I was pretty soon disillusioned with the whole thing. The ones you could make weren't worth making, you know what I mean? Is that how you got involved?" He greedily finished the Charlotte Russe and unfurled the cardboard base. "False bottom. Deceiving. The C.P. was just like a Charlotte Russe. Very little you could really sink your teeth into. So, tell me about your case." he said, tossing the empty container remnant into the trash basket beside Les's desk.

"I didn't know I was a case."

"Whatever. Let me see what's on your record."

Les withdrew from his desk drawer the carbon George had given him. Herbie Moscow inspected the sheet and clicked his tongue against his teeth. "They've really got you nailed, kid. I know these organizations. I remember these petitions. I was a Young Communist myself."

"I was still just a teen-ager when all this is supposed to have happened," Les protested.

"That doesn't mean you wasn't old enough to be hooked," he said. "But no matter what you were, you're not a Communist now, right?"

"I just told you that."

"You didn't have to tell me, Rose," he said, addressing Les as if he was still some sort of student. "I can always tell if there is a Communist in the room. Because I was one myself. It's a feel you pick up that never leaves you." Herbie Moscow suddenly leaned forward and stared into Les's eyes. "Take you, for example," he decided. "You're definitely not a Communist now. Not even a sympathizer. I can also see that you've never been lacking in the intelligence department. So, why did you sign all this shit?" He pointed to the list on the sheet. "Who did you think you were, John Hancock?"

Les smiled. "Mostly for the same reason—or one of the same reasons—you joined the Communist Party."

"For the gash?"

"Yes."

"And did you get any?"

"No."

"Of course, not. What'd I tell you? The Communist Party is the biggest crock going. It's as wrong about politics as it is about gash and just as deceptive. So, I feel sorry for you. And maybe I can even help you?"

"And how much is that going to cost me?" Les asked.

"I'm insulted," said Herbie, jumping to his feet. "Do you think I'm like that cheap *goy* who jews you to death two dollars here, five dollars there? I don't need your money. I get paid. Well paid. I'm an expert. I work for the FBI. I work for the House Committee. They know me in Washington. I'm a personal friend of Joe McCarthy and Roy Cohn and one hand washes the other. I don't need your money."

"Then what do you need? Tell me what I have to do to get myself cleared?"

"It's very simple," said Herbie. "You just have to come clean."

"But I have nothing to come clean about," Les pleaded. "I just signed a few stupid things, that's all. These sisters had these Friday night hootenannies down in their basement. I was still in high school."

"But what about the other people?"

"What other people?"

"The other people who were there."

"Most of them were in high school, too. Or college."

Herbie ran his across his mouth and licked it. "But were any of them anybody?"

"What do you mean?"

"Were any of the other people there—whether they signed anything or not—somebody whose name might mean something."

"I don't understand. Mean something to who?"

"To the newspapers."

Les shook his head. "We were just a bunch of kids in a Brooklyn basement listening to records."

"Well, I don't know if I can do anything for you then," Herbie said, and moved toward the door. "The way it works, you see, is I need a name. You give me a name bigger and better than yours and I get your name cleared. Even Stephen. I mean because I got a bigger fish. It's a good deal for me. It's even a better deal for you."

"But I can't come up with a name," Les shouted. "There were no fish there, big or little, I told you. Just a bunch of Brooklyn kids in a finished basement."

"And you're the one, Rose," Herbie half laughed, "that's going to get fucked."

"What do you mean?"

"I mean, they'll write about you in *Counterattack*. They'll list you in Red Channels. They'll make you more famous than you ever dreamed. And you can say good-bye to your job and the entertainment industry because you'll be blacklisted forever."

"It's not fair," Les protested.

"Nobody's talking fair," said Herbie. "Whenever you're involved with Commies, it's a war in a world of danger."

"But I'm not a Commie," Les insisted. "You even agreed."

"But you still have to prove it. Not to me, but to everyone else." Herbie patted his briefcase and looked out into the corridor. "Alot of action here?"

"What do you mean?"

"Gash."

"I wouldn't know."

"And you might never find out either, Rose. Better think of a name. A couple of names. Then call me again." And he was gone, clutching his brief case up high, under his arm pit.

Les did not particularly want to call Doug. He had steered clear of him as much as possible since his affair with Lisa. And although he didn't feel guilty, Les also didn't feel exactly comfortable about it, either. But now he needed advice and he needed it badly. He didn't have the money to go to a high-priced lawyer. All he could do was go to older and more experienced friends. Like Doug. So he had called him that night and asked him to meet him for dinner. Doug chose Filene's, the bocci place on Thompson Street, and Les found him waiting at the bar when he arrived. And it was only after Doug had greeted him warmly with a big, bear hug that Les noticed Lisa seated on the stool behind him. She looked good up there too, her short legs folded in behind the rungs. Les went to hug her, but she just turned her head and politely offered him her cheek to kiss. Which he did.

In a few minutes they were seated at a table, studying the menu, Doug telling Les how proud he was of him and the progress of his career; Doug had even heard that Les would soon be having a show of his own. Was that true? Yes, Les told him and said he owed it all to him—and Lisa. And after they had finished ordering and were folding away their menus, Lisa informed Les she was working as a receptionist at Elizabeth Arden between "gigs," but was up for a part in a "soap" and Doug talked about his teaching at an acting school while waiting to get work as an actor himself. "But, at least," Doug lifted the now emptied beer glass he had brought to the table with him, "you're working." Les responded by pouring half of his beer into Doug's glass and drinking the rest of it while signaling the bartender for refills.

It was not until they ate their pastas and salads and were shmoozing over coffee that Les finally got to the point and told them all about his problem and the pickle he was in. Lisa gasped audibly and Doug ordered a grappa.

"There are lawyers who handle this sort of thing," said Doug.

"I don't know if I can afford one."

"And there are groups," said Lisa, "to help people in just your position. I'm sure the union would help."

"Nobody is just in my position," Les said sadly. "And I don't want to go near any groups—that's how I got into this trouble in the first place—and I don't want to get any unions involved."

"Les may have a point there," agreed Doug. "Then they have something else on you."

"That's madness," said Lisa.

Les had planned to tell them about Herbie Moscow's proposed solution and of the idea he had for implementing it. But then he thought better. Even though Doug was the most professional theater person he knew, Doug would never understand. As for Lisa, she would be hopeless. His surrogate parents, which is what Lisa and Doug essentially were, Les decided, were turning out to be as useless as his real parents would have been.

On the subway back to Brooklyn that night, he even considered talking about the problem to his parents. But once he walked in the door of their apartment above the store he realized how absurd that notion was. His father was asleep in his chair before the Dumont TV set and his mother was mending socks while watching a panel show drone on. In that setting, how could he possibly begin to explain that the political climate in the great land of freedom and opportunity they had struggled so to reach was threatening to destroy the fruit of their lives, the nectar of their happiness, their only son?

5

It was as if *Monty* enjoyed being on the highway, like a skittish colt at last let loose from the coral. Especially once they were through New Jersey and past the cobblestoned expressway in Philadelphia that ran alongside the gray, rippling river. After a traffic circle, Les noticed a sign saying Valley Forge and considered stopping off there and saying some sort of secular prayer to the nation's founding father. He would tell George Washington that he had spent his cold winter there in vain. That his vision of the country was being subverted, not by revolutionaries of the left but by reactionaries of the right, who were out to destroy his very dream. And, more importantly, the dream of Les Rose. But what good would that do, his going there as if on a pilgrimage, and sending up his lament and prayer? Les did not believe in prayer and he knew George Washington was not buried there anyway.

He drove on through the green Pennsylvania countryside over well-paved ribbons of flat blacktop, passing neat, tidy Federal houses with sturdy rock foundations and rolling farm land behind them, across bridges that spanned racing rivers and fast running streams and winding railroad tracks, until he descended into a valley full of smoke stacks and coal bins and more railroad lines. Here the houses were made of wood and lacked eaves, stacked next to each other like crates delivered on a sidewalk before a store that had not opened yet. Downtown there was rock and stone masonwork again, especially in the bank buildings and city hall and a magnificent railway station of Beaux Arts design that reminded Les of the Frick Museum on Fifth Avenue with its Roman arches and deep-set stained glass windows. A president could have surely once stopped there on a whistle-stop campaign tour and spoken from the rear platform of his private train. But then behind the station was a jumble of tracks lined with more freight cars and cabooses and refrigerator cars and coal cars and oil tank cars and passenger cars and locomotives than Les had ever before seen assembled in a single place. It was like a boy's dream of Christmas—or Chanukah—a gift of the world's greatest electric train set brought to life.

Next to the station was a diner, also shaped like an old railroad car, and Les stopped in there for a cup of coffee and directions. The address he wanted was on Hillside Avenue. And Les was told he could reach it by turning left at the red light and following that street up until it crossed Hillside which, the cashier laughed, "Was not on any hillside."

He followed the directions and came to a level but tree-lined street of large wooden houses with big front yards that had all seen better days. The house he parked in front of had white shakes and green trim. As Les walked up the cracking cement path that led to the porch, he could see that it was obviously in need of a new paint job. The white shakes were peeling and streaked with gray. On the porch was a rusty old hammock. Les pushed it and a spring wailed as if he had stepped on a sick cat.

The door was open. In the entrance foyer on a walnut paneled wall was a row of mailboxes with bells beneath them. What once had been the grand home of one of the privileged few was now a multiple dwelling divided into many apartment units. Les rang the bell beside the nameplate he wanted. No answer. He looked in the mail box behind it. Empty.

But who knew if these old electrical systems worked anyway? Les decided to see for himself if anybody was home. Naturally, the apartment was on the top floor in what was originally a storage attic or servant's quarters. Climbing the stairs, Les told himself, that he should have called and let him know he was coming. After the visit of Herbie Moscow, Les knew he had to talk to someone and who better to turn to? Because he needed someone in his corner, advising him as if he was a fighter on a stool in need of a big round near the end of a losing bout. Someone who had the street smarts and gut instincts for the job. Someone he could count on to never let him down.

The door was closed but Les could hear a radio or record playing within. He knocked loudly. Soon he heard steps and then the familiar voice calling out, "Who's there?"

"Les Rose."

The door shot open and Chicago welcomed him into his arms like a brother. He was wearing a yellow cashmere sweater over a black sport shirt and gray checked pants and his impeccable dress was in sharp contrast to the fading wallpaper and the rain streaked ceiling and the buckling linoleum on the hallway floor. Les followed him into the apartment. To a small living room that looked as if it had been furnished out of old Sears Roebuck catalogs or current Salvation Army thrift stores: a colonial scatter rug on the floor, a maplewood benched couch covered with a quilted pad, a black rocking chair, a mahogany based floor lamp—all a far cry from the decor of the Brooklyn apartment he had recently left behind.

Chicago pointed to the still swinging rocking chair and the newspaper laying beside it, open to the sports pages. "I was just dozing."

"I rang the bell downstairs," Les said. "Nobody answered. But I figured I would give it another shot."

"Smart," Chicago nodded, turning the radio down. "Because the bell don't work. Coffee?"

"No, thanks. I just had some at the diner downtown."

"Near the station?"

"Yeah."

"They have good muffins for breakfast there," said Chicago,

sitting down again in the rocker. "So, who told you I was here and why didn't you call first?"

Les sat down on the couch. The apartment had a musty, oily smell as if too many eggs had been fried and too many strips of bacon grilled in the kitchen he could but half see. Also, it seemed, as if windows had never been opened. Les felt claustrophobic. "Do you want to take a walk?" he asked.

"What for?" Chicago shook his head. "So, why didn't you call me first? I could have been out."

"It was a spur-of-the-moment thing," Les explained. "I just decided I wanted to see you, that's all."

"And she told you I was here?"

"Yes," Les nodded.

"One thing you didn't warn me," Chicago smiled.

"What?"

"That she could be such an awful pain in the ass."

"Was that before or after you decided to leave?"

"Both. First, I could see she was trying to steer me toward getting a regular kind of job. Which, if that's what I wanted, I could have stayed home with my mother and father and worked in the store and never quit high school in the first place."

"Is that what Vivian actually said she wanted you to do?"

"No." Chicago took out a pack of cigarettes and lit one with a gold Ronson. "But I could tell that's what she wanted." He exhaled in Les's direction. "And I never could get used to the idea of her fucking around with Michel DuChamps, either."

"Whoa!" Les put up his hands. "That was long before you were married. That was in Paris and only for a week."

"That don't make it right," said Chicago. "I guess if it was with somebody nobody ever heard of, it would have been different. Or maybe, if it was somebody from outside the neighborhood. Or if it was somebody who wasn't at the wedding, I don't know. But whatever—our marriage was all wrong. It's like after you make a bad bet, you know it the instant you lay it down and then you try to forget all about it, but it's too late." He suddenly smiled. "How's your mother?"

"She's fine," Les said. "Both my parents are fine."

"And *nookie?*" Chicago smiled. "Are you getting any *nookie?*"

"Enough," Les said.

"Stay off the high-class stuff," said Chicago. "But maybe you know that already, since you went to college."

"Only for a year."

"A year is enough, if you're smart. How's your job?"

Les told him. And about his problem. In describing the political situation, when Les mentioned the name of Joe McCarthy, Chicago reacted quickly. "I never liked him when he was managing the Yankees, either." For a second Les was not sure whether Chicago was joking or not, but then he laughed reassuringly. And so Les finally got down to the nitty gritty of his predicament.

"So, if you give them Michel," Chicago slowly nodded, "you think they might lay off you?"

"Yes."

"But how do you know they won't come back for more?"

"Because I have nothing more to give."

"They sound like cocksuckers," Chicago said. "And you never can trust cocksuckers. You let them suck your cock once and they think they can screw you up the ass, too."

"Then what should I do?" Les asked point blank.

"You should play it smart."

"Which would be what?"

A key turned in the door and Glenda appeared, her arms cradling two bags of groceries. When she saw Les, she smiled without the least show of surprise, as if he had just reported for work as a busboy at her station. Chicago sprang to his feet, kissed her on the cheek, and relieved her of her bundles.

"I figured on fixing hamburgers for supper," Glenda announced.

"Great," said Chicago, already on his way into the kitchen. "I'll put the stuff away."

Glenda took off her hat and coat and hung them in the hall

closet and came back fluffing out her hair but not saying anything, instead just smiling as if Les understood that she never was supposed to say anything anyway. She sat down beside him on the wooden couch and they both waited for Chicago to return. But Les had to admit to himself that she looked better than he had remembered, both her face and body having filled out. Still, Glenda was very much the traditional thin *shiksa* type, a far cry from *zaftik* Jewish beauty. And it was still hard for him to see what Chicago saw in her.

"You sure you don't want coffee?" Chicago asked returning to the living room.

"No, thanks."

"Tea?"

Les shook his head again.

"You'll eat with us?"

"No," Les said. "You'll eat with me. I want to take you out to dinner."

Chicago turned to Glenda. The expression on her face was blank. But evidently Chicago was able to read something into it. "Okay," he agreed. "But we come back here for dessert."

They drove downtown in *Monty,* Glenda seeming to enjoy riding in the back, holding on to the crossbar, the wind in her face and her hair streaming back. They directed Les to a spaghetti and pizza joint on the same street as the railway station that had billiard tables between the bar and the familiar-red checkered cloth-covered tables. It seemed any advice he might receive about his blacklist problem was destined to involve an Italian restaurant. But meanwhile, Les was surprised at how delicious the pizza was, the sauce rich but not too oily, the crust moist but still firm. Les even remarked that it was as good as any New York pizza.

"They're okay with *guinea* food," agreed Chicago. "But when it comes to deli, they ain't worth shit. Because all they got is *guinea* deli. Right?"

Glenda looked up from her slice and nodded in expert agreement.

"What I wouldn't give for a nice piece of *kishke*," Chicago said wistfully.

Les snapped his fingers. "I should have thought of it and brought some."

"Next time," said Chicago.

It was not until after dinner, when they returned to the Hillside Avenue apartment with two pints of ice cream, maple walnut and chocolate mint, and Glenda said that she had to go to bed early because she had to get up early and work breakfast the next morning that Chicago and Les got past all the small talk.

Chicago told Les that he felt there was something special between himself and Glenda that had never ceased to be so from the moment they first met in the mountains. So, when Glenda married the ex-tackle after he returned home from the Air Force in Germany it did not work. Just as Chicago's own marriage did not work. Glenda and the ex-tackle and he and Vivian simply weren't meant for each other in the same special way he and Glenda were. It was as simple as that.

Les asked him if he might have felt differently and his marriage might have worked out better if he had not been informed of Vivian's loss of virginity and with whom she had lost it. "Then it would have been even worse," Chicago smiled. "The marriage could have gone on longer."

They spoke of Chicago's economic problems and how he expected to make a livelihood. "I tell you one thing," Chicago said. "I won't handle any action up here. The *guineas* have a lock on it. And there's no way I'm going to give them any trouble."

"Maybe you should open a Jewish deli," Les joked. "They won't give you any trouble on that score."

"Maybe," Chicago seemed to consider seriously. "Meanwhile, I'll look around and Glenda's working."

"But doesn't it get boring?"

"Only in the daytime," said Chicago.

Les then returned to his problem and asked Chicago what he

should do in order to play it smart. "It's no contest," Chicago replied. "You got to take your chances and fuck him."

"You mean I should give them Mickey's name."

"Sure."

Les was still wavering. "But is that the right thing for me to do?"

"It ain't the right thing for you to do," Chicago said. "But it is the only thing for you to do. Besides," he laughed, "it is the right thing for you to do for me. And think of it this way: You owe me one."

Although Chicago kept insisting Les stay the night, Les knew he did not have his heart in those requests. So he said that he had to get back to New York to work in the morning. Which was not true. He had already arranged to have the day off. They embraced like brothers and Chicago walked him down to *Monty* and they embraced again. Then Les drove downtown. He could not stop at the local hotel because Glenda worked there and would be serving breakfast. Les turned onto the highway and drove all the way to Valley Forge before he found a motel to his liking. And the next morning he drove through the memorial park in his purloined army jeep, slowing down just enough to read the historic markers about the hard times of America's first patriots.

6

"Well, I've been thinking it over. I do have a name for you."

"Somebody who signed the same petitions and went to the same meetings?"

"Yes."

"Who?"

"Can I trust you?"

"Trust me for what?"

"Trust you to get my name cleared."

"I told you I could do that if you came up with a big enough name."

"What if the name isn't big enough?"

"Then I can't promise to help you. But I'll do what I can. You never know how these things work out."

"What's a big name?"

"What do you think is a big name? Any movie star is a big name. Any recording artist is a big name."

"What about television?"

"Of course, a television star is a big name. It's show business. So, tell me the name and we can start straightening out your entire problem."

"Myron Feldstein."

"Myron Feldstein? Never heard of him. Who's he?

"Michel DuChamps."

"The French kid on the TV sitcom?"

"Yes."

"Michel DuChamps. That's good. I don't think you'll have much to worry about in terms of your career."

"What about Michel DuChamps?"

"Him? He's got a lot to worry about."

7

"Isn't that where Lincoln spoke?" asked Herbie Moscow. He and Les were on the Lexington Avenue subway going downtown and Les had just told him that he had visited Valley Forge recently.

Les regarded Herbie with disbelief. He knew he had disappointed Herbie by not springing for a cab, but now he was completely unnerved by him. After all, this was the man Les was counting on to get him out of his patriotic—or rather unpatriotic—pickle. "Aren't you thinking of Gettysburg?" Les suggested.

"Okay," Herbie said, "Gettysburg." As if he were conceding some minor technical point in a tedious argument.

"Anyway," Les said, "they're both in Pennsylvania."

"Who the fuck cares?" Herbie said. "Look at that."

Sitting across from them was an Oriental girl with her hair combed back in a tight chignon. Herbie was staring straight at her. But she was ignoring his look by casting her eyes above it, as if the placard ads for vocational training schools and credit loans and analgesics were the only real points of interest within her line of sight. "If you eat Chinese gash, do you get a little slip with your fortune printed on it?" Herbie asked.

"No," Les said. "You just get hungry for more an hour later." And that tired twist of the old joke broke Herbie up. Set him to slapping his knees and patting Les's back and trying to catch his breath all at the same time. Les tried to both apologize for—and disassociate himself from—Herbie's behavior by innocently smiling back at the Oriental girl. But she missed making eye contact, her gaze still going way over their heads.

"Ever fuck a slant?" asked Herbie after he had finally stopped laughing.

"No."

"There was one in my party cell, but she was a dog," said Herbie, again staring straight ahead at the Oriental girl.

"Did you fuck her?"

"I don't fuck dogs." He abruptly stopped studying the Oriental girl. "I told you we should take a cab. I got to prepare you for the meeting and the subway is too fucking distracting."

After work the previous evening, Herbie had taken Les to a high-ceilinged apartment with parquet floors on West End Avenue to meet the ideological commissar of the Hearst press, a portly, bejoweled old Jew who reminded him of a "Cuddles" Zakal until he began waving his cigar around and barking orders at his thin, neurasthenic wife because his glass of tea was not hot enough. Then, somehow, he reminded Les of the labor leader David Dubinsky.

The commissar wrote editorials for the *Mirror* and a column for the *Journal American* and was the definitive Hearst arbiter on all matters Communistic. When Herbie first introduced Les to him, the commissar acted engagingly and with great charm. But he dropped the effort—or effect—when he soon realized that Les was the one who had to sell him, that he was the customer and Les was the peddler. It was then that he dumped on his wife and Les watched her scamper down the long hall from the living room, not so much to fetch fresh tea but rather simply to retreat. She did not reappear until he and Herbie were set to leave, sneaking out of the kitchen as if she was the maid whose duty it would be to close the door behind them.

Meanwhile, Herbie and the commissar—who Herbie addressed as Mr. S.—were bantering back and forth, as if contesting who could drop more names: Joe and Roy and J.B. and Peg and Vic and

Don and Vince and J.G. and Louis and Elizabeth all whirled by Les, all without apposition, as if their first names alone provided identification enough for any knowledgeable person. Then the name-dropping contest extended to groups and organizations and publications, all equally unfamiliar to Les. Finally, Herbie did mention one name Les could recognize, that of a semi-prominent character actor.

"Yes," the commissar rubbed his hands gleefully. "Isn't it terrific."

Herbie, who until that moment had genuinely surprised Les, by dropping his crude, rough edges and matching the commissar in almost every facet of professional anti-Communist erudition, suddenly seemed confused and lost. "Terrific?" Herbie asked, and nervously lit a cigarette. "What's so terrific?"

"Of course, it's terrific," smiled the commissar. "He's taken my advice and is preparing a statement that he wants me to go over."

"This afternoon," Herbie said, snapping his lighter shut, "they found him dead on the sidewalk on Central Park West."

"What?" The commissar bent forward.

"He either jumped or fell from the terrace of a friend's penthouse apartment."

"The son of a bitch must have jumped," the commissar decided and leaned back into his chair again. "And after all the work I did with him." He sounded like a professor disappointed by the decision of a favorite student to drop a course.

"Yeah," Herbie agreed. "It's a shame he died before he could make a clean breast of it."

Les was appalled by their callousness. He had never come into contact with the man personally and yet he was shocked to learn of the actor's death. But Herbie and the commissar, who had both trafficked with him, were now reacting so coldly. What kind of people was he dealing with? It was not too late to just turn around and bolt out of the apartment. But bolt to where? Where could he run to and still have a future?

Herbie had already begun to discuss him, pointing out to the commissar that even though Les was far from the jumping—or fallen—actor in stature, he still had a breast to be bared. Which was their business at hand. Herbie became more and more deferential in tone to the commissar as he sought his advice about the best way to handle "Les's case." Les had forgotten that he was a case and suddenly realized they were like two kidnappers determining his ransom, the ransom he would have to pay in effect in the Rose case, to free himself as a victim.

"I checked the petitions and the lists that Les signed," Herbie was now saying. "And there's only one name that he could possibly give us and I must say, to his credit, Les suggested that name himself. Which is why I think we should clear him."

"What's the name?" the commissar coughed as he relit his cigar.

"Myron Feldstein."

"Who the hell is he?"

"Tell George," said Herbie.

"Michel DuChamps," Les said in a voice barely above a whisper.

"Who?" the commissar thundered.

"Michel DuChamps," Les said, managing to raise his voice but slightly.

"Who the hell is he?" the commissar repeated.

Herbie told him that Michel DuChamps was a French singer with a running part on a popular TV sitcom.

"Well, you know about such things," the commissar said to Herbie, adding very snidely. "After all, you're our youth expert. So, let me check with the boys downtown and see if they're interested."

"I'm sure they'll be interested," said Herbie. "Because I've figured out just the way to handle it." And Les listened with openmouthed amazement as Herbie proceeded to outline his proposed scenario. But Les did not say a word. He had chosen not to bolt and run. He had decided to offer Mickey's past in sacrifice for his own present—and future.

And evidently, the boys downtown were interested. Because Herbie had called Les just a few hours earlier to say that they were in business and that Les was wanted downtown as soon as possible.

They got off the subway train at Brooklyn Bridge, with Herbie looking back and waving good-bye to the Oriental girl. She dropped her self-assigned typecast role of inscrutability and suddenly glared right back at him as if he was Jack the Ripper himself. In reply, Herbie blew kisses to her through the departing train's window. And he was in a chipper mood as he and Les climbed the iron-lipped stairs of a kiosk that surfaced onto Park Row across the street from City Hall.

The branches of the trees in the park were as bare as the slats of the benches and Les felt a chill. "Now," he said, "we can take a cab," and looked down Broadway in search of one.

"Save your money," said Herbie. "Here, we don't need a cab. They got a free bus door-to-door."

"You're kidding?" Les had never heard of a free bus before in the City of New York. Much less one that went door-to-door.

"I never lie except on the witness stand," said Herbie. "Power of the press." And as he was explaining how a shuttle bus was provided to transport workers to and from the newspaper plant on South Street to the Park Row subway stop, indeed, a municipal bus soon appeared from the east carrying a small complement of passengers. While Les watched them get off, some with the brims of their fedoras pulled down way over their faces, he wondered if any of them were former Communist Party front sympathizers, like himself, who had just made a deal.

Into the early morning hours of the previous night, Les had thought deeply about the implications of his action and had finally reached the conclusion that all artistic acts involved informing and betrayal. That one informed on one's parents, one's lovers, one's own inner emotions. That one betrayed one's friends and acquaintances. That society encouraged and even rewarded such actions for good reason. Because in the act of baring and revealing himself the artist had to endure great pain—just as he, Lester Rose, at the moment was personally undergoing—and so certainly such individuals deserved to be acclaimed and applauded for that.

Furthermore, since everyone had to admit that even the purest artistic impulses were rooted in some very murky, gray areas, the conventional moral and ethical standards had little application when it came to judging any of an artist's expressions. Sometimes you just had to betray and inform in order to be able to continue practicing and developing as an artist. It was like the Merano Jews of the High Holiday *Kol Nidre* prayer having to say all sorts of terrible things about their fellow Jews and the Hebrew God in order to survive as Jews in the first place. It was as simple as that. It was the artist in Lester Rose that had determined his decision and he would be the better artist because of it.

The bus drove through Chinatown, Herbie and Les its only passengers, and turned on to the waterfront, passing low-huddled bars that reminded Les of the setting of the Eugene O'Neill one-act plays Miss Vickie Levine had made them read aloud in class. He tried to recall if Mickey and he had once been cast in such a reading together, but could not remember.

The building housing the newspaper was not very impressive by high-rise standards, but its ornate stone facade completely overwhelmed its rundown warehouse waterfront neighbors. But once inside, despite the marble entrance lobby, its interior matched the neighborhood exteriors in grime and dirt. Also, it wreaked of the sulphurous smell of newsprint, the lung-hollowing aroma of printer's lead, and the oily stench of ink. Les had never been in a newspaper office before, his conception of newspapers at that point in his life deriving solely from movies and plays, and so the smells took him by surprise. After all, the building he worked in did not smell of television. If it smelled of anything, it smelled of radio.

Herbie rang the button for the elevator and it soon appeared. The elevator operator seemed to know Herbie and did not even ask him what floor he wanted. He just swung the gate shut and stared straight ahead, moving his wheel as if he were the captain of a ship steering his vessel through dangerous waters. There was a copy of the newspaper on his stool. The headline across the top in red was PARK AVENUE MATRON SLAIN. Below that in black was another headline IKE SENDS MESSAGE TO CONGRESS.

"You must be very lucky," Herbie said.

"Why?"

"The way this whole thing is going to work out."

The elevator opened onto a large dark floor with desks extending in every direction and noise seeming to emanate from all of them. At the head of a cluster of desks arranged in a semi-circle sat a bald man who was talking into one of three phones on his desk and nodding to a person standing over his shoulder at the same time. Herbie headed straight for that man. Les assumed he was the editor. He even wore an eyeshade, just like in the movies.

While continuing to talk on the phone, the editor rose and extended his hand for Herbie to shake and held on to Herbie's hand until he completed his conversation. Then he embraced Herbie and turned to Les, asking, "Is this him?"

Herbie nodded.

The editor took Les's hand, shook it firmly and said, "You're a very lucky young man."

Everybody seemed to be considering Les lucky—except himself. As far as he was concerned, he was still not out of the woods yet by any means. But Les nodded and smiled back at the editor politely, as he rambled on that the reason for Les's luck was his having such a great American as Herbie in his corner. Then the editor unexpectedly picked up a cowbell, stood up on the chair he had been seated on, and vigorously shook the bell back and forth.

Conversation died down, typewriters stopped clanging, it became semi-quiet, like a ball park before the singing of the national anthem or a high school assembly before the Pledge of Allegiance. The only sounds in the vast room were those of unanswered telephones ringing and tickers clicking, mechanical voices impervious to cowbells.

"Gentlemen," the editor was shouting. "Once more we are honored by the presence of that great American, Herbie Moscow. I wish the presses were running so I could stop them in his honor. But meanwhile, at least, we can all rise and show him how much we at this newspaper appreciate everything he has done in the trenches to protect this nation from the Commies. Let's hear it for this hero." He pointed down at Herbie and waved the bell enthusiastically as chairs were pushed back and men rose, clapping their hands in Herbie's direction, and suddenly the office had been transformed into the kind of scene that few newspaper movies had prepared Les for.

At a signal from the editor, everyone stopped applauding and abruptly returned to work. A tall lean man approached the editor's desk carrying a pad and a pencil. He and Herbie knew each other and Herbie introduced him to Les. He was the reporter who was going to write the story and the editor repeated the scenario that had been previously agreed upon. Les was to tell the reporter all he knew about Michel DuChamps and the meetings he had attended and the petitions he had signed. But since Les had no credentials as an expert on Communist youth, and Herbie was an important informer and Commie fighter, it would make for a much better angle if all of Les's information was attributed to Herbie. In other words, Herbie would get the headlines for exposing Michel DuChamps and Les would be spared any public notice as Mickey's finger-pointer. They would all get what they wanted. Except, of course, Mickey. And that just could not be helped.

It was his professional and artistic life against Les's. And Les would survive. Which, Les guessed, ultimately did make him comparatively lucky. But he certainly did not feel that way.

BOOK IV

1

At night the beachfront synagogue seemed larger to Lester than it had in the daytime. And since the sign posted by the L.A. fire department warned that occupancy by more than 399 people was dangerous, Lester figured he was in no great peril. The place seemed less than half filled, not more than 200 people in the house. Mostly bearded guys with *yarmulkes,* who would bounce one kid on their knees while another kid ran in and out of the row and then up and down the aisle. Men and women were segregated, about one third of the seating set aside for women, and it was to and from their mothers and grandmothers that most of the children were racing.

Lester recognized a few familiar faces from the business in attendance: a female agent from CAA. A lesbian developist from MGM. A macho TV cops and robbers producer. But no real industry heavyweights. None of the top brass from Disney or Universal or Warners. Lester's wife, Jean, who always point-blank refused to enter any religious structure—not even Notre Dame or Saint Chappele or the Cathedral at Chartres—had, of course, not come with him. But he was not without feminine accompaniment. His daughter Monica, home for Christmas—or rather Chanukah—had volunteered to come instead. Along with her college roommate, Jill, a girl from New York who was staying with them. Monica had assured Jill that it would be a more interesting evening than taking in a movie in Westwood, especially since they had already seen everything good playing there anyway. Rhonda from Lester's office was also there along with her boyfriend, Jeff, who worked for a small production company that made documentaries. And as the synagogue doors were about to close, Lester noticed Max Isaacs and Susannah Troy hurrying in and then being asked to go their separate seating ways.

When the crowd—or audience—quieted, the kids obeying the *shahs* of their parents and the admonishing fingers of any angry looking old man in their vicinity, a rather pleasant pink-faced young man wearing a small white *yarmulke* ascended the *bimah,* positioned himself at a lectern on which stood a candelabra with a single unlit candle on it, and introduced himself. He was the president of the synagogue, he said, and was glad so many people had all come together on this joyous evening to celebrate the most joyous of the Jewish holidays, Chanukah, in the most joyous possible way, with an evening of joyous song. And he hoped that this evening's joyous concert would set a joyous custom and precedent and become joyously remembered as the synagogue's First Annual Chanukah Concert. He then took the opportunity to thank all those assembled before him for buying tickets and coming out on a night when there were holiday specials on television to watch and so many other things to do and predicted that no one would be sorry that they had come. For while the only thing the coast of California ever sent to the Jersey shore was a candidate for Miss America, tonight on the California shore with the ocean at their very doorstep, New Jersey was sending a gift of infinitely greater value, one of its finest cantors, a man the *Forwards* had once called "a legitimate throwback to the age of golden throated cantors," the world renowned Ben Sirota.

Lester had forgotten that Michel had a stage name. Lester also wondered in which world Michel was renowned. Certainly, not in any world he knew. And then the synagogue darkened and Lester heard Michel's familiar tenor voice before he saw him, as the rear doors of the synagogue swung open and Mickey dressed in a tuxedo, but wearing a white satin, fluffy cantors's crown and illuminated solely by the light of the single candle he was holding before his face, entered intoning the words of the blessing for the lighting of the Chanukah candles, caressing each syllable of every word playfully and lingeringly until he reached the *bimah,* where he lit the solitary candle in the candelabra with the dripping candle he had been carrying and placed it beside the other, two flickering flames in the dark.

Then the lights rose and Mickey sang two gay Chanukah songs in Yiddish with some members of the audience knowledgeably accepting his invitation to join in on the choruses. He told a few jokes before becoming serious and singing *Hinnini,* the cantor's showpiece aria from the Yom Kippur Service. It required acting excellence, as well as vocal prowess, and Lester thought Mickey did it well. Lester was also surprised at the richness in the timbre of Mickey's voice considering his age. It was the voice of a young man. And as Mickey proceeded through the rest of his program, varying from folk Yiddish to liturgical Hebrew, Lester remembered the fabled cantors he would strain to hear outside of the Jewish community center's windows during his boyhood. But then Mickey suddenly segued into singing a medley of show tunes from Rodgers and Hart and Jerome Kern and Cole Porter. And, of course . . .

> *C'est si bon!*
> *Lovers say this in France*
> *When they thrill to romance.*
> *It means it's so good.*

and finally:

> *Hold me close and hold me fast*
> *The magic spell is cast*
> *This is La Vie en Rose.*

When you kiss me heaven sighs
And though I close my eyes
I see La Vie en Rose

When you press me in your heart
I'm in a world apart
A world where roses bloom

And when you kiss me angels sing from above
Every day words seem to turn into songs of love
Give your heart and soul to me and life will always be
La Vie en Rose

It was hard for Lester to tell what was going over best, since there was never any applause within the hallowed confines of the synagogue, but according to his show-biz savvy house-sense it seemed to be *C'est si bon.* Even Monica and her friend Jill over in the women's section, Lester noticed, were sitting up for that one.

And in less than seventy-five minutes without a single intermission—faster than some Woody Allen pictures—the concert was over and the president was back on the *bimah* besides a perspiring Mickey, who was patting his brow and neck and throat with a blue polka dot handkerchief. The president shook Mickey's hand and made an announcement inviting the audience to stay for a joyous party to honor both their renowned guest and *freilichah* Chanukah, which would commence as soon as the ladies of the sisterhood had time to set everything up. Which would take five or ten minutes at best but, he promised, would be well worth waiting for. Lester looked toward Monica and Jill questioningly, expecting them to opt to leave immediately, but they just shook their heads and giggled something to each other. So, he walked down the aisle by himself and out onto Ocean Front Walk to get a whiff of ocean air before taking on the lure of the *kosher* but calorie-laden refreshments.

He knew none of the people milling about in front of the synagogue. The sun had already set and behind him on either side were the art deco skeletons of newly remodeled condominium and apartment complexes in magic lantern silhouette. Looking out toward the ocean, he could also see the reflection of the moon rippling on the horizon line. And if he listened carefully he could just barely hear the waves washing up on the beach and then receding again.

A handsome woman came walking toward him, a smile on her face. There was something familiar about her walk and carriage. Was she an actress who had once read for him? A bit player in a movie he had seen recently? A fellow guest at some dinner party? The hostess at some charity luncheon? Somehow Lester seemed to associate her with food, even though he could not place her precisely. She stood before him still smiling without uttering a single word. Finally, he broke the silence himself. "Hello," he said.

She just continued to smile back at him without saying anything and the longer she was silent the more familiar she became. Then suddenly she fell against him and embraced him warmly. He looked past her shoulders at the hungry group of loiterers in front of the synagogue as if pleading for someone to come forward and identify for him the woman in his arms. Her fingers dug into his back and she started to sob lightly against his chest. He did not know what else to do so he whispered into her hair, "Happy Chanukah."

"Lester Rose," she said, and looking up thrust her face before his. And then for the second time Lester found his past projecting itself into his present unexpectedly in the most unlikely of settings, a synagogue at the foot of the beach not far from Pritikin's.

"Glenda," Lester kissed her. "What a wonderful surprise! What are you doing here?"

"I live near here. In Venice," she said.

"I didn't know that."

"Oh, yes, I moved out here two years ago to be near my daughter."

"Why didn't you call me?"

"I once did. But you never called me back."

"I never got your message. Honestly. My secretary must have screwed up. Anyway, I'm delighted to see you," Lester hugged her again. "Also surprised. Whatever made you come here tonight?"

"Ben Sirota called and told me about the concert."

"You know him?" Lester was shocked. "How do you know him?"

"He came out to see Leon. Back East before he died. Just like you once came to see him. Not before he died, but a long time ago."

"I would have come, too. I had no idea how ill Chicago was at the time. How many years is it now?" Lester asked mournfully.

"Three," she said, and her hand went to her eye again.

"And you're still a Jew?"

"Of course."

"And have you found another fellow?" Lester smiled.

She shook her head. "Leon was the man in my life."

"C'mon," Lester took her arm and guided her back toward the synagogue. "I want you to meet my daughter. She's just like Cosby's kid on his TV show, the oldest one, only white."

As she walked beside him, Lester could see that Glenda had put on just a few pounds since that summer back at the Levine Family Diplomat, but her essentially thin face had filled out, giving her the character and substance it had seemed to lack when she was young. And for the first time, he could see why Chicago might have found her so attractive. Perhaps Chicago had anticipated in advance the job that age would do. Too bad he wasn't still around to enjoy it.

2

After that chilly night years ago, when Chicago had walked Lester to his jeep *Monty* in Pennsylvania, they had pretty much lost track of each other. Lester continued on with his career and they simply just never connected again. Somehow, Lester did learn that Glenda had become Jewish and that she and Chicago married, but that was about all. Then one morning—as Groucho Marx once said, in L.A. you sit down and stand up and years have passed—Chicago called Lester at his office on the lot. He was in San Diego, he had a few hours between planes in L.A., and could he and Lester have lunch together. Naturally, Lester told him to come on over and cancelled his scheduled luncheon appointment.

When Chicago arrived in Lester's office some two hours later he was nattily dressed as always. In his British tweed sports jacket, a designer shirt, finely tailored double knit slacks, and loafers of Moroccan leather he looked more like a successful producer or director than Lester did himself. Chicago's remaining hair was gray and thinning but his face sported a Palm Springs tan, and, he had added very little weight. But somehow he seemed smaller than Lester had remembered him. His eyes flitted up and down the posters on Lester's wall very much the same way they used to survey the chalked odds posted on the price board in the poolroom. "I didn't know you made all these pictures," Chicago said. And then not as a put down but rather as complement he marveled, "I never even heard of some of them."

Lester laughed: "This studio has made alot of pictures you never heard of."

"How many have they made?"

"All together?" Lester said. "Over the years?"

"Yeah."

"I have no idea," Lester said. "But a lot. Thousands. Probably several thousand."

"Then no wonder I never heard of some of them," Chicago said seriously. "But television is funny. They keep showing pictures either I never heard of or I've seen a thousand times." He scanned Lester's office again. "How long you've been here?"

"In these offices?" Lester scratched his head. "Three, four years. I keep moving around."

"Why's that?"

"It all depends where I make my deal. Look," Lester put his arm around Chicago's shoulder, "I'm hungry. Let's eat. Then I'll explain the whole business to you."

In the commissary they were seated in the inner-sanctum, the power place, where the executives, producers, agents, and directors dined. There were few women seated at any of the tables except for a developist and a lady from William Morris. Chicago surveyed the room in disappointment. "No real *nookie*," he said. "I thought Hollywood was full of *nookie*."

"It is," Lester said, "but this isn't Hollywood."

"What do you mean? How far is Hollywood Park from here?"

"Not far. But that isn't in Hollywood, either."

Chicago picked up the menu the waitress had deposited before him and opened it. "So where's the Hollywood *nookie* then?" he asked, as if it were an item that he had been assured would be found on the menu.

"How long will you be in town?" Lester smiled.

Chicago looked down at his watch, a gold Rollie. "My plane leaves at four ten," he said sadly and they both laughed. Then they ordered and as they ate Chicago brought Lester up to date on his life. He and Glenda had a daughter who was going to law school in San Diego. "Imagine," he said, "My ex-wife and my only child both shysters." Lester asked him if he ever saw Vivian or was in touch with her. "Are you kidding? The only thing I ever had to do with her after the annulment was when Laura died, and I sent her a card or flowers or some money for something." He stopped slurping his soup and looked down at his hands and memorialized. "That was a shame: brilliant girl. A young doctor. Her whole life ahead of her." He snapped his finger together and slowly shook his head. "Cancer is a terrible disease." And then he repeated, "Her whole life was ahead of her."

Chicago asked Lester about himself and Lester dutifully told him how his first two marriages had been disasters because he had made the mistake of marrying what should have been just one-night stands but that Jean, his third and final and present and future wife, was a terrific woman and that they had terrific kids and that emotionally it seemed to him that his first two marriages had never really happened and would never have happened anyway in today's climate. "Nowadays I would have moved in and then I would have moved out," he said, "And the only papers involved would have been from Bekin's or Mayflower or Allied Vans."

Chicago laughed. "That's why I flew out here. My daughter's living with a guy. When I heard it, I went through the roof. But Glenda said, 'Calm down, it's nothing, that's the way it is these days, and besides we did it ourselves.' And I told her, at least, we were still married to somebody else when we did it. So anyway, I flew out here to see how much 'nothing' it was. And you know something? It is nothing. I like the guy. He's studying law, too. So, I'll wind up having connections with three lawyers."

Lester passed on dessert, but when Chicago ordered a pecan pie he reached over and took a forkful to go with his decaf. Chicago smiled and said, "Remember Ethel?"

"No," Lester swallowed the sweet, gooey cholesterol-laden pie.

"Once, after Vivian was giving you a hard time, I fixed you up with her."

"Oh, Ethel," Lester said. "How is she?"

"Who knows? How should I know? But she gave me terrific *nookie*. Not as terrific as Glenda, but still terrific. But between you and me, you know who was—" his hand wavered and his eyes narrowed "—not so great in the *nookie* department?"

Lester knew the answer and did not try to ward it off, but somehow mentally cringed upon hearing it.

"Vivian," Chicago said and dug back into the pie.

"I wouldn't know," Lester said. "But I remember she told me you were great in bed."

Chicago stopped eating and smiled across the table at Lester. "How would she know? All she had before me was Mickey. Maybe a couple of Mickeys. Say, whatever happened to him?"

"I have no idea."

"His career certainly went down the toilet."

"Apparently," said Lester.

"Anyway, it looks like you've had a career, kid. A great career," Chicago laughed. And Lester laughed, too. No one had called him "kid" in years.

After lunch Lester walked Chicago around the lot. Only one picture was shooting and the studio's TV series were in hiatus, so there was really little to show him. Empty soundstages and unpeopled sets did not seem to interest Chicago, not even when Lester mentioned the great pictures in the past that had been shot on those very streets. Anyway, Chicago seemed more intent on recounting to Lester his own success as a Jewish bookmaker in a Pennsylvania city of honkies run by the Mafia, than to be impressed by any cinema lore. "I guess Glenda's being *guinea* really helped do it for me," he said, summing up his own career rise.

"I didn't know Glenda was Italian," Lester said. "Her maiden name wasn't Italian, was it?"

"The family changed it."

"And she always seemed so un-Italian. I mean, so calm."

"She was anemic and had a low thyroid, besides. But now, she's Jewish and even makes *kishka* for me."

They were back in front of the administration building and

shaking hands. "Me and Glenda are very proud of you," Chicago said, taking in the lateritic brick building and the brown stucco soundstages behind it.

"Thank you."

"And you know who else is proud of you? She's always talking about you and goes to see every movie you ever made. Millie."

"Millie?"

"From the Levine Family hotel there. She was your waitress, too."

"Millie."

"Her kids are all married and she lives in Florida. Glenda and her always get together whenever we go down there. You fucked her, didn't you?"

"I guess so."

"You guess so?" Chicago laughed. "Sure you did. It was the same night me and Glenda met. How could you forget it? Anyway, I could reminisce all day, but I have a plane to catch."

"Do you want me to get a car for you?"

"Like some jeep, for example? What did you call it?"

"Monty."

"Yeah, *Monty.* Anyway, I got my own car waiting." And he pointed to a limo parked down near the gate, a liveried chauffeur standing beside it.

Then suddenly Lester did not know what on earth got into him but out of his mouth, as if he were some third person, came the words: "Before you go, Chicago, tell me one thing I've always wondered about?"

"Sure."

"How many balls do you have?"

"How many balls do I have?" Chicago's sun-burnished face blanched. "How many balls do you have?"

Lester held up two fingers.

"Then how many balls you think I have?" Chicago challenged.

Lester shrugged innocently and waved the same two fingers.

"Then why do you ask such a stupid question?"

"I was only kidding," Lester said. And went forward and embraced Chicago. "Just joking?"

But Chicago remained stiff in his arms. "Balls are no joke," he said. "Two is more than one. And one is more than none. But balls are no joke."

"I'm sorry," Lester said. "But it's so good to see you. Take care of yourself. And give my love to Glenda."

"Okay." He shook Lester's hand and patted him on the back before turning and walking toward his limo, waving his hand behind in the air, either in abrupt dismissal or a final farewell.

3

"Leon always said you were his best friend," Glenda was saying as Lester steered her back into the synagogue.

"He did?"

"Yes."

"Well, he was very important to me. I owed a lot to him."

Children were still scampering about the synagogue, but most of the concertgoers were now part of a slow moving line that was passing through a doorway to the right of the holy ark over which a red and white fire EXIT sign was posted. As he and Glenda joined the line, Lester felt like a theatergoer after a performance, waiting to go backstage through the house entrance rather than the stage door. Glenda pursed her thin lips into a smile and Lester smiled back and asked, "Where's your daughter?"

"She'd never come to something like this. She's always rebelled against being Jewish."

"That's funny," Lester said. "My daughter's here. And I'll bet it's the first Jewish function she's been to since junior high when her friends were all getting *bar mitzvahed* and *bat mitzvahed.*"

"Judy was *bat mitzvahed.*"

"Monica wasn't. My wife doesn't believe in any religion."

"That's a shame," said Glenda.

Lester couldn't believe the conversation he was having with Glenda. First, because he couldn't believe he was having any conversation with Glenda period. Second, that summer in the mountains Glenda had struck him as the ultimate *shiksa,* dull and silent and good looking, especially if your key aesthetic standard consisted of not looking even a taint Jewish in the slightest. And there he was standing alongside her in a crowded synagogue aisle during Chanukah in Santa Monica.

When they passed through the doorway under the EXIT sign, it was as if they were entering a different world. If the Pacific Ocean washed upon the shore before the synagogue, somehow Middle Europe lay behind it. Two long tables filled the back room. Men sat at them, children on their laps, toasting each other with wine and whiskey glasses, while women scurried about producing heaping platters of potato pancakes and apple sauce and pitchers of sour cream. It was an up-to-date Breughel interior and only hungry dogs barking and sated cats sleeping in the corners were missing.

Near the head of one table stood Michel, surrounded by admirers, among them Lester's daughter, Monica, with her friend, Jill; Lester's assistant, Rhonda, with her boy friend, Jeff; and Lester's writer, Susannah, with Max Isaacs. He and Glenda pushed their way through the crowd.

"Congratulations! You were terrific," Lester greeted Michel.

Michel poured a shot glass full of rye whiskey and handed it to Lester. "Then make me an offer." He poured a glass for himself and tilted it up against Lester's. *"L'Chaim!"*

The whiskey burnt its way down Lester's throat distastefully. He never liked whiskey, especially rye, anyway. And if he was going to fill himself with calories, there was certainly a better way to go. He reached over and loaded a paper plate with potato pancakes.

"Daddy," said Monica. "You shouldn't eat that."

"Why not?" said Max Isaacs. "They're *kosher.*"

"He knows what I mean," Monica told Max, her eyes grimacing toward Lester as if she were his mother rather than his daughter. He had never seen Monica look so Jewish before.

"Just one bite," Lester said. And swallowed a pancake whole.

Monica abruptly snatched the plate out of his hand. She had never acted so Jewish before, either.

"What do you think?" asked Susannah Troy.

"About what?"

She nodded in the direction of Michel who was still busy receiving the plaudits of other concert goers. "He's very good, isn't he?"

"He was always very good," Lester said.

"It's a shame about the blacklist," Susannah said. "All that talent. I guess he could be called the unknown victim."

"There were a lot of unknown victims," Lester said. "Excuse me, I've got to get something to drink." But he did not look for a soda or tea or coffee. He looked for the nearest exit and rushed through it to an areaway of garbage cans leading onto a dreary street called Speedway Alley and then walked to the parking lot, found his Porsche and, thankful that Monica had come in her own car, gunned it home.

There was no review of Mickey's concert anywhere in the trades. Nor was there any mention of his being signed for an important role in an upcoming major film. So, Lester assumed that the scenario God had concocted for Mickey—or vice versa—had bombed out. And since the film idea sparked in him seemed to have also died in the embers of Susannah's script, he was more than ready to forget all about his reinvolvement with Mickey Feldstein.

Until one day a phone call from Paris: It was Marie Carol, Lester's femme fatale in *Alice in Paris,* who he wished had been his own Paris mon amour but instead had been Michel DuChamps' pick-up date at his dinner party for her. They small talked on Marie's international dime until she got to the point. Seemed Michel had sent her the "God Was My Co-Cantor" draft. With a star's instinct, she knew there was nothing in it for her. But the script was laying around her dressing room until one day Bernard Rogers who was visiting her on the set, picked it up and, *voila,* he was interested. Did Lester know Bernard?

Of course, Lester knew Bernard Rogers. One of France's leading stars, he was an American singer-actor who had settled there in the fifties and had gone on to a successful career playing hard-boiled, soft-hearted gangster roles, a sort of combination James Cagney and Jacques Brel. None of his pictures ever came to America, but they all did well in Europe. Bernard by now seemed too long of tooth for any possible role in either the story that Lester had envisioned or the script Susannah had turned in. And even Lester himself had come to realize that his heart had never really been in the basic story anyway. Perhaps he had been attracted to the project more as a kind of dare, a sort of metaphysical game of chicken, than anything else. In any event, he was no longer interested in the project and no one else at the moment had shown signs of any interest, either. "Please have Bernard call me," Lester said.

"Bernard is right here," Marie sang out. "Shall I turn him on?"

"You mean put him on."

"Yes," she giggled. "Of course." And soon Bernard was on the horn, helloing and bon jouring, and telling Lester how much he liked a picture he did fifteen years ago and how much of a pleasure it was to finally meet him, even if it was just over the phone. And Lester told Bernard how long he had been a fan of his. The warm-ups over, Bernard told Lester there was something in the script that appealed to him very much, that touched him deeply and in a very meaningful way. Perhaps it was because he was Jewish himself on his mother's side. But, in any event, of course, the script needed a great deal more work. And he had a few ideas about the direction in which that work should go. Would Lester be interested in hearing them?

"I'm always interested in hearing how to make a movie work," Lester said.

Well, Bernard began, he liked the idea of a blacklisted singer, at the height of his career, having to find a new way to perform his art. But perhaps he would lose some of the cantor, but not all of it. And make the story more universal and more real by having the blacklisted singer go to France where after first performing as a cantor he goes on to become a French movie star playing American gangster roles. He wanted to, said Bernard, in other words, put more of himself into it. Anyway, it was something he could relate to, even though he did not have a complete take on it yet.

"Are you thinking of it as a role for yourself?"

"Possibly," said Bernard. "I do not know at this point. I am not certain. But it is, I think, a project that has an enormous appeal to me. A great relevance and personal meaning, as I say. Something not only to consider acting in. But something I could direct or produce—"

"Or co-produce," Lester corrected. After all, he still owned the script.

"Yes," Bernard said. "Or direct," he repeated.

"Well, then the first thing we would have to do is come up with a new script?"

"Yes," said Bernard.

"Which costs money. And I'm not so sure just now the studio would be willing to put up the money."

"I see," Bernard said.

"Especially since you seem to envision it as a project that would appeal primarily to a French audience."

"At the moment."

Lester was silent.

"Then perhaps I should talk to some people here about it."

"That would be a good idea," Lester agreed. "And then we could talk some more."

Indeed, they did talk more, Bernard Rogers's phony English always reminding Lester of Michel Duchamps's in its contrivance. Nevertheless, Rogers eventually came up with enough French money to buy another pass at a script. In French. Lester did not consider the English translation of that draft very great, but it was no "God Was My Co-Cantor," either. It had very little resemblance to either his original vision or Susannah's abomination. But perhaps it read better in Japanese. Because, with Bernard Rogers in the leading role, they put up enough money to make it a French *go*.

BOOK V

1

Lester Rose was on his way to Deauville. What was he doing going to Deauville? Because Deauville was where you went when you couldn't get into Cannes. And everyone was saying that *Chanukah in Santa Monica,* starring Bernard Rogers, was basically "a Festival picture." Which struck Lester as strange since it couldn't get into any of the other festivals.

Actually, *Chanukah in Santa Monica* was one of those movies which was neither fish nor fowl. It had attempted to be both commercial and artistic and instead had wound up like a duck that could neither swim nor fly. As an art movie it was too mawkish and sentimental and as a commercial film it was too arcane and inaccessible. And although not a bad movie, it was just not a very good one. It was shot in France completely, even though some scenes were supposed to take place in Santa Monica. But you didn't have to be a native Angelino to spot the fact that it was not Southern California but Southern Cannes. Bernard Rogers had also insisted upon the title, claiming it would have an exotic ring to the French. Lester felt that was a mistake, too. If he wanted exotic, Lester thought, Bernard could just as easily have called the picture *Life in Venice.* Or even *Tennis in Venice,* for that matter. But maybe Bernard was already dreaming of sequels in case it was a hit. *Purim in Pasadena. Shevouth in Silver Lake. Tishabov in Tiburon.* The possibilities were endless.

Anyway, *Chanukah* wasn't a Lester Rose film; it was just a picture based on a Lester Rose film idea. And since he really didn't have anything else to do with it, his billing was *avec participation*. Which meant that if *Chanukah* somehow managed to escape its limited, initial target audience in France, and possibly Japan, and got a wider release pattern, the gift of a sou—or a yen—or two might dribble his way eventually. But Lester wasn't holding his breath. Stranger things may have happened in the annals of cinema —but he had not heard of many lately.

Travel is the perk of the movie business. Free travel. Lester did not know any other way to travel. The last time he had paid for his own travel may have been paying the toll going over the George Washington Bridge on some ill-fated pilgrimage into New Jersey. Otherwise, it was always the studio or the network or the production company picking up the tab. And Lester had traveled all over the world—Japan, India, Australia, Argentina, Brazil, Columbia, Europe, Iran, Israel, the Soviet Union—scouting location sites, casting actors and directors and cinemaphotographers, and just simply for exploitation, helping to sell one of his pictures by checking into the best hotel in town and having reporters and television girls and all sorts of news media people come up to his suite and interview him.

With *Chanukah* Lester had figured his actual participation long over, when just two days before the Festival screening the Japanese money people called and asked him to come to Deauville: they hoped that his attendance could be of some marketing help. Lester would never have accepted the nod, no matter how low they bowed to him over the phone—France was no big deal to him—but it so happened that his daughter, Monica, was spending her *wander yahr* abroad headquartered in Paris and this provided a first-class boondoggle opportunity to visit her and see how she was doing.

For two days Lester tried to reach Monica to let her know he was coming. But she was never in. No answer. Not even a machine. Probably wandering *somevahr* around Europe, Lester assumed.

Still, he stopped off for an overnight at the Athenée and tried her again first thing from the hotel that afternoon. But again no answer. So, he took a stroll down the Champs.

No matter how many times Lester visited Paris, he was always overwhelmed by the magic and the miracle of the city, the sounds hitting him as if he were Gershwin himself, and the sights, of course, moving him like a whole gallery of Impressionists. And the years would suddenly seem to peel away and make him feel young and idealistic and vulnerable again, open to a world of both endless possibilities and infinite pain. Until he would remind himself of the simple truth: All Paris really was just a Coney Island of the soul.

Lester strolled up and down the Champs, window-shopping and movie-marquee-studying and then, instead of returning to the hotel, he impulsively hopped a taxi over to Monica's apartment on Montparnasse. Take a shot on her just being there, he figured. And at least he could walk around the neighborhood and see what he was paying for. If only from the street level. Lester always liked that neighborhood anyway. Him and Hemingway.

It was a gray Paris day, the air almost moist to the touch. As if they ever had any other kind of weather. One of the world's best kept secrets, Lester knew, was that Paris's weather was even worse than London's. Gene Kelly could have made *Singing in The Rain* and *An American in Paris* there on one shoot. And, in fact, as if to prove his point, it actually began to rain as the taxi was crossing over Quai D'Orsai and by the time they reached Monica's address it was coming down hard.

Through the sleeting rain, Lester looked up the freshly sand-blasted facade of the elegant gray building to the green mansard roof and tried to guess which apartment was Monica's. She had written it was on the top floor, but had not told them in which direction it faced. Because of the rain he should have stayed in the cab and just headed straight back to the Athenée, have a bite and scoot on up to Deauville. But instead, Lester paid the driver and got out of the cab. Which rushed away, leaving him in a cold, driving rain. And so just for quick shelter, Lester hurried into the doorway of the building. And rather than just stand there and do nothing but drip, he pushed Monica's bell.

Almost immediately, to his surprise a male voice came back over the intercom. *"Qui est là?"* Lester's ears perked up like a rabbit's; he could almost place that voice; He knew it was not that of the concierge or anybody like that. Lester wondered if he might be hallucinating as he replied to the voice with the same question it had asked him. "Qui est là?"

> *"Je suis un ami de Monica."*
> *"Je suis le père de Monica."*

Long silence. Not a sound coming from the apartment over the intercom, only the rain hitting against the great oak front doors. And then a steady beep on the return buzzer. Lester pressed down on the handle and pushed the door open, the beep droning on as it closed behind him.

Lester had expected to find an elevator. But there was none. Just flight after flight of worn maple-stained wooden stairs. Okay for young legs like Monica's, but not his. And he was winded by the time he reached the top floor. Also confused. Because by then he had definitely placed the voice behind the return buzzer. Beyond the shadow of a hallucinatory doubt. And what the hell was that voice doing in his daughter's apartment? Unless it was his sick idea of some sort of joke. Or revenge. But revenge for what? Lester was just a Brooklyn shopkeeper's scrawny son who had gone on to become an obese Hollywood director. The stuff of light comedy, not heavy drama.

The door to the apartment had an oval ceramic tile with a stenciled number ten in blue-black nailed to it. Lester rang the bell on the framing doorjamb. A large bell, oversized like a gigantic nipple, it made such a puny sound that Lester could barely hear it ringing through the thick door. Which soon pulled open at an angle, and in the backlighting revealed the very person Lester feared he would discover.

"What the fuck are you doing here?" demanded Lester.

"Come in," said the figure, opening the door wider, and smiling. "Don't just stand there like a peddler."

2

Lester entered Monica's high-lofted Montparnasse studio apartment, a skylight slanting down overhead, ivy clinging to it. There were greens everywhere, a miniature jungle sprouting up out of clay pots and wooden barrels on the terra cotta tiled floor; and ferns of all sorts lined the stark white walls. There was not much furniture, though. Just a drop leaf table, two chairs beside it; an armoire; a sofa and marble-topped coffee table; a leather chair; but all the furniture had that handled-with-care look that upgrades secondhand and used into antique and period. Along the far wall, rain beat down against muslin curtained French doors that led out onto a balcony with an iron-grill rail. It was an upscale—or the original Gallic—model of the studio apartment Doug and Lisa had years ago on Ninth Street in the Village. Monica had chosen well and Lester did not begrudge her the rent he was paying. But what the fuck was Mickey doing there?

"Relax," Mickey said, as if reading his thoughts. "I don't think Monica was expecting you."

"Where is Monica?"

"Austria. Skiing. She's not due back until tomorrow. But when the bell rang, I thought it just might be her anyway."

Mickey now had a *Miami Vice* beard and looked like the villain in *The French Connection*, as if his facial and tonsorial style inspirations were derived from the end of a cable remote switch. His dress too seemed strictly out-of-touch to Lester. Fifties' European working class: thick pin-whale rust colored corduroys and a shaggy black cable knit sweater topped by a beret. Lester went over to the French door windows, drew back the curtains, and looked down through the rain at the railroad yard below that fed into Monteparnarse station. It reminded him of Pennsylvania.

"Can I get you anything?" he heard Mickey behind him. "Wine? Beer? *Un* Pernod?"

Lester turned around and laughed. "Are you offering me my own liquor?"

"Apparently," Mickey said.

"What are you doing in Paris?"

Mickey laughed. "First, you wanted to know what I was doing in this studio. Now you want to know what I'm doing in Paris. And the next thing you'll want to know, I suppose, is what I'm still doing on the face of this earth?

"No," Lester said. "The next thing I want to know is, if in addition to alcohol, there might be some herb tea here?" He had returned to the Pritikin diet. It almost seemed as if whenever he was back on that diet, he ran into Mickey.

"I don't think there's any herb tea, but I'll see," Mickey said, heading for what Lester assumed was the kitchen. Meanwhile, he tried to flesh out the worst case scenario. Mickey had wooed his daughter, seduced his daughter, screwed his daughter. After all, just a generation ago, hadn't Mickey screwed both Davis sisters in this very same city? But, then again, Monica was of this generation and had to be too smart for him. She was a brilliant girl, a Princeton graduate magna cum laude, and certainly knew better than to fall for his line of shit. Yet, on the other hand, Monica had been charmed by Mickey at the party at their house. And she had actually wanted to go to his dumb Chanukah concert. So, maybe she was eventually taken in by him. Even Marie Carol, a world-class French sophisticate by any standards, seemed to fall for Mickey's Michel shit. And after all, Monica was basically the product of a privileged and sheltered Southern California upbringing, naive and trusting.

Mickey returned from the kitchen with a small jar of instant coffee. "No herb tea. No any tea. Just this."

"Is it decaf?"

"I don't think so."

"Then I'll pass."

"Anyway, sit down."

Lester lowered himself on to the sofa and Mickey hovered over him, smiling. "Well, we've finally gotten together in Paris. It's a shame it's decades too late. Remember how I used to urge you to come over and join me?"

"That's neither here nor there. How do you know my daughter and what are you doing here?"

"I know your daughter because God meant for me to know her."

"Don't be ridiculous."

"Alright, have it your way then. Because you introduced her to me."

"I've introduced Monica to a lot of people but they're not here. In her apartment. Right now. What are you doing here?"

Mickey continued to just smile.

"Quit being a fucking Mona Lisa," Lester said.

"Relax," Mickey said, and sat down at the other end of the couch. "Did you know that Laura Davis died?"

"I think you told me that years ago."

"She died years ago while still quite young. Cancer."

"A lot of doctors get cancer."

"And remember Vickie Levine? Victoria Levine? Our high school drama teacher?"

"Don't tell me she's dead, too."

"No," Mickey frowned. "She's retired."

"You've kept up with her all these years?"

"No. Vivian Scott has."

"Vivian Scott?"

"Vivian Davis."

"You've kept up with Vivian?"

"Only since she's become my lawyer." Mickey leaned toward Lester. "It's interesting how Vivian happened to become my lawyer. Let me tell you how it happened."

Lester rose and went back to the French door windows and looked down through the rain at the railroad yards below, flashing again on that Pennsylvania town where Chicago had settled. He also remembered Glenda's saying that Mickey had once visited Chicago there and wondered if Mickey was now somehow asking him to play mouse to his cat. "First, tell me," Lester repeated, "what you're doing in Paris."

"First, I'll tell you how Vivian became my lawyer," Mickey said. "Then, I'll tell you what I'm doing in Paris."

"And what you're doing in my daughter's apartment?"

"And what I'm doing in Monica's apartment." Mickey smiled. He rose from the sofa and came to the windows and stood beside Lester looking down into the rain. "Do you remember the blacklist?"

"Of course," Lester said. "But I don't have all day to hear the story of your life, either."

"The blacklist is not the story of my life. But it is an important part of it. I would have been an important international star if I had not been blacklisted."

"You never know," Lester said.

"I know," Mickey insisted. "*Prisoners* was the number two top-rated TV show in the country, I had a record contract with Decca, MGM had signed me to a long-term features deal. I couldn't miss."

Lester turned away from the window. "I've seen a lot of 'couldn't misses' miss. It's the nature of the beast."

"I wouldn't have missed. Do you happen to remember how I came to be blacklisted?"

"Not the details," Lester said. "Not exactly."

"Well, let me refresh you." Mickey reached into his back pocket, pulled out his wallet and extracted from it a faded clipping. "Some professional stool pigeon named Herbert Moscow gave my name to the Hearst newspapers and Red Channels." Mickey waved the clipping before Lester, yet seemed to be reading from it at the same time. "Claimed that Myron Feldstein had been an active member of several Communist Front groups. That Myron Feldstein had signed numerous petitions including the Stockholm Peace Petition. That Myron Feldstein had marched in many picket lines and demonstrations staged by Communist sympathizers and fellow travelers. And that Myron Feldstein and Michel DuChamps were none other than one and the same person."

As Mickey continued to wave the clipping in Lester's face, he could not help but recall Senator Joseph McCarthy himself brandishing documents in a similar manner at the televised Army hearings. For a moment it seemed Mickey was consciously trying to parody the Wisconsin senator.

But Mickey was deadly serious. "Of course, I immediately denied all these allegations," he said, refolding the clipping and returning it to his wallet. "But it was already too late. In those years, as you may recall, the accusation was fact enough and denial just further compounded the crime—or sin. My movie deal was cancelled, my TV sponsor fired me, the record company took a walk, and the promising show business career of both Michel DuChamps and Mickey Feldstein was nipped in the bud." He pulled a leaf off a potted plant, tore it in two, and dropped the severed remnant of the leaf from each hand, watching them flutter to the floor. "Do you remember anybody named Herbert Moscow from those hootenannies in the Davis sister's basement?"

"I don't remember anybody from that period. It was too long ago and in another country. Anyway," Lester said. "I have to be going."

"In this rain?"

"There are taxis."

"Not when it rains."

"Then I can take the Metro."

"Wait, and I'll give you a lift."

Lester did not know why he was so surprised, but somehow he was. "You have a car?"

"Yes, I have a car. I don't own it. It's rented. But it's a car."

Even if the rain had stopped there really was no way Lester could just leave. Because he still had to find out exactly what was going on between Mickey and Monica. And also if it had anything to do with a suspected blacklist grievance from way back in ancient history. How much Mickey may have discovered, Lester did not know, but he was sure that he could argue or explain most of it away. In any case, he did not want Mickey fucking around with his daughter. Because if that was Mickey's sick idea of some sort of revenge, it simply was not permissible. He would not tolerate it. "I'll have a Pernod after all," he said.

And he followed Mickey into the kitchen, which wasn't bad for a French apartment. Everything that should be there was there: a stove, a sink, a refrigerator, but all a generation behind, appliances that back in the States would long ago have been thrown out and replaced. Mickey, still acting like a host in Lester's own daughter's apartment, set up glasses, removed ice from the refrigerator, and poured splashes of Pernod, all the while continuing to talk. "Herbert Moscow was the son of a bitch who came up with my name. So for years I used to wonder how this Herbert Stoolpigeon could know so much about me, when I couldn't remember a thing about him. Especially since I have a good memory for faces; I have an actor's memory. And the more I studied pictures of him, the more certain I became that I had never seen his face before. That he had never once set foot in the Davis basement on a Friday night. Then one day it suddenly dawned on me: Herbert had his own stool pigeon. A little more water? No calories in water?"

"Okay," Lester said and Mickey further clouded his drink.

"But who was the stoolie's stool? I gave it a lot of thought, until I finally decided who it had to be." Mickey led Lester back to the studio atelier. "Guess?"

"I have no idea."

"*L' chaim!*" Mickey touched his glass to Lester's. Lester acknowledged the toast and they both tasted their drinks. "Vivian Davis," Mickey said. "I figured it had to be Vivian for several reasons. First, she had the motivation: Rejection. After all, I had rejected her twice. Once after I came back from Paris and was so involved in getting my own show business career started I didn't have the time or energy to think of anything else."

"And the second time?"

"The second time was after your friend Chicago left her. She was having a hard time of it and would write me and call me and tell me how much she had always loved me. That I was the true love of her life. All that kind of stuff. But by that time my career was taking off," he laughed, "and I didn't have the time or energy to think of anything else."

"So," Lester took another sip of his Pernod, the taste reminding him of the licorice drops he would suck on as child while watching a film unreel in a darkened Brooklyn movie house. "Vivian told this Herbert guy about you."

"That's what I used to think," Mickey nodded. "I thought so for many years."

"And what did you do?"

"I didn't do anything. How could I be vindictive toward a woman? Especially Vivian. Besides, I had become a religious man. Maybe religion had worked into me from the outside. Like Laurence Olivier putting on a Richard the Third nose. But anyway, whatever, I had become a very religious man. And it didn't behoove me to judge and inflict punishment upon people for their mistakes; that was the function of my God."

"And you weren't even bitter?"

"How could I be bitter about God's will?" Mickey smiled benignly. "If it weren't for the blacklist, I would have wasted my life in show business. Just as you have wasted yours. Instead of posing as a phony Frenchman, I became a real Jew and served God rather than agents and directors and producers and studios. I've lived for Him rather than for other people's fleeting dreams and mundane projects. And, through it all, I had a wonderful life and found spiritual serenity and artistic peace. What more could a man want? I could almost thank God for the blacklist."

Lester could not quite believe Mickey's religious declamations; they seemed half-baked, they didn't square. Because if Mickey had actually achieved such peace and serenity, why had he held that concert in Venice? Why had he been so intent on a movie career? Why had he screwed around with Susannah? But still, Lester was more than ready to let all that pass and accept whatever Mickey said. But what he could not ignore or allow to pass was that he had just found Mickey in his daughter's apartment. Worse, there was some sort of tie between that fact and the blacklist. Yet Mickey said that he was convinced that it was Vivian who had given his name? But Mickey also had referred to Vivian as his lawyer. Lester could not understand that at all. Unless the man was definitely crazy. Certainly his costume alone was evidence that he was either a certifiable religious nut or a certified anachronism. "Why are you wearing a beret?" Lester suddenly asked him.

"You prefer I wear a *yarmulke?*" Mickey laughed. "But a beret is better in this weather." He stirred his drink with his finger. "Anyway, as I was saying, I could almost thank God for the blacklist. But not quite."

"What do you mean?"

Mickey rolled his eyes and smiled again. Now Lester recognized that smile. It was not Giaconda's but more like a druggie's, sweet and sorrowful, otherworldly clever yet sickly naive and paranoid at the same time. "God does not commit injustices," Mickey said. "Men do."

Lester was not about to try to follow his theological arguments. It was better, he decided, to treat him just like a druggie. Like some overage flower child. "Sure," Lester nodded, as if in total agreement.

"I had always assumed that Vivian was my betrayer, the person who had informed on me," Mickey continued. "Until one day—or rather evening—she came to our temple. For a fund-raiser for the American Civil Liberties Union. She was affiliated with them and was one of the featured speakers. Well, afterwards we hugged and kissed and reminisced and all that. And then I put it to her rather bluntly: How could she go around presenting herself as a Civil Libertarian after what she had done to me? Unless, of course, she was performing some act of atonement? She claimed she didn't have the foggiest of what I was talking about? What had she done to me? And I told her exactly what I was talking about and precisely what she had done. Well, she said, she was shocked. Definitely shocked. And that I was wrong. Dead wrong. But that I could be relieved of my misconceptions by filing under the Freedom of Information Act for all the FBI and Congressional Committee records. Which, with her help, I did." Mickey paused, took a swig of his drink, and smiled at Lester. "It took a lot of time and energy because of the bureaucracy and all that. But Xeroxes of the files finally came and they clearly indicated that, indeed, somebody had informed on me. But not Vivian."

Lester took a long swallow of his Pernod and asked. "Then who?"

"The name was almost always all blacked out."

"Oh," Lester exhaled.

"But there was enough between the lines to indicate that the fink who fucked me had been in television production at the time."

"Oh?"

"Everything seemed to indicate that the fucking fink was you."

Mickey was looking Lester hard in the eye. And Lester stared right back at him. "By name? By exact name?"

"No. Not legibly."

"So you had discovered nothing. *Bupkes* as we used to say in the mountains."

"Except Vivian had an idea. She said, and I remember her exact words, 'Leon and Lester had a very strange relationship; they knew most of each other's secrets.' So I phoned Chicago, as you called him, who was quite sick at the time. And I went to Pennsylvania to see him. And he told me: 'Yes, Vivian was right. Yes, it was you.' That in exchange for my name they had let you go."

"You believed him?" Lester laughed. "You believed Chicago?"

"Why shouldn't I? The man was dying."

"More reason to lie."

"It was you, Lester."

"That's what you think."

"That's what I know."

"If that's what you think," Lester repeated, "then why haven't you ever confronted me before?"

"Confrontation isn't my style," Mickey said, putting his Pernod down on the marble coffee table. "I don't believe in it."

"What do you believe in? What is your style?"

"I believe in God," Mickey said solemnly. "In letting God work things out."

"And God has decided to let you work things out for him?" Lester reflexively clenched his fists.

"It's too late for that," Mickey pointed at his fists, wagging his finger. "And, as I say, it's in God's hands anyway."

"Never mind God's hands. Have you touched my daughter?"

"I'm not an informer," Mickey laughed.

"Have you told her I'm responsible for your having been black-listed?"

"I could never sink as low as you, Lester." His lips parted in that nutty smile again. "I would never betray my best friend."

"You were never my best friend," Lester said, as a key turned in the door, the door pushed open, and Monica stood there, looking like a little girl beside her tall skis.

3

"Daddy," she sang out in a voice that usually was to Lester as sweet sounding as any string instrument, but now cut through him like a rusty razor. "What a wonderful surprise!" She dropped her skis and ran into his arms. "I didn't know you were coming."

"Neither did I until two days ago," Lester said as they hugged and kissed. "It was a last minute business." And then she slipped out of his arms and was on her way into Mickey's. Lester watched her kiss him, their heads bobbing in and out and from side to side French style. "Michel," she said, standing back and surveying the apartment. "Everything looks marvelous."

"You look marvelous, *mon petite,*" he said.

But nothing looked very marvelous to Lester. Indeed, at that moment he felt Monica needed his protection every bit as much she had as a toddler when he would swoop her up in his arms and harbor her from angrily barking dogs and disturbing nightmares and sudden sirens wailing in the night. Now he had to shield her from that three M madman, Myron-Mickey-Michel, and not allow her to get drowned in piss aimed at himself.

Mickey picked up a coat that had been laying on the back of the leather chair. It was a Humphrey Bogart raincoat with flaps and belts everywhere that didn't seem to fit in with the rest of his outfit. He poked his arms through the sleeves, wiggling his fingers in the air. "I will see you soon. *Demains?"*

"Mais ouis, demains," Monica said. "But why are you running off?"

"I think I should leave you two to talk," he rolled his eyes and his lips pulled back into that druggie smile. "You must have much to talk about."

"Who writes your dialogue, Myron?" Lester asked.

"God," Mickey replied. "But only because Billy Wilder isn't available." And he and Monica both laughed and she took his arm and escorted him to the door.

"The rain's really coming down," Monica brushed his sleeve. "Do you need an umbrella?"

"I have my beret," he touched the top of his head as if to see if it was still there. As if he knew Lester was aching to knock his head out from under it. "And my *deux chevaux* is parked just around the corner."

Mickey waved to Lester and Lester waved back and watched him and Monica go into that French cheeking routine all over again. And then Monica led Mickey out into the hall, as if there actually was some elevator to be shown to. And it seemed to take forever before she returned to the apartment, bright and happy. Too happy. "Michel said you two had a talk you should have had ages ago."

"Yes," he nodded slowly. "How was Austria?"

"Weather-wise, fine. Otherwise," she wrinkled her nose, "the most interesting people there seemed to be Italians who couldn't speak English or French."

"Where were you exactly?"

"Kitzbuhl," she said.

"Good skiing?"

"Better than Baldy."

Lester sat down on the sofa and Monica took off her ski jacket and leaned over and kissed him again. "So, tell me what you're doing here? And how long you're staying? And how's Mom and Peter, and are you working on anything new and exciting? Tell me everything."

Then, as she wandered in and out of the room, unpacking and

stowing away her clothes and stuff Lester told her that her mother hadn't come with him because it was a last minute thing and she knew how her mother could never do anything at the last minute. That her brother was fine except the New York police were after him for being a scofflaw with eighteen parking violations. That he himself had a couple of exciting projects in development and had been offered a few interesting scripts, but nothing that really started his blood flowing. Which was why when the Japanese had called him because of his participation in *Chanukah in Santa Monica* he decided on a whim to come to France. "And it was a chance to see you. I'll be leaving Paris tomorrow and so was hoping we could have dinner together tonight."

"Of course, we can," she said. "It's really great I came back to town early and you could catch me. Because I have so much to talk to you about."

"Are you enjoying it here?"

"A lot," she said and went into the bathroom. Lester returned to the kitchen for a refill. But after dropping an ice cube into his glass, he began to tremble and the glass shook. Was he that afraid of what Monica had to tell him? He flashed on a rainy day in Brooklyn years ago, not unlike today in Paris, when he drove around in his trusty jeep *Monty* listening to Vivian Davis's account of her holiday liaison with Mickey. Mickey and Vivian together had betrayed him as surely as he could ever have betrayed Mickey. They had destroyed his romantic dream and left him only with the practical one of a career to yearn for. So, when he had given Mickey's name, he really had no choice. There was nothing else he could do. He had nothing else to give. So there was no need for Mickey and Vivian to track him down like a runaway convict. There was no call for vengeance—or revenge—on anyone's part—then, now or ever. And it was not as if going into the blacklist he and Mickey had been all that even. So as far as he was concerned, the accounts had all been balanced out long ago.

Lester stilled the glass long enough to pour more Pernod into it. And after drinking it down straight, he was all right again. Almost.

4

"I've been craving Vietnamese food all week. Austrian food is so heavy," Monica said as the waiter deposited before them steaming wooden trays containing all sorts of dumplings and noodles and platters of sauteed fish and stir-fried vegetables and bowls of rice.

Lester would have preferred—after all, this was Paris—to take Monica to a fine French restaurant. But neither of them wanted to dress and it had been really too late to make a reservation at any Guide Michelin multi-starred type bistro. Not if they wanted to eat before nine-thirty or ten. Monica was into Vietnamese food, anyway, and this was a place she liked to frequent. With its storefront window it didn't look like very much to Lester, but Monica had assured him, as they stepped out of the still softly drizzling rain, that many real food *mavens* actually dined there.

"I eat here a lot and always tip very well," Monica said, expertly picking a dumpling off its sticky bamboo bed with her chopsticks. "You know why?"

"Because it's my money," Lester said, helping himself to the fish.

Monica made a face, curling her upper lip against the bottom of her nose. It was the same face she used to make when Lester would tell her to do her homework or not to stay out too late. "In case I'm ever broke, I want to be sure I can always get a meal here."

"In case you're ever broke," Lester said. "You can always call us. Or call Marie Carol. I gave you her number?"

"Yes."

"Or call the studio office here. Tell them who you are and they'll take care of you."

"I know, Dad. But I also like to think adventurously."

"Maybe you're having too many adventures anyway," Lester said. And the moment the words left his lips, he felt as if he were reading lines from a familiar script but one in which he was now cast in a different and most unsympathetic role. His own mother used to address him with just such sarcasm. And just as he disliked her when she did it, he now abhorred himself. But it was Monica's fault. Your own children were your parents' best and last revenge.

Monica lay down her chopsticks. "What do you mean by that?"

"Nothing," Lester backed off. And they both resumed their eating in silence. He ordered another beer and she poured more tea for herself. And then Lester leaned across the table and again his mother's voice—or words—flew out of his mouth. "What the hell is Michel doing in Paris?"

"Didn't he tell you?" she looked up from the bowl of rice she was holding. "I would think it's the first thing he would tell you. It was the first thing he told me. And it's kind of funny. And charming.

"Charming? What is?"

"He's giving a concert."

"Here in Paris? They've sent for him to give a concert here in Paris?"

"No," Monica laughed. "He's sent himself. Like he did in California."

"What is he going to sing here? California songs?"

"Very funny. But I don't think so. It's in a synagogue. A Moroccan synagogue. This Saturday night."

"Are you going?"

"Of course," she smiled. "I go to all of his concerts."

"How did you meet him?"

"You introduced us."

"I mean in Paris."

"I ran into him on the Boulevard."

"What boulevard?"

"Monparnasse. At the Select."

"I thought nobody goes to the Select anymore."

"He did. I did."

How do you ask your daughter if she's been sleeping with an old friend, who's out to screw you by fucking her? Lester guessed you don't do it directly but you sort of sidled up to it. "And have you been seeing him since."

Monica smiled and nodded. "Michel's been very kind and helpful."

"In what way?"

"He's helped me with my French. And my plants. He's wonderful with plants and flowers. Whenever I'm out of town he comes in and waters them."

"And that's all he's done?" Lester heard himself saying in his mother's voice, "Is water your plants?"

"Daddy," Monica lay down her chop sticks again. "Stop it."

But he couldn't help it, he had to know, he had to hear it from her mouth. "Have you been seeing him a lot?"

"Yes."

"Should I ask you the next question?"

"Depends upon what it is?"

"Are you in love with him?"

She seemed genuinely surprised. "Michel?"

"Yes."

"Of course not."

And Lester should have left well enough alone. Finished the meal, never brought up the subject again, and left Paris a winner. But he couldn't stop, he couldn't deceive himself for a single second. Michel had a history and no one knew that history better than him. And once more words, as if propelled by some sort of special genetic power, were suddenly and irretrievably out of his mouth. "Have you slept with him?"

"What a question!"

"Why?"

"Because you know I can't answer it."

"Because I'm your father?"

"Not only that," she frowned. "But also it wouldn't be fair to Michel." She slowly began to laugh. "Either way."

Lester was dying inside because he knew the truth. Did all the paths of his life from Brooklyn to the mountains to summer stock to NBC to Hollywood lead to this end? Was it all going to come down on him finally in this way? Somehow, he managed to hang on and finish dinner and even take Monica to the Select for coffee and dessert after. But the next day he did not leave Paris for Deauville. Nor did he stay in Paris either. He returned to America immediately. To New York.

5

There were certain streets in the Village that, to Lester, just never seemed to change. Even the trees, almost leaf for leaf, were the same as they were thirty years ago. Even the garbage piled high before the iron grill fences seemed the same, eternally waiting to be picked up by a sanitation truck forever clanging away somewhere on the next block. And sometimes, as Lester walked along those streets, in addition to the kids in great coats and vinyl jackets and long thriftshop skirts with white flesh showing above their black ankle socks, he imagined figures from the Village past scooting by: Maurice, clutching in his arms bundles of old Partisan Reviews and French magazines, as if he has just wrested them from the pyres of a book burning; Joe Gould, the original dirty old man, in an over-sized winter coat drawing in on a stubby cigarette through his long, gray bearded face; or a redhaired moustached gay, whose name Lester could never recall, cruising in orange leotards and green tights with the stern visage of a British naval commander about to lead men into battle.

On one such street just north of Washington Square in a white brick building Lester had a pied d'terre he rarely used. The street even had a protective association he paid dues into whose real function Lester decided was to protect the block not from muggers but architects. He had bought the apartment for a song years before when he was making a picture in New York and was able to charge most of it off to the budget. And like most real-estate investments it had become too good to sell. When Monica began at Princeton, he and Jean had let her use it on weekends. Also Peter when he started going to Sarah Lawrence. Which turned out to be a mistake. For soon Peter was living there full time and loudly moaning about how much he needed a car in order to commute to classes in Bronxville. Another mistake. Lester gave in and let him have a car. The dreams of a father, it seemed, were not only visited upon a son but also answered by the old man himself.

After getting in from Paris, Lester called the apartment. No answer. Not even the machine. Rather than go to a hotel directly from JFK he took a cab there, figuring he could always go to a hotel but if Peter was around they could have dinner together. But there was no answer when he rang the downstairs bell—even though he fantasized for a quick, nightmarish second that he would hear Mickey's voice replying over the intercom, "I am bisexual and I'm making all your children." So Lester let himself in and took the elevator up.

The moment he had turned the second key in the door, pushed it open and switched on the light Lester was appalled. It was as if a set dresser had been instructed to undress the set. The place was a disaster area. The convertible sofa in the living room was open, wrinkled blankets and sheets upon it, pillows and cushions and bolsters scattered about the floor around it. Also, ashtrays and pieces of Danish and styrofoam coffee containers and empty beer bottles were everywhere. Lester ran his finger over the singe of a cigarette burn he had never seen before on the cherry wood coffee table and it came up dust.

The kitchen was even worse: An opened box of Froot Loops lay on its side across the dirty dishes stacked precariously high in the sink. Other Froot Loops were sprinkled on the tile floor, like some warring insect brigade caught in a sudden nerve gas attack. Lester opened the refrigerator: a lemon. A jar of mayonnaise. A bottle of A1 sauce. A bottle of oyster sauce. A carton of soured milk. Two cans of beer. And an apple. In the freezer were two containers of ice cream, Black Cow and Strawberry Amaretta. He lifted the lids. Ice-like, grizzly beards had formed on the half-eaten contents. There was also an unopened box of Mrs. Paul's Frozen Fish Sticks and a can of frozen daiquiri mix.

In the bedroom both beds were unmade, rock publications and music magazines and Sunday newspapers strewn at their feet. Clothes were everywhere: draped on the backs of chairs, hanging from dresser drawer handles, or like puddles springing up from a leak in the floor. Lester went to the windows overlooking the garden below. It was as if they were capped with a strange green-black-brown filter or gel. They were covered with pigeon shit.

He knew he should immediately go uptown to a hotel. The Plaza. The Pierre. The Sherry. But instead, Lester took off his jacket and proceeded to clean the place. Like a Beverly Hills Hispanic housemaid. Like a road company Lady Macbeth. Whatever, it felt good. He made the beds, vacuumed the floors, dusted the furniture, collected two Jiffy bags of trash and garbage, washed the dishes, rehung jackets and jeans and dresses and skirts in the closets and returned shoes and dance slippers to the shoe racks, bagged two pillow cases of laundry, and even wiped the pigeon crud off the rear windows. Intense work that warmed his soul, but left him hot and sweating. Just as he was relaxing over a cold glass of running water and about to take a bite out of the solitary apple, he heard keys turning in the locks and the door opening. A pretty Asian girl, her hair braided in long pigtails appeared in the doorway. She frowned for a moment, and then said, "Hi."

"Hi," Lester replied.

"I'm Elaine."

"I'm Lester Rose."

"Oh, Peter's father?" she closed the door behind her. "Peter'll be right up. He's parking the Rabbit."

"What rabbit?"

"His VW Rabbit."

"Oh yes, of course. Do you want a glass of water?" Lester offered. "Or a lemon or a beer or some A1 sauce?"

"No thanks," she laughed.

"How about some frozen fish sticks then? Mrs. Paul's?"

"No, thank you."

"An apple?" He held up the one in his hand.

"No, thank you."

"Well, at least sit down while we wait for Peter."

"Sure," she said. "Was he expecting you?"

"I don't think so."

"I didn't think so, either. I mean, he didn't say anything. Except
—" Her forehead frowned again in puzzlement. "Then why is this
place so—" her eyes flitted about the apartment, until she found
the precise word she was looking for "—clean?" She seemed to
pronounce "clean" as if it were some quaint foreign expression.

Lester saluted himself with his glass of water. "Because I cleaned
it."

"Gee," she said, nodding her head as if to acknowledge the
possibility of just such a phenomenon, and smiled.

Lester smiled back and they were sitting there smiling wordlessly
to each other when Peter walked in the door, surveyed the room,
and exploded, "What the fuck have you done?"

"Aren't you going to say hello to me first?"

"No," Peter slammed the door behind him angrily. "Who gave
you the right to barge in here and put me down?"

"Put you down?" Lester could neither understand the ferocity of
Peter's attack nor what he was actually saying anyway. "Barge in
where?"

"Okay," Peter threw his books down on the coffee table. "So this
place wasn't so neat according to your standards. But it was fine
with me. And I was going to clean it this weekend anyway, wasn't
I, Elaine?"

Elaine seemed to shrug and nod her head at the same time.

"But this shit," Peter pointed at the clean apartment all around
him. "This is insulting. It's putting me down. It's saying I am
unable to take care of this fucking apartment myself."

"Who said that? I never said that," Lester sighed. "Although that's something we might talk about later. Meanwhile, why haven't you introduced me to Elaine?"

Peter looked at Elaine and then at Lester. "I figured you'd already met. And you have. You know her name already and Elaine looks like she knows who you are. Anyway, what are you doing here? You're supposed to be in France visiting Monica."

"I was. And now I'm here."

Elaine rose and went over to Peter and played with the buttons on his jacket. "I think I'll be going," she said.

"Wait," Lester said, "don't run off. I was going to ask Peter to dinner and you're most welcome to join us."

She studied Peter. "No. I don't think so," she said to him rather than to Lester.

"No, come on along," Peter told her. "You haven't eaten yet and you could protect me from him." Then he turned to Lester. "Anyway, Dad, you shouldn't have cleaned this place. You really shouldn't have. That's invading my privacy."

Lester could have argued about whose privacy was involved. After all, it was his apartment not Peter's. But what was the point? He was only in town for the night, he would not see Peter again until the semester break, and he had not yet even begun to discuss the matter of the parking violations.

It seemed to Lester that neither of his kids had heard of the invention of the fork. Because it was rice and wood in his mouth again. Also Peking duck, sizzling scallops, moo shu pork, and some flat noodle dishes he'd never heard of before. They were in Chinatown where Elaine had done the honors ordering in the mother tongue to a waiter who evidently knew her very well. Lester figured it was because all Chinese must know each other very well. Until Peter explained to him that Elaine's family was in the restaurant business, too. But out in Brooklyn. And he told Lester about her big kick of reading the list published each Sunday in *The New York Times* of restaurant closings ordered by the Health Department because of violations, laughing and gaffawing in particular over which chop suey joints had got caught and which hadn't.

Later in the evening they dropped Elaine off at her great aunt's house at the Chinese housing project for senior citizens on Broadway where she was going to spend the night. Lester had made it abundantly clear that it was okay with him if they both returned to the apartment and screwed to their heart's content, while he went off to a hotel. But no, Elaine insisted, since he had cleaned the apartment he should stay there and, besides, it would be good for Peter to spend as much "quality time" with Lester as possible. Her own father had died two years ago and she was still sorry that she really had never gotten in enough "quality time" with him.

So, Lester returned to the apartment with Peter and got in some "quality time" discussing the eighteen unpaid parking tickets, summons for which kept coming to his Santa Monica, California, address. Peter said it was probably more like twenty-one by now and that it was "no sweat anyway." It was his problem and that Lester should let him handle it.

"But you're not handling it at all."

"Well, I've got to park somewhere," Peter said. "And every place I park, they slap tickets on my windshield."

"Well, what do most New Yorkers do?"

"They garage their cars."

"Well, why don't you put your car in a garage?"

"This is boring, Dad. Let's talk about something else."

"Tell me why it's boring."

"Because I can't put my car in a garage."

"Why not?"

"Because I can't afford it. Do you know how much it costs to garage a car in New York? Three, maybe four, five hundred dollars a month."

"That much?"

"Sometimes more."

"But those traffic violations add up to a lot of money, too."

"Not if I don't pay them. Anyway, let's go to sleep. Where do you want to sleep?"

Lester shrugged. "Anywhere."

"Okay. You take the bedroom. You're the guest."

"I'm also the host," Lester said. "You can have the bedroom."

Finally, they decided that they could both have the bedroom. After all, there were twin beds. And Peter showered and got into the bed near the window and put out the reading light. "Aren't you going to study?" Lester asked, pointing toward the living room and the books that Peter had left there. "Tomorrow," Peter said. "I brought them for tomorrow." Lester showered and expected to find Peter sleeping, but instead, he was up watching an old Dan Duryea movie on television.

"Any good?" Lester asked.

"Haven't you seen it?" Peter replied with a sudden surliness.

"Yes."

"Then why do you ask?"

"Because I've forgotten it."

There was a long pause. "It's not bad," Peter said.

Lester got into bed and tried to sleep but he was over tired, jet-lagged beyond the point of sleepiness. "Peter," he asked, as he tried to focus his eyes on the screen. "Do you mind if I ask you something personal?"

"What?"

"Did I upset any of your plans by showing up here tonight?"

"What plans?"

"I mean, you may have planned on spending the night here with Elaine."

"I told you before, it's okay. In fact," he smiled, his eyes still glued to the screen, "I might get a good night's rest for a change."

Lester smiled back. "Let me ask you something else? And you don't have to answer me if you don't want to: But how old were you when you first had sex?"

"You mean like with a girl?"

"Yes."

"You mean like all the way?"

"Yes."

"Why do you ask?"

"I'm curious."

"Well," Peter considered, "it was pretty late. I was like pretty old."

"How old?"

"Maybe fifteen."

"Fifteen?" Lester looked over at Peter while Dan Duryea on the TV screen was tilting his head trying to comprehend something else at the same time. "Fifteen? That's late?"

"In Santa Monica, Dad," Peter shifted his eyes from the screen over to Lester, "fifteen is late. Like very late."

"And how many girls and women have you had since?"

"I don't know. A dozen? A half dozen? Maybe a dozen and a half? Anyway, a father shouldn't ask a son these questions," Peter said. And then added. "How's Monica?"

"She's fine. She sends you her love."

"Dad?"

"Yes."

"How about giving me enough money to garage the Rabbit?"

"How much would that be?"

"Five hundred a month."

"I thought you said three hundred before."

"Okay. Four hundred."

"We'll talk about it in the morning. Good night." And Lester tried to fall asleep while the light from the TV screen blinked on and off in his eyes and the sound droned on in his pillow flattened ears.

The next morning, when Lester went down for a newspaper and bagels and coffee, the streets of that Village neighborhood were again intensely familiar to him, as if time still stood still, forever frozen in memory. When he spotted a short woman on high-spiked heels coming out of a drugstore on Sixth Avenue, he was sure he knew who it was, even marveling at the coincidence, and glad of the prospect of running into her after all these years. He followed her for almost a block before she stopped at the corner, waiting for the light to change, and he got a good look at her face. No, it was not Lisa. This woman was twenty years too young to have been the age Lisa must be now and there really was no resemblance between them from the front. And hadn't he heard something about Lisa having wound up teaching acting out at a college in the Midwest, in Illinois or Wisconsin, some place like that? Or was that Doug? Anyway, he had not come to New York to see Lisa.

Back in the apartment, he read the newspaper and had a good dump and tried to interest Peter in some bagels but Peter insisted he never ate breakfast and closed his eyes and proceeded to sleep away the morning. Lester woke him again near noon. Didn't he have any classes?

"Not today," Peter said and turned over.

What about studying? Didn't he have any studying to do?

"Not today," Peter repeated. And then he mumbled. "What's today?"

"Friday."

"What time is it?"

Lester told him.

"Then it's too late," he said.

"Too late to study?"

"Too late to move the Rabbit. It's alternate street parking. Or they have to clean the streets. Or something. It's always something. Anyway," he yawned, "it's another ticket."

Lester finally managed to get Peter out of bed and watched him go through the prolonged rituals of showering again and greasing his hair. He had seen stars take less time getting made up for a role in which they had to age thirty years, than Peter took grooming himself to prepare for a single day.

Since they were in the Village, Lester thought they might have some Italian food for lunch. But Peter insisted on sushi. And he had his favorite restaurant. Again no forks. This time not even any chopsticks. Both of his kids were certified members of the rice generation.

When they returned from lunch, Elaine was in the apartment waiting. Evidently, she had her own key and had let herself in. Evidently also, Peter had promised her they would be back on campus that afternoon because she had a conference with her don she couldn't miss.

"Okay," Peter said to her. "Good-bye, Dad," he said to Lester, and picked up the books he had dropped on the coffee table the evening before. "And don't forget about the garage money."

"Nice to have met you, Mr. Rose," said Elaine.

"Lester," Lester corrected.

"Lester," she accepted. And they were gone and he was left with the rest of the afternoon to himself. Which was what he wanted. Which was why he had not called anyone, not even Jean, to let her know he was back. Not even his assistant, Rhonda, to let her know he was in town. He was still in France, in Deauville as far as the world—except for his kids—was concerned. And for all he knew the Japanese producers were showing *Chanukah in Santa Monica* at that very minute without his participation.

The gift of a limbo day in the city, even just a few hours, to be spent anonymously and without appointments was like a secret pleasure—or vice—to Lester. He considered renting a car and going out to Brooklyn and just driving around the old neighborhood. But then he quickly reconsidered. He just was not up to seeing boarded-over windows and burnt-out buildings and dirty streets in what once had been a vibrantly thriving place to live. Besides, he had not come to New York just to see slums, even those that evoked a very special and familiar past. He had come to New York for a very specific reason. To see a very specific person. And at last he called her.

Lester got through with surprising ease, considering it was a law firm, and found her not in the least surprised to hear from him out of the blue. But, alas, she was sorry, she was busy for dinner.

"How about coffee or a drink before dinner then?" Lester asked.

"Almost anything is out for tonight. I'm going to the theater."

"Which theater?"

"The Public. Downtown."

"Perfect. I'm downtown. In the Village. How about meeting me here for a drink?"

"Where?"

"I have an idea," Lester said. "A terrific idea." And he told her where to meet.

Lester enjoyed the rest of the afternoon, walking around the Village and then listening to some old Fats Waller records that he had forgotten he had left in the apartment. And soon it was time for that drink.

6

As Lester walked through Washington Square Park, where the branches of the trees were bare but there were still uncollected leaves gathering under the benches on the cement spoke path ground; past the NYU students rushing to class and the clerical workers hurrying home; past the few mothers and nannies still wheeling carriages and the anxious druggies looking to make a sell or a buy; and past the chess players still congregating in the southwest corner of the park, impervious to both the hour and the weather, huddled over each other's shoulders; and the joggers in earphones seriously squaring the perimeter of the park, Lester thought about his kids and how different they were from him. Who was he to worry about the sexual activities of the rice generation? Look at Peter and how matter-of-factly he seemed to take sex and interracial screwing. What a contrast between the old man and his son at the same age! And Monica—who he knew for a fact had left her virginity behind in Malibu years ago—starting on the pill the summer before her junior year in high school. So she was certainly old enough now to lay for whoever she chose. But then, why did it have to be Mickey? That's what was gnawing at him. Why did it have to be fucking Mickey who was choosing to fuck him by fucking her. He didn't mind Mickey's trying to hurt him. But he didn't want him hurting Monica. And he was sure, sooner or later, Mickey would hurt her. Otherwise, what Mickey was doing just didn't make any sense. But Lester knew that if he had tried to come on anymore strongly about it with Monica in Paris, it would only have aggravated matters. He also knew he had very few options at his disposal.

Lester arrived at the cafe first. The Reggio was still standing there, the wire-framed chairs and round tables in the display-like windows unchanged, even though he noticed the espresso machine looked new. But how could he have expected it to last thirty years? Lester took a table in the back and ordered an espresso while he waited for her to arrive.

And then she came in, her coat slung over shoulders like a cape, an unmasked intruder, her flannel skirt furling. In addition to a purse, she carried a briefcase. She looked around the small room clockwise, stopped and turned her head back until she settled upon him, and smiling, headed for the table. Her body seemed to have become fatter and her face thinner at the same time. She set down her briefcase on the empty third chair at the small table and bent across it to kiss him just as he was rising to greet her. Their lips almost missed and they both laughed.

"It's been a long time," Lester said.

"Nonsense," she peeled her coat off her shoulders. "I don't recognize time. I've banished time, Rose. What are you having? I think I'll have one, too."

He signaled the waitress and ordered another espresso. "Wait," Vivian said to her, "make it a cappuccino." She turned back to him, "I know it's more calories, but who gives a damn?"

"Busy?" Lester looked over at the briefcase.

"Very," she said, patting it. "I always have homework." And then rubbing her hands. "Tell me how you've been."

"Busy," he said. "If it's not one picture, it's another."

"Well, at least, you're doing what you always wanted to do." Then she smiled and added, "Almost anyway."

"And you?" Lester asked as the waitress deposited Vivian's cappuccino before her."

"Oh, I love what I'm doing." She looked around the cafe. "I was still married to Leon when we met here once. Right?"

"Right."

"Poor Leon," she shook her head.

"He had a good life from all I heard," Lester said. "Including what I heard from him."

She blew across the top of her cappuccino and then spooned the froth to her lips. "I mean, he was still young."

"Laura was still younger."

"That was in another world. In another life." She waved to the side with her hand. Lester noticed there was a ring with a huge stone on it.

"How old was she?"

"Just thirty."

"And what did she die of exactly?"

"Cancer, also."

"Anything to do with her medical work?"

"I don't think so. It's in the family. My mother died of it, too."

"Oh, I'm sorry to hear that."

"After Laura died," Vivian leaned forward, "I remember writing to you because we were setting up a memorial scholarship fund for disadvantaged minorities in her name."

"I don't remember ever receiving any such mail, I swear."

"It was mailed to your studio office. But no big deal, Rose. The fund's doing fine and so are some of its recipients."

"Laura would have liked that," Lester said. "Did she leave behind any kids?"

"She didn't have any. Neither have I. My own that is, biologically." Vivian reached down and opened her purse and pulled out pictures of two girls and a boy. One of the girls was about Monica's age. She and the boy were black. The other girl was an Asian. Reminded him of Peter's Chinese girlfriend, Elaine. "But these are my stepchildren. My husband's from his first marriage. And Sookie, who is Vietnamese, we adopted together."

"Handsome kids," Lester said. "What does your husband do?"

"Wilson's a judge now," she closed her wallet. "But we were equals before the bench when we met. Both working for the same public interest group. I was his senior. You have two children, right?"

Lester nodded.

"Mickey told me." She returned the pictures to her purse and looked at her watch. "I'd really love to shmooze and reminisce but I don't have much time, Rose. I've got to meet Wilson for a quick bite and then run over to the theater. What is it you want to see me about?"

"I want your professional advice."

"That might cost you."

"Fine," Lester nodded. "It's about Mickey."

"Then there might be a conflict of interest."

"It's in his interest. I want you to find out exactly what I have to do—just what is it that he wants—to lay off my daughter."

Vivian laughed out loud. "Is that what he's doing now in Paris? Going after your daughter?" And she laughed again, peal after musical peal, and some of the additional years she had been wearing that half-masked the Vivian Lester remembered seemed to fall away from her face. "Mickey," she caught herself between giggles. "He's still so incorrigible."

"You know he thinks I'm responsible for his being blacklisted."

"Aren't you?"

"Certainly not. There were Congressional Committees and Hearst newspapers and witch hunters of all kinds. It was the climate of the times. And he has no proof linking me, anyway. But that's beside the point. The point is, that no matter what he thinks, it's not right for him to try and get back at me through my daughter. That's utterly wrong and as a parent you know it."

"Look, Rose, I know this may be difficult for you to accept, but I'm sure Mickey isn't out to get back at you personally by laying your daughter. He'd be out to lay your daughter even if she wasn't your daughter. Just because she's a woman is more than reason enough for him. No matter how many religious mantles he wears

—or mantras he inveighs—he's an inveterate Don Juan, Casanova, or whatever they're called these days. Why do you think his congregation sent him off into early retirement? It was just getting too scandalous. Why do you think all of his wives left him?"

"He didn't tell me his wives left him. He just said his wife died."

"One of them did die. Probably of a broken heart. But the others left him. So, my personal advice is to let whatever is going on between your daughter and Mickey run its course. And knowing Mickey it surely will." She opened her purse again and dropped some money on the table.

Lester picked it up and handed it back to her. "Don't be silly."

"No, let me," And she shined her hazel eyes on him. "If I can recall, you picked up the check the last time we were here." And then, "I can understand why you might think Mickey would stop at nothing in order to get back at you."

"You think I'm guilty of some terrible thing?"

"Unpardonable and unforgivable," she slowly pronounced. "And unredeemable."

"Not even if I get a note of excuse from my mother," Lester began to joke. But went no further. He saw it would be pointless to go on. To even try to explain that his unrequited love for her had been the cause of the "unpardonable and unforgivable and unredeemable" thing he was supposed to have done. So, he just slowly kept nodding as Vivian continued on, raking the ashes of burnt-out platitudes until she came to the old saw, "I really don't see how you could live with yourself all these years."

"Easy. Very easily," Lester said. "We're both grown ups, Davis. And you very well know by now that people can live with anything. Weren't you just telling me to sit back and live with the fact that Mickey is fucking my daughter?"

"I didn't say that," Vivian said. "You can always tell your daughter what you think is the real basis of Mickey's interest in her and see what effect that has."

Lester laughed disparagingly. "What a phoney liberal solution: asking me to commit the very wrong you accuse me of."

"What do you mean?"

"To inform. You're asking me to inform on myself."

"Maybe you should have become the lawyer instead of me." She smiled. "Except there's a vast difference between informing on others and informing on yourself."

"Speaking of informing," Lester said, "have you informed yourself that perhaps you still may be in love with Mickey?"

"That's absurd," Vivian said as the waitress brought her change and Lester slapped a few singles down on top of it.

"Mickey told me all about how you kept writing to him after Chicago left you. He even *informed* me that you said he was the best lay you ever had."

"This is a silly discussion. I don't know what to believe about what you claim Mickey says I once said." She handed Lester his money back and added her own onto the change in the tray. "Mickey may have been the first, but he was not the best I ever had. That honor, if you want to know, goes to Leon."

Then she rose and he rose, too, to help her on with her coat. Now, they were standing face-to-face and he expected her to say something else hurtful to him about his betrayal those many years ago. But instead, there were tears in her still beautiful doe eyes. And she leaned forward and kissed him, saying, "There was a time, Rose, and I can still remember it clearly which is why I came, when you were not despicable."

Lester followed her out the Reggio door and walked silently behind her to the nearby corner at West Third where she stepped into the street to hail a cab going crosstown. He planned to just continue walking north on MacDougal to the apartment and pick up his bags and head out to JFK for a flight back to L.A. But then Vivian said something very strange, almost clinically strange. There was a faraway look in her eyes as she returned to the curb, her head tilted like a Dan Duryea to one side. "Remember how curious you used to be about Leon's balls?" she said. "About how many he had?"

"Vaguely," Lester said, "but not really." A cab pulled over and waited for her to get in.

"Well, you were," Vivian smiled. "And for your belated information, Leon had two testicles. One was smaller than the other, shrunken because of the mumps he had as a child. But there was never any question as to the quality of his balls."

"If I was still interested in knowing anything about the quality or the quantity of Chicago's testicles," Lester said, "I could have always asked Glenda."

Vivian turned away, the small of her back constricting and her shoulders hunching together as if struck by a sudden spasm of pain; and she opened the door and stepped into the cab. Looking in at her as she began to settle deep back into the torn black Naugahyde seat, her still shapely legs sprawled forward, but her knees pointing at either door and her feet at each other, Lester saw scarcely a face that could have possibly launched a betrayal, most unpardonable and unforgivable and unredeemable. But rather the *punim* of a middle-aged Jewish lady, not unlike his own mother's or that of any of his aunts', crow's-feet forming at the doe eyes, turkey wattles beginning to show on the neck, hairlings on the chin and the cheeks more concave than convex; and an anger flashed through him. Because who the hell was she, that old *yenta,* to accuse him of anything? What ordeal by fire had she ever passed through? When had she ever had to make the kind of choice that he had had to make? And what great courage had she ever displayed? Hell, she had surrendered her artistic dreams of acting almost as easily as she had given up her virginity to Mickey, by deciding to cop out and become a lawyer. Why even little Lisa, with literally less going for her, had had more guts than that. So who was she to come on as nobler than thou, as Miss All-American Virtue? Wasn't she also guilty of an action that was unpardonable and unforgivable and unredeemable? Hadn't she led him on only to let him down? Couldn't she recall how intensely the flames of youth burned? Didn't she realize that after all those yearnings of youth had been doused, the rest of one's life was just so many ashes and embers to be forever sifted through? No, it was never easy to be an artist and you had to make all kinds of devilish deals to become one and survive as one. And in his years in television and film he had had to make compromises and choices every bit as heinous in their way as giving Herbie Moscow Mickey's name. Anyway, in Hollywood you were always making lists, preparing lists, contributing to lists—of cameramen who were available, editors who were acceptable, actors who were castable—and he himself was always on lists of directors and producers to be approved by stars and studios and networks. In show business everyone lived by lists and so it was only normal that some people had to die by them. But Mickey could have come back years ago and had a career if he had the talent, the drive, the art. Others did. Writers and actors and directors. Lester had to think that any artist who could not come back and triumph over such adversity could not have been much of a heavyweight in the first place. Of course, if push came to shove, he, Lester Rose, would have to solemnly swear that he had not done the right thing in supplying Mickey's name. But who was to say that he had done the wrong thing, unless they were in the exact same situation he had been in? In fact, it was ironic that of the three of them, Mickey, Chicago and himself, he was the only one who would remain to the very end, and unredeemably so, a virgin to the ideal Vivian had once represented. And, instead of a holier-than-thou lecture and accusation from her, he would be willing to settle for that as the punishment that ultimately fit his crime.

Lester closed the door and Vivian's cab pulled away. He crossed the street and headed uptown.

7

A few days later back at his office an item in the trades about Deauville and the action there caught Lester's eye. Orion was reported to be negotiating for worldwide distribution rights to *Chanukah in Santa Monica*. Lester immediately buzzed his business manager, Arnie, and asked him to check it out with a tennis crony of his, one of this week's triumvirate running Orion. After lunch Arnie called him back. Yes, Orion was interested in the picture on a negative pickup. And for a very nice price. So Arnie was pretty sure Lester could eventually count on a healthy taste. Except, of course, assuming the Japanese were no different from the French and the Italians, he would have to sue to get it. But that would be an if-come down the line of worry.

Later that same afternoon, after his assistant, Rhonda, had gone for the day, Lester wrote out two hefty checks for Peter, one to pay for his parking violations and the other to garage the car; and then he put through a call to Paris—2:35 A.M. Paris time. He let the phone ring ten times. But there was no answer. Monica was out.

No point getting too upset, Lester tried telling himself at first, she was probably off skiing or some such thing. But then, he decided, who was he trying to kid? Maybe things did have a way, just as the ballplayers—and, come to think of it, T.S. Eliot—said, of coming around.

Because, no doubt about it, he had done a rotten thing. But who

311

didn't do rotten things? Sure, he had betrayed a friend. But who was he supposed to betray? Some stranger? Would that have made it right? Of course, not. Yes, he was a shit and had acted like a shit instead of like some dumb hero. But wasn't it the assholes who always pinned the medals on the heroes anyway?

Vivian had wanted to know how could he live with himself? Easy, very easily, he had told her. Because who else was he supposed to live with? The simple fact of the matter was the world was a venal place, no matter what the legends were. And he was just an infinitesimal part of it and no one man made a difference. Not even, it pained him to think, the great artists. It was all bullshit. And if that was being negative, very well then, he was negative. Because that was the deep reality of human existence as he had so far experienced it. And he wasn't holding his breath for any last minute developments that might make him change his mind.

Lester went to the water cooler, watched as it bubbled out a drink to him, and downed it in one gulp. Anyway, at this point, he told himself, it was Monica's life, not his. True she was flesh of his flesh—but that's all she was. She was not *his* flesh. She was her own flesh and what she did with it was her own business. What the fuck did it have to do with him? She had no more to do with him than he had to do with his own parents. She was no more him than he was her. Each generation had to start from scratch, write its own ticket, commit its own sins, stumble over its own ethics. It was Sisyphus, as far as he was concerned, uphills of useless sacrifice and unnecessary worry. That was the deep reality of the situation.

Lester crushed the paper cup in his hand and dropped it to the floor for the sweepers. He closed his studio office door behind him and wondered, as he walked down the empty hallway, pictures of stars and scenes from Academy Award-winning films looking down at him from both walls, if Jean had prepared dinner or if they'd be going out to eat tonight. He hoped they'd be staying home because he was still a little jet-lagged and wanted to watch the Laker game.